W0473321

ANNIE MURRAY

Annie Murray graduated from Oxford in 1983. She has worked as a journalist and a nurse, has had short stories published in several magazines, and won the *SHE*/ Granada Television Short Story Competition in 1991. She now lives in Reading with her husband and four small children. *Kate & Olivia* is her second novel.

Also by Annie Murray in Pan Books

Birmingham Rose

Annie Murray

Kate & Olivia

PAN BOOKS

First published 1996 by Pan Books
an imprint of Pan Macmillan Ltd
Pan Macmillan, 20 New Wharf Road, London N1 9RR
Basingstoke and Oxford
Associated companies throughout the world
www.panmacmillan.com

ISBN 0 330 33659 2

Copyright © Annie Murray 1996

The right of Annie Murray to be identified as the author of this work has been asserted by her in accordance with the Copyright, Designs and Patents Act 1988.

All rights reserved. No reproduction, copy or transmission of this publication may be made without written permission. No paragraph of this publication may be reproduced, copied or transmitted save with written permission or in accordance with the provisions of the Copyright Act 1956 (as amended). Any person who does any unauthorized act in relation to this publication may be liable to criminal prosecution and civil claims for damages.

11 13 15 17 19 18 16 14 12 10

A CIP catalogue record for this book is available from the British Library.

Typeset by CentraCet Limited, Cambridge
Printed and bound in Great Britain by
Mackays of Chatham plc, Chatham, Kent

This book is sold subject to the condition that it shall not, by way of trade or otherwise, be lent, re-sold, hired out, or otherwise circulated without the publisher's prior consent in any form of binding or cover other than that in which it is published and without a similar condition including this condition being imposed on the subsequent purchaser.

For Peta, with thanks

ACKNOWLEDGEMENTS

I should like to express my warmest gratitude to the following:

For particular help with the research for this novel by generously giving their time and conversation: Mrs Iris Deathridge, Mr Terry Leek and Dr Marcellino Smythe.

My agent Darley Anderson for his galvanizing encouragement, faith and friendship.

My editor Peta Nightingale for her sharpness and dedication and for keeping going with it in testing circumstances.

All those at Macmillan involved in the various stages of production and promotion – in particular my copy editor Penny Rendall and illustrator Gordon Crabb.

Belatedly and long overdue to my former editor Jane Wood.

Birmingham's Tindal Street Fiction Group: Gaynor Arnold, Alan Beard, Julia Bell, Mike Coverson, Stuart Crees, Godfrey Featherstone, Barbara Holland, Alan Mahar, and Penny Rendall for their ongoing support and expertise.

Finally, and above all, my family: to John – and to Sam, Rachel, Katie and Rose. Thank you.

In fact in almost every family, one sees a keeper,
or two or three keepers, and a lunatic.

Florence Nightingale

Prologue

ANNA

Birmingham, 3 August 1981

My mother is dead.

Anna repeated these words to herself, still trying to make it real as they walked along the cemetery path under the dripping trees: rain had fallen briskly after a hot day, clouds piling suddenly across the blue. Smoke was still wafting from the squat chimney of the crematorium. These places removed death so far from you.

But she had seen Kate dead. The day of the Royal Wedding, when the hospital was festooned with red, white and blue, flags waving on the ward TV and everyone carrying on about Diana's dress. The nurses put a yellow rose between the papery flesh of Kate's hands. And they prepared Anna for days before by avoiding her eyes, by which she knew for certain Kate was dying. It was obvious anyway. The cancer sucked her down to a tight-skinned puppet, eyes closing against the world. Astonishing that a woman as big as her mother could ever shrink so thin.

She sat quietly touching Kate's arm for an hour or more after she died, though the moment it happened she knew her mother was gone, absolutely. Mom. Strange and silent. She didn't know then that the changed form on the bed was more of a stranger than she imagined. Kate was the one person of whose past she thought she could be certain. She had known it the way a child knows the rhythm of a fairy story, secure and unchanging for thirty-four years. Until yesterday. Why couldn't she have said something before it was too late?

'Sure you wouldn't like me to drive you, my dear?'

Anna smiled, squeezing the fleshy arm that was linked with hers. 'No, I'm fine thank you, Roland. And I'm sure it's me who should be offering you. You're the one who's been of most support to her.'

The chubby cheeks next to her creased into a melancholy expression. Now his hair was so thin on top, Roland's face seemed even more naked and expressive. 'Not a lot I wouldn't have done for the old girl – you know that.'

'I know. You've been so good. Thank you.'

'Want to be on your own for a bit?'

She nodded. 'Yes. I think I do. I'll go and face the house. But it'd be lovely to see you again – soon. I haven't been coming back often enough, I know that.'

Roland gave her hand a final pat as if to absolve her from any sense of guilt, put his little tweed hat back on his head, and with his usual supreme tact walked on ahead of her. She watched, eyes full of affection. He was squeezed into an ancient black suit, a fraction too small, and the hat looked quite incongruous with it, but that was all Roland – one of the things for which they had loved him.

Not wanting to run into anyone else, she followed swiftly past immaculate borders of marigolds to the wrought-iron gates. As she reached her car, the clouds started to let rain fall.

*

The cutting from the *Post* about Kate's retirement was pinned to the noticeboard in her kitchen with a yellow-tipped tack.

'"Aunt" Kate to retire after forty years', it read, and beside the caption a photograph of Kate's round face beaming at a baby in her arms. She was restraining the plump hand that was reaching up towards her face.

'He was a little demon,' Kate had told Anna, laughing. 'He was determined to pull my glasses off!'

> Kate Craven, known as 'Aunt' by generations of the city's children, retires this week after nearly forty years' Health Visiting.
>
> A motherly, if often outspoken character, Kate will not be forgotten by the many women whom she has advised and supported over the years.
>
> Her career began in 1938 as a nurse at the General Hospital and in her time she worked in most areas of South Birmingham, as well as being an ardent promoter of Health Education in schools.
>
> From her final post at Poplar Road Clinic in Kings Heath she was given a send off today by staff and parents.
>
> 'She's a lovely lady,' said one mother of three. 'Flexible, honest, and always kind. Everyone will miss her.'

Anna stared at the picture again, the smile on that round, generous face. *What is all this? What have you kept from me?*

The phone started ringing. She knew it was Richard. She should have unplugged the thing.

'How was it then?' he said. She could picture him standing in the hall of their house in Coventry, still in his casual social-worker clothes, moss-green cords, brown jacket, shirt open at the neck. No tie of course.

'It was a ball, what d'you think?' He should have taken the day off and been there with her.

'Sorry.'

Anna didn't say anything.

'So you're not coming back tonight then?'

'No,' she agreed flatly. 'I'm not coming back tonight. Nor tomorrow. I've got all the house to sort. There's no point in driving up and down now it's the holidays, is there?'

'If you say so. Only I could do with the car. It's a bit awkward.' There was a sigh in his voice, but then he always sounded rather long-suffering on the phone.

She tried being conciliatory. 'All right, I'll come over tomorrow night. I'll be able to use Mom's car – OK?'

'I could cook,' Richard offered.

'That'd be nice,' she said, thinking she'd believe it when she saw it. 'How was today?'

'A pain. Delays in court all morning. Gerry Kinsella this afternoon.'

Gerry was one of Richard's most intractable probationers. Normally she'd have felt obliged to ask about it. Today she didn't think she'd bother.

Richard sighed wearily. 'I suppose I'd better go and find something to eat then.'

'Yes, you had, hadn't you?'

Anna put the phone down hard and said to it, 'You've just lost your mother, Anna, so how are you feeling? Well funnily enough I'm pretty cut up about it, Richard. Really nice of you to think of asking.'

The box, with its card pinned to the top, 'FOR ANNA', was in one of the bedroom drawers.

She had not been long in the house when she started prowling restlessly round the rooms, as if to make absolutely sure it was empty. The bedroom door opened with a squeak and she felt her palms sweating, somehow nervous of invading Kate's privacy. It was a pretty room: floral curtains and bedspread to match in soft pinks and greens, and a cream carpet with sprigs of pink roses. Kate had moved into this house only a year ago, preparing for retirement and a bigger garden. Anna remembered the austerity of her mother's room when she was a child, the brown lino and old iron bedframe, the lodgers.

She opened the wardrobe and looked inside, but found at once that she couldn't bear it. Kate's clothes, her shape, the skirts limp and slightly pushed out at the back from being sat in, the broad, still creased waistbands. And shoes, her second, very personal skin. Kate's shoes, squatting there in the bottom of the wardrobe, defeated her. She lay on the bed, her hair draping her face like a shroud, and cried. She hugged the flowery quilt with its familiar scent, trying to feel her mother's once plump arms round her, soothing her out of the pain of her own death.

It was after this she found the box, a carton covered with Christmas wrapping paper. Inside were a photograph, two letters and a thick bundle of paper pushed into a pink file. These were all tied together with the thin white elastic Kate used to thread through Anna's school socks to keep them up.

She had never seen the photograph before. It was from an old newspaper, the paper yellow and the print grainy. She knew at once that the two children in the picture were Kate and Olivia. There had evidently been bright sunlight in their eyes, adding crinkled noses to their smiles. It was quite obvious which was which. Kate's wide, friendly face, the glasses, well-defined eyebrows above them, her dress looking a bit too small. And Olivia, beautiful right from the first. Anna squinted at the image. She had never seen any picture of Olivia before. She was thin, shorter than Kate, with a mass of wavy hair and dark eyes which dominated her face. Her dress was of a pale, frothy looking material. Anna thought she could just make out the tips of Olivia's fingers round Kate's waist. Beside the two of them stood a very tall dark-haired man, and behind, a ring of people watching a roundabout, its movement slightly blurred in the picture.

Handwritten in the margin were the words, *Onion Fair. Birmingham 1929.* The girls had been eight then, though the writing in blue biro looked recent.

Anna picked up the shortest of the letters. It was on a good quality sheet of blue paper. Beneath the Birmingham address appeared a mere lineful of words written with beautiful evenness: 'I'm here to stay now. *Please.* Olivia.'

Anna's heart started to beat faster. So often at storytime in her childhood: 'Mummy, tell me a story about you and Olivia when you were little girls.' And Kate had seemed to relish this talk while Anna sank into sleep. Idyllic summers spent in the languid gardens of Moseley, their endless talk, piano playing, their laughter and games. Talented, lovely Olivia, who was killed in the war in 1944.

Anna looked up slowly, frowning. The date at the top of Olivia's letter was December 1980.

She reached for the pink file.

Part One

Chapter 1

KATE

Birmingham, 1929

'Kate Munro!'

Miss Pardoe's voice rang down the school corridor. I jumped guiltily, wondering what I'd done wrong. When Mummy spoke to me in that tone it meant Trouble. I had forgotten for a second that that was the way Miss Pardoe always talked.

'Come here,' she commanded. I walked up to her, trying to interpret the expression on her handsome face. At least she didn't look cross. 'It's all right. You're not going to be punished. I've a little job for you. Olivia Kemp has been taken ill, and I'd like you to go and sit with her until she goes home. You'll find her in the lost property room.'

I scowled at Miss Pardoe's back as she strode off towards the staff room. Just my luck.

The lost property room was a narrow hole next to the changing rooms with a cold stone floor and a stained enamel sink on one wall. There were a couple of hard, ink-stained chairs inside and a small cabinet screwed to the wall, always locked and containing a rudimentary first aid kit. Apart from that there were two disintegrating baskets into which were thrown any items of lost clothing or kit found round the school. The room stank of sweaty Aertex and rubber pumps, and there was only one high little window, so it was gloomy as well as smelly.

And on top of that it had to be snotty, top-of-the-class Olivia Kemp. Although we were in the same class, I'd mostly kept out of her way until now. For one thing Olivia was glorious to look at, skinny, with those huge brown eyes like a puppy's and thick, curling brown hair. I was plump with hair that was neither blond nor mousy but somewhere in between, and I had to wear specs that crouched across my nose like black crows. Olivia sat in the corner desk at the front of the class, head bent, working and working, or listening with wide eyes and what seemed exaggerated intentness to whatever the teacher was saying. She got marvellous marks and we all thought her frightfully stuck up. And she was Councillor Kemp's daughter. Everyone in Birmingham had heard of Alec Kemp. He was the youngest yet one of the most prominent councillors in the city, and a very handsome one at that. You could see where she got her looks from.

I had enough friends to pair off with in class or at games if I needed to – Marjorie Mantel and Celia Oakley were always available. Now I actually came to think about it I wasn't sure who Olivia's friends were. She seemed to keep people at a distance. But I was sure she had much bigger fish to fry than me. Shame one of them hadn't been landed with the job of looking after her. I hoped her mother would be quick. No doubt she would be utterly ravishing and think to herself what an ugly lump I was while being sweetly polite to me.

I flung open the door of the little cell-like room so

violently that the brass handle banged hard into the wall behind it. Olivia was sitting on one of the two upright chairs, feet in white ankle socks and black shoes, not touching the floor. On her lap was a white enamel bowl. Her eyes widened as I crashed into the room. She looked very small alone there in the murky light. I could see her eyes were full and her cheeks wet.

'Oh, it's you.' Quickly she rubbed the backs of her hands across her eyes as I shut the door behind me. 'I do feel rotten.'

I stood opposite her, hands on hips. 'Miss Pardoe says I've got to look after you.'

Olivia looked up at me doubtfully. 'You look very cross,' she said. 'Actually, you very often look cross.'

Did I? I wondered, intrigued by this observation. Against my will I felt sorry for her. 'I'm not cross. I say, you do look awfully seedy. D'you still feel sick?' It would be rather interesting to see Councillor Kemp's daughter being sick in a bowl.

'Not at the moment.'

We eyed each other warily. I sat down on the other chair, opposite her.

'I suppose they've sent for my mother?' Olivia looked across at me. She had tears in her eyes again.

'I expect so,' I replied gruffly. 'Doesn't she like you being ill? My mother says we make enough mess when we're well.'

In fact I said this mostly to cheer her up, our times of illness being those when Mummy seemed to find us most tolerable.

Olivia giggled suddenly, a rippling, infectious sound, and surprisingly loud. 'D'you like your parents?' she asked.

I thought about it. My parents felt like shadows who hovered round the edges of my life. My father was forever working. 'No, not all that much,' I said.

Olivia looked perturbed for a second at my response, then she gave a strange smile, her teeth almost bared. 'My parents are absolutely marvellous.' Her expression changed to one of curiosity. 'D'you always say what you think?'

'Mostly.' No one else at home did, so I felt I might as well.

Olivia considered this. 'You can probably get away with it because you're rather plain. If you're pretty, everyone seems to expect such a lot of you.'

'Thanks very much.'

She clapped one hand to her mouth, eyes wider, laughing with embarrassment. 'Golly, I shouldn't have said that. I didn't mean it really. I think you're nice.'

'That's all right.' For the first time I smiled at her. She wasn't really a bit stuck up, not the way I'd imagined. 'Anyway, it's not true – that I get away with it, I mean. I always seem to be in trouble with Mummy, and she thinks my brother William's the bee's blinking knees.'

Olivia was quiet and I realized she was only half listening to me.

'Are you going to be sick again?' I felt slightly less hopeful about it now.

Olivia nodded miserably. Her face had gone very pale and her forehead had broken out in a sweat. Her head lolled forward, her thin hands clutching the bowl tightly. Surprised at myself, I went over to her, put one hand on her shoulder and with the other held back some loose wisps of her hair. I could see ginger lights in it. Green liquid gushed suddenly from her mouth into the white of the bowl. She retched and I felt the force of it go through her. She gulped and panted. I fetched her a cup of water.

'Here.' My feelings of protectiveness took me totally by surprise.

'Ugh.' She wiped her mouth and sipped the water as I emptied the bowl into the old sink and rinsed it out. 'That was horrid. Thanks though. I feel better.'

From that morning on, we were inseparable.

My life changed when I got to know her. We were besotted with each other in the way young girls can be. Both of us had been lonely and needed someone to talk to. We loved each other's company. At home there was only William, and sometimes Angus from next door. Marjorie Mantel and Celia Oakley were pale substitutes for such a friend. I felt butterflies of excitement in my stomach at the thought of seeing Olivia. She was above all things lovable, and for that you could forgive her a great deal.

As well as being in the same class she lived less than half a mile away from us. We'd sit in her huge bedroom on Park Hill, its bay windows letting in sheets of sunlight, happy for hours, talking and laughing together. Often I don't think we even knew why we were laughing. It was just pleasure in being together.

I loved that room. It was such a pretty, girlish place, stuffed full of things: a flowery chair on which dolls and teddies and other animals snuggled together, their glass eyes or button replacements peering out between each other's furry limbs, a grand doll's house on a table, her shelf stuffed with books and her cupboard and drawers full of pretty, feminine clothes. We weren't allowed pets at home, but they even let Olivia keep her two budgerigars in her room, and they flapped around and rang their little bell in a cage near the window.

'Don't they keep you awake?' I asked her.

'No, silly. I cover them up and they go to sleep on their perches.' Even this made us laugh.

Best of all, though, was Olivia's little dressing table with its dainty drawers, its embroidered mats on the top and its bright, slanting looking-glass. The ones in our house looked as if someone had gone over them with sandpaper and they made your face look squiffy. The top of the dressing table was covered with all her pretty things, her silver-plated brush and comb, her jewellery box from which tumbled a muddle of hairslides and combs, necklaces, rings, and a little woven basket with a few of Elizabeth Kemp's discarded lipsticks and powder compacts. She had perfume and ribbons, she had cushions on the bed and pretty prints on the walls of flower fairies and some chubby children playing with a spaniel pup.

My own room was comfortable enough, but very plain. Candlewick bedspread, my old doll and my favourite teddy, Bosey. A small table, books . . . And usually the only other rooms I saw were William's, which was very dull, and Angus's, with his model aeroplanes everywhere and the smell of adhesive. Olivia's room seemed a place of enchantment.

And she made me feel like a girl.

'Come on, Katie,' she'd say. 'Let's make ourselves up.' She'd daub my face with rouge and powder, pencil in wobbly lines along my eyebrows and smooth on lipstick with a flourish. Then I'd do her, once she'd taught me how. My mother never wore make-up, except the odd dab of powder which she applied as a kind of nervous habit like some people smoked cigarettes.

Then we'd sit squeezed side by side on the silky-seated stool in front of Olivia's toilet mirror, our faces close together, admiring the effects we'd created. At other times we did clown faces. Or Livy would just paint her lips thickly with scarlet, and pout and roll her eyes at the glass until we were both laughing so much we couldn't paint anything straight.

We played the piano together. We helped each other with our prep from school. Although she was usually top of the class I was sometimes able to help her, especially with arithmetic, which boosted my confidence no end because William was always held up as the one with the brains.

And most importantly, I could tell Livy anything.

'You're so lucky having a brother,' she said to me wistfully one day.

'No I'm not. I hate him.'

'You don't.'

'All right. Not hate. But he's such a smug boots. He's always got to have done something marvellous all the time. He has to be best. And he's smug to Angus too, and Angus is really good at some things and much kinder than William.'

'Well I think it's nice. Much better than being the only one all the time, like me.'

But I felt that being on your own would be quite all right if you had parents like Olivia's: a beautiful, sweet mother like Elizabeth Kemp with her soft, blond looks, and Alec Kemp. The amazing, glorious Alec Kemp. He was the most exciting man I had ever met. For the first time in my life he and Olivia made me feel pretty. Since I met the Kemps I felt I had become a different person: more appreciated and contented than I had been since I was a very small child.

Chapter 2

I remember the shiny perfection of that day.

The Onion Fair – and with Olivia and Alec Kemp! We sat in the back of his Bentley, every line of it sleek and gleaming, singing, 'We're going to the fair, the fair, the fair,' to the tune of 'The cat's got the measles . . .'

'I want to go on everything!' Olivia cried, bouncing excitedly in her seat as we swept towards the centre of Birmingham.

'Oh, I expect we can arrange that,' Alec said easily from the driver's seat. The two of us shivered and giggled with delight.

Olivia was wearing a very pretty dress in cream broderie anglaise, a matching strip of the material holding back her wild hair. My dress was of course much plainer and more 'serviceable' as Mummy would say, in blue and white gingham. But I did have a beautiful tortoiseshell slide to fasten my hair, which Livy had given me. She was forever giving me things.

She peered out of the window. 'Are we going past the factory, Daddy?'

'No,' Alec Kemp replied, steering the huge, smooth-running car along the cobbled streets. He had a deep voice and was proud of his Birmingham accent. 'No need today. We're going out for some fun, aren't we, girls?'

I stared at the back of his neck, the dark brown hair

cut in a precise line above his white collar and beautifully tailored suit. It was a surprisingly sober suit for his tastes, in grey worsted. He seemed so much bigger than my father, who always had a stooped look as if other people's problems were actually fixed heavy on his shoulders. Alec Kemp stood very tall and he was jaunty, engaging, with large brown eyes and a vivacious face.

People turned to stare at us as the Bentley eased to a standstill at the edge of the Serpentine ground in Perry Barr. The two of us must have looked very small sitting on the plush back seats, peering out eagerly, our feet not touching the floor. Most people came to the fairground by bus or tram, but we were arriving with Councillor Kemp.

'Will people recognize him?' I whispered.

'Of course.'

Of course. Pictures in the *Mail* and *Gazette*, always immaculately dressed in expensive suits with suave, black hats, or clad in vivid Prince of Wales checks. He would smile genially from the photographs, his image of himself carefully presented.

'Will you have your picture in the papers today?' I couldn't resist asking him.

'We'll have to see,' he said. 'I could have my photograph taken with my daughter and her lovely friend perhaps?'

I squirmed with pleasure. Alec Kemp had a way of making you feel like a princess in gold slippers, even if you knew you really looked more like one of the pumpkins.

The fairground was already packed and milling with people. As we walked from the car we could hear shouting and screams of laughter from some of the rides, the throb of hot engines driving the roundabouts and a band playing. Everywhere we looked was a blur of curved, coloured movement: merry-go-rounds turning and the twirl of dancing skirts and lights flashing on the machines and sideshows. And smells: a delicious mixture of potatoes baking, fried onions, cigarettes and sweat and the sharp whiff of blue smoke from the engines overlaid by sweetness of candyfloss.

'Don't get lost now, girls,' Alec said. 'I'd have one heck of a job finding you again in this throng.' With his pipe jutting from the side of his mouth he took our hands and I felt the smallness of my hand in his huge palm. I was almost bursting with pride. As we walked along he smiled and raised his hat to people, took his pipe out of his mouth, loosing us each time and then reaching for our hands again. The smell of his tobacco smoke wafted down to us. I looked up at the tall, athletic figure beside me. I saw women of all ages blushing as he smiled and spoke to them.

One young woman approached him, smiled coyly and said, 'Aft'noon, Mr Kemp.' And Alec replied, 'Good day, Violet.' She walked away giggling with her friend, casting backward glances over her shoulder.

'How does she know you?' Olivia asked.

'She's from the works,' he told her.

Alec Kemp was one of Birmingham's darlings. Born and educated in the city, he had won his way to grammar school and become a self-made man without ever leaving the place. He had taken over his father's mediocre firm and used it to prove himself. Kemp's was squeezed into a plot of land behind Birch Street, near the heart of Birmingham, round which were crushed streets of grimy dwellings, and tiny workshops and chimneys pouring out black smoke into the already speckled air. But Alec's reward for economic prowess had been to move from the terrace in Sparkhill where he grew up, to one of the huge, ornate houses gracing the streets of middle-class Moseley. And this was considered quite fitting for a young, successful man so obviously destined to become one of the city's aldermen, and particularly one who had taken the condition of the city's housing so much to heart. He had already completed a successful campaign to demolish one of the decaying blocks of Victorian slums in the Birch Street area and build innovatory flats to house the occupants. His campaign slogan was 'Prosperity and Responsibility'.

And it's Livy and me who are with him, I thought. No one else. I felt more presentable than usual, wearing that frock instead of the cut-down pair of William's shorts that Mummy so often dressed me in. If only I didn't have to wear my ugly specs . . .

Alec treated us to everything that afternoon. 'Here, you'd love a go on this,' and 'Come on girls, I remember this one from when I was a kid.' He lengthened his stride towards the biggest merry-go-round with the horses gliding up and down so high above us, its banner reading 'Rides for Young and Old'.

'I wish Daddy was like your father,' I said excitedly to Olivia. 'He'd never spend money on things like this.'

Olivia grinned mischievously. 'He's all work, work, work. That's no fun, is it?'

My father was forever working, busy with his patients or in the study. Reading, writing: Christian ethics, papers on improving the health of the nation. His work as a doctor and his Christian Socialist principles didn't leave him much time for leisure. Quite unlike this glamorous, thrilling, all-providing Father Christmas who was Olivia's father. No wonder Elizabeth Kemp adored him so. How could you not envy her, being married to such a man? Largesse flowed from his fingers, pouring out over the whole city.

The horses slowed suddenly, people climbing down before they had stopped, and it was our turn. We rode together on one of the painted horses, knees gripping the cool smooth flanks. I sat behind, my arms tight round Olivia's waist, and her hands gripped the twisted metal pole. We laughed and screamed to the loud music. 'I'm flying!' I shrieked, and Olivia just giggled and giggled.

He took us on the helter-skelter and the Big Bens, the steam yachts which swung up until they were at right angles to the ground, leaving your stomach behind as they came down again with everyone screaming. We laughed our way helplessly along the shuddering cake walk. He bought us hot potatoes, balloons, furry stick-fuls of candyfloss.

'It's like eating knitting,' I said cheekily, and Alec lunged for it, teasing me. 'All right. If you're going to be fussy, I'll have it!'

But Olivia stopped suddenly, taking in the sight of one of the traction engines which pulled the trailers, right in front of us. It was a brilliant emerald green, the sunlight catching its polished brass funnel.

'I've got to go on one of those!' she cried and, candyfloss still in hand, she dashed across the dry ground, wisps of her hair and her cream skirt flying behind her. I followed, letting go of Alec Kemp's hand, scared for a moment by her impulsiveness. Only days ago I'd watched her climb the parapet of a little bridge over the River Cole, scrambling up, shouting triumphant, then falling. She was unhurt but wet and scared. But she could make you frightened for her. Sometimes I wished I could tie her down. I felt staid and solid beside her.

'That's not a ride, Olivia!' Alec shouted. He strode after us. 'Come back. You'll get lost.'

But she was already standing next to the majestic machine. She had to have what she wanted. By the time he reached her she was already climbing up into it. We could hear its throb, the power of it. She was chatting to the men working the engine, who smiled back, captivated but bemused, caps on heads and their hands black with grease.

'We've told her we can't move it, sir.' One of them climbed down to speak to Alec Kemp, who raised his hat to him. 'Not now, in this crowd.'

'That's quite all right. She shouldn't be up there,' Alec replied. I saw him slip coins into the man's hand. 'Thank you.'

That was the one cross moment. I had seen the panic in his face as Olivia dived into the crowd. Now he gripped her so hard that she yelped. When he let go there was a pink, suffusing mark on her arm.

'You must never go off like that again, you silly girl. D'you hear?' I could hear the anger like needles in his voice. 'Now stay close to me all the time or you'll get into trouble.'

Olivia stared at the ground, lower lip thrust out. I could tell she was near tears.

'I'm sorry,' she said in a little high voice. 'But it was so exciting.'

'Never mind, princess.' Alec recovered quickly and swung her up into his arms for a moment. 'Daddy doesn't want to be cross. Come on. Let's go and find something else you can have a go on.'

The photograph was taken after one of our merry-go-round rides. A young fellow with sticking-out teeth and a badly fitting suit approached us with his camera. 'Councillor Kemp, I'm from the *Gazette*. Could I trouble you for a picture?'

'Of course. It's no trouble, is it girls?' He smiled amiably. Courtesy to everyone, he maintained, was the trick. He was a great one for presenting the right image. 'Would you like the girls in as well?'

'That'll be a treat,' the young man said, squinting into his lens. 'Stand nice and close together now.'

We were both still alight with the thrill of it, standing warm together, arms wrapped round each other's back, utterly friends and absolutely happy.

The picture made the evening edition.

* * *

OLIVIA

They moved the piano forward in the drawing room, left music open on it and a vase of huge chrysanths on the top, which spread a heavy scent through the room.

'Don't make me,' I begged Mummy. 'Please. I don't want to I can't.'

'Oh, Olivia.' Mummy knelt down beside me immediately. Her face was white. She implored me with her eyes. She had to make me, had to, for him. 'Daddy's so proud of you. Do it for him, please, my darling. You must do things for Daddy to make him happy.'

She put her arms round me. She was so thin and pale. I could smell her cologne. 'Please Olivia, my pretty darling. You're so clever.'

She cupped my face in her hands, stared into my eyes and she was frightened, I knew. She stroked my hair as if I were a pony. I had no choice. I was only ten and they expected me to play in front of all those people: councillors, aldermen, even MPs like Neville Chamberlain.

'We'll ask Kate to come along and keep you company,' Mummy said.

It was 1931, the summer leading up to the formation of the National Government. They were all smug and expectant, of course, much talk of the eclipse of Socialism, Ramsay MacDonald having fluffed it. Waiting like vampires to do their duty for King and Country.

Daddy held a party, which meant giving orders for a marquee, terracotta pots with cascades of geraniums and busy Lizzies spilling from them like blood, lanterns strung between posts in the garden for when dusk came, and days of frenzied preparation of food. Mummy was pretty and charming but she was a draper's daughter. She had a little green book called *How to Entertain*, and kept it by her bed like a Gideon Bible. The responsibility made her eyes bulge. It took away her sleep.

I went to talk to Lady and King, my budgerigars. They were in my bedroom. I was allowed them there as long as I kept them clean. Lady was an unpromising-looking creature, pale sulphur colour with a smudge of green down one wing. King, though, looked perfectly splendid. A green-patterned bird, he lived up to his name, mottled with black and majestic. But they were such mute birds. They made sounds but they didn't speak. I wanted them to talk to me.

Sometimes I got angry with them. 'Say something. Speak, will you? Say, "Pretty Livy." Don't just sit there looking stupid like that!'

They'd chatter together sometimes, harsh, shocking outbursts of noise like dried beans falling on lino, but usually when I wasn't in the room. I'd listen from outside, hearing them gossiping, confiding things between them or fighting over the seed. They fluttered around in a frenzy, pattering their droppings down on the floor of the cage for me to clear up. When I went in they'd go silent suddenly, as if I was interrupting something.

It was like that that morning. As I climbed the soft, red stair carpet, I could hear them chirruping from the other end of the corridor. I tiptoed, my feet making no sound. I stepped over the raised, creaky board on the dark landing, knowing exactly where it was. I even held my breath when I reached the long strip of light by my bedroom door. They were hopping round the circular cage, chatting like an old couple reminiscing. Cosy, it was. I stood at the door listening, feeling angry. One of them rang the little bell I'd hung in there for them. They hopped and fanned with their wings.

Slowly and silently I slid into the room. They didn't see me at first. When my shape and movement came to their attention they stopped. They sat quite still, watching me warily, like they always did.

'Go on,' I said sweetly, squatting down beside the cage. 'You don't have to stop because of me. Keep talking – I like to hear you.' I pressed my nose against the bars. They fled to the opposite side of the cage and stood on the bottom, shifting nervously from one horrible naked pink foot to the other. I hated to see their scalded-looking skin and the way they were so scared and shifty.

'All right,' I wheedled. 'If you've got nothing to say, I'll talk to you. Daddy's having one of his parties tonight and there's a big tent on the lawn in case it rains, though it doesn't look as if it will. And all the important people Daddy knows are coming. And he's going to make me play the piano in front of them and I don't *want* to! I HATE THEM ALL STARING AT ME!'

My shouting made the birds panic. They crashed around the cage, nowhere to escape to, their wings clumsily hitting each other, beaks open and vicious. Sometimes I thought they might peck each other to death to escape me.

'It's all right, I'm sorry,' I soothed them. 'I'll tell you something nice now. Something that makes it better. Katie's coming. My best friend Katie. You like her, don't you? She doesn't scare you. She's coming to keep me company and stop them all pressing in on me with their eyes. Katie doesn't mind it. She doesn't see it. She loves me.'

And I loved her. How I loved her

'Much more than you ugly little pigs,' I said to Lady and King. I stuck my tongue out at them.

Dear Kate. She was so overwhelmed by it all. So impressed. Her family were restrained and colourless. She was always wide-eyed and in love with us, her round face pink at a word from Daddy. He charmed her as if with a magic pipe and she lay squirming at his feet. She was so sweet. Of course she was plump and she had to wear those dreadful glasses, but she was a darling behind all that gruff self-protectiveness. Win Munro never gave her an ounce of self-esteem. She had no idea how to say anything warm or caressing. It was my parents who did that for her. And Daddy was so fond of Kate back then, giving attention in a way that he never normally did to women who weren't beautiful.

But you couldn't not like Kate. She was full of innocence and fortitude. She'd go to the ends of the earth for you in her tight cotton frocks and buckled sandals.

'Gosh, Livy, it's beautiful!' she cried, looking round the garden with her mouth open. The wisteria was hanging in flower and there were garlands of lilies round the entrance to the marquee. The servants were on the run, Dawson and O'Callaghan heaving a huge side of cooked meat on a platter.

'My feet are killing me already,' O'Callaghan moaned. I hadn't got the measure of O'Callaghan yet, she was a new one. The maids were always coming and going. Except Dawson. Dawson was a very sensible woman. She'd learned: she lived out and had a small child and no husband. She hung on to her job with us.

It was already nearly dusk when the guests arrived. Lanterns glowed between the leaves in the garden. Mummy had dressed me in a white bridal frock like Betty McNamee wore for her First Communion. Kate's dress was pale green and as frumpy as ever, poor thing, but I could never lend her one of mine because she couldn't fit into them.

'It's gorgeous, Livy,' she said wistfully to me. She wasn't jealous. That wasn't Kate. She just admired. Her heart was so whole. She didn't see bad things and I didn't want to make her. I needed her to believe in us, in our fairy tale, so we could have her wonder, her adoration.

We stayed at the edge of the crowd, darting to the table to fill our plates. Kate ate, I picked at the food, the meats and sweet tomatoes and eggs and prawns trapped in aspic. I gave my most angelic smiles to those who stopped me and spoke.

'You're not eating much,' Katie said, as we sat in our spot near the shrubbery and watched.

I was sick with nerves. 'Oh, I've seen the food going past under my nose all day,' I said. 'Dawson and O'Callaghan gave me some bits to eat. I've no space left.'

We gazed up at the shadowy figures around us, the men in their dark suits and the shimmering, coloured silks of the ladies' long dresses which swished across the grass as they walked. I pointed to a tall, lean man talking earnestly near us. 'Neville Chamberlain,' I told Kate. 'Look, there's his wife over there.'

'She's gorgeous,' Kate breathed, peering over at Annie Chamberlain, swathed in pale violet silk. 'Look at that dress.'

We took in fragments of conversation. There was much talk of the election and the downfall of Socialism, and of riots breaking up meetings of the New Party. Labour's darling MP for Smethwick, carried on shoulders through the street after the 1929 election, dark and dashing with a red rosette, had soon fallen foul of the Prime Minister, Ramsay MacDonald. Oswald Mosley's meetings in the Bull Ring were now broken up by hecklers, bottles and chairs flung into the crowd by irate members of the Labour Party.

'Quite extraordinary, Mosley's lot seem to be,' a voice said. 'Bunch of thugs. Fearful tribe.'

Oswald Mosley had become the *bête noire*, but of course the Tories weren't complaining. I was fascinated by Mosley. He was so attractive. There was something diamond hard about him, and everything dark: his hair, clothes, heart, black and dangerous as a cobra.

'Olivia?' Daddy's voice cut across the chatter of the guests. 'Have you seen my girl? Where are you, Livy?'

I loved him so much I wanted to run into his arms, do anything I could to please him. My daddy, my handsome, adoring father. I was all to him, his kitten, his princess. He wanted to show me off in front of his friends. The piano. I felt my stomach lunge and buckle.

'Olivia?' Kate cried in alarm. I stood retching in the darkness behind the blossoms of buddleia, its drugging scent all around me. The guests couldn't have noticed.

Wiping a spot of my mess from my shiny black shoe on to the grass, I walked from behind the leaves, standing up very straight.

Kate was big-eyed. 'Here, drink this.' She handed me her glass of ginger beer.

'Been over-eating, Olivia?' Daddy teased softly. He loomed over us both, immaculate in his evening dress. Kate beamed up at him. 'Come on now, they want to hear you play.'

The piano was my passion. I knew I was good, brilliant perhaps. It was something I was sure of, deep in me. But my music was precious, intimate. I liked playing for myself, and for Kate, not for strangers. But I had to do it to make him happy.

A semi-circle of them were sitting, polite and expectant, in the drawing room, skirts carefully arranged, on chairs and on the sofa, some of the men standing and smoking, wafting the smell of it round the room. As I walked in and the talk lowered I could hear the ladies exclaiming to each other how pretty I looked, what a darling child.

I tried to pretend they weren't there. I walked to the piano and sat down, closing my eyes for a second. But when I opened them I saw Kate had slipped into the room and was standing blushing by the door. I remember feeling aggravated by that. They weren't looking at her, so why was she all tomato red?

'Tell us what you're going to play, Olivia,' Daddy prompted me.

I looked up. They were all smiling. Lipstick lips, moustaches, rows of teeth. I knew I looked sweet and pretty and small. I was too short to reach the pedals.

'M-Mozart,' I said. The stammer was deliberate of course.

I chose something easy and rattled it off, badly. Three sonatas played perfunctorily. I kept my face down, my heart pounding. The music did nothing for me. I wasn't lost in it. I was outside it and hating those people. Hating them all.

Of course they all clapped. They had to. I boiled inside. Clapping something bad. Hypocrites.

'Bravo!' a voice boomed.

'What a lovely child.'

'Credit to you, Alec!'

My feet took me across the cream Persian rug and out of there, running up the stairs to my room and my sleeping birds. Kate followed me. Moments later I was sobbing, held in her round, comforting arms.

Chapter 3

Devon, July 1935

'Livy? I love you.'

'You shouldn't say that.' Olivia sat up abruptly in her bed across the room. 'Girls aren't supposed to love girls. Not like that.'

'Not like anything,' I protested. 'Why d'you have to twist things? I just love you. You're my best friend.'

Olivia relented and rolled sleepily across the bed again, grinning through strands of hair. 'Funny old thing. I love you too.'

I lay back on the firm pillow. I was so happy. On holiday with the Kemps – in a hotel! I stretched and wiggled my toes, the dry grains of sand scratchy between them. The cotton sheet felt delicious against my bare legs. I couldn't see anything clearly because my specs lay on the chair next to the bed. The light in the room was a blurry green, filtered through curtains which wafted by the open window, through which we could hear the waves.

Our first full day there and everything about it felt right. The sun was shining and only tiny puffs of cloud shifted slowly across the sky. We had swum and climbed on the rocks all morning while Elizabeth Kemp lay back in a chair on the sand and Alec had taken a boat out. We were now resting to let our lunch go down before swimming again. And the best thing of all was that we'd talked and laughed together all the morning, just her and me as close as close.

Before lunch we walked up the steep path from the beach to the cliff top, our legs scratched by gorse as we climbed the path of compacted mud, small stones rattling away from our pumps. We found a place to sit on the wiry grass which topped the headland, and looked out over the hazy blue of the estuary, tiny white sails in the distance.

Olivia sat leaning back on her hands, her legs stretched out in front, the warm wind blowing her hair back from her face.

'I found a piano in that back sitting room in the hotel,' she said. 'So we shan't have to do without playing after all.'

'No music.'

'But we'll remember it, won't we?'

When she said we I knew she really just meant herself. She sat for hours at a time in front of the piano at home, whereas I was forever looking for excuses to get out of practising, and Mummy didn't pay too much attention to whether I did or not.

'It'll be something to do after dinner,' Olivia said. 'If we're not already done in from all this fresh air.'

She leaned her head back and closed her eyes. I could see the shape of her eyes moving restlessly under the lids. I sat watching her. Both of us had changed in appearance since we first became friends, but we had spent so much of our time together that I barely noticed Olivia's looks alter any more than I did my own. Since she had been away at school in Staffordshire and I didn't see her for weeks on end, though, I'd begun to notice things. Livy's voice, which was deep and strong, had become even more forthright with a confidence that the school had given her, its Birmingham intonation fading. Her hair was thicker and glossier. She was thinner, had a waist suddenly, and breasts. Curiously I looked down at my own body. I'd certainly not been short-changed on that front. Just like my Granny Munro. My legs looked much pinker and rounder than Olivia's slim ones.

'I wish they hadn't sent you away to that school.' It was far from the first time I'd made this complaint. 'It's not the same without you around.'

I was waiting for Olivia to agree and say how much she missed me during the term time and how there was no one else at school who was half such a good friend. This familiar conversation was like a ritual seal on our friendship.

But this time Olivia said, without even opening her eyes, 'Well, it could be worse. Gets me away from them at least.'

'Who?'

'Mummy and Daddy, of course.'

'But they're marvellous, your parents!'

Olivia started laughing, sitting up hugging her knees, her body shaking.

'What? What did I say?'

'Oh, Katie. You're so innocent, aren't you?'

I felt cross suddenly. Olivia was putting on that superior tone she sometimes used, as if the fact that she was a mere six months older let her into all sorts of adult secrets.

'I'm not,' I said sulkily. 'Granny Munro tells me all sorts of things.'

Olivia laughed again. 'How is your mad granny?'

'She's not mad,' I protested, with a reluctant grin. 'She does it all on purpose.'

Granny Munro, Daddy's mother, had come from Scotland to live with us only three months ago, after my grandfather died. She had made up a little bit for Livy not being around. Already she had appeared at the breakfast table with no clothes on, told the local grocer's that she needed biscuits and cheese on tick because we wouldn't give her any money and set up a trestle table at the front of the house in Chantry Road in order to hold her own jumble sale because she had brought too many possessions to Birmingham with her. She was driving Mummy nearly demented.

'It's been really fun having her living with us,' I said. 'She tells me all sorts of things Mummy would never dream of saying.'

Olivia had lain back suddenly, head among the blades of grass, her eyes closed. 'Lucky old you,' she said in a bored voice. I felt rather hurt and didn't bother telling her any more.

She'd never explained what she meant about her parents, I thought, lying on the warm bed. Perhaps it wasn't anything. Maybe it was just one of those Olivia things to say, making a drama out of nothing much.

'Livy?' I lifted my head, resting it sideways on my tanned arm.

'Mmm?'

'Let's take the boat out later?'

Olivia nodded, eyes closed.

I took a deep, contented breath, enjoying the smells of the little hotel: floor polish and cabbage and Rinso on the sheets. I'd have liked Angus to see the place. In fact I was feeling so well disposed towards everyone that I'd almost have liked William to be there.

I knew Olivia's parents were having a rest in the next room. They had the very end room along the corridor facing the sea, and ours was next to it. A touch ashamed of myself I tried to imagine Alec and Elizabeth Kemp lying together on the bed which I'd glimpsed that morning through their door. Elizabeth would have unpinned her soft, fair hair. Perhaps she would have changed into a loose gown for taking a rest. My imagination skated quickly over Elizabeth's slight body. Beside her I pictured Alec's darker, more robust one. His handsome face with those brown dancing eyes would be close to Elizabeth's. Was he leaning over her? I wondered. I thought I could hear their voices through the wall. Was he about to kiss her? Would he then do *that* to her? What Granny Munro had told me about that I knew my parents could not bring themselves to mention?

For a moment I allowed myself to imagine Alec Kemp leaning over me, his lips moving closer to mine . . . Of course Alec was my best friend's father and I was a rather lumpish fourteen-year-old with thick spectacles. But he was also the prince in every story. Kiss any frog, I thought, and it would transform instantly into Alec Kemp.

I heard a door open, close again. Growing sleepy I followed the faded pattern of dog roses and convolvulus on the wallpaper, hearing the rustle of the sea. As my eyes closed and I began to drift into sleep I heard noises from next door and was suddenly awake again. The sounds were soon unmistakable. I held my body absolutely still, listening, me heart starting to beat very fast. The sound of weeping was so desolate, so intense, and it could only be coming from Elizabeth Kemp. At first her crying was quiet and muffled. I waited, expecting to hear Alec's voice comforting her, but there was nothing except these terrible broken cries. For a few moments

Elizabeth sobbed loudly and uncontrollably before the sounds died down. Then there was silence.

When I woke, Olivia had already gone.

I stood by the window, enjoying the salty air and looking for her. From below came the sounds of children shouting, a dog barking, a boat's engine in the distance somewhere. The hotel was sited in the angle of a narrow bay with only a few cottages for company and a narrow road passing through. Round the headland was a small holiday town, which could be reached by the road or a short ferry ride.

The tide was out and shadows from the cliffs were already beginning to edge across the sand. Everything had turned the richer colours of late afternoon and children were busy digging on the wide shiny platter which was now the lower half of the beach.

The memory of Elizabeth Kemp's crying shifted uneasily round my mind. I had always liked Elizabeth. She was very gentle, a timid person who I had scarcely heard utter an angry word since I'd known her. She wasn't a vibrant woman. She was unsure of herself and she provided a counterbalance to Alec, his restlessness and drive. But there was a sweetness about her and she always gave me a warm welcome. Above all she obviously loved and admired her successful husband with wholehearted devotion. So what could have brought on such broken-sounding grief? I tried to persuade myself that I'd been mistaken and the noise had been coming from somewhere else.

The boat was drawing closer. It was the ferry. The red paint on the hull became visible, the engine droned louder as it advanced on the low stone jetty, pulling in with a churn of reversing engines.

As the passengers climbed out, a movement caught my eye, something known, familiar. Alec Kemp walking the tapering jetty among them, jumping down athletically. He was dressed in navy trousers and a white shirt, unbuttoned at the neck, and already his arms and face had lost their city pallor. He looked tanned and healthy. He held a cigarette in one hand; on his face was a look of satisfaction, amusement even. When he reached the hotel he stood, facing the beach, to finish smoking. I knew instinctively that there was something wrong in his being there. I drew my head in quickly, closed the window and waited a few more minutes before going down to find Olivia. By then he'd gone.

Olivia was down near the sea, scraping wet sand out of the blue rowing boat, *Serenade*, which Alec had hired for the week. The breeze puffed out the yellow blouse she was wearing over her swimming costume. She was not alone. Three boys were standing round her, and as I drew closer I saw that they were much our age, perhaps older, locals by the look of them, who were watching Olivia, giving unwanted advice, bantering with her. Olivia had let her hair loose in a wavy curtain down her back. Uncertain, I went and stood by them, wishing they'd go away.

'Need a bit of help pushing her off?' one of the boys said in his curvy Devonshire accent.

'We'll give you a push off all right!' another said, and they all sniggered. 'Want us to come along with you?'

To my surprise, Olivia, instead of telling them to get lost, was smiling impishly at them. 'I don't think you'd better come in the boat,' she said, 'but we could do with a bit of help getting going.'

'Getting going!' the third lad echoed, and they all

laughed raucously as if she'd said something funny or dirty.

'This your friend is she?' one of them asked, eyeing me up and down. 'Shouldn't think you'd need much of a hand with her to help you.'

I scowled at them. I didn't like being compared unfavourably with Olivia. I stood there awkwardly, dressed in an ungainly old pair of William's shorts.

'Ooh – she don't like us!'

To my fury, Olivia carried on smiling and humouring the boys long enough to let them help us drag the boat the final few yards to the sea. The bow slid into the water, rising and dropping suddenly as the force of each wave broke over it, and we clambered in.

'Right, here you go,' the boys shouted, standing thigh deep in the water, the edges of their shorts wafting with the water's movement. The boat was already well afloat, but they pushed us off, cheering and waving exaggeratedly as Olivia started to row. She stopped and waved back. I kept my hands by my sides, frowning.

'We didn't need those idiots!' I exploded furiously as soon as we were a distance from them. 'Why did you let them?'

'Oh I know we didn't, but you have to keep them happy, don't you?' she said in a pettish voice. 'Anyway, what's eating you?'

I didn't answer. I watched the water curl away from the oars. Peering down I could still see pebbles and sand on the bottom and trails of green weed. I screwed up my eyes against the white light on the water. I hated it when Olivia was like this. She had suddenly gone into what I called her witch mood, when she was sharp and mean and stirring up trouble and I couldn't get near her.

After a while I said, 'I saw your dad. He'd been to the town.'

For a second Olivia hesitated, frowning, the oars stilled at right-angles to the boat. Then, abruptly, she carried on rowing.

'Can I have a go now?'

We swapped places and I started off, enjoying the pull against the water, the feel of using all my strength. I dug in hard, trying to force the boat fast across the bay.

'Don't pull down so deep,' Olivia snapped. 'You'll catch a crab.'

'Look. What's the matter? What've I done?'

'Nothing.' Olivia stared down miserably into the bottom of the boat. 'You haven't done anything.'

The breeze helped propel us back towards the beach. Soon the prow jerked the boat to a halt against the sandy bottom and it tipped sideways so we were forced to jump out.

'One, two, three, pull!' we cried, hauling the little boat along the beach with exaggerated effort. Several times we fell over backwards and lay side by side, helpless with laughter, the sharp words forgotten, our hair getting thick and gritty with sand.

'Come on, you daft thing,' Olivia giggled weakly. 'Or we'll never get it up there.'

The beach was in shade now except for a slice down one side. Picnickers were packing up their windshields and Thermoses.

'Girls!'

Shading our eyes, we saw Alec Kemp moving towards us with his long stride, the dark trousers flapping round his legs in the breeze. I was squatting down next to the boat. Olivia stiffened.

'Don't move.' He grinned at us. 'That'll make a lovely picture.' He raised his Brownie camera, legs bent slightly and elbows out to get the angle right, and clicked down the shutter. 'One more.' Another click. 'There. That'll do nicely.'

He helped us position the boat up by the sea wall and we went to the hotel. As we crossed the road, quiet as it was, he took our hands as if we were small children before walking across. I was thrilled.

We ate each evening in the dining room of the hotel at tables with stiff white tablecloths and vases of miniature silk roses. It was a family hotel, not a posh establishment, but it had a wine list and tried to keep up certain standards. I was allowed to drink wine – wine! Alcohol was something my parents didn't hold with.

It was several evenings into the holiday and it had been raining most of the day. We'd woken to a fine mist of it over the sea and had barely been out all day. And it was mackerel, shiny metallic blue across our plates, the eyes still in. Fish made Alec Kemp irritable, if he hadn't been already. He liked to do everything properly and with style, but boning fish defeated him.

'Blasted things,' he said, pushing small bones out between his teeth with what seemed to me disproportionate fury.

Elizabeth had come down to the meal with her face clearly blotchy and pink from recent tears which even the carefully applied powder could not hide. I hadn't heard her crying again since that first day and had tried to forget what had happened, but seeing her that evening, the sound of it resurfaced disturbingly in my mind. She had composed her face now in its habitual lines: gently upturned lips, her glances towards Alec conveying, so far as I could make out, only attentiveness and appreciation. But her left hand fiddled restlessly with the string of seed pearls at her neck.

Elizabeth usually spoke very little as we ate. Alec liked to perform. Elizabeth would watch him, the smile fixed on her lips, letting him entertain us all.

Alec would tell stories about his Birmingham childhood – he and his two brothers – or the way he had taken over the firm, Kemp's Foundry Supplies Ltd, from his father and built it into something that really counted. There was no doubt he was doing well. The 1930s were such a desperate time for many people, but while laid-off miners were demonstrating on Birmingham's streets and queues reached round the corner from the Labour Exchanges, Kemp's Foundry Supplies was prospering. We'd all heard much of what Alec said before, but we let him talk. The couples and families at the other tables were talking quietly, except for one where the children were squabbling over bread rolls and cutlery.

'The old man didn't have the know-how to make the business really thrive,' Alec might say. 'He didn't lift a finger to improve the products. Of course in the end all the customers started to move to the firms that did. That's business. So I had to win them back – and more. And that's what I've done. You have to remember that, young Katie. If you want to get on you have to keep on your toes.'

Sometimes he leaned across the table and very softly sang 'K-K-K-Katie, beautiful Katie...' to me in a wooing voice which made my cheeks go red as I squirmed with pleasure and embarrassment.

But this evening there seemed to be barbs at every point in the conversation.

'Flaming fish.' Alec slammed his knife and fork

down. 'Flaming, bloody mackerel.' He pushed his chair back and lit a cigar.

'You should persuade your father to take a bit of a holiday,' he said, the cigar nipped between finger and thumb. 'Works far too hard.'

'He never seems to have the time,' I told him. 'I wish he would. He's always working. I don't think he'd know what to do if he wasn't.'

'Not good for his health though, is it?' Alec took a long pull on the cigar. 'He's a quack. He ought to be the first to know that. Sand, sun, fresh air – all the pleasures life can give you. Keeps a man, well, on top, so to speak.' He smiled engagingly at Olivia and me, but there was a glint in his eye, something I couldn't read but which made me feel uncomfortable.

'Alec.' Elizabeth's voice held a warning, though she was still smiling. Her hand gripped the pearls, knuckles whitening.

Alec's dark brows sank into a frown. 'I bet that idiot Parker's making a right balls-up of everything.'

'Kemp's will be quite all right without you,' Elizabeth reassured him. As she moved her hand to lay it on his sleeve I noticed the startling blue of the veins in her thin wrist. 'Even if Reg Parker doesn't get everything quite right, he can't possibly undo all your success in one week, can he? Don't worry, darling.'

I looked at Olivia, who was pushing peas on to her fork. For a second she glanced up and caught my eye, then looked away with determined nonchalance over towards the lights on the far wall with their little tasselled shades. I saw the blood rising in her cheeks.

'I wonder what all these people do for a living,' Alec said aggressively, looking round the room. 'What they do to deserve a holiday by the sea.'

Olivia clenched her teeth tightly together and stared at her plate. I could sense panic around me and I was filled with sudden dread, though I had no real idea why. I knew I wouldn't be able to finish my food.

'Daddy.' Olivia's cheeks were flaming. 'Don't start here. Please.'

Alec angled his body close to Olivia, who flinched visibly away from him.

'Well, you provide some of the conversation then, since you don't like mine.' He leaned back pretending to be genial and conversational. 'We could talk about – pets, let's say. The care of birds, for instance. Budgerigars in particular.'

I was bewildered. Olivia's beloved birds had become ill and died months ago. She'd cried over them for ages afterwards. Why was he being so cruel now, baiting her as if suggesting she hadn't looked after them properly?

'Livy loved those birds,' I said indignantly. 'She did everything she could for them.'

'Oh yes,' Alec agreed smoothly. 'Absolutely everything.'

Olivia swallowed, spots of red burning in her cheeks. 'I was thinking,' she said in a high, fluttery voice. 'It's funny being here with different servants. No Dawson or Radcliffe.'

'Your mother's missing them I think,' Alec said. He was unsmiling, spoke very deliberately, watching his wife's face. 'Bit of female company round the house. Even if they are common little tarts.' He spat the words out.

'Alec.' There was an appalled, begging note in Elizabeth's voice and her eyes were full of tears.

'They know how to please, though.' His tone was casual now, almost chatty. 'Never had cause for complaint, have we, darling? Worth bearing that in mind, Katie. Always be eager to please. Gets you places.'

Elizabeth stood up and left the room, walking through the stares of the other diners. Olivia was sitting rigid in her seat. I felt sick.

'Look.' Alec was suddenly sheepish. 'Sorry about that, Katie. Olivia? You're not cross, are you? You know your mother never is much good at taking a joke!' He tried to laugh it off. 'Never mind us, Kate, don't take any notice. Have a nice pudding, eh? I'll go and get her.'

Olivia stared stonily at her plate as Elizabeth followed her husband back to the table. Her expression was completely collected as if nothing had happened. We sat through the rest of the meal, Alec back to his ebullient, entertaining self. I felt very edgy still and could not help glancing at Elizabeth Kemp. But if it had not been for Livy's mutinous silence I might have begun to think I'd dreamt it all. Alec was affable, able to bring out jokes. And Elizabeth's face wore its mask of gentle, affectionate amusement.

'Livy?'

We were preparing for bed after the meal.

'I don't want to talk about it.'

'But what did . . .?'

'I said I don't want to talk about it.'

'Is it – are they often like that?'

Olivia stood with her back to me, pulling her dress on to a coat-hanger. After a moment she turned, suddenly giving me a dazzling smile which also managed to convey bafflement. 'Whatever do you mean?'

* * *

Did they really never know I heard them? Of course they assumed my deafness, my innocence. And when Daddy was aroused he bellowed, locked in his own needs and urges. I listened to their ritual through the smooth wood of the door, through keyholes, cracks between hinges. My room was safely far away, they thought, at the opposite end of the house. But I was there: nights when the maids had left or were up in bed and occasional afternoons when they assumed I was well occupied elsewhere.

Why did he pursue it? I used to wonder. Why humiliate them both? Sexual intercourse petrified my mother. I suppose my mind couldn't take in the contradiction that he really did love her and want her. That the others were all substitutes, not additional pleasures.

That afternoon they thought I was asleep in the gazebo. Carelessly they left ajar the door to their delicate nest of a bedroom, its windows edged with draped chintz the colour of clotted cream, stained with bright crimson flowers.

'It's been so long,' he begged. I had a wider viewing strip than usual. I had learned to move absolutely silently. He was kneeling at her feet naked, offering himself to her, his erection a dark branch in front. I called his penis his pleaser. I didn't know the proper name for it then. 'Please, my darling. I need you so much.'

'No. Don't, Alec. No.' Mummy's voice came out as a moan. I could just see the edge of her silky, peach-coloured gown and imagined her with her arms clasped across her breasts, shutting him out, her face distraught.

'Let me just touch you. You know sometimes if you relax you can . . .'

'No – I can't.'

'You won't have a baby – you know you won't. It's all right.'

'Please, Alec, why must you do this? It's so horrible, I can't bear it. Go to anyone you like if you have to but please leave me.' Her voice was high and tearful.

'But you're my wife, Elizabeth.'

She moved over to the bed and backed up against the pillows, pulling her knees up. She looked so little with her wispy hair all hanging down, sitting there, cornered.

'Come on,' he wheedled. 'Just unfasten it, that's a good girl. Just lie back. There. Isn't that nice? You like this, don't you?'

He latched his mouth on to one of her breasts. She gave a whimper of distress. I suppose he fooled himself it was pleasure.

'Now – there's a good girl – ' His voice was low and hypnotic. 'Just open up now – let me in and it will all be all right.'

I couldn't see their faces. He had climbed over her, his body, strong and agile, already moving above her.

'No!' she cried.

I pulled my arm across my mouth and bit into it, hurting myself, listening to their sounds.

'I've got to,' he grunted. 'You've got to let me. You cold bitch!' His voice rose to a great roar. 'Let me in – *now.*'

Her sobs filled the room. I bit myself harder, harder. 'I can't. I can't bear it.'

'Touch me then, quickly for God's sake – hold me. Tighter. That's it – yes – harder . . .'

Something I hadn't seen before. He came with his pleaser spurting between her tiny hands, his noises ecstatic, angry, all at once. There were a few seconds of silence. My arm was smarting, indented with deep pink curves.

Mummy cried and cried. She always did.

'I'm sorry, Elizabeth.' He lay contrite beside her. 'I'm sorry, my lovely. Stop that now. Stop.' Then loudly, 'Stop that fucking noise can't you, you stupid cow?'

He moved from the bed and I knew he would leave the room. I whisked along to my end of the house taking in tiny shallow breaths.

When I closed my bedroom door behind me the birds grew silent. Lady fluttered up from the bottom of the cage to one of the wooden perches, shifting her claws back and forth along it, her eyes black and cold like pellets in her yellow face. King was clinging to the bars, his bill hooked round one of them, gnawing at it.

I leaned against the door, watching them. King suddenly made a flurried movement as if something had startled him and launched himself, feathers fanning violently, until he landed on the bottom. They had no practice in using their wings properly. There wasn't the space. I saw then how they'd never move from there. Never do or be anything else.

'You're stuck in there, aren't you?' I said softly, sliding across the carpet to them. 'Nothing you can do about it in there all day every day, is there?'

Their dark eyes fixed me with metallic stares. They didn't care what I was saying.

'It's not right, is it?' I unfastened the door of the little cage and reached inside. King panicked again, wings beating madly, their cool draught against my hand. He flapped round and round, evading me. Lady sat quite still as if frozen.

Carefully I lifted her from her perch and drew her out, one hand cupped round her body, the other underneath, supporting her gnarled feet. Her little life pulsated against my palm. I squeezed her, my fingers pressing tighter and tighter until I was shaking and the effort made me dizzy. Lady struggled for a few seconds but I had her too hard and I kept holding her with all my strength until she was still. Her little head flopped to one side. I laid her in the bottom of the cage. Then I chased King. He didn't want to come but I was faster than him and I killed him too and left him lying beside Lady. Their beaks were touching. They looked as if they loved one another.

Dawson found them like that. I came in later and found her standing bent over the cage.

She turned her brown eyes on me. 'Oh, Miss Olivia, what on earth've you done?'

Mummy and Daddy said the birds had both caught a chill. They kept telling me so.

I was so happy when they sent me away to school.

* * *

Chapter 4

Birmingham, 1935

Granny Munro was standing quite naked in the drawing room.

'Kate!' My mother's voice from the wooden balcony was shrill with barely concealed rage. Strands of greying hair hung limp on each side of her thin cheeks as she looked down at the upturned faces in the garden, our eyes screwed up against the bright summer sun. 'Get in here quickly. She's doing it again!'

The vicar was due round any minute, I remembered. One of Mummy's parish meetings. I threw down my cricket bat and ran towards the house. Even Olivia perked up. She had been pouting on the bench in front of the hollyhocks because William had caught her out. She and the others weren't supposed to know about Granny, but of course they did.

'She must've taken all her clothes off again!' Olivia cried, almost clapping with delight.

The four of them left in the garden watched as I scurried into the house. They stood in silence, unable to resist trying to hear what was afoot: Olivia, William looking embarrassed and Angus and John from next door.

The house felt very dark and cool as I ran inside. Mummy emerged from the kitchen and seized my arm.

'Do something with her quickly,' she hissed, unrestrained now we were alone. I was startled, feeling her hand on my arm. We hardly ever touched each other. 'The wretched, selfish old woman. This is too much. Mr Hughes could be on the doorstep for all I know.'

Clenching her hands into fists to try and quell her frustration, she retreated back into the kitchen. She must have thanked heaven for the nets in the front windows, or anyone passing along Chantry Road might be treated to a glimpse of her mother-in-law. It wasn't just embarrassing that she was standing there starkers like that: it made it look as if Granny wasn't being cared for properly, and Mummy was supposed to know about taking care of people.

I tiptoed nervously along the tiled hall. The drawing-room door was not quite shut and I tried to peer through the crack between the hinges but my specs got in the way, so I pushed the door a little further open.

Granny was standing with her back to me. She had not a stitch on. Her hands were clamped to her waist, and she was taking in deep breaths through her nose and letting them out through her mouth like a steam train mustering force. Though I'd never in my life seen Mummy naked, the sight of Granny was something I was growing used to. Sometimes I helped her dress, and very often I sat perched on a cork-seated stool as steam curled round the bathroom, and kept her company while she bathed. In fact that was when we had our best talks.

I could talk to Granny Munro about anything. What was such a relief about her was the way she was so straight and open, just came out with it when she was thinking something. And I could tell her so much, like how I got fed up with Mummy lumping me in with the boys all the time and never buying me anything pretty like Olivia had and how I wished Angus was my brother instead of Wonderful William.

She'd tell me stories about her childhood and her life in North Berwick with Grandpa Robert and how she swam in the grey foamy sea every day up until she left. We said things to each other we knew mustn't be repeated.

'When you get to my age,' she'd say, soaping her vanilla blancmange of a belly, 'and you've had as many children as I have, you get past modesty and all that sort of nonsense.' Then, with a conspiratorial little smile, she'd add, 'I don't suppose your mother will though, do you?'

Despite this, it was odd seeing her there in the drawing room. I smiled, half in amusement, half pity. Sarah Munro had always been a big woman – I was left in no doubt from where I'd inherited my solid figure – and had not shrunk much in old age. The years had just made everything droop a bit. Her bottom was large and squashy and her back covered by sagging folds of flesh. But she stood good and straight, her soft, steely-grey hair still neatly pinned up. She was a strong woman for seventy-five.

I suppose I'll be like that one day, I thought, looking down at Granny's plump, mottled legs.

I clicked the brass door-handle to give her a chance, let her know she wasn't alone. Granny whipped round, glowering, her long, pink breasts swinging as she moved. I saw she still had her half-moon glasses on the chain round her neck. When she saw me her expression lost some of its defiance.

'Ah, it's you.' Her Edinburgh accent was broader than my father's, who had long moved south, the tone of her voice surprisingly soft. 'I suppose you've been sent to tame me?'

I, at fourteen, was the only one who could 'deal with' Granny Munro. Even her son, doctor or no doctor, could make little headway with her.

'Mummy's afraid Mr Hughes'll see you.'

Granny's broad, pink face broke into a grin. 'I'll bet she is. The sight of me would be enough to give that namby-pamby little preacher a turn.'

Anxiously, I peered back into the hall to see if Mummy was coming, but there was no sign of her.

'Granny, look, I'll help you get dressed, shall I? You'll only get into more trouble if you don't. Shall we go upstairs, and I'll bring you some tea up afterwards?'

'I suppose if I stay here I'll be shot at dawn. Or it'll be rat poison in the tea. That'll be the next thing.'

I gathered up the clothes that she had apparently not just discarded but hurled all round the room: garters and bloomers, the heavy dress and shift and her stiff whale-boned corset. Her stockings had landed on the standard lamp.

'I'll check the coast is clear and then we can get back upstairs.'

The doorbell rang as we were crossing the hall. My mother dashed out from the kitchen and made frantic flapping motions at us, her body taut and furious.

'Oooh,' Granny said, stopping in full view of the front door and clasping her hand to her chest, 'I think I can feel a funny turn coming on.'

'Just get up there,' Mummy snarled at her, gesturing at Simmons our maid, whose eyes were goggling, to wait before opening the door.

Granny suddenly dropped the pretence and shot with impressive speed up to the first floor.

'Why d'you *do* it?' I panted when we were up in her

room overlooking the garden and I was rolling her stockings up her legs.

'Got to get someone to take notice of me somehow, haven't I?' she said petulantly, perched on the pale blue candlewick bedspread. 'Locked away up here.'

I clicked my tongue. 'You know you can come down any time you like.'

'Yes, but with her around . . . Heavens, no wonder your father's wrapped himself up so tight in his work.'

I'd heard these complaints so many times now that I didn't rise to them. 'I'll go and fetch you some tea now, shall I?'

I settled her in the easy chair in what was in fact a light, comfortable room with many of her possessions round her. I carried up tea and slabs of shortbread and stayed while Granny enjoyed them, sitting with the window open over the garden. It had gone quiet outside. I sat on an upright wooden chair, my tanned legs spreading over the seat.

'I gather you managed to behave yourself while I was away?'

'You deserted me.' She looked at me out of the corner of her eye with mock reproach.

'It was only ten days.'

'And it was lovely,' Granny stated.

'It was . . .' I hesitated. Since the holiday I had tried to push the disturbing elements of it to the back of my mind. 'Yes, it was lovely.'

Granny ruminated on her oblong of shortbread.

'I'd like to marry someone like Alec Kemp,' I said, dreamily.

Granny snorted. 'Nonsense. He's a Tory.'

I giggled. 'And he's married already.'

'And he's old enough . . .'

'... to be my father!' I finished for her, laughing.

Granny sat re-stirring her tea. She dropped the spoon noisily into the saucer and said, 'No. The one you ought to marry is Angus.'

'Angus?'

'Yes, Angus. If ever I saw a nice boy it's Angus.'

'But he's only fifteen.' Set beside the glamour of Alec Kemp, Angus seemed a mere child.

'And you're only fourteen.'

'But Angus is just a friend. I mean he's just, well – Angus. And he's so quiet and serious all the time.'

Granny shrugged. 'You don't want to get married. Get a job instead. Far better paid. If I hadn't got myself married and tied down out in the sticks I'd have had a much better time. Out there, marching with them all.' She held her arm out as if to indicate a column of militant women parading through the garden. It was a cause of continuing regret to her that she hadn't been able to take an active part in the Women's Suffrage movement. She switched into her rhetorical tone. 'Marriage is pure slavery anyway. Look at your mother. Frustration, that's her problem. Don't think I don't sympathize, because I do. Much too full of ideas to be married, that one.'

Suddenly she flagged, and sank back in the chair. 'Where's my book? You get out with your friends. I'll be good, I promise.'

The others had moved down to kneel round the pond at the far end of the garden. They had a net and a bucket and were looking for tiddlers. Butterflies were slowly folding and unfolding their wings on the buddleia.

As I walked across the lawn, I saw Angus coming back in from next door carrying another net. There was a gate between our garden and the Harveys' which enabled us to pass freely between them.

Angus was a tall, slim boy with a pale complexion and dark brown hair cut very short at the back but longer at the front so that it tumbled over his forehead. He had serious eyes and a more uncertain manner than William's, whose body had a kind of physical arrogance about it. Like me, William had inherited a solid figure, but in him it was expressed in muscle: a brawny torso, thick, rugby-playing legs and a broad, freckled face topped by wavy fair hair. Angus was much lighter and more delicate looking, and dressed as ever in the careless Harvey way, in long baggy shorts and a buff-coloured shirt that looked a size or two too big.

William and I tolerated each other just about, but I always liked Angus better. William was self-confident, an achiever both in class and sports. Angus appeared less certain of himself and William often put him down.

'Oh, come on,' William would shout, exasperated, during a cricket game. 'If you're going to bowl at least put a bit of elbow into it. Even Katie could do better than that!'

And Angus would try harder, very seldom rising to William's needling. It took me a long time to realize how much he minded it.

'Is she all right?' Angus asked. He sounded concerned, and I was grateful to him for being so and for not poking fun.

'She's had a cup of tea. I waited with her for a while.'

Angus nodded. 'Poor thing. She's missing Scotland I expect. My mother says she's welcome to call round at our place any time, you know.' He gave me his sudden smile which made his grey eyes crinkle at the corners.

'We thought we'd go into the park. We were waiting for you.'

The gardens on our side of the road all shared their boundaries with a private park which had a lake in the middle.

As we neared the pond, Olivia looked up from where she was kneeling beside William on the rough slabs round the water.

'About time!' she called, jumping up. 'Let's go! There's nothing to catch in here. Come on, William.'

To the equal astonishment of me and William, who was nearly sixteen and felt himself to be above our company nowadays, Olivia thrust her arms through each of ours and pulled us with her to the gate at the bottom of the garden. William strode along, apparently unable to resist but looking most uncomfortable.

We walked down the leafy path and round the still water of the lake to a shady spot from where you could look back up to the line of Chantry Road's huge, ornate houses, their windows catching the light of the afternoon sun. Leaves rippled white, green, yellow. Moorhens and mallards slid over the surface of the lake. The boys started off with the nets. Olivia and I lay on our stomachs on the cool ground waiting for a turn and looking down into the dark water.

'I look like the full moon,' I sighed. My round face shuddered in the water's surface. 'Except the moon doesn't wear specs.' With her big dark eyes and long wavy hair Olivia looked like a wispy Ophelia in the water. 'I wish I was pretty like you, Livy.'

Olivia smiled. She could be a minx when attacked but when I made a comment like that it brought out her better nature. 'You've got a lovely face. All sort of big and generous.' She called out to the boys, 'Come on – let us have a turn now, won't you?'

I took one of the long-handled nets and dipped it into the water. It came up containing nothing more than a coating of green slime.

'Try again.' I found Angus at my shoulder. He watched seriously as I dipped in the net and on the fourth attempt brought it up with something tiny flapping in the bottom amid the leaves and weed. Carefully we turned the net out into the enamel bucket. I saw the deft, precise movements of Angus's slim fingers. Heads together, we watched the tiny, almost transparent creature struggle into the water.

'We shall let it go, shan't we?' I asked.

'Oh yes – it'd be cruel not to.'

For a second I became aware of Olivia watching us, her brown eyes puzzled. Suddenly she twirled round, floral skirt dancing about her legs, and skipped over to William.

'William, will you help me? I can't seem to catch anything either.'

William picked up his bucket looking surprised, walked over to Olivia and squatted down, his thick legs bent up on each side of the pail. Olivia inclined towards him as if she had a secret to tell him, and William, startled, jumped back and overbalanced, sitting down suddenly.

Olivia let out peals of giggles. 'What are you doing?' she cried. 'Here – let me pull you up.'

'I can get up myself,' William said crossly, with a flushed face.

She kept on at him all that afternoon: 'William, will you help me? William, walk with me. Will you carry my bucket?' I couldn't understand this sudden attention paid to him, nor his passive response to her clamouring. If I'd carried on like that I was quite sure he'd have told me to leave off. Finally he did say gently to her, 'Can you leave me alone for a bit now, Livy, eh?'

Pouting slightly, Olivia stepped over to me.

'William's being rather mean.' She turned her head to look at him over one shoulder, coquettishly, strands of her chestnut hair half covering her face.

'Just leave him alone for a while,' I replied, carefully moving my net through the water. 'Anyone'd think you've got ants in your pants this afternoon.'

I was so absorbed in helping Angus to release some more tiny fish into the bucket that it was some time before I noticed Olivia was crying.

'Hey, what on earth's the matter?' I flung an arm round her slim shoulders, but she wriggled uneasily.

'Come over here,' Olivia said. She seemed all twitchy and strange. We left the boys and walked back up slowly under the trees towards the garden.

'I feel so peculiar,' Olivia sniffed. 'It's – Katie, I got my – you know – today.'

I turned to her, baffled.

'My – when you become a woman.' Olivia seemed to have to wring the words out of herself.

'Oh,' I said. 'Gosh. I see. Your periods.' Thanks to Granny Munro I knew all about those. 'Bad luck. Is it making you feel rotten then?'

'No. My tummy hurts a bit. It's sort of gripy, down here.' She laid a hand on the lower part of her stomach. 'But it's not that. I feel awfully queer. I've never felt like this before. As if I want something very badly but I don't know what it is.'

'Oh,' I said again. I hadn't the remotest idea what Livy was talking about.

'And when I told Mummy about it, she got all cross and then started crying. It's made me feel awful.'

I was astonished. Hoping to cheer Livy up, I said, 'Never mind. Let's go in and have some tea before you have to go. Mrs Drysdale's made shortbread and there's chocolate cake.'

Olivia burst into tears all over again.

'What's up now?' I cried.

'I don't know.' She was wiping her face with her hanky. 'It's just how I feel.'

When we got inside, Mummy seemed to have calmed down. Her meeting was over.

'Well, you look like a wet weekend,' she said briskly to Olivia in her best nursing sister tone. 'Where are the boys?'

'Coming,' I said.

We sat in the kitchen and Mrs Drysdale poured tea for us all from the big brown pot with its green and orange knitted cosy. I loved the kitchen. It was warm and steamy in winter with the range going full blast and cool in summer with its dull red quarry tiles and shady atmosphere.

We all sat round the table, Mummy with her thin body quite upright, as if she had a steel bar up the back of her blouse. She had fastened her hair up again at the back and it waved neatly round her face. She was wearing a moss-green cardigan which had a tie of braid at the neck.

'You've got so much on, Mummy,' I exclaimed, looking at her. 'It's such a boiling day!'

'It may be outside,' she replied as she sliced up the moist cake, a smooth ridge of butter icing between the two layers, 'but I've been in sorting out this parish work.'

'Oh yes,' I said. 'Sorry. I forgot.' I always seemed to say the wrong thing.

'Your father's going to be late.' I wondered why she was even commenting on the fact since Daddy was late almost every day. 'Sometimes I don't know why he doesn't take a truckle-bed and go and sleep in the surgery.' She checked herself, remembering that Mrs Drysdale was still working over by the sink. Mummy pointed at the ceiling. 'I take it she's quietened down?'

'She's all right,' I assured her, glad I'd managed to do something right. 'And she's promised faithfully to be as good as gold from now on.'

'Well,' Mummy said drily. 'I'll believe that when I see it.'

Chapter 5

'Can I come with you, Daddy? Please?'

He hesitated over his boiled egg, not meeting my eye. William was scraping his toast with irritating loudness so that charred black crumbs dusted his plate.

'I don't think so,' Mummy intervened abruptly. 'You haven't been down there for years. You're too old.'

'What your mother means,' Daddy said, his manner less harsh than Mummy's, 'is that you might find some aspects of it rather unappealing at your age. You were just a little girl when you used to come before.'

Occasionally as a small child I'd gone down to the surgery with Daddy and sat in the corner of the drab waiting-room with my colouring pad and crayons, amid all the coughing and sighing and complaining about things I couldn't understand. I was curious, hungry to see my father's other life. It was the very fact I might now be able to make more sense of it all that attracted me. And Granny had supported me. I think she hoped it might bring Daddy and me closer.

'And the patients wouldn't like it either,' Mummy said, sniffing. She had a heavy summer cold and would have been feeling very sorry for herself had she ever permitted indulgence in such emotions.

'I think you should go,' William said, taking an enormous mouthful of toast and speaking through it.

'The sight of you would shock them all into feeling better. Either that or finish them off altogether.'

'William!' Mummy said.

I scowled, and Daddy pretended the conversation wasn't happening, a tendency of his which I found hugely aggravating.

'This is not just a game,' I said. 'I really do want to come.' In my enthusiasm I knocked over my egg cup and Mummy tutted.

My father wiped his mouth with his napkin. 'No one'll object,' he reassured Mummy. 'Katie seems interested in looking after people. You do wonders with your granny after all, don't you?'

My mother buttered her toast in silence.

'You don't mind, do you Mummy?'

She looked up, tight-lipped. 'Why should I mind? I'm just thinking of your health – all those germs. But your father's the doctor. I was only a nurse, after all, so what do I know?'

Having to abandon her job as a children's nurse on marrying Daddy was a sacrifice about which she had never ceased to feel bitter.

Daddy pushed back his chair, ignoring this remark as he tended to blank out all such expressions of emotion. 'I'll be leaving in ten minutes.'

I sat in the passenger seat next to Daddy, nervous at being alone with him. We turned into the Alcester Road, the Austin shuddering on cobbles and tramlines, swooping downhill from the fresher air of Moseley towards the lower-lying, smoky atmosphere of Balsall Heath, two miles from the middle of Birmingham. Daddy's surgery was on the inner edge of this area, in St Joseph's parish, with its hotch-potch of dilapidated back-to-back houses, and workshops and factories all squeezed in together, its life altogether louder and more public than in our suburban street. What would it be like to live here? I wondered. I was seeing everything with new eyes today, alert suddenly to these differences. Both my father and Alec Kemp moved daily between these two contrasting areas, both able to afford houses in prosperous, tree-lined Moseley. The surgery was in the Birch Street area, only streets away from Kemp's Foundry Supplies.

I eyed Daddy's profile, his neatly trimmed dark hair, the little moustache and tired blue eyes, every line of him dutiful and serious.

He cleared his throat. 'I gather you managed to settle your grandmother down yesterday,' he said in the objective voice he always used when speaking of her, sounding as if he was discussing one of his patients.

'She took all her clothes off in the drawing room again.' I saw him flush slightly and wondered if I'd said the wrong thing. I couldn't always work out what I was supposed to say to my parents. One minute they were talking about patients and illnesses and bits of bodies, some of which I knew you didn't refer to, even in Latin, in polite company. Then at other times if you mentioned something, especially if it was to do with the family, they'd go all stiff and embarrassed. It was very confusing.

'Why did Granny come and live with us? She could have managed on her own, couldn't she?'

'It seemed the most practical thing, after your grandpa Robert died. North Berwick's a long way off and it made sense for her to be near her family.'

'But we're not her only family.'

'We were the ones who were able to have her. The

others have commitments which made it impractical for them.'

'But I don't think she's very happy. And she and Mummy can't stand one another.'

Daddy was silent for a moment. I looked out as we passed the ornate red-brick bathhouse on the Moseley Road.

'It always takes families time to adjust to new arrangements – particularly people who are above a certain age. Three months is not a very long time in that situation.'

What situation? I wondered. We were talking about Granny, not some situation. I sat in silence. Whatever the reasons she was here I thanked God she had arrived, like a bracing gust of wind from north of the border.

We turned into a side street and parked outside the surgery. I squinted myopically at the brass plaques. *Dr. W. Munro*, and underneath, *Dr. J. Williamson.* I hoped I shouldn't see sour, bad-tempered Dr Williamson.

'It needs a polish,' I said.

'Well, there's a little job for you then.'

A line of people were already waiting outside by the step. Daddy raised his hat and greeted them. One of the women, tight-faced, held a silent baby. An elderly man was coughing, bent over by it, his lungs sounding drenched.

The waiting-room was dark, the walls painted brown. There were wooden benches against three of the walls and in one corner stood a small table and two chairs. In the fourth wall a door, through which Daddy disappeared, led out to the two consulting rooms at the back, and there was a little trapdoor for the dispenser.

I was just settling myself down at the table when my father reappeared, hurrying across the waiting-room.

'Dr Williamson is going to handle the start of surgery. I have some urgent calls to make. Won't be too long.'

'Oh, let me come. *Please* let me!' It seemed very important that day that I see everything.

He had no time to spare for discussion. 'Come on then, quickly.' He was already going out of the door. 'None of them is too far. It'll be easier to walk.'

It was a humid day, warm and cloudy, threatening storms. We hurried along the crowded pavement of Birch Street past rows of shops, their blinds slanting out over the pavement. Everything seemed colourful, absorbing. Each shop gave off its own special smell: the warm, fleshy smell of sides of meat padded with yellowed fat, fresh bread and burnt currants, the tangy sweetness of strawberries and the bitter smells of metal and rubber from the hardware shop. Mixed with this was the ripe whiff of horse manure from the road.

I followed Daddy into another side street, hurrying to keep up with him, he striding and I trotting.

'Here we are.' He knocked on the door of a house. 'You'd best stay outside, I think. Old Mr Fenton has his bed downstairs now.'

The house was run-down and filthy, the windows so thick with grime that they must have let in very little light. There were signs that the paint on the bleached window frames must once have been blue.

A woman with a large, sagging face and a wart sprouting whiskers on her left cheekbone appeared at the door. The rest of her hair was wrapped in a washed-out brown scarf. As the door swung open a waft of stale air hit us, stinking of sweat and urine. I shrank back.

'Oh, it's you, doctor,' the woman said lifelessly. 'He's bad today.' She talked of a turn in the night, said she was sorry for having to bring the doctor out. My father gently dismissed the apology.

The woman left the door ajar and I peered in. I could see a bed with a heavy wood headboard, covered by old grey blankets. Propped against the pillows was a yellow face, so shrunken that it seemed not to be living at all but a mask, something out of an old tomb. The head was bent back slightly so that the nose pointed at the ceiling. The old man was struggling for breath, his lungs making a terrible rattling sound.

I had expected to feel afraid or repulsed, but I found I was looking at him with a detached kind of pity. He was dying, clearly. He appeared to be at a distance from us already, as if death had moved in and taken possession before life was extinguished.

I watched my father bend over the bed and take the old man's hand tenderly from under the bedclothes to feel his pulse. He spoke a few soft words. 'Easy now,' I heard him say. His daughter stood at the end of the bed with her arms folded across her large breasts.

Daddy turned to her. 'There's nothing more I can do, I'm afraid. You're doing the best that can be done.' The woman sighed and nodded stolidly and kept thanking Daddy before we left.

As we approached the next house, two children who had been waiting on the front step came running at the sight of the doctor, cheeping like young birds: 'It's the babby – he's took real bad!'

They were both girls, both dressed in very worn gingham frocks, too big for the elder girl and too skimpy for the younger.

'Our mom's worried it's the diphtheria or she'd have brought him to you.'

I stepped into the house with Daddy. The room was spotlessly clean, though with very little in the way of furniture. There was the black iron range, a table and two wooden chairs.

The young mother was pacing the cold bricks with bare feet, the baby in her arms. His eyes were half open and he was breathing in quick, panting breaths.

Daddy gently opened the child's mouth. In a voice that was low but urgent he said, 'Kate – outside. Now.'

I watched from the doorway with the other girls, whose eyes moved enviously over my dress.

'You were right Mrs Smith,' Daddy told her. 'It is diphtheria. Little Tom is very ill. We'll need to get him to the fever hospital.'

He spoke further of the child needing a hole in his windpipe to help him breathe, and of arranging transport, a blue-windowed diphtheria van. When we left I had even more trouble keeping up with him. He strode down the street, lips pressed tightly together. I wondered once more whether I'd done something wrong.

In the end I asked timidly, 'That baby was very ill, wasn't it?'

'We ought to be able to do something.' The words burst out of him. 'We ought to be able to prevent children from getting terrible diseases like that. It's a scourge – it's dreadful. I can't bear to see it.'

I'd never seen this grief in him before. I felt like crying myself, and could only trot along silently beside him.

He looked down at my miserable face and suddenly smiled. 'Hey now. Don't you go worrying, Katie. It's not your fault.' He laid his hand on my shoulder for a moment. 'Come on. We've one more call to make.'

I waited downstairs in a filthy room in one of the back-houses, facing out over a yard strung across with washing. The room was very dark and stuffy and on the table were the remains of what looked like several days' worth of meals. The old oilcloth was soaked with spilled tea and the remains of some kind of stew. There were plates covered with congealed gravy, several jam jars with a crust of dried tea-leaves at the bottom and an old heel of bread. The floor was strewn with food remains and dirty clothes from which rose a rank, sweaty smell. And there was another terrible odour about the house which I couldn't identify but which turned my stomach.

Across the table from me a scrawny girl who I thought was about thirteen sat picking her nose and sniffing, her brown hair in two rat's-taily plaits. Round her feet a baby crawled on the floor, its nappy hanging heavily round its bottom and stinking of faeces. The child's face and limbs were streaked with filth. I found myself bearing in mind one of Mummy's nursing sayings: 'Always breathe through your mouth.'

'What's the matter with your mother?' I asked her.

'She's took bad after the babby,' the girl said matter-of-factly. 'Can't get out of bed no more.'

'This baby?' I pointed at the infant who was now sitting down, having found an old scrap of bread to chew off the floor. Shiny worms of snot trailed from his nose.

'No, the littl'un – she 'ad 'im last week.'

As we spoke I became aware that the sound I could hear of a small baby crying was coming from upstairs.

'Have you got any other brothers and sisters?' I asked. I supposed the girl must think me awfully nosy, but she didn't seem put out by my asking.

'Ar – there'm six of us. Three older 'uns, me, and then me dad buggered off, an' then Bob moved in an' she 'ad the two babbies.'

'Oh,' I said, barely able to imagine such a household. 'So is Bob out at work?'

'Nah. 'E's buggered off an' all.'

We heard Daddy's tread on the bare boards of the stairs.

'Now Lisa,' he said carefully to the girl. She had a certain spark to her and was evidently taking everything in. 'You know your mother is very poorly?'

Lisa nodded.

'She's got childbed fever and I'm afraid she's so sick that we're going to have to take her into the infirmary. She says you've been helping her a great deal, but she's fretting about you missing work and about little Sid here.' He glanced at the youngster by his feet who was staring up at him with enormous blue eyes. 'She said your neighbour Babs Keenan would look after you both but she's not well at present. So what I'd like you to do now is to clean Sid here up a bit. A new napkin at least, eh? This afternoon I'll come back and take him on a little journey in my car. You'll have him ready, won't you, Lisa?' Looking at me he said, 'He's coming home with us for a few days. Just until Mrs Keenan's herself again.'

At the surgery I heard him explaining to Dr Williamson. 'Puerperal fever, poor woman. In a shocking state – she should have been in days ago by the stench of her. The child didn't look too hopeful either.'

When we drove home in the car with baby Sid Blakeley, he wasn't looking in a much better condition than he had been that morning. Lisa had evidently tried to give his face a wipe over because the dirt was smudged and differently distributed. She had changed his nappy but this one was now nearly as full as the last, and the ammonia smell of it filled the car. I held the child beside me on the back seat.

'Hello, little fellow.' I smiled at him. The boy turned his pasty, snub-nosed face towards me with interest. He had not seemed disturbed by being taken away from home. I pushed my little finger into his palm and he gripped it tight. I giggled at him, leaned my face close, and he reached up and tried to snatch at my specs.

'Oh no you don't!' I laughed, pulling my head back. 'I like him, Daddy!' There were no young relatives in our family so babies were a new experience. I liked Sid's little fat wrists and soft, dirty feet. 'How old is he?'

'About a year.'

'His sister – she's younger than me, isn't she?'

'Oh no – couple of years older. She's been out at work for a time now.'

As we drove back up into Moseley I asked, 'Daddy, why did you become a doctor?'

'I suppose for the reason anyone does. Because I wanted to help people who were sick to get better.'

'Do you like people?'

I couldn't see his face but heard the rare smile in his voice. 'I suppose I do.'

'Does Mummy like people?'

'I would think she does, yes.'

'She doesn't always seem to.'

'Now, now.' He stopped the car outside our house.

The questions I hadn't asked him were, how long is the baby staying for and, above all, won't Mummy be *furious* with you?

I carried the smelly child into the house and went

nervously upstairs to find her. This was the greatest moment of surprise of the whole day.

She took one look at the little boy and launched herself straight back into her element. 'Right. The first thing that child needs is a jolly good bath. Go and get it running, Kate. I don't have the baby bath any more, but at least he can sit up by himself. Not too hot – dip your elbow in. And a new bar of Sunlight. Here, give him to me.'

She took Sid to her with no sign of hesitation, filthy as he was. 'Hello, young man.' She looked intently into his eyes as I watched in astonishment, seeing a new softness in her thin face I had barely remembered her capable of. 'What you need,' she went on, 'is a wash and a good big bowl of something to eat. Do you like porridge, eh?' Seeing me in front of her still, she said impatiently, 'Go on. Stop dithering. This child needs looking after. And when you've run the bath, go down and ask Mrs Drysdale to put some porridge on for him.'

Sid appeared later with a face of a quite different and more wholesome shade, and bolted down a dishful of sweet porridge. My mother settled him down to sleep in William's and my old cot. To my surprise she had pulled out from various recesses in the house almost all the paraphernalia needed for looking after a baby: cot, sheets, blankets, bottles, terry nappies and toys.

'Why on earth did you keep it all?' I asked.

'Well, as you can see,' Mummy said stiffly, 'you never know when it might come in handy.' Of course she couldn't express the fact that she simply couldn't bear to part with these things.

I went to Granny's room to tell her the news. 'I've had a simply marvellous day!' I was glowing with it all. I plonked myself on a chair beside her. Her cheek was pushed out by a sweet she was eating.

I told her about the surgery and the visits to the houses.

'It was all so interesting, seeing all those people. And Daddy was so different from how he is at home.' Granny was listening attentively. 'D'you think I could do something like that when I grow up?'

'With a family like yours,' she said serenely, holding out a little white paper bag, 'I should think it would be almost a foregone conclusion. Bullseye?'

Sid Blakeley stayed in our house for only four days before Babs Keenan called at the surgery to say she was ready to take him home. But for a short time he turned our house upside down. Though he couldn't speak, he was able to express himself, his needs and his joy with a directness of which no one else in the house was any longer capable. His small body and nose-wrinkling grin softened the lines of my mother's face and pulled unusual smiles from my father. I even found William now and then chasing him about the room, both of them on their hands and knees. As for me, I was besotted. And I took secret pleasure in reciting to myself the new words I'd learned out on the rounds that day: diphtheria, puerperal, buggered.

Chapter 6

Birmingham, 1936

A humid night in August. There was no breeze to stir the curtains at my open window, and I was lying restless, under a sheet. The sound of the front doorbell startled me out of my half sleep. It sounded twice, long and hard. For a few seconds I lay listening, trying to guess the time. It was already dark and felt like the middle of the night. A door opened downstairs. Daddy and Mummy must still be up.

Out on the landing I saw my mother moving quickly down the stairs, still dressed but with her hair pinned up for bed. The old wooden cased clock on the shelves by the stairs said ten past eleven. I peeped round the banisters into the hall.

They opened the door to Elizabeth Kemp, her face very white, eyes like huge dark wounds against her skin. She had on a cotton dress with a white shawl half covering it. Her pale hair was loose at her shoulders like a young girl's and in her agitation she had evidently not thought to put on a hat. I watched, absolutely still.

'I'm sorry. You've got to help me.' Her voice was low and hoarse. 'I shouldn't have come here. I know you're not my doctor, but I don't know where else to turn.'

She started to cry, weak, tired-sounding sobs. My

mother steered her into the study and Daddy went in behind, shutting the door.

'What's going on?' William was standing sleepily at my shoulder with only his pyjama trousers on. 'Did I hear some sort of rumpus down there?'

'It's Elizabeth Kemp – crying her eyes out,' I whispered.

'Why?'

'Don't know. Can't hear now anyway. Ssh – let's go down and listen.'

'Kate, we shouldn't . . .' That was William for you. Rather stodgy.

But he followed me part of the way down the stairs. I stood at the bottom, listening so intently that even my own breathing felt like an interruption.

For a time the three adults in the study talked in low voices. There were questions, answers, short exchanges, but I could only hear the tone of their voices and not the words. But suddenly there came an anguished outburst from Elizabeth that sent William and me haring back to the top of the staircase.

'I can't. I can't do it. I just couldn't bear it!' And the sobbing began again.

'Whatever's the matter with the woman?' William asked. 'I've never heard anything like it.'

For a second I felt annoyed at his superior tone, his implying that Elizabeth was making an unnecessary fuss about something. Of course our own mother behaving in this way was quite unimaginable, but I felt churned up inside by the sounds of such terrible unhappiness downstairs, even though I had no idea what the matter was.

After more quiet talking the door opened. We squatted down, one at each side of the top step, hidden by the carved wood of the banister. I was astonished to see that Mummy had her arm round Elizabeth's shoulders.

In an exhausted but formal voice Elizabeth Kemp said, 'Thank you for your advice. I'm sorry to have put you in such a difficult position.' She glanced distractedly at a half sheet of paper she was holding. 'I'll do something as soon as I can. Next week.'

With a strange gentleness my parents closed the door behind her and Mummy turned and leaned wearily against it. She looked unusually vulnerable, standing there like that in those hairpins, her emotion all clenched up inside.

In a high voice she said, 'Heavens above.'

My father shook his head sadly. 'Sometimes I wonder if the middle classes don't have it worse. All this business of keeping up appearances.'

'Thank goodness we've not had that to contend with.' Mummy sounded close to tears. Daddy went over to her and took her in his arms and she leaned against him, both of them standing in silence.

Unused to witnessing such intimacy, William and I avoided looking at each other. As our parents moved apart, the two of us shot into our bedrooms.

* * *

OLIVIA

Before she had me, Mummy gave birth to her first baby at home. I know because she told me, early on sometime. Though she very seldom spoke to me of her feelings, there was no one else she could confide in, only her little girl. Who was too young. She couldn't seem to let things out gently. Her words were like shards of glass coughed up from her throat. She was in labour for five days, and the baby, who would have been my elder brother, was born blue and without breath. They had to stitch her up inside, tight like a hessian sack.

So when she was expecting me she chose to go to hospital. She waited for me, settled on stiff white sheets. Although I was small I wouldn't come out. She lay on her labour bed for four days with her feet up in leather stirrups while the doctors tried to decide what to do. The pains were mild at first. Then her body pressed down tighter and tighter and she was in agony back and front but they wouldn't let her move. She cried out, 'My baby's dead.' One of the nurses slapped her and said, 'Pull yourself together.' They wouldn't let her eat.

On the third day when they unstrapped her legs she tried to jump out of a window. The next day they cut me out by Caesarean section and by a miracle I was still alive. They told her one of my hands was tightly gripping the umbilical cord. They instructed her not to have 'relations' with Daddy for four months after. She swore never to let him touch her again. She didn't quite manage that.

Usually she is sitting in the drawing room. She hasn't been well these last weeks. She seems exhausted and her face is white.

'What bad luck to be off colour while the weather's so good,' Daddy jokes. 'Poor old girl. At least you've got Olivia home to keep you company.'

Dawson eyes her knowingly. Later I realize you can never fool Dawson.

I come skipping down Chantry Road from my piano lesson at Mrs Weiss's cosy house, wearing my little leather sandals and a silk frock. I've had a lovely afternoon and I want to tell Mummy about it. I run inside, leaving Dawson to pull the door closed by its cold iron knob.

'Mummy? Mummy?'

My feet thud up the stairs and Dawson looks up at me from the hall with her dark, handsome eyes. 'You should leave her to sleep, Olivia,' she calls, but there's a smile in her voice. Along the dark corridor, shadowy after the brilliant day outside and the more so because their bedroom door is closed. My feet slip on the red carpet.

'Mummy?' I knock. There is silence. Softly I turn the handle and push the door open. I stand in the doorway unable to move.

The bed has turned red. Even her hair is soaked almost to the roots as she lies askew across the covers, her eyes closed. Her face is chalk white, the cheeks drawn in tight. She still has a satin slipper on one foot.

I cross the room. By her feet is the deep blue and white chamber pot, full to overflowing with blood. Next to it on the floor something long and sharp, streaked red.

I find my voice. 'Dawson!' I scream. 'Dawson!'

It was only when my mother went secretly to a doctor that she realized how much an abortion would cost. She had no money – none of her own. Without asking my father for the price she could not even contemplate it. Rich as we were, her choice was as limited as so many others in her position and she resorted to the same thing: a sixpenny knitting needle.

If I had not been at home she would have died.

* * *

Within a fortnight of her visit to our house, Elizabeth Kemp suddenly became gravely ill. I could get almost nothing out of Olivia.

'She's in a private nursing home,' was all she'd tell me. She sat, pale and tight-lipped in one of the cream chairs in the Kemps' beautiful drawing room.

'Can I come and see her?'

'No, I told you. She's very ill. She can't have visitors.'

'Well, when will she be better?'

'I don't know.' Olivia put her hands over her face and burst into tears. 'I wish I knew. I just want her back home.'

'Your father must be able to see her, surely?'

Olivia looked guarded suddenly, as if afraid. 'Yes. Sometimes.'

When Alec Kemp came home later that afternoon his face was grey and exhausted.

If Granny Munro had any idea of what was happening in the Kemp household she chose to keep silent. She was blunt, but not brutal. And she was in the same position in the house as a child: an eavesdropper, not a person responsible enough to be automatically party to information, though she was shrewd enough to guess most of it.

By the autumn of 1936 she had settled in much better. She was keeping her clothes on and she and my mother had reached an uneasy truce.

One Saturday William and I were talking to her while she tidied her room – or at least I was in there and William had to come barging in as well.

'Goodness, Granny,' William said. 'What a mess.'

'I think it looks rather nice,' I said loyally, staring round at the tottering staircases of drawers she had removed from the chest, the rush-seated chairs tilted over on the bed amid the letters and diaries, the full skirts of dresses in sea blue and grey and her tweeds, the tangles of pearls and heavy amber and jade beads, all of which she was evidently trying to sort into piles. William blushed at the sight of some of her more personal items of underwear: huge brassières and corsets and bloomers strewn across the bed.

'Ah, spotted my dreadnoughts have you?' she laughed. 'Poor William. I tell you what, you go down and fetch us up a nice cup of tea and Katie and I will have them stowed away by the time you get back.'

With relief, William squeezed out of the door.

'The poor lad, I shouldn't tease him so,' Granny said, winking at me over her glasses. 'But he is a bit of a stiff fellow, isn't he? Very like his father, I'm afraid, and his before him.' She sighed, folding an enormous pair of pink bloomers. 'You don't really remember your grandpa Robert, do you? He was a good man. Truly good. You can't argue with that sort of goodness – it wouldn't be fair.' Her face wore a wistful expression. 'But oh, I did long to let up occasionally and do something really wild and *bad*. I'd have to go for a good stump along the beach or a bracing swim to get it out of my system and then I'd feel better. Until the next time, anyway.' She smoothed down the bloomers and picked up another pair. 'You know, Katie, you can spend all your life keeping your feelings packed tightly away. I'm not sure it's always the best thing. Trouble is, after years of doing it you don't have much practice at showing how you do feel.' She peered at me with her watery eyes, looking suddenly sad and vulnerable. 'I know I rather overdid it when I first came here.'

I went and flung my arms round her. She smelt of camphor and rose water. 'Granny – it's been absolutely lovely since you came. You're the best thing that's ever happened!'

And she laughed tearfully and hugged me back.

In the evening when Daddy went to look in on her there was clearly something wrong. She was lying at an angle across the bed in silent distress. She had spent most of the day seeing to her room and it was immaculate.

'Win,' Daddy shouted. 'It's Mother.'

I came running immediately. 'What? Granny, what's wrong?'

I knelt down and took her hand. It felt cool and clammy, like the feet of those birds Olivia used to have. She was trying to speak, but nothing came out that made sense. 'Granny, Granny!' I sobbed, leaning my head against her fulsome body, feeling the stiff corset under my ear through the silky stuff of her dress. 'Don't be poorly, Granny, please.'

All I had from her in reply was a low, frightened whimper.

It was agreed that we'd care for her at home. We could see in her eyes that she'd prefer it. Her stroke had in fact been a mild one, and within days her speech began to unfurl into something we could recognize. The left side of her body slowly began to tingle back into life.

'I'm not done yet,' she said defiantly, one corner of her mouth lurching up unasked. 'I'll be out in the breakers.' But just then she couldn't even get out to the bathroom.

My mother rose to the occasion and nursed her with a kind of objective professionalism. She was brisk and detached and left me to provide the other components of nursing: company and affection. As soon as I came home from school I spent every moment I could sitting in the easy chair next to Granny's bed.

'You've got to get better – please, please,' I kept saying to her. 'Please try, Granny.'

With huge effort she'd manage the words, 'You're not nagging me – are you?'

Granny's illness pushed everything else to the back of my mind. Olivia was away at school and normally I missed her every single day. We wrote long letters full of details of our days and jokes and anecdotes about school. I wrote to her still, but the letters were shorter and full of my worries about Granny. I had almost forgotten that unseen, at home, Elizabeth Kemp was dragging herself very slowly, painfully back to health. But that was something shut away from my understanding then. Olivia never even hinted to me what had happened. She tried to preserve her parents, present them to me perfect as seahorses on a bed of wax. I had no idea just how much she needed me.

Angus often came to see Granny after she fell ill. They had an affinity with each other. She liked him to read to her and I'd often go into her room and find Angus's dark head bent over Wilkie Collins or Edgar Allan Poe. ('Anything with a really good story,' Granny would say.)

One wet winter afternoon I sat listening as Angus finished off a chapter from *The Woman in White*. After a few minutes Granny coughed gently and interrupted him. 'It's all right. You stop now Katie's here. You're a good reader, Angus Harvey, I'll say that.'

'I suppose you'd like tea?' I asked.

'Of course. What other pleasures do I have left in life

now apart from my food? Well, and your company of course.'

Simmons had a kettle on the hob downstairs. I carried a tray up and we settled down by the fire. She left the light off so the room was lit only by the flames. Rain flung itself at the window. Granny sipped her tea carefully from one side of her mouth, some of it spilling into the saucer which she held underneath. She tutted with frustration until she saw Angus and me watching her anxiously. She smiled lopsidedly at us. Tiny flames danced in the lenses of her specs.

'Don't you worry about me.' I heard a mischievous twinkle in her voice. 'I must say it's lovely seeing the two of you together. You make a lovely pair. Or am I embarrassing you?'

It was too dark for me to see if Angus blushed as I did. He was still smiling affectionately at Granny.

I jumped up, anxious to find some activity to hide behind. 'Yes you are. Now – shall I do your hair for you?'

She shuffled over a little so I could sit on the edge of the bed and I pulled the pins gently from her long grey hair. It reached half way down her back, thick and soft. I felt Angus's eyes on me, watching the two of us together.

'Tell me,' Granny said to him. Patiently he waited for her to manage the words. 'What is it you want to do with your life, Angus?'

After a moment's thought he said, 'What I'd really like is to invent something. A machine or tool that would be very important to people. Make their lives better or make it easier to build something else. Or create something really beautiful that people could enjoy looking at.' He hesitated. 'I don't think I'm brainy enough to go for anything really academic like William.'

Granny waved her good arm dismissively. 'Never mind William. I wasn't talking about him. William will do whatever William does. I'm interested in you. Are you saying you plan to be an engineer?'

He looked into the fire, his thin face serious. 'I think what I'd like most is to learn the basics of something really well. Get an apprenticeship somewhere.'

'What about the university?'

'Perhaps later. I want to work in the real world a bit first.' He seemed embarrassed to be talking about himself like this.

'You're good at Meccano,' I said eagerly.

Angus laughed. 'That's a start, I suppose.'

I realized with surprise that for all the years Angus and I had grown up and played together we had barely ever had a conversation without the others around, when of course there was a lot of ragging and we were always intent on cricket or some other game. We didn't have serious conversations. Self-conscious suddenly, I concentrated on the soft feel of Granny's hair sliding between my fingers. I hoped Angus would think the pink of my cheeks was only from the fire.

'What will you do after school, Katie?' he asked.

'I think I'd like to be a nurse.'

'You've made up your mind then?' Granny said.

'Only just this minute.' I laughed. 'But I've really known that's what I want to do for ages. I want to look after people. It seems the obvious thing.'

I felt Angus watching me again. I knew there were new feelings between us.

'You've always been good at looking after people,' he said. 'Your grandmother, Olivia . . .'

'Olivia?' I was startled. 'What d'you mean? Why does Livy need looking after?'

'It's always looked to me a bit as if that's how it is, that's all. Sorry. Perhaps I've had it all wrong.'

'Livy's all right!'

'Well anyway, I think you'd make a very fine nurse.'

'What's this,' Granny interrupted, 'the mutual appreciation society?' She was smiling, her face cock-eyed and rather comical-looking. 'You two want to look out.'

Seeing she'd embarrassed us again, she added, 'I think I need a doze now. And you must need a rest from me. Thank you for your company, Angus. I'm most grateful.'

She was already sinking into sleep as we left the room's cosy light and went downstairs. William was studying in his bedroom.

'I suppose I should be going,' Angus whispered. 'William's putting me to shame.'

But he stood with me in our big family room at the back of the house where there were old easy chairs, a Welsh dresser and a piano. He seemed reluctant to leave, and I found I didn't want him to. I perched on the arm of a chair, woollen skirt pulled tight across my knees, a compromise between remaining standing and committing myself to sitting down in the chair.

'She's a fine person, your granny,' Angus said.

'Everything changed when she came,' I told him. 'I love having her here.'

Cautiously Angus said, 'I suppose your parents aren't always the easiest people to talk to?'

‘No.’ I felt grateful that he’d noticed. His own family were freer, more scatty. ‘They’re certainly not. But with Granny – it’s hard to explain. I know she did some peculiar things when she first came. She was so used to being in charge of her house and everything, going down to the beach for a swim, even in winter if she wanted. And suddenly she was expected to come and settle down here with everyone telling her what to do. But she’s just so different from everyone else . . .’

The tears came suddenly, streaming down my face with so little warning that I couldn’t control them.

‘I just can’t bear the thought of her dying.’ I felt silly blubbing like that in front of Angus, I who had always been so much one of the boys, their games from which you didn’t run off in tears. I took my specs off and put my hands over my face.

‘Katie, don’t – ’ His voice was gentle. He took one of my hands gently away from my cheek and drew me to my feet. ‘She’s doing well, isn’t she?’ He looked anxiously into my face. ‘She’ll be all right.’

‘But you can’t just say that,’ I retorted. ‘She’s old and sick. People *do* die. Daddy’s patients are always dying.’

‘I’m sorry,’ he said, shrugging awkwardly. ‘It was a stupid thing to say. I just wanted to make you feel better, that’s all.’

I looked up at him. His face was rather blurred even at this distance. ‘I must look such a fright.’

‘No. You look lovely.’ He spoke so kindly that I nearly started crying again, but he was embarrassed and covered it with a joke. ‘My, my, grandmother, what big eyes you’ve got!’

We laughed together. ‘I’m sorry, I don’t have a hanky to offer,’ he apologized. I pulled out my own and he wiped my face softly with it, then leaned forward, coming suddenly into focus, and kissed my damp cheek. It didn't startle me as much as it did him, and he leapt away from me almost as if he'd been electrocuted.

Then he went all brisk and said, 'I'd better be off now. Prep for tomorrow. Do cheer up, won't you?'

Confused, but warmed, I watched him go.

Chapter 7

'What's going on with you and Angus?' Olivia demanded. Her voice was tight and angry. 'You're all sort of stiff with each other. And he keeps eyeing you up all the time.'

I tried to look surprised. 'Nothing – really.' Even now the new emotions between Angus and me were too fresh and untried to talk about, to Olivia or anyone. And I didn't like her phrase 'eyeing you up'. It sounded dirty.

'Katie,' Olivia wheedled, putting on her very best appealing face. 'We never keep secrets from each other, do we?'

I shook my head, though I knew this was far from the truth nowadays: I couldn't talk about Angus; even less could Olivia bring any words to the surface about her mother, and I no longer dared ask. When Elizabeth had returned home she had been frighteningly thin, her face drained white with bruise-coloured dents under her eyes. Even her hair had a deadened look, its sheen quite gone. Very slowly over the months her colour had begun to return. Smiles appeared dutifully at her lips. She was forever resting. I visited. I tried to be concerned and helpful. But not once did we talk of what had happened. And I knew instinctively that I must never mention Elizabeth's visit to our house last summer. I was afraid. I could feel changes nudging at us. Although mostly we tried to put aside any difficulties and were as affectionate with each other as ever, there were times when these things which I knew, or half knew, became a burden, and an obstacle between us.

As soon as she noticed the changes between Angus and me it got much worse. It's hard for me to express my feelings for Angus, how they gradually grew and intensified. I'd known him for so long and our lives had been very much a part of each other's. Our more adult feelings grew directly out of that. But of course it meant letting go a part of our childhood which had always included Livy and William. And I assumed Olivia was jealous, simply that.

'I wondered if Katie'd like to come for a walk with me?' Angus asked shyly.

He had appeared at the front door instead of coming round the back, in the hope of avoiding William. Mummy was startled. The realization that she had a daughter who was now sixteen and who might not want to wear hand-me-downs and be counted for ever as one of the boys had scarcely dawned on her.

I was up with Granny, who beamed triumphantly on hearing Angus's invitation. I was immediately flustered. 'Me – on my own?'

'Go on with you,' Granny commanded. 'I told you he'd get round to it one day. He'll not bite you. Just relax and enjoy yourself. After all, you've known the boy since you were knee high.'

He watched me walk downstairs, smiling. He was dressed in cream flannel trousers and a pale blue shirt and I laughed nervously and said, 'Look – we match today!' My skirt was pleated cream with a print of cornflowers. I had slimmed down a bit now I'd grown taller and liked to think of myself as 'curvaceous'. I took more trouble with my hair too, curling the ends and pinning it back so that it waved round my shoulders instead of pulling it into any old Alice band. I did feel self-conscious about the size of my bust, though. It pushed rebelliously at the buttons of every blouse I wore.

'It's so heavy and embarrassing,' I complained to Granny.

'Never you mind,' she told me serenely. 'You may not appreciate it, but believe me, there'll be others who will. Now stop finicking. You're lovely.'

'I was wondering if you'd fancy a walk to Cannon Hill Park?' Angus said. 'It's such a good day.'

'I'd love to come.' Then just in case I'd got him wrong, I added, 'Shall I fetch William as well?'

'I'd much rather you didn't,' he said quickly.

It was beautifully warm outside, with lilac and laburnum coming into flower and bluebells still in some of the gardens. We walked through the shade of the mature trees at the end of Chantry Road and down the hill towards the park.

I felt very conscious that we were alone. Since Angus had kissed me that day we had scarcely had any time without someone else's company. We had all met, of course, with Olivia home for the Christmas holidays, had talked and joked together and been to the park and the pictures. And Angus had often called round at the house, but everyone assumed he had come to see William and we'd ended up as a threesome or more. But even then, I knew that every time Angus and I were close there was more between us than was spoken. We were inhibited of course. Angus was shyer even than I was, but an undercurrent of glances and thoughts developed between us, which of course Olivia had not failed to notice.

At first we walked in silence. I was acutely aware of his every movement, as I'm sure he was of mine. Eventually I said, 'So next term's your last? Things won't be the same when you get a job, will they? No more long hols.'

'I'll still be a student really. Though I don't know what we get in the way of time off yet.'

Angus had gained a place at the Vittoria Street school to learn jewellery-making and silversmithing.

'I thought when you said you wanted to make things, it would be cars or furniture or something?'

'There's a lot of design involved in those, of course. And it'd certainly be a challenge. But when I saw the sort of work you can do in the Jewellery Quarter I knew I should like that much better. I'd like to make things that are beautiful as well as useful.'

'You're lucky.' I sighed. 'I wish I was good with my hands. Olivia's clever at the piano and there's you . . . Granny says William and I are doomed to be ham-fisted for life, and I'm afraid she's right.'

Angus laughed. 'Yes, I wouldn't set William loose on a lathe or any other kind of tool. But he's got more than his fair share of talents I'd say.'

I knew William often went out of his way to appear superior to Angus.

'But William's so ridiculous!' I protested. 'I know he's awfully brainy and all that, but you can't have a decent conversation with him. It's like trying to talk to a shire horse – big and strong and quite intelligent but awfully dopy. I can talk to you so much more easily.'

Angus laughed. 'Well, that's something anyway.'

We turned through the wrought-iron gates. It was

Birmingham's biggest and proudest park, the expanse of grass sloping softly down from the bandstand under the chestnut trees to the fish ponds where there were boats for hire in summer.

We strolled round the murky oval of water. Ducks slid alongside us in hope of food.

'I don't know,' I said gloomily, after a while.

'What? What's the rest of that sentence?'

I smiled. If I'd said that to William he'd just have ignored me. One of the things I'd always liked about Angus was the way he listened to you.

'I'm not sure I like growing up really. The way you realize certain things suddenly.'

'Such as?'

'Mummy and Daddy were talking about those poor people in Spain this morning.' The bombing of Guernica had reached our households in bold newspaper headlines. 'How can people do things like that? I thought the League of Nations was going to stop there being any more wars?'

'Not if countries defy the League. The Germans already have, remember.'

We found a spot to sit on the grass in the shade of a tree, near the park's large war memorial. I was frowning. I felt heavy and preoccupied when what I really wanted to do was laugh and be good company. But I was already wondering whether our walk would cause trouble.

'I can tell there's a thought in there trying to get out,' Angus said, leaning round to look into my eyes.

I laughed reluctantly. 'It's just, Angus, would you say your family was happy? I mean they seem happy to me.' I'd thought a lot about the Harveys recently.

Angus's father, James, owned a business crafting pianos and harpsichords. He was kind, jovial. There was Mrs Harvey with her friendly, welcoming face, who spent her time reading and reading, and John and Mary, Angus's younger brother and sister. I'd begun searching for undercurrents, wondering if there was something I'd missed in every family, even my own.

'Yes, I s'pose I would,' Angus said. 'You know, just normal. We rub along.'

I told him some of my feelings of unease about Olivia, though I didn't mention Elizabeth's mysterious visit. 'I don't know what it is I'm trying to tell you really,' I said. 'It's just that they can behave rather oddly. I've been noticing it more recently, but even that holiday I went on with them – you know, a couple of years ago – they were certainly different from how they seem normally.'

'Wouldn't any family be if you were living closely with them for a week or two?'

'No. Not like that. There's something not right, but Olivia won't talk to me. I can't seem to get near her any more. And I don't like that.' I looked into Angus's face. 'I know you all find her a bit of a trial at times, but she's so nice really, and so different when we're on our own. I'm really very fond of her.'

'I know. I can see. But if there's something she doesn't want to talk about then you can't make her, can you? You know Olivia, she likes attention. If there was anything she wanted you to know she'd soon tell you.'

'We used to be able to tell each other everything,' I said sadly. 'And now she's gone all chilly because she thinks you and I . . .' Face burning, I stared down at the grass, feeling I'd said too much.

I sensed Angus waiting tensely beside me. We sat in silence for a moment. Then he reached over and gently took my hand. I felt him trembling slightly.

Neither of us could think of anything to say. The silence grew longer, our shyness and lack of certainty about what to do next inhibiting us completely. We sat for a time, the palms of our hands growing sticky from being pressed together.

In the end I slowly withdrew mine. 'Shall we go back now?'

'Where were you this morning?' Olivia demanded, marching across our lawn towards me. 'I came round looking for you and your mother said you'd gone out with Angus.'

'I did. He came and asked me to go for a walk with him in the park. I'm sorry.' Immediately I resented feeling obliged to apologize.

'Did William go too?'

I shook my head. Olivia looked at me through narrowed eyes. 'You could have waited for me. I spent the morning on my own.'

'I'm sorry – I wasn't expecting it. He just came over and asked me. Look, sit down and I'll go and fetch something to drink.'

But she couldn't leave the subject alone. 'Well,' she demanded harshly when I returned to the garden with a jug of lemonade and biscuits. 'Did he kiss you?'

I flushed, annoyed now instead of apologetic. It really was none of Olivia's business, but I tried to keep calm.

'No, I told you, we just went for a walk, that's all.'

'But he's obviously sweet on you.' She looked shrewishly at me. 'Do tell me what he said.'

I remembered the awkwardness of that part of the

morning when Angus had held my hand. 'Really, nothing very much,' I said, selecting a biscuit as casually as I could. 'We talked about the League of Nations if you must know.'

Olivia brought out a mirthless laugh. 'Really? How dull of you!'

'Well if my walk with Angus was so dull, why are we discussing it?' I retorted. We teetered on the edge of a serious quarrel. But I couldn't bear to fight with Livy.

Eventually I persuaded her to go inside with me and play the Chopin waltz she'd been practising. The piano was a fine one, from James Harvey's works. Absorbed in the music, Olivia's mood softened. I watched her, my anger dying. I loved it when Livy played. I was always moved by the sight of her, taken up by it, her body no longer deliberately poised as it usually was, coy yet somehow closed. She was more fully herself than at any other time when she played for me. I'd seen her play for her father's guests and I knew she found it a torture. Then she was formal, mean with the music, giving nothing of herself. But now she was playing without a score in front of her, and at times she leaned her head back and closed her eyes, her long hair reaching down her back against her sea-green frock. She finished the Chopin and, not heeding my applause – 'That was wonderful, Livy' – moved straight into a Beethoven *adagio* which was one of my favourites. This she knew very well so she had no need to look at all. I watched and listened to the notes flowing from the piano. Olivia's eyes fluttered closed and her body swayed, taut and sensual.

She was oblivious to the fact that as she was reaching the concluding bars of the piece the boys slipped into the room, William, Angus and John, all lured by the sound of the music as they came in from cricket. They sat quietly, wiping their hands on their thighs, foreheads beaded with sweat, and waited for the end.

Olivia played the final chords and lifted her hands, wrists leading, from the keys. When she opened her eyes she leapt to her feet as if boiling water had landed in her lap.

'Oh!' she cried. 'How could you? How *could* you?' She rushed from the room, out into the garden.

'What on earth have we done?' William asked, laughing in total bafflement. 'Honestly, she gets more peculiar by the day, she really does.'

'Don't laugh at her,' I snapped. 'You probably just made her jump. I'll go and see.'

I found Olivia sitting curled on the slabs by the edge of the pond, her head resting on her bent up knees.

'How could you?' she said again as I knelt down beside her. She reached for her hanky, her face already pink from crying. 'How could you let them see me like that?'

'Like what, Livy?' I was rather frightened.

'So abandoned-looking. When I play like that I'm . . . naked. I can't bear the thought of them seeing me . . .' She began to sob, her voice rising. 'It doesn't matter in front of you because you really know me.'

'Do I?' I asked sadly.

She cried in my arms, shuddering with the strength of it like a small child. Then she raised her head and stared up at the sky, a desperate expression on her face.

'Livy – darling. What's the matter?'

Olivia didn't answer. She sat shaking her head.

'Look.' I spoke briskly, trying to overcome the disturbed feelings welling inside me. 'That lot are all as thick as two short planks anyway. All they saw was you playing the piano and making music, nothing more.

Now do come in with us, or they really will start wondering what's going on.'

'Just wait one moment, will you?'

I sat down beside her and waited as she tried to compose herself. I put a warm hand on Olivia's arm, and she leaned over and rested her head on my shoulder. I stroked her wild hair.

'I'm sorry.' She sounded exhausted. 'I didn't mean to be such a witch earlier.'

'It's all right.' The skin of her upper arm was cool and smooth where I touched it. It reminded me of when we were younger, comforting Olivia in some quiet place at children's parties when the clamour of it all had proved too much for her. 'You know I'd do anything for you, don't you?'

Olivia twisted her neck and looked solemnly round at me. 'I do believe you would.'

We walked slowly up the garden together. Olivia seemed tired, almost dragging her feet along. When we went inside the boys had started on a game of bagatelle. Olivia and I stood behind them quietly. I watched as Angus concentrated, pushing the wooden stick, flicking one of the small metal balls so that it flew round the board. I felt very tender towards him too.

When his go was finished he straightened up and turned to Olivia, deliberately including her. 'You know your piano playing is just beautiful. Have you ever thought of applying to a music school?'

Olivia let out a harsh laugh. 'Oh, I've *thought* about it,' she said. 'But Daddy would never let me. I thought you knew – when I leave school I'm to take my place as a breeder of sons.'

* * *

I wasn't supposed to go up to Izzy's attic, but she never minded and that day Mummy was out. I called Izzy by her Christian name. She liked children, was still almost a child herself, with hair the colour of rust curling round her face and deep blue eyes.

It was two days before my seventh birthday, back in those days before I had started to watch and listen at doors. I was lovely then, clean. Life was sweet, mutual adoration. Daddy. My beautiful, talented, worshipping Daddy. I was his princess in white gossamer dresses, his fairy, his angel. Comfort and trust: his embrace, his tobacco smell, the scratchy worsted of his flamboyant suits, bright checks dazzling my eyes and the strong warmth of his long, long body.

A thin carpet curved up the attic stairs, the colour of green baize. But at the top the floor was bare for the maids, a peg rug or two in their rooms. I had new shoes: black patent leather, rounded toes, with a strap and a button to fasten them. I watched my feet as I ran up the stairs, my thin brown legs beneath a cherry-coloured skirt, white ankle socks, the shoes . . . They tap-tapped loudly on those wooden boards. I ran to Izzy's door, rapped with my fingers, didn't wait –

'Izzy, look – I've got new shoes!'

It was his face. For seconds as I burst in on them, Daddy was in crisis, deep in his body's pleasure. He curved back over Izzy's little body, pushing down on his arms, her knees very white drawn up each side of him as she held him. His face was thrust back, red and sweating, mouthing the air, eyes squeezed shut.

Before he could recover himself enough even to speak my name I was downstairs in my room with my birds, bent up rigid on my bed with the eiderdown over my head. I was too sick even to cry. What they were doing I knew, and I didn't know. He had showed me all his weakness.

'Olivia?'

He'd pulled clothes over himself quickly and come down to sit on my bed. He was scared and I hated him for it. He lifted the eiderdown and laid his big hand on my back, but I curled myself tighter, squirming.

'Princess? Come on – there's no need to be upset. Izzy and I were just playing a little game and it's all over now. It's nothing to worry about. You can just forget it.'

His voice was light and wheedling. He tried to lift me on to his lap but he had a new sweaty smell and I pushed him away. But then I started to cry on my bed and I crawled back into his arms. He stroked my hair. His hand smelled of her.

'We'll let that be our little secret. Mummy needn't know our secret, need she? Just you and me, my pretty angel. You're good at keeping secrets, aren't you?'

I nodded, sobbing into his chest. The birds shifted on their perches.

The next day he came to me holding a box tied with extravagant pink ribbons. 'Angel – this is for you.'

The dress was also pink – taffeta, with silky bows sewn round the full skirt and lace petticoats.

By the end of the week, Izzy was gone.

* * *

Chapter 8

Birmingham, 1938

That terrible July evening.

The four of us were at the Kemps. We had lain in the sun most of the afternoon, drugged by the heat. The boys, shirts unbuttoned, sprawled side by side on a rug. William's solid, sporty frame was tanned and muscular from a summer term of tennis, cricket and swimming, his broad chest covered by a down of fair hair. His face was freckled and rather bullish. He lay with his arm under his head, his wavy hair bleached on top by the sun, blue eyes moving over a book on the Renaissance. The pages were dwarfed by his large hands.

Angus, much slighter with only a few dark hairs visible on his chest, was reading poetry, propped sideways on one elbow, but often stopping and looking up at the mellow brickwork of the house, with Virginia creeper trailing between the windows. Sometimes he looked across at me and we exchanged a secret smile.

Olivia lay on her back beside me on another rug, her vivid blue dress pulled up so the hem barely covered her knees, and a wide-brimmed straw hat shading her eyes. She seemed to be asleep. I sat up, sated with sunshine, pulling my skirt down to my ankles. The colours of grass and sky looked dark and intense after I'd lain so long with bright light beating on my eyelids.

The garden was immaculate, laid out on two levels, the upper area where we were lying edged by tall privet hedges. Around us were the scents of guelder roses, buddleia, mock orange, and in the middle of the lawn a fountain played out from the mouth of a stone dolphin on to a bed of water lilies and fish with feathery tails. The cool, sprinkling sound of water was constant. On the lower level of the garden, screened off by conifers from the vegetable patch, stood the round summer-house which the Kemps called the 'gazebo'. It was made of varnished wood with high windows and had inside a couch and chairs. I'd spent hours playing in there with Livy, in its shadowy light, its musty, exciting smell.

Elizabeth Kemp was sitting in a wicker chair in the shade of the house, a finely woven straw hat on her head, lifelessly turning over the pages of the *Queen*. She saw me turn to look at her.

'Would you like a drink?' she asked in her thin voice. 'There's a jug on the table. Or I could have Dawson bring something out?'

'It's all right,' I said, standing up slowly and stretching. 'I think I've had enough sun for now, thank you. I'd like to go and sit inside, if you don't mind.' I saw Angus raise his eyes from his book, and knew that if I moved inside he would soon join me.

'William?' I called, making sure. 'Are you all right here?'

'Mmmm. Want to get through some more of this.'

Olivia didn't stir.

I walked into the cool of the house, poured a drink of blackcurrant juice, and took it through into the informal sitting room which looked over the garden. It was the more attractive of the two rooms, I thought, the plump settee and chairs covered with trailing flower patterns in pinks and greens, and plants on the windowsills. After a moment, holding the glass against my warm cheek, I saw Angus get up and move towards the house. I smiled, waiting for him to find me inside. As the months passed we were overcoming our inhibited shyness, but our time alone together still felt furtive and stolen.

Angus came in and stood behind me.

'I can feel you,' I said. 'You're giving off heat like a boiler.'

'Not very flattering!' He moved my hair aside and I felt his lips warm on the nape of my neck. 'Couldn't you think of a more attractive comparison?'

I reached round and took his hand behind my back. 'You're the poet round here.'

'I only read it.' He came and stood beside me, his arms lean and tanned. 'Olivia seems to be out for the count.'

'Good.' I turned to him. 'D'you want some blackcurrant?'

We went and fetched him a glassful and sat side by side on the settee. After a few moments his slim fingers closed round mine. He sipped the rich-coloured drink.

'That's good stuff.' He indicated the glasses on the low table in front of us. 'Homemade?'

'Oh, I should think so. Can't imagine Elizabeth Kemp having shop-bought cordial, can you?' We laughed together.

'Everything just so,' Angus said. He nodded towards the garden. 'Even out there.'

'Makes our gardens look a bit ramshackle, doesn't it?'

He looked down at me. 'I want to see your eyes.' Sliding my specs off carefully with one hand he put them on the arm of the sofa. 'There, that's better.' He ran his hand over my hair, gently lifted my chin with his fingers. Both of us were nervous, and within seconds there were footsteps in the hall. We sat up and I quickly put my specs back on. Elizabeth put her head round the door and found us sitting sedately side by side, looking through a book on Wedgwood china.

'I'm just going to slip up for a wash and change,' she said. 'I'm glad you've made yourselves at home.' A few moments later we heard water running upstairs. I took my glasses off again. We laughed, our eyes meeting.

He was very correct when we kissed, as if he was slightly afraid of me. He kept his arms stiffly round my shoulders or waist, or caressed my back. Both of us sat skewed round to face the other so our legs got in the way.

'Angus?' I looked into his eyes and saw in them such strong feelings that I wanted to say something, tell him I loved him, but it felt too soon, the words too important.

We leaned back in each other's arms. Moments later, very softly, he laid his hand on one of my breasts, hesitantly at first, then more firmly, and I so big, filling his hand. He unfastened a button of my dress and for a few seconds his fingers reached in to touch my bare skin. It sent such an extraordinary sensation through me that I arched my back. Angus withdrew his fingers as if he had been burnt.

'Did I hurt you?'

'No. It felt lovely.'

He got up abruptly and stood with his back to me, looking out at the garden. 'I'm sorry.'

'Whatever for?'

'For – perhaps going a bit far. I don't want to do

anything to offend you, Katie. I wouldn't dream of it. It's just that I'm new at all this – knowing how to behave and what you expect of me. I feel I ought to know exactly what to do.'

I went over to him and put my arms round him. He felt rather stiff and reluctant at first. 'Angus – I don't mind – really. Perhaps I'm supposed to, but I don't!'

Laughing now, he pulled me into his arms. We stood holding each other more easily, kissing, the house quiet around us.

'It must look very dark in here from out there,' Angus said after a while, looking over my shoulder towards the garden. 'There's no one out there now. They must have come in.'

A few moments later, hearing the sound of the front door, we sprang apart again. There were brisk footsteps along the hall and Alec Kemp appeared at the door.

'Hello, you two,' he said, with that smile he could bring out, mischievous and complicit as if he guessed exactly what we were doing there. 'Got all you want?' He stood loosening his tie and removing the studs from his collar. His suit was a loud tweed. 'Elizabeth upstairs?'

We heard her voice from behind him. 'Darling, hel*lo*. Did you have a good day?' Her tone was caressing, solicitous, as if addressing a convalescent. 'Poor thing, having to work when it's so hot.'

'Oh, it wasn't so bad. Where's Olivia? Upstairs?'

'I thought she was with you,' Elizabeth said to Angus and me. Her right hand moved nervously to her throat, fingers nipping a fold of skin. 'She'll be around somewhere.'

Ten minutes later, when Angus and I were ready to

leave, Alec came down from changing into more casual clothes.

'I gather that brother of yours is here too,' he said to me tersely. Every trace of mischief was gone from his voice.

'He was,' I told him, bewildered. 'But he must have gone on home.'

'Well,' Alec replied grimly. 'We'll see.'

Outside, the only signs of life were two magpies, stalking across the grass.

Alec strode down the lawn, tensed and threatening, his hands clenched. The sight of him filled me with a terrible sense of dread though I could make no sense of it at the time. Angus and I followed.

Our feet were silent on the grass as we approached the gazebo, neat as a doll's house in the corner of the lawn. We were right behind Alec as he pushed the handle then stood across the doorway. The scene came to me in painful, jumbled images, like a cubist painting. Olivia's face, hair loosened in thick waves, her expression frozen; long, brown arms, the blue dress startling at her waist, her white, white breasts. And William's hand, arrested in the act of touching her, looking huge and dark as it was snatched away. I found my eyes moving anxiously downwards to check the extent of my brother's embarrassment, but he was fully clothed, everything fastened. His face was enough, flushed red like raw meat, eyes childishly wide. He could not speak. The two of them sat like trapped rats.

There were no smiles from Alec this time, no knowing looks. This was his daughter, matured and ripe as a siren, legs spread on the striped couch, pulling the blue cloth up fast now to cover her nakedness.

'I knew I'd find this.' His voice came low, more broken than angry. He stood over her, trembling. 'Oh God – Olivia. You were supposed to keep yourself clean. Clean.' In an anguished whisper he hissed at her, 'Have you any idea what you've done?'

She stared ahead of her sullenly, wouldn't face him. He leaned down, provoked into anger now, and took her chin roughly in his hand. 'Look at me – ' He jerked her face up violently, but her eyes still didn't meet his. 'You filthy, disgusting . . .'

'No, Mr Kemp, no!' William cried, jumping up, his face gleaming with perspiration. 'It wasn't – that's not fair!'

'Fair?' Alec shouted at him. 'What the devil has fair got to do with it? Are you telling me it wasn't her leading you on, getting you so wound up you couldn't resist her?' William couldn't seem to deny this. 'I know what they're like.' Suddenly he slapped Olivia hard across the face. I saw the pain flare in her eyes but she made no sound. She carried on staring sullenly across the room.

I slid past him. 'Livy – are you all right?' My friend's face was hard and full of hatred.

'Course I'm all right,' she spat out. Then more softly to me, 'Thanks.'

Alec marched her to the house and the rest of us followed. He had Olivia by her upper arm and she acted as if she was oblivious to the stream of abuse that he directed at her as they crossed the lawn. She was a bitch, filthy, too clever for her own good. She looked round, up at the trees, anywhere. By the time we reached the house I was choked with helpless rage.

'Get in the house,' Alec ordered. 'You won't be going anywhere for a while, my girl.'

He tried to bundle Olivia into the house while the three of us watched aghast from the bottom of the steps. I caught a glimpse of Elizabeth Kemp, her face a terrible white in the shadowy hall.

Olivia grabbed hold of the heavy iron door-handle and held on tight, her hair tumbling all over her face. 'You know why he's like this, don't you?' she shouted shrilly. 'Because my mother won't do it with him – never – '

Elizabeth Kemp stood absolutely still behind her, her mouth open, one hand at her throat. In panic, Alec clamped a hand over Olivia's mouth and pulled her with all his strength to loose her hands from the handle.

'Just get out of here,' he shrieked at the boys. 'And take your hideous sister with you. Out – now!'

Alec finally succeeded in wrenching Olivia's hands away from the door. For a second she shook her mouth free. '. . . so he does it with tarts and whores.' She spat out the words, '*Councillor* Kemp!' and then the door slammed shut. Through the coloured glass we saw their movements receding from the door, heard Olivia's cries.

My legs nearly buckled under me. William was silent, standing quite still.

'My God,' Angus said. 'D'you think there's any truth in that?'

I burst into tears then, and felt Angus's arm round my shoulders. He put out a hand to touch William's shoulder, but William shook him off.

The three of us walked home in silence. As we passed under the sweet-smelling trees in the dusk I felt hatred sinking deep in me and settling there.

'How could you be so *stupid*?'

I felt like killing William. We'd sat through tea,

through the passing of plates of bread and butter and jam and stewed fruit and junket, saying nothing to our parents, while misery and rage nearly choked me. What was happening to Livy? I wanted to rush back to the Kemps' house and break glass to get in.

Afterwards I cornered William in his bedroom. He was sitting on the edge of his bed, elbows on his solid thighs and a book between his hands. He didn't look up at me.

'Didn't you think?' I hissed at him furiously. We didn't want anyone else hearing this conversation. 'And put your flaming book down, can't you? Don't you care what you've done? What that bastard might be doing to Livy?'

William looked up, shocked. 'Katie – language.'

'You weren't such a prig with her.'

He laid his book face down on the eiderdown and looked up miserably at me. His face with its freckles and boyish looks appeared very young suddenly, but it did nothing to melt my heart. 'It wasn't my fault.'

'Oh no – of course not. Nothing to do with you at all.' I stood haranguing him, hands on hips. 'Anyway – I never knew you liked Olivia – like that, I mean.'

'I don't.'

'So what the hell did you think you were doing?'

'Look,' he said, standing up suddenly. His face had turned red to the roots of his hair. 'You've got a nerve coming in here lecturing me when you know perfectly well that you and Angus – '

'Angus and I what?'

'Were up to exactly the same thing, weren't you?'

I stared at him, my fresh-faced, good all-rounder, oh-so-wonderful brother, and I could see him, ten, twenty years on, pompous and self-justifying. I'd never disliked William before as I did at that moment.

'The difference with Angus and me, if you must know, is that we love each other and we know when to stop. Whereas you apparently have no idea what might be appropriate and you don't care a fig about Livy.'

'It wasn't like that.' William's voice turned small and pitiful. He sank down on the bed again. 'It's true I've never felt that way for her. I can see she's pretty as well as anyone else. But recently she's been behaving so oddly. She's too moody for my liking.'

'Well, something obviously changed your mind.'

William shot me a look of appeal, then stared down at the worn green carpet. 'One minute she was asleep, or I thought she was. Then when you'd gone in, she suddenly got up and came and sat down, right next to me.' He shuddered slightly at the memory. 'She was like a snake. She started touching me, just my hands, very softly, but you know – seductively, and staring me in the eyes. Then she just said, "Come on – come with me." So I went with her to the summer-house.'

'But why did you go?'

'That's the thing.' He seemed relieved now to be talking. 'She has this way with her. You can't refuse her. If her father hadn't come in like that I don't know where it would have ended. She just took me over.' William looked away towards the window. 'She kept touching me, and I couldn't ... You always feel with Olivia as if, if you disagree with her or refuse her, she'll crack. She always seems fragile.'

I found my mind following this remark like a dog after a stick. It was true. Olivia had this quality that made you want to care for her, to succumb to her. I remembered Angus's comment 'You look after Livy.' I felt sick inside now with my longing to care for her, to rescue her from her father. My brother meant nothing to me. I could think only of her.

William suddenly burst out, 'No one ever talks about it, do they?' I dragged my thoughts back to him. 'Dad, Mum. I'm eighteen and I've never kissed a girl before and I couldn't even think straight. And girls aren't supposed to do that, are they? My mind was telling me one thing and my body wanted to do another. And Olivia wanted me to, that was the thing. It was she who took her dress off, not me. You must believe me, Katie. But now she's in such trouble and I feel it's all my fault. I should have stopped her, been stronger.'

'Yes, you damn well should,' I said heartlessly.

'What if they tell Dad?'

'Oh, they won't do that. Think about it.' I tried to be more sympathetic. 'Look, don't worry. I'm sure nothing will happen to you. In fact I don't suppose they're thinking about you at all.'

He kept Olivia locked in her room for nearly four days. Nothing was supposed to pass her lips except water. Elizabeth Kemp was under strict instructions not to let her out, and she was too afraid to defy her husband.

I was frantic. Granny was the only one who knew. I paced restlessly up and down by her chair in the garden. Nowadays she did very little but sit. Her speech was reasonably distinct, but slow. We were patient waiting for her words, like listening for the voice of an oracle.

'There's not much you can do, I'm afraid.'

'But they're starving her.'

'Oh, I expect you'll find someone's feeding her something on the quiet. After all, Mr Kemp can hardly do nothing but sit at home like a guard dog. He has a business to run. All you can do is to be as staunch a friend as you can when she comes out. Whatever's wrong in that family, you can be sure it didn't begin yesterday.'

I tried to see Olivia. Elizabeth Kemp's spidery fingers twitched along the collar of her blouse as she stood at the door. 'Alec says I musn't let anyone in.'

I felt complete contempt for Elizabeth Kemp at that time. Even in my fury with Alec I wondered whether he was owed sympathy. Was he married to a woman so cold, so selfish that she wouldn't even let him touch her? Had her illness, secret and undefined, been simply a ploy to gain his attention and keep him physically at a distance? Warmed by my own new relationship with Angus I found it hard to imagine feeling so negative. It was clear to me, though, that this woman in front of me was frightened.

'Will you tell Livy I'm here?' I asked. 'Please? Perhaps she could just come to the window?'

Elizabeth glanced wide-eyed down towards the road as if fearful that Alec might appear at any moment. Then she nodded. 'Be quick though, please.'

As I started walking round the back of the house towards Olivia's window, Elizabeth called out in a high, childlike voice, 'It's not his fault, you know.'

I didn't bother to reply. I didn't care about them any more. I cared only about Olivia.

She appeared at the window still wearing her nightie, sleeveless, in white organdie. We stared at each other in silence for a moment.

'Are you all right?'

Her face looked different: naked, like a statue from which rain has washed the dust. I could tell she had spent hours crying, though her eyes were not red. They were wide and sad, yet I could see in them something else, hints of other submerged emotions. I thought I detected a kind of exultation about her which disturbed me because it was so incongruous.

She nodded at me.

'Are you on your own all the time?'

'No.' She spoke so quietly I could barely hear her, as if she was afraid of being overheard. 'Mummy slips up and keeps me company. And she sends Dawson up with food although she's not supposed to. I'm supposed to fast like Joan of Arc. The servants think it's mad of course, and who can blame them?'

'But for goodness' sake,' I exploded, 'when's he going to stop all this nonsense? He's got you imprisoned up there – and William's feeling awful.'

She pressed a finger urgently to her lips. 'Shh – please. Sometimes he comes home to check . . .' She smiled suddenly, an odd, amused smile. I felt she was removed from me, untouchable. 'Please tell William I'm sorry. He won't get into any trouble, I promise.'

'Why on earth did you do it, Livy?'

'Oh,' she said dismissively. 'I had to know I could, that's all.' She wavered for a moment. 'I don't know really . . .'

'Was it because of me and Angus?'

'Oh no. No – I'm very happy for you,' she said smoothly.

I heard light sounds to my left, and saw Elizabeth Kemp tiptoeing round the house towards me.

'What are you supposed to do to get out?' I asked quickly. 'What are the terms?'

'Oh, I have to apologize, and give up any notion of a life of my own, and promise I'll never go near another boy again and be Daddy's little girl for ever and ever until they find the right man for me to marry. Not much really.'

'You must go,' Elizabeth said to me. 'Please. Don't keep coming. It'll make things worse.'

I looked into her pale face, lined now round the mouth and eyes and taut with fright. I wanted to take hold of her and shake her and tell her she was weak and pathetic. Instead, all I could say, contemptuously, was, 'This is ridiculous.'

'Katie!' Olivia appealed to me as I was about to move away. 'We didn't want you to know any of this. You know Daddy's a good man really. You won't tell anyone, will you?'

I stared up at her. 'No,' I said in the end. 'I won't tell anyone. But for your sake, not his.'

When Olivia finally came out of her room she looked even thinner. Her manner was taut and she was sardonic and hard to reach.

'Did you apologize?' I asked.

'Not exactly,' she quipped. 'I just told him I'd spend my days up there writing up his story for the *News of the World*. He soon let me out then.'

* * *

OLIVIA

Katie was so lonely when we first became friends. She needed me. And oh, yes, I needed her. She was the only one I ever came near telling about home. But I didn't want to spoil it. I wanted her to love me. I wanted her admiration, her worship of us, of Daddy. It meant that I could pretend, and believe in it all sometimes too, like

I did when I was a little girl, and for Mummy's sake no one should know. Katie was so innocent. Sometimes she saw things but I glossed over them. I became closed by habit and could not open myself again.

Katie gave me herself. No one took much notice of her at home, and I made her flower, I know I did. But then people kept taking her away. That grandmother of hers. She was barmy but Katie had to love her of course. That was the difference between us: she could love people properly. Before, she talked only to me. And then Angus. I could see it coming long before either of them. The way he looked at her secretly. I couldn't endure it.

What she never understood (how could she?) was that I, Olivia Kemp, had to be the one, not her. The one that men wanted. I was the pretty one. I knew what my body had to do. If my existence taught me anything it was that the way to get anywhere is to give them what they want and plenty of it and they can't resist you. You've got them caught like flies in honey. Mummy couldn't do it. It wasn't her fault, I know that. I know she spent every waking moment trying to compensate Daddy for her inability to service him. But I was going to please them, to have them. I had to be the one.

Poor stupid William. Quite handsome in an obvious sort of way, but so middling and happy with himself. As soon as I touched him I knew my power.

'Come on,' I whispered in the garden. 'Come with me. I'll show you how to enjoy yourself.' When I saw the look in his eyes my body was turning inside. I fancied I had a thick scent coming out from me like an orchid. I wanted scarlet silk wound about me.

He was so easy. I made him shudder trying to hold himself in.

'Oh Olivia,' he kept muttering in the stupid way they all do. 'Oh God, Olivia.'

I had no intention of letting him enter me, oh no. I let him kiss me, and when I undid the top of my dress – his face! His eyes were almost bulging in his head. I spread my legs to let him imagine things, let him put his hand up my skirt.

I moved my hand over his pleaser, all hard and tight. If they hadn't all come crashing in like that I would have unfastened him. Taken him in my hand – mouth even – made him lose control of himself.

Poor Daddy. His princess dethroned, if not deflowered. But he was a hypocrite locking me up like that. I couldn't forgive him. And I told them about him. I let some of it out. I didn't want to – to spoil things like I did. It was seeing them all there at the bottom of the steps – Kate and Angus all close and united of course – looking so shocked and righteous. I wanted to tear through that, to smash it all up. I'm a bad, bad woman.

But the days when he had me locked away up there, he came to me on his knees, weeping, begging me, 'I love you. I worship you. Say you'll never never ever . . .' One day he knelt with his arms around my back, face pressed against my belly like a child, his tears wetting the light cloth of my nightdress. I stood stiff as a tree, not touching him, just looking at the dark curls on top of his head. In that moment I knew I could do anything.

* * *

Part Two

Chapter 9

Birmingham, 1939

'Katie – darling!' Olivia gave a discreet wave, arm half extended as I panted across the polished floor of the Ranelagh Room in Lewis's department store.

'It's all right. Don't rush. I haven't been here long.' She raised herself from the chair smiling broadly and leaned across to press her face against mine. Her lips brushed my cheek. 'Oh, sorry – I've left lipstick on you. Where's my hanky?'

'Not to worry. I've got one.' I wiped my cheek, handing my coat to the waiter, stowed my gas mask under my chair, then sat beaming at Olivia. 'It's so lovely to see you.'

For a moment we were silent, looking at each other as if unsure where to begin, and finally both burst into laughter at our awkwardness.

'You're all aglow,' Livy said, once we'd settled into being with each other. 'Still in love with nursing then?'

'Absolutely.' I pulled the comfortable chair in closer to the table. 'Yes, it's marvellous, especially now they've let us loose on the patients. The classroom part's a real slog, but it's worth it once you get out there on the wards.' I had been nursing now for over a year and I knew I had made the right choice. I was being sucked into the rigours and rituals of the General Hospital which took us young and unformed and bent us to its demands, its disciplines.

'I'm sure you're terrific at it,' Olivia said. It was typical of her to have such implicit faith in me.

'I just can't imagine wanting to do anything else.' I smiled back at her, taking in her appearance. 'I say, Livy – you look marvellous. So glamorous.'

She was wearing a perfectly tailored suit in royal blue and her hair was pinned stylishly, swept back from her forehead. Beside her on the table lay a wide-brimmed blue hat and leather gloves. She was made up, lips a rich scarlet, and she looked stunning.

Of the four of us she seemed suddenly the most grown up. William had taken to Oxford with apparent ease, his conversation when he came home full of rugger and student pranks. Angus was enjoying his training at Vittoria Street. But both of them seemed comparatively unchanged, except that they had moved on to something new. Whereas Olivia dressed now with sophistication, made her face up routinely in a way I never did and seemed suddenly adult.

'You'll have to take me in hand,' I teased as we sipped our white wine. 'There's you looking like something out of *Harper's* and me in my frumpy old uniform . . .'

Olivia grimaced and rolled her eyes to the ceiling. 'There've got to be some compensations, I suppose.' She picked up the menu and laid it in front of her but didn't read it. The band was playing 'Blue Moon'. A shaft of autumn sunlight fell into a warm rectangle across our table.

'The job's not getting any better then?'

'I hate, hate, hate it!' Suddenly she was storming at me. Olivia had not been given a choice. The Kemps decreed that she should do a year's secretarial training, something useful, not these airy-fairy notions about study and music. She was to become versed in Pitman and commerce. As well as the proverbial 'something to fall back on' (which I'm sure in their hearts they never thought she'd need) it was to be her entrée to a suitable marriage. She would rise through a prominent company and marry well, preferably the boss. She had worked now for six weeks at Leggett and Martin, an insurance company which occupied prestigious offices in Colmore Row.

The smile had dropped from her lips. 'It's so tedious and arid. I can't bear it.' She looked into my eyes. 'I know I may not be brilliant at music or anything else – '

'You're exceptionally good, though,' I interrupted fiercely. I felt frustrated on her behalf. It wasn't as if the Kemps were short of money. They could have allowed her more freedom to choose.

'It's what I really wanted. Was that so wrong of me?'

I reached over and squeezed her hand. 'Of course not. Look, they're far too protective. They're trying to run your whole life for you.'

I had spent much less time at the Kemps' house over the months since Alec found William and Olivia together. That summer of 1938 had felt like the end of our childhood, changing all of us. Alec and Elizabeth were civil enough to me still – more than civil in Alec's case. He was clearly very embarrassed and went out of his way to win me over. But I was on my guard now and couldn't trust him as I had before. I avoided the Kemps as much as possible.

Although I'd tried to talk to Livy about what happened after it was over I couldn't get her to open up on the subject. I knew she was aware of my stinging censure of her parents. When we met now it was nearly always somewhere away from either of our houses. It was sad. Both of us knew we had lost something.

The waiter approached our table and hovered discreetly. Olivia forced her attention to the menu. When he had taken our order and departed with dignity Olivia leaned closer and whispered across the sugar bowl, 'I've got to get away. It's suffocating me. I've got to do something.' She seemed frantic.

'Gracious, Livy – '

'I've thought about it over and over. I was going to try and find a job in London. But now with the war everything's changed. It seems so trivial and selfish to think about it. After all, we could all soon be dead . . .' She pressed one hand over her eyes, trying to hold back tears. Her nails were the same colour as the lipstick.

I reached out again and took her other cold hand across the table. 'Livy, darling – don't. I do wish there was something I could do for you. Can't you ask your mother? No, I suppose she wouldn't put her oar in for you.'

Wiping her face, Olivia said, 'Don't be too hard on Mummy. It's not her fault. Not really.'

'She said it wasn't *his* fault,' I said, more harshly than I'd intended.

Olivia looked me in the eyes. 'I wish I could hate them. I wish it so much.'

'Livy – can't you tell me what's so wrong at home? Is it – what you said that day – about your father?'

She rearranged her cutlery with nervous movements, half looking up at me, a fierce blush rising in her cheeks. 'No. I can't talk about it. I'm sorry, Katie.' She tried to sound brisk. 'I really shouldn't have said anything that day. I must have given you quite the wrong impression. Please forget I said it. Mummy and Daddy are just a bit over-protective. That's all.'

Our food was served: roast chicken and vegetables. Livy was treating me.

'This is so nice,' I said to her as the waiter spooned potatoes on to our plates. 'Thank you for it – very much.'

'Oh, I'm glad to.' Her smile was warm again now. It was such a reflex with her, being able to rally herself and change the subject. 'What are best friends for?'

We sat talking and laughing over our meal, and I enjoyed watching her pretty face across the table, thinking how the war was beginning to bring things like this into focus, things we had taken for granted.

'How's dear Angus?' she asked.

She often called him 'dear Angus', with a shading of irony in her voice.

'He's thriving. Loving the training. Of course I don't see very much of him – we're both so busy. And now, who knows what's going to happen?' In those early days of the war we were all galvanized by the expectation of being bombed or invaded any moment. 'Do you think it's all going to be over soon? Daddy's taking a very pessimistic line: Fascism is the dark force of evil in our time and won't be easily overthrown, and so on.' I imitated my father's sober Scots voice and Olivia grinned. 'Feels so normal sitting here like this though, doesn't it?'

'All these gas masks and shelters and everything certainly bring it home though, don't they?' She grew solemn again, reverting to her own frustrations. 'Honestly Katie. The only way I can see to get out of this is to get married. And that's not much of a motive for giving your life to someone, is it?'

In November Granny Munro lay dying. Another stroke felled her so that she couldn't speak and could barely move. She lay in her room, inert as lard, one side of her pallid face the only real register of her feelings.

Angus and I were able to spend time with her together one evening. We sat leaning forward so she could see us, the room lit only by the low sidelight on her bedside table. I held hands with her, with Angus on my other side. My emotions were very mixed. Here I was with two of the people I loved best in the world, together in this strange, silent intimacy. Granny's eyes moved over our faces. Her hair was white now and thinner. She was less considerable in size. I hadn't seen Angus for some time and was acutely aware of the novelty of his presence beside me: the soft curve of skin I loved at the back of his neck where the hairline ended, his hand warm on mine, eyes serious and affectionate.

Coal burned with a hiss in the grate. We talked softly from time to time, both of us telling her about our different jobs: my patients, Angus's hours cutting sheets of metal into fine shapes with a tiny fretsaw. We knew she liked to hear. Eventually her eyes closed.

'We'll be back soon,' I said softly. I laid her hand on the bedcovers. 'I'll bring you up some soup later.'

Outside the door we stopped and put our arms round each other.

'You smell of work.'

Angus laughed. 'Not surprising. I came straight here.' He looked at me sadly. 'She's very bad, isn't she?'

'She's dying. There isn't much can be done. We just have to keep her as comfy as we can.'

'What if there's an air raid? You can't very easily lift her down to the cellar.'

'I don't know.' The long looking-glass at the top of the stairs showed my face white with exhaustion. My legs felt weak and shaky. I'd just come from a long spell of duty on a women's surgical ward. 'We'll have to think of something.'

We went to join the rest of the family for dinner. It was unusual to have everyone at home. William had asked for permission to leave Oxford to see Granny. The house felt sombre with swathes of blackout material at all the windows. The panes were criss-crossed with tape to shield against blast. There was talk of food being rationed within the next couple of months: bacon, sugar, butter. Even the light in the dining room felt thinner, as if they were diluting the electricity.

As we ate our boiled ham with carrots, potatoes and dried peas, I stopped feeling so low and tired. We sat under the high, coved ceiling with its ornate rose at the centre, all painted white, and the walls a paper pattern of buff and brown. My father was at one end of the table and William at the other, Angus and I sat opposite each other, Mummy next to Angus.

I glanced at each of my parents as we ate. Both of them looked very tired too. Daddy was mostly silent and preoccupied. The war was constantly in our minds, yet of course at that stage no one knew exactly what it would entail. Poland was overrun, the seas had become menacing, trawled by U-boats and malevolent ships, magnetic minds floating unseen just below the surface. It was as if the world had a pall over it. And of course Daddy felt involved in every detail, as well as that of the health care of the city of Birmingham. His eyes were focused far from those around him. If he had taken the trouble to adjust them so that he could see my mother, he should have noticed the pale, pinched look on her face, her tense angry movements, evident even in the way she was eating, stabbing at the ham with her fork like a hen after corn. I watched her uneasily.

'How's Oxford?' Angus asked William, since no one was speaking, though I felt sure he must have asked him earlier. 'Still doing well?'

'I'm enjoying it enormously,' William said. He was looking very well, thinner and alight with the stimulation of it. 'I've got an absolutely first-rate tutor this term, and the chap I'm rooming with is very decent – we fit in a lot of sport together. All in all it's exceeded expectation. Pity about the war, though. Even if it is only "Bore" War at the moment . . .'

Daddy cleared his throat. 'I doubt if the Merchant Navy would see it that way.'

William gave a nervous laugh, embarrassed at expressing any uncertain emotion in front of his father. 'Yes, well I suppose we all really know our days are numbered now. Waiting to be called up and all that. It's all rather disturbing.'

'Well, it'd be terrible if anything happened to disturb your little life, wouldn't it?' I said. I saw Angus look at me in surprise.

'Kate, how can you say that?' Mummy snapped. 'Heaven only knows what your poor brother might have to go through. And Angus too, for that matter.'

'D'you think it hasn't crossed my mind?'

The terrible thought of Angus going away: it was like a hand closing tight around my heart, making my breathing go shallow. Our generation was brought up on images of the Great War. The trenches were woven in to every family history.

'If it comes to it, Angus,' William said, 'who are you going to join up with?'

My father's voice sliced unexpectedly across the table. 'You take it for granted I suppose that you have to follow the herd, like thousands in the last war who thought it was a heroic and glamorous thing to do. Have you not considered that there might be other alternatives?'

'But you weren't a conshie in the last war,' William protested, his face as usual turning red easily. 'And if you had been they'd have given you a pretty thin time of it.'

'No, I wasn't a conscientious objector then.' His voice had dropped but it was clipped and precise, his accent coming out more strongly than usual. 'I was a medical student. I chose to direct my energy to the preservation of life instead of its annihilation.'

The four of us sat watching him awkwardly. He discussed his thoughts so rarely that we felt at a loss as to how to communicate with him. His fervour usually expressed itself quietly, in his writing.

'But Father, this Adolf Hitler fellow is a raving lunatic. You can't just let him march across Europe taking away people's liberty and get away with it. Where's the justice in that?' William had assumed his debating chamber tone. 'We have to fight. Doesn't it bother you, the thought of other people doing all your fighting for you?'

'*Bother* me?' Daddy's pale blue eyes swept round the table coldly. 'Does it bother me? William, it appals me. But I can't believe there's any such thing as justice in a war. There's nothing just about it. And I have to stand against it with every fibre of my being. Can you understand that?'

William stared at him, then said stiffly, 'I'm sorry, I can't agree. When the time comes I shall offer myself to the army. I can't do anything mechanical of course, but they might find me something clerical or educational. I'm sorry I can't share your ideals, Father, but that's just the way it is. What about you, Angus?' He spoke with a note of appeal, needing Angus to support his point of view, but there was a challenge in his voice as well, the old competitiveness. I watched Angus anxiously.

'I shall volunteer for the RAF. I'm going to offer to train as a pilot.' As he spoke, his eyes met mine, but I could hear a certain kind of assertion in his voice and knew it was directed at William.

'Mummy, what's the matter?'

I'd taken the presumptuous step of following her upstairs after the meal and knocking on her bedroom door. There was no reply but I opened it and stood in the doorway. 'May I come in?'

'You already are in.' She had her back to me.

Timidly I walked towards her. 'You seem very upset about everything. Is it William – having to leave Oxford when they call him up?'

She went to her dressing table with an agitated pretence of sorting through one of the drawers, though I could see she was achieving nothing. She couldn't seem to bring herself to speak. Her thin, deft hands folded handkerchiefs, tinkered with the contents of a sandalwood box, jewellery she almost never wore.

'Mummy?' I forced myself to move closer. My experience in nursing had at least made me more at ease in approaching people.

'You know I'm no good at talking about things,' she

said. 'Never have been. You just have to get on with life, not keep blathering about it all the time.'

I felt encouraged. Even this much expression of her inner feelings represented progress.

'You must feel very hard-pressed now you've taken on so much more in the garden – and Granny. You're doing such a good job with her. It must be jolly tough. You two never exactly got on well, did you?'

Mummy ceased her activity suddenly and stood still. Her shoulders began to shake and I could see from her twisting lips that she was trying to ram her feelings back down inside herself.

'Look, you were a nurse,' I said gently. 'You know you're doing the best job you possibly can.'

Her voice came out in a kind of screech. 'But it's not a job, is it? It's an imposition. He just takes it for granted that I'm here to do it all. He always has done. And I can't make a fuss – not with the war . . .'

'But you always wanted to carry on nursing – '

'Nursing's not the same as this though, is it?' she cried, whirling round to face me. What I had intended as a sympathetic conversation seemed to be fast turning into a row. 'It's one thing to be a professional and be paid and be able to walk away from it,' she said, slamming the drawer shut. 'It's quite another when it's family and you have feelings all tied up with it and you can't just go off duty. Oh, I can't bear it.'

Her whole body seemed to crumple and she sank down on the green sateen eiderdown. Cautiously I sat down as well, not daring to touch her. A tear ran down each of her pale cheeks and then there were no more.

'I can't tell you how much I loathe it, having to clean up day after day when she soils herself. The indignity of it – for her. And I can feel her eyes watching me as if she's trying to say something and I feel it's a reproach. We're alone together so much, you see. Just her, quite silent, watching – and me. I try to be detached. I stand there wiping her up and think, "You're a nurse. This is a patient." But my patients were babies. I always loathed nursing old people. I was no good at it.' She looked round at me suddenly with frightened grey eyes. 'When I look at her I see myself. She reminds me this might happen to me. When you nurse people when you're younger it's not the same. And the worst of it is, the more time I spend with her the more I can't help admiring her. Her stubbornness, her independence. Bull-headed as anything . . . Qualities I've never . . .'

She sniffed and got up from the bed with renewed briskness. 'I never thought I'd be saying any of this. It's ridiculous and self-indulgent. Come along now, we must go down. The others will think we've deserted them. Those poor boys could be going off soon to get themselves killed.'

Chapter 10

Granny died shortly before Angus went away to begin his initial RAF training. He came to her funeral, of course, walking with Olivia behind William and me, when I would much rather have had him by my side. My father was silent, slightly stooped, displaying no emotion. Mummy looked haggard, exhausted from the nights of waiting while Granny had been lulled finally to death. To my surprise she wept at the sight of the coffin being lowered into the dark grave.

'In the midst of life we are in death: of whom may we seek for succour, but of thee, O Lord . . .'

I watched numbly then, wondering whether Granny would have been offended that she was being committed to the earth by this rite of the Church of England, but I decided she would have been amused by the irony of it. I found my sadness in our ring of black shoes round the grave, the wind flapping trouser legs and Mr Hughes' alb and rich purple stole, and Mummy having to hold on to her hat, and thinking how small and defenceless we booked standing there beneath the heavy sky.

My tears came later as I walked back between the silent stones and trees of Lodge Hill Cemetery, this time with Angus beside me. Mummy and Daddy walked slightly ahead of us, slowly, as if they had lead ingots strapped to their feet. I felt I ought to go to them, though I knew no comfort would be possible between us.

'I shall miss her so much.'

Angus put his arm strongly round my shoulders. He was wearing a black suit which made him look thin and older. 'Your house will certainly never be the same again. Even though she didn't get out of her room much by the end, it's going to feel very empty.'

'Not as empty as it'll be in a couple of days,' I said forlornly, tears running down my face. 'Oh Angus, I can't bear the thought of you going.'

I was really crying now and he stopped me and took me in his arms and I could feel his heart beating against me. He held me close, his cheek against mine, arms tight around me.

'I'm sorry.' He drew back and looked into my eyes with a troubled expression. 'I wish it didn't have to be now, so soon after this. But you'll be busy too, won't you, and I'll be back on leave like a shot as soon as I get the chance. Katie, you know I love you so much?'

'I know.' Thankfully I laid my head against his shoulder. The suit smelled strange, seldom used, with a whiff of camphor. 'I love you too. And I'm glad you were so fond of Granny as well.' I looked up at him. 'I suppose we all have to do our bit now.'

Angus grinned, suddenly, eyes crinkling at the corners. 'I couldn't help having a little smile to myself when he read that psalm – "I will keep my mouth as with a bridle", or however it goes. I think she would have enjoyed that, don't you?'

I laughed, tears still on my face, and hugged him again. 'Yes, she would, and she wouldn't like to see us being miserable either.'

Olivia approached us, dressed to the hilt as usual. She had on a very stylish black coat and hat and vivid red lipstick. Her cheeks were pink from the cold wind.

'Now now, you two,' she said archly. 'You've only just dispatched your grandmother, Katie. Surely you should save the billing and cooing for later?'

I turned to her, stung by the insensitivity of her remark, but seeing her smile I relented. It was so hard to get cross with Livy. She took my arm and we all walked on together.

'You're off on Thursday then, Angus?' She spoke to him in a caressing way, turning on the charm.

'Yes – basic training. It'll be a good stretch yet before I'm qualified to fly.'

'Have you any idea how much I envy you?'

'Really? Well, I suppose if you're that keen you could join up yourself.'

'Me?' Olivia looked astonished. 'What on earth would they want me for?'

'They need everyone they can get, especially if you've got something to offer. You could go for a clerical job, couldn't you – in one of the women's forces? I should think you're pretty well qualified by now.'

'Angus,' I protested. 'Don't give her ideas, please!'

But Olivia had stopped, excitement lighting her face. 'My goodness, of course! Why didn't I think of it? It's so obvious.'

'Oh, Olivia,' I wailed. 'You can't go away as well. Anyway, I've heard the women's forces are full of rough types who you wouldn't feel comfortable with at all. You know how you like your home comforts, the piano . . .'

'Kate,' Olivia said determinedly. 'I wouldn't care if it were full of the most uncouth Amazons to walk the earth if it means I can get away.' She ran round in front of me and kissed Angus so extravagantly that he blushed.

'Thank you, Angus. It's been staring me in the face!'

'Oh well,' I said gloomily. 'With any luck they won't take you.'

We linked arms again. The rest of our small party was standing by the iron gates of the cemetery. I felt a great rush of affection go through me – a sense of the preciousness of people I knew so well when everything around was changing.

'My best friends.' I reached up and kissed each of them and we walked to the gate with our arms round each other's backs. 'At least love is something they can't ration, even if they are taking you away from me.'

I spent the evening before Angus left round at the Harveys'. It was a comforting household with its littered, nestlike clutter of newspapers and periodicals, books and music scores and dogs' baskets. Two black Labradors sprawled snoozily in the hall beside a deflated football, a stack of the family's gas masks in their boxes, a carton full of Meccano and an assortment of old shoes and galoshes. John's clarinet lay askew across a chair. Mary was sitting at the table in the living room in a cone of light surrounded by algebra and *Paradise Lost*. On the mantelpiece a round-faced clock was just visible between John's swimming cups, sheaves of paper and invitations, candlesticks, receipts, ration books and good wishes cards. Mrs Harvey, who resembled Angus facially but was much rounder and had hair several shades lighter, sailed cheerfully through the mayhem apparently oblivious to it.

We all ate together. They were comfortable people. Being with them was like wearing a very old coat, so much so that I realized regretfully that evening how much I had taken them for granted. I had been beguiled by the Kemps for so long. My hatred for Alec Kemp seethed in me now, a revulsion born of former adoration. But it allowed me to appreciate the Harveys at last, and their home which was so familiar, into which I had run freely for so many years and always been made welcome.

Peter Harvey was black-haired, balding, thin. He smoked and smoked cigarettes and his chest sounded as if it was full of dried peas when he coughed. He had gnarled, prematurely arthritic hands which meant that although his firm produced beautiful instruments, he could no longer play them. But he was not downcast. He had a jovial, slightly sardonic way with him. Ruth Harvey was kind and comforting, though often with a rather distracted air, as if any question you asked her cut through a train of thought which brought her back from somewhere quite different and she was uncertain for a second quite where she was.

We didn't talk that evening of Angus going away. We sipped sherry and listened to the seven o'clock wireless broadcast, the nation's ritual. The Red Army had invaded Finland. The Western Front still ended short of France. Every bulletin was listened to with rapt attention and a strong sense of dread.

'Oh dear,' Ruth said as Peter got up to switch off the wireless. 'It's so awful not knowing what's going to happen.'

'Well, let's face it, you never know that at the best of times,' Peter said, clicking the round dial to cut off the radio announcer and picking up his glass again.

'It doesn't seem to matter as much normally, though,' Ruth said. Then she jumped up from her chair. 'Anyway, let's not be miserable on Angus's last night at home. Come on through and eat, everybody.'

We tried to keep the war out of the conversation as Ruth dished up beef casserole and potatoes and home-grown carrots and greens. We talked of the past, of childhood, until we were all laughing and joking. John and Mary both stayed quiet, though they joined in the laughter, Mary watching us all with her heart-shaped face and serious eyes.

After we had talked over coffee and it grew late, they left us alone.

'I know you'll be thinking of Angus and praying for him as much as we shall,' Ruth said to me before she retired.

'Of course.' I smiled at her.

She laid her hands on my shoulders, looking into my eyes, and I saw Angus's eyes in hers. 'It's a great support to us to know that, Katie.'

Peter Harvey gave me a peck on the cheek. 'If we don't see you again before you go back to work, come round when you can, won't you?'

They were as tactful and generous as it was possible to be. If I had stayed there all night with Angus I felt they would have passed no comment. They were open-minded people, and in any case, the war changed so many things.

'Are you scared?'

'Not scared, I don't think. Just nervous. A bit excited in a way.'

We lay side by side on the plump green eiderdown on Angus's bed. His arm was round my shoulders and I rested my head on his chest.

'I hate the idea of you doing something so dangerous. Couldn't you have chosen something a bit less heroic?'

'Well, that'd make a change for me, wouldn't it?' His tone was ironic, almost bitter.

'What d'you mean?' I half sat up and looked at him. 'I don't understand why you seem to feel – well, whatever it is you do feel – not very able physically, or a coward or something. It's just not true. Is it because of William, because he's always trying to put you down?'

Angus shrugged. 'There are things everyone feels they have to prove, I suppose. I need to be able to know I can do this. It's a challenge. And I've always wanted to learn to fly.'

'Yes, I'd almost forgotten.' I looked round the softly lit room. Like the rest of the house it was cluttered. There were old models, childhood preoccupations: a de Havilland DH–4 bomber, Bristol fighter, planes from the last war settled like moths on Angus's bookshelf, fuselages resting on school exercise books, volumes of poetry, encyclopaedias.

'D'you think Livy will really join up?' I asked him.

'She sounded serious enough.'

'I can't really imagine it. Though God knows, she needs to get away from those two.'

'Is Kemp's going over to the war effort?'

'I imagine so. I'm sure the war will increase dear Alec's sales figures enormously. Couldn't be better for him and his reputation, could it?' I added almost automatically, 'Poor old Livy.'

Angus pulled me closer to him. 'Livy, Livy, Livy. You can't take on her life for her, you know. If anyone's going to rescue her from her stifling parents it's going to have to be herself. After all, she can do a job now and earn her own money. It won't be long before she's twenty-one.'

'I know, but the hold they have on her. They're so over-protective.'

He leaned over and kissed me to stop me talking. His lips tasted faintly of coffee.

'Let's leave Livy out of it for tonight,' he said, looking into my eyes.

Slowly he undid the buttons down the front of my dress, removed my specs and unfastened the front of his shirt, and we lay holding each other, in the shadows from the little bedside lamp, warm skin touching. The house was silent. From the garden we heard an owl.

Angus ran one finger along the strap of my bra. I sat up. 'I'll take it off.' He helped me pull it away, releasing my breasts, full and heavy. I felt the heat of him against my back as he sat up behind me, his hands reaching round to touch and stroke me.

'There's so much of you.'

'You mean you don't get many of those to the pound!'

'No – you're wonderful. Like touching life.'

We seldom allowed ourselves to go this far. Opportunities were few in any case, and it was hard to draw back, not to take it further. He kissed my neck, lowered his hands so they were round my waist.

Holding me, he said, 'Katie, what I'd really like to do now is to ask you to marry me. But it doesn't feel right with the war on and everything feeling so uncertain. So I'm not actually going to ask you, but I wanted you to know that I'd like to.'

I turned my head and pulled him close so our cheeks touched. 'Well, if you had asked me, I'll just tell you that I'd have said yes, but since you haven't, I haven't!'

We laughed, lying down in each other's arms. 'Kate,

I do love you. But I don't want to make you a war widow.'

I felt chilled. 'Don't say that, please.'

Angus pulled me on top of him, his hands stroking my body. 'I love the feel of you. You're so beautiful.'

We kissed each other hungrily and I felt him move under me, his hands pressing into my back.

After a time he said, 'Katie, I'm sorry, you'll have to get off.' He looked at me shyly. 'It's just – if we carry on like this I'll go too far.'

I moved beside him again and he sat up, sighing, running his hands through his dark hair. 'I've been longing to have you – completely – for such a long time.' He looked away from me, embarrassed.

'Darling – ' I sat beside him and kissed his face. 'I want it too.'

'Do you? Don't you think it's wrong – outside marriage and all that?'

'Probably. But that doesn't stop me wanting it.'

Angus laughed delightedly. 'I love the way you're so honest. D'you mean you'd really . . .?'

'Yes. Especially now you're going away. If it wasn't for the war it would be different. Only I'm not sure about in your parents' house.'

'I can't think of anywhere better. Trouble is – I don't have anything in the way of protection. I certainly don't want to go and leave you pregnant.'

Hesitantly, I said, 'It's all right – as long as you don't actually come into me, isn't it?'

I moved my hand down and touched him, hearing him take a sharp intake of breath.

'You don't mind – if I touch you?'

I guided his hand to my body. We unfastened our

clothes, timid, then bolder, learning each other, lost in it. We lay together for a long time.

Much later I let myself out into the starry darkness of the January night.

It was a month of partings. William left shortly afterwards for the army. After a restrained farewell to Mummy and Daddy, he kissed me goodbye stiffly, suddenly garbed in adulthood and self-importance in a way that I found mildly ridiculous. He'd grown a little moustache which had gingery lights in it.

'Take care of yourself, Kate.' The whiskers prickled against my face. 'Keep an eye on the parents, won't you?'

'I will,' I promised, absolving him, as required, of any guilt on that front. 'Good luck, William.'

A week or two later Olivia came to see me at the hospital. I'd just knocked off from my shift and had invited another of the nurses to my room for a cup of tea. Brenda Forbes had a room close to mine in the nurses' home and we spent quite a bit of time together. She was a sturdy down-to-earth girl from a family of nine children. Her father owned a hardware shop in Alum Rock on the east side of the city. I found there was no side to Brenda and I enjoyed her sense of humour.

'Been up and down like a fiddler's elbow all afternoon,' she groaned as we walked along the corridor to our rooms. 'My feet are killing me. Don't half stink after work, don't they?'

'Yes – since you put it so delicately, I must say washing my feet is the first thing I want to do after a shift.'

Brenda pulled the starched cap off her long dark hair. 'One of these days I'm going to get myself a glamorous job.'

Laughing together, we burst into my room. And there was Olivia. She sat on my one hard wooden chair, her hat still on, face all made up, her smart suit looking incongruous in my austere little room. I felt strangely deflated at the sight of her.

'Oh,' Brenda said rather curtly. 'You've already got company. I'll see you later then, shall I?'

'No – Brenda, do come in. I'll make us all a cuppa.' I was embarrassed that Brenda should feel she had to leave.

'You're all right,' Brenda said. 'You talk to your friend. I'll get back and sort out my washing. See you later, Katie.'

I was relieved. Trying to juggle Olivia and Brenda together would have been pretty taxing. Olivia's eyes followed Brenda from the room, bemused.

'Gracious,' she said, eyeing me up and down.

I pointed out the landmarks on my apron. 'That's sputum, that one's vomit, and this wet patch, you'll be relieved to know, is only water.'

She took in my sudden tired irritation. 'Sorry, you must be exhausted. And missing dear Angus.' I chose to ignore the arch tone in her voice.

Tears filled my eyes. 'I am. I feel so worried, and I don't even know what there is to worry about yet.' A sense of foreboding that I could barely put into words had weighed me down ever since Angus left. I missed him with an intensity I hadn't expected. Now he was gone I knew just how much I loved him, and that feeling was private and couldn't be shared with anyone else.

Not even Olivia. I had had a note from him, though, saying he was settling in and learning a great deal. Apparently he was in Cornwall.

'Poor Katie,' Olivia said. Carefully she lifted off her bright cherry-coloured hat and laid it on my table. 'Come here – ' She held out her arms to me, then withdrew them again. 'How about taking that apron off?'

I unbuckled my belt and lifted the apron off and then we hugged each other and I felt her soft hair against my cheek. She felt like someone from a different world, beautiful and sweet-smelling: Givenchy perfume, her favourite.

I held her at arm's length, smiling. 'It's lovely to see you.' Then I narrowed my eyes suspiciously. 'What are you doing here?'

'I've got news to tell you. I've got to tell someone or I'll burst.'

I stared at her. 'You haven't?'

Her face broke into a delighted grin. 'I have. I had a letter today.' She held it out for me to read. 'On behalf of the Naval Ministry I should like to invite you . . .'

'I've been accepted by the Wrens!'

'Oh no, Livy – not you as well!' I said without thinking. 'I'm sorry, I suppose I ought to be congratulating you. I'm happy for you if that's what you want. But what on earth have your parents said?'

'They don't know. I'm not going to tell them until the last minute.'

'D'you think that's wise?'

Olivia nodded emphatically. 'Oh yes. They'll be hopping mad when they hear.'

I handed her a cup of tea. 'It's been difficult at home, hasn't it?'

'Difficult?' Olivia shrugged as if she couldn't find the words. 'I'll say.'

'I don't understand your parents, I can't pretend I do. I know there must be things you're not telling me and I don't want to pry.'

She didn't meet my eyes. 'It's not your problem. You've made that very clear.'

I was stung both by the injustice of this and the bitterness in her voice, but before I had time to respond she had done one of her quick changes and was on to something else.

'You're nearly done aren't you – qualified, I mean?'

'Yes, in the summer. I can't wait.'

'What will you do?'

'Depends a bit on the war. I want to get out of the hospital. I'll go for the Health Visitor's training if I qualify. There'll be a stint of midwifery first of course. But I'm set on that. "Prevention is better than cure" as they say. And I could do with getting away from all the petty rules in here. Matron saw me with a bit of my hair hanging loose from my cap the other day and I thought she was going to send me to the gallows!'

We sat talking for a long time. I felt like hanging on to her, delaying her leaving because I knew I was unlikely to see her again for a good while.

'It's going to be awful not having you around,' I said. 'You will write to me, won't you?'

'Of course I shall. After all, whether we've got men in our lives or not, we're still best friends, aren't we?'

I reassured her. I knew she felt pushed out because of Angus. 'Of course we are.'

But as she left, I knew, sadly, that there were more and more things in our lives that we were unable to talk about. I couldn't automatically confide everything to her now that Angus was gone. Our lives were increasingly separate and we couldn't hold on to the absolute closeness of childhood.

Chapter 11

'For goodness' sake Katie, find something useful to do,' Mummy said, though in a less acerbic voice than she was capable of. She was almost smiling.

I couldn't settle to anything. I was home after my exams and Angus was about to arrive on leave to 'await further instructions'. Now all I could do was to wait. Restlessly I kept going to the window and pulling back the nets to look out along Chantry Road, willing him to be there against the bright flowers of the gardens.

'There are endless things need doing in the garden,' Mummy went on. 'The lettuces are going to seed already – oh, and my blue dress needs rinsing through. You could peg that out for me.'

Dreamily I stood and washed out the faded blue dress in the scullery's deep white basin, silver bubbles of water tickling up round my hands, my thoughts far away. It seemed so long since I'd seen Angus.

'I've passed!' I had written to him ten days before. 'It seems like a miracle. After all, this has hardly been the ideal time for performing in exams.'

Everything was heaped against us that summer of 1940. The Dutch had fallen, the Belgians capitulated, then Dunkirk and the advance into France. And the Italians took against us as well. The Channel saved us, and all those young men in their tiny planes. But at the time I wrote to Angus in July, the Battle of Britain was still beyond the horizon.

'How small our personal concerns seem in the face of all this. But I miss you so much, my darling. Life here has been very busy, and I'm glad of it. It's in the quiet moments that I long to see you and feel very low at the thought of how little we can be together. Brenda came in and found me actually hopping up and down with excitement when I got your letter about your leave next week! I'm certain she thought I was quite cuckoo. But I can't wait to see you, my love.'

Angus had been moved from Cornwall to Cambridge.

'I never thought I'd end up attending lectures at Clare College,' he'd joked in his first letter from there. 'That's much more William's sort of territory. But at least it's taken some of the mystique out of it for me.'

After wringing out the dress, twisting it round and round into a tight snake, I went into the hot garden and hung it, the thin straight shape of my mother, on to the washing line. Then I tried to turn my attention to the vegetable patch. Mummy, in her gristly way, had dug out, single-handed, another long strip of bedding for vegetables in the place where we all used to play cricket, and radishes were growing roughly where we positioned our homemade crease. Angus, William, Livy . . . I had to hold on to each day for what it was. The future was too uncertain and frightening to think about. And what was precious about today was another of Livy's frequent letters, to which I would reply as promptly myself, keeping the threads of our friendship alive. And today – today I was going to see Angus.

For about half an hour I stooped and squatted round

the bed, tugging at groundsel and grass, my summer dress tucked round my legs. I pulled lettuce and carrots for lunch, then sat staring in a dazed way at the rows of spinach and beetroot. I heard the latch on the gate behind me and, turning, was on my feet in an instant and running to him.

'Oh darling, my darling!'

'Katie!'

Laughing, almost crying, I ran to him and we were in each other's arms, pressed close, quiet at first, suddenly shy.

'I've missed you so much,' Angus said after we'd kissed. I touched his face with my fingers, seeing his eyes full of love.

'You've still got your uniform on.'

'I've just walked in. Went up to change and I saw you through the window tinkering with the weeding.'

I laughed. 'My mind wasn't exactly on the job!' I looked at him in silence for a minute, then said seriously, 'It is so wonderful to see you. I love you.'

'And I you. More than ever.'

The week passed with terrible speed. We saw each other so rarely that Angus's leaving again seemed to overshadow even his arrival home. In many ways it was a blissful week, but for the sense of what was brewing in Europe. And I noticed a strange restlessness in Angus.

I sat beside him one evening in the Harveys' house on their battered, comfortable sofa. Angus had his arm around me and we had been talking softly, but I noticed that he seemed tense. I leaned round, holding his slight body, trying to take in the fact that he was here with me. All that was in focus was the front of his white shirt, the row of translucent pearl buttons. I stroked my hand over his ribs. He felt even thinner than when he'd left.

'What's the matter?'

'It's odd being home.' He sighed. 'All the time I've been away I've been dying to be back here with you. That's the most important thing, seeing you.' I pushed myself up so that I could look into his face. 'It's nothing to do with you,' he assured me. 'It's just so comfortable here. I feel as if I'm being cosseted like a child again when I'm supposed to be out there doing a job.'

'But they're only trying to make you welcome. Give you some home comforts.'

'I know. It's quite unreasonable of me. I feel … everything's changed. This wretched war has turned us all upside down. But you must know, Katie, nothing could change the way I feel about you.' He leaned towards me for a kiss.

One baking hot afternoon we caught a train to a country station outside Coventry, with our sandwiches and lemonade, fruitcake and apples that Mrs Harvey had packed for us.

'You have a lovely afternoon now,' she'd told us. 'You both deserve it.' Her voice was wistful on our behalf, knowing how rare and brief were our times together.

We walked out into the Warwickshire countryside, finding fields into which it was possible to believe the war had not yet slunk its tentacles. The corn was turning yellow. Bees moved in and out of the poppies and morning glory and a breeze moved the wheat stems.

'It's so beautiful,' I said, stopping, breathing in the smell of the fields, the air free of smoke. 'It's so long since I've been out of Birmingham. You almost forget there is anything else.'

We stood quietly for a few moments looking out over the gold field edged with the trees' black shade and sprinkled with red.

'I do think it's right to fight for it,' Angus said suddenly. 'I've thought a lot about what your father said, before William and I joined up, and I can see he's probably the most, I don't know – saintly of us. But I do feel with every fibre of me that you have to stand up to the likes of Hitler, and I want to be part of defending all that this country stands for against what they're doing.' He spoke with a forced casualness, avoiding sounding pompous as William would have done. I reached out and squeezed his arm.

After a time we came to an oak tree providing a patchy ring of shade between two fields and sat on the soft grass edging the barley. I opened the packet of beef sandwiches. Angus's mood was changeable that afternoon, sometimes joking, the next moment quiet and serious as if preoccupied, and then I could tell his thoughts were elsewhere.

'It was odd travelling up to Cambridge,' he said, pouring lemonade into our two enamel cups. 'Now they've made all the signs so small we couldn't always tell where we were. It's quite a haul from Cornwall too. We thought we must be going to Scotland, but then it all looked too flat!'

'I wonder what they'll do with you next?'

'More training somewhere. Has to be. I'm a way from getting my wings yet.'

'D'you really like flying?'

'Oh yes.' He sat eating with his knees drawn up in

front of him, shirtsleeves rolled up to the elbows. His forearms were tanned under the dark hairs. 'I enjoy it even more than I imagined. I wasn't sure when we started off, of course. All those talks. It was all airframes and aerodynamics and navigation, and the hangars were horribly cold.' He gave me his wide smile. 'But as soon as they started teaching us to fly – oh, it was marvellous. Hard to describe it – it's like another dimension to life. I'll have to take you up for a spin one day, then you'll see what I mean.'

He talked with enthusiasm about all he was learning and the other cadets training with him.

'They're a real mixed bag of course, but we've got used to each other now. We had to pull together against a couple of officers who are right – '

I could tell he was biting back a swear word, another symbol of forces camaraderie.

' – well, tough sorts, let's say.'

I laughed. 'I do have more than the odd patient who curses, you know!'

Angus grinned sheepishly. 'Of course. I'm sorry. I keep talking as if I'm the only one who's doing anything.'

'It's all right.' He'd already asked me about my plans. 'The war hasn't touched us all that much yet, except for there being so many people missing. I sometimes feel so stuck here with you all gone.'

To my annoyance, tears filled my eyes. The past months had been so lonely. I had poured all my energy into work. I didn't want to be blubbing in the few days I had with Angus.

He shifted over to me, pushing aside the packet and cups and apple cores from our picnic. The grass was soft beneath us. Crows called in the branches.

'Here, let me hold you.'

We lay in each other's arms, looking up at the thick, strong branches of the tree, sunlight skewering through into our eyes now and then as the breeze shuffled the leaves.

'I wonder what you make of it all,' I said. The solid girth of the trunk was behind our heads. 'You'll still be here long after it's all over.'

I rested my head on Angus's chest, listening to the sound of his heart, one arm across his body. A daytime moon hung in the sky, remote and white like a slice of pumice.

'How many children shall we have?' I asked playfully, making believe we lived in a wholesome world to which there was no threat.

'Oh, six at least.'

I leaned up on one elbow. 'You are joking?' But he was looking very solemn.

'Katie – ' He hesitated. 'If I wasn't to make it through all of this . . .' I wanted to stop him, not to hear, but I knew I must let him speak. 'We've none of us any idea how it's all going to go, but I want you to know – I love you. Whatever happens, I'll always love you.'

'Oh God,' I said, beginning to cry. 'This is awful. Why did this have to happen? Those damn Germans messing up everyone's lives. Angus, I love you, that's what matters. Wherever you are you know you can always carry that with you.'

He pulled me strongly towards him.

'I love you,' we said again and again between our kisses. 'I love you, I love you.'

Angus pushed himself into a sitting position, his jacket for a cushion, between the roots of the tree. I sat on his lap facing him.

He ran his hands over my shoulders, dark eyes watching my face. 'You're thinner,' he said. 'Heavens, I can feel your bones. Don't disappear, will you?'

I stroked his hair, cropped RAF-style now, smiling at the bristly feel of it. Gently he tugged my thin red blouse out from the band of my skirt and reached round to free my breasts.

'Oh God, I've missed you.' His hands were warm on my skin, holding me close.

'Katie – ' He hesitated. 'I've got some, well – protection this time. We could make love properly. That's if you don't think it's wrong?'

'You've been planning this!' I teased him.

'Not planning. Hoping.'

Without answering him I sat back, and to his surprise, unfastened first my clothes, then his.

'I take it that's a yes.' Again he slid his hands under the red cotton of my blouse. As we touched each other I was aware of the muscular strength of him, the force of another body so close to my own. We were nothing but gentle with each other, but in our excitement I understood how lovemaking could so easily fall over into a fight.

After, we lay close, quiet in the dappled shadow of the tree, our heads on Angus's brown jacket. That day is one of my most precious memories of Angus. The intent, tender expression in his eyes when he moved into me for the first time, the haze of leaves and blue sky behind his head and my hands pressing into the flesh of his back under his shirt. His cry, 'It's lovely – God it's so lovely,' at the height of it. And our 'thank you, thank you' afterwards as our cheeks touched, mine wet with tears.

Lying together, we heard the planes, the sound half

obscured at first by the breeze, then swelling towards us, engines straining across the sky. Angus sat up.

'They are ours?' I asked, only half joking. Without my specs I couldn't even see the planes, let alone their insignia.

'Yes, definitely ours. Off on a practice run, I expect.'

The sight of the planes had pulled his mind back to his training, his job.

'Can't escape it for long, can we?' I said, sitting up. 'Oh, I do wish we could see what's going to happen.'

Seldom has a wish been more ill-guided. In our ignorance of the future that afternoon we sat, peaceful and loving in our barley field between Birmingham and Coventry, cities whose solid, familiar faces would be shattered almost beyond recognition by the approaching storm.

Chapter 12

As we waited through the intense days of the Battle of Britain, Angus was sent to Canada to complete his training in Moose Jaw, Saskatchewan. The inhabitants of Apple Valley en route to Moose Jaw stopped their train and deluged the lads with the red fruit which gave the place its name. Before he left again, Angus gave me a book of poems.

'Some of them are my favourites,' he said. 'I want you to keep this for me.'

The collection was by Gerard Manley Hopkins. I found them hard to understand but for glimpses of beauty in them and my favourite was the simplest: 'Heaven–Haven – A nun takes the veil':

> I have desired to go
>   Where springs not fail,
> To fields where flies no sharp and sided hail
>   And a few lilies blow.
>
> And I have asked to be
>   Where no storms come,
> Where the green swell is in the havens dumb,
>   And out of the swing of the sea.

I kept the poem in my head as a charm, a conjuror of peace, even if there was none in the world.

'Every day I thank God selfishly,' I wrote to him, 'that you have, as yet, no wings on your uniform.'

God was on people's lips more than usual in any case. With autumn came the bombing. At the height of the blitz on Birmingham I went to church with my mother. I had moved to live back at home now my training was complete.

'Lead us, heavenly Father, lead us, o'er the world's tempestuous sea,' we sang. The church was packed and people stood in the aisles. We all needed something to hold on to.

Mummy was tense as a trip-wire. I stood with her one day while she was wrenching the pale flesh from a boiled pig's head for brawn.

'Wouldn't this be a good time for you to go back to nursing?' I ventured. 'They're short-handed everywhere.'

Daddy was working incessantly it seemed. Days, nights, any demand that came he tried to meet, as if he had something to prove.

'How can I?' Mummy said briskly. 'There's the house to run, all the garden – there's so much to do. And no Simmons.' Simmons had volunteered for the ATS.

'But I'm here to help,' I urged her. 'I thought you wanted to do more nursing?'

'What's wanting ever had to do with anything?' she snapped. She handed the bowl of pig's flesh to Mrs Drysdale. 'Here, you could finish this off for me, please.' We went through to the living room. 'She's so wasteful getting the meat off,' she murmured.

Mummy was up to her eyes in make do and mend. There were old cut up shirts and curtains strewn all over the living-room sofa. She held up a length of curtain material in a yellow and white regency stripe.

'I thought this would run to a skirt. Or do you think you'd look too much like a stick of rock in it?'

'No, that would suit me very well.' I smiled cautiously. 'It's just – I've decided to delay my midder training for a few months and work in casualty for a bit. Extra help's needed everywhere.'

Mummy stopped again and looked up at me awkwardly. 'I suppose I could fit in a few hours at a first aid post. It's not as if you and William are holding me back any more.'

'I'm sure they're crying out for you,' I said.

The first bombs had fallen on Birmingham in August 1940. The bombardment crescendoed through that foggy, blacked-out winter, right through until April 1941. So much that we had thought solid and sure, familiar landmarks made of weighty stone, caved in like plywood boxes. The bombs destroyed the Market Hall, smashed to rubble sections of Fort Dunlop, Marshal and Snelgrove's, the Bull Ring, the BSA. People pushed the remains of their belongings from bombed houses to the emergency centres in wheelbarrows and babies' prams. In November, the fires from Coventry's sacrifice bled into the sky.

I worked nights in the casualty centre at the Queen's Hospital in Bath Row. Mummy was doing two-night stints in the first aid post at Moseley Baths.

On one of the heaviest nights of the blitz I set off late for work. Pushing down feverishly on the pedals of my bike I turned into the Moseley Road. There was a light mist which made the going slower with my muffled headlamps. I breathed in mouthfuls of the damp air. Abruptly, the air-raid sirens let out their terrible wail into the night.

'Damn and blast it!' I stopped, my stomach churning with nerves. Gas mask. I couldn't go without it tonight.

I tore back home to fetch it and set off again, balancing the box in my wicker bicycle basket.

I had only gone about a mile when I heard the sound of the first planes. In panic I dismounted, and finding myself against the wall of a churchyard, left the bicycle and ducked down in the graveyard, somewhere I would never normally have gone at night on my own. Squatting, head down, hands against the lichen-covered brick of the wall, I became aware of my quick breathing, the beat of my heart, close and hard, and in the distance the drone of the planes.

They crossed the city, coming in from the east. There was a swell of sound: ack-ack guns, the impact of the bombs, muffled explosions in the distance, then the noise dying. And here was I shouting 'Damn you, damn you!' at the top of my voice, furious at having to squat terrified in my own city while they knocked the stuffing out of it. It was clear they were aiming for the centre, hoping to destroy aeroplane and weapons factories, though in fact the extra 'shadow' factories to fuel the war were built on the edges, so shops and houses took it instead.

I had not long set off again when I heard the next lot. I had suddenly grown wings. I flew down the sweeping slope of Belgrave Road as if I was parachuting and pedalled madly across the Bristol Road towards Five Ways.

What little traffic was on the roads had come to a standstill. I slowed, looking upwards. The searchlights jittered and crossed over us, lighting up the bellies of barrage balloons like bloated silver fish, and now there was extra light from fires. The planes were very close. I was only yards from Bath Row, already off my bike and pushing it, when the first wave of bombs fell. I flung myself against the nearest building, shielding myself behind my bicycle and with my free arm wrapped round my head. The gas mask tipped on to the ground. Our ack-ack guns were going again, hammering into the sky. There was a terrible pause, then the impact. In seconds there were more explosions, close, but not in my street. Panting, I waited for the one that was going to fall on me. There came what seemed hours of sound, the whistle of the bombs, the echoing, shaking impact as they fell, glass shattering and debris falling and the smell of cordite and the air thickened with dust and smoke. But the sound of the impacts grew more muffled. They were moving over. The guns held fire, no doubt predicting the positions of the next wave of planes that I could already hear. I knew this was the moment to move.

I pushed my bike upright. Flames lit the sky from the next street and I could hear fire-engine bells in the distance and shouts from firewatchers high on one of the buildings near by. As the planes roared overhead I dashed towards the entrance to the hospital, thanking heaven I could at last get under cover.

There was an ambulance parked outside. At the Casualty entrance I held the door open for two ambulance volunteers coming out with an empty stretcher.

'Won't be Bournvita and slippers tonight,' one of them said to me cheerfully. 'Not for a good few hours yet, anyway.'

I smiled at him, reassured. My legs were like jelly, but at least I would be inside now. These people had to go out and face it all over again. 'I wish I could get you some.'

'Oh, you'll have enough to do, love.'

But we at least had an illusion of safety here, the generous layers of the hospital stacked above us.

Hurriedly I hung up my coat and pinned on my white cap, feeling at home now, able to be competent. Doctors, already looking exhausted, were scurrying between the new arrivals in the reception area. 'Fractured tibia – needs casting', 'This one – theatre – quickly', 'That one can hang on for a bit'.

Nurses were collecting valuables from the wounded, writing rapid notes on casualty record cards and trying to exude calmness and reassurance. There were already more casualties coming in.

'Where the hell have you been?' one of the other nurses demanded as she rushed past me.

'I got caught out in it.'

She didn't comment further on my lateness. 'At least you can hear ours going out there.'

It was always a great boost to people to be able to hear the ack-ack guns, though we had no idea how accurate they were. Our defence was comforting. We were fighting back. But it was hard, even while rushing to and fro paying attention to the job you were doing, not to strain your ears, constantly wondering what was going on outside, wondering how close they were. Often we felt the vibrations of the bombs' impact.

I was sent to theatre to help prepare trolleys. I recited the items in my mind trying to keep my thoughts away from the bombing, from my parents, both out there working. Saline, hydrogen peroxide, sterilized dressing drum, Cheatle's forceps, tray of instruments, bandages, iodine . . . the reassurance of routine.

I'd no sooner got going on that, though, when Sister hurried over to me. 'Nurse Munro, we need you to come and help with some of the new arrivals . . .' and once I'd got started on that one of the doctors sent me scurrying back and forth for dressings. As I completed this task we heard a loud groan of pain from one of the two men lying to the side of the reception area waiting for further attention.

'Nurse!'

'Go and see,' the doctor ordered me.

A middle-aged man, face a ghastly white, was lying stoically pressing a pad to his wounded head. When I approached him, he said, 'I'm all right love. You see to 'im.'

The sounds of distress were coming from the younger man beside him. He had a padded dressing which had been hastily applied to his left cheek and was already bloodstained. The clothing had been cut from his upper torso, presumably because it was soaked in blood. There was no other apparent injury to his body.

I bent down beside him. 'What's the matter?'

Few of our patients made much of a to-do when they came in. Some, of course, were very frightened or in pain, but many of them were in shock and lay there numbly like sacrificial lambs.

'God,' he groaned. 'I'm in such bloody agony.' He twitched his body angrily from side to side. 'I can't stand it. It was numb to begin with, but now it's getting worse every minute.' He spoke painfully out of the side of his mouth, trying not to move the left side of his face.

'It won't be long,' I assured him. 'A doctor will see to you properly soon. It's busy tonight, I'm afraid.' I felt a bit irritated at the fuss he was making, but at the same time there was something about him which intrigued me. I think it was partly the strength of feeling that came from him, even though it was expressed through frustration, and partly the glimpse I caught of the side of his face not covered by the dressing. I saw the contours of a prominent cheekbone, a strong chin and eyes of the brightest blue I'd ever seen. I found myself staring in fascination.

I thought I'd try and take his mind off the pain. 'My name's Kate,' I said. 'Yours?'

'Douglas Craven,' he grunted, then added ironically, 'Pleased to make your acquaintance.' He spoke very carefully, wincing as he did so.

'It's bad out there tonight, isn't it?'

'Of course it's bad,' he snapped. 'What the hell d'you think?'

'What happened to your face?'

'Don't know exactly. I was on firewatch. There was stuff flying all over the place. Something stabbed right through my cheek – metal. I can feel it's gone into the bone . . . Aagh – God!'

He started giving dry, tearless sobs, his lips contorting miserably. He had a little moustache which was clotted with blood so I couldn't see its colour. His hair was blond though, so I assumed the moustache might be. For a moment I took his hand.

'They'll soon look at you. It must be quite awful for you.'

'Damn it!' He writhed beside me. 'This is terrible.'

He communicated the powerful outrage of a fit man who has been struck down and slowed.

A commotion suddenly started up at the entrance, raised voices and more stretchers arriving.

'I'll be back.'

Everyone was talking at once, the ambulance workers, a doctor trying to be heard above everyone else. Then everyone saying 'Ssssh.'

'It's the Carlton Cinema up Sparkhill,' one of the

ambulance workers told us. His eyelashes were white with dust.

'The control centre warned us you were coming,' said a voice. Everyone had fallen silent. 'What's the damage?'

'Direct hit. Straight down in front of the screen.' The man speaking looked really shaken. 'There's God knows how many gone. The blast got their lungs. They were all sat there in the front rows as if they were still watching the film. Never seen anything like it. Eerie as hell. They're taking the rest straight to the General, and Selly Oak, I think.'

I hurried back to Douglas Craven. 'It's going to be very busy.' I told him what had happened.

'Oh damn, damn,' he groaned.

'Whatever's wrong? Was someone you knew at the Carlton?'

'I should have been over there.'

I stared at him in disbelief. 'What are you talking about?'

'I'm a reporter. If I hadn't been on bloody fire-watch I could have been over there – got the first look at it ... And now I'm stuck here with my face in shreds ...'

I knelt down close to him so that no one else could hear, and between clenched teeth I said, 'You stupid, self-pitying sod. You ought to be ashamed of yourself.'

I turned away and busied myself with what I considered to be more deserving patients.

The next day I was ashamed. It was very bad form to talk to any patient like that however much they provoked you. It had been a very hard night and I was exhausted, but I went to enquire with the casualty register.

'Douglas Craven? Looks as if he was admitted for the night.'

The morning, after the all clear, had brought news that the total dead in the Carlton Cinema was nineteen. It was the first thing my mother told me the next morning. I resolved to take this news to Douglas Craven, to show him the consequences of what he had seen as a 'story'. I suppose I felt rather self-righteous, and it didn't occur to me that the reason the city was reeling with the news this morning was that someone like Douglas had done the job of reporting it.

We didn't recognize each other to begin with. They'd cleaned Douglas up so that his hair and moustache were the same colour, and the dressing was neat and not seeping.

Now it was more reposed, his face was even more striking, with its chiselled bone structure and those vivid blue eyes. He was sitting in bed in the pale light of the ward eyeing the morning paper.

'Hello,' I said gruffly.

He looked up, baffled. I didn't have my uniform on.

Speaking rapidly, I said, 'I owe you an apology – for last night. I shouldn't have said what I did. You were in pain and in a state. I'm sorry.'

His blue eyes suddenly showed recognition. 'Kate, isn't it? My Florence Nightingale.' He appeared still to speak with some difficulty.

'Not all nurses are Florence Nightingale,' I pointed out stiffly. 'We're all different. We have personalities of our own actually.'

'Yes, quite. I'm sorry. And thank you for your apology. You're quite right, I was in a state, but nothing to some of them who came in. I'm afraid I was having a bit of a tantrum. Do sit down by the way.'

Reluctantly I perched on the chair by his bed. I wasn't at home as a visitor in a hospital, nor was I sure how I felt about being in his company.

'Surely you should be asleep in bed after last night, not visiting me?'

'I've slept. I'm used to night work. How're you feeling?'

'Oh marvellous. Actually – ' he tried a rueful smile, putting the palm of his hand cautiously against the dressing – 'my face is dreadfully sore and stiff. They managed to yank out a great shard of something.' He spoke in a sardonic tone, but I saw a blush seep across his face. 'I'm afraid I was an awful baby.'

Disarmed, I said, 'That's all right. It's the pain.' I added untruthfully, 'Anyone'd be the same.'

'You're very kind,' he said. 'Do you enjoy being a nurse? Seems a frightful job to me.'

'Oh yes – on the whole.' I told him of my longer-term plans. I found that he asked a great many questions, and that by the time I left I had told him a surprising amount about myself, my work and my family. I supposed he was at ease asking questions. It was his job, after all. His eyes watched me with intent interest. To my surprise I realized I was enjoying the conversation. I found myself telling him I was engaged, which seemed the easiest way of explaining my relationship with Angus.

'Ah,' Douglas said. 'That explains it. Your face has a kind of glow about it.'

I smiled wryly. In fact I was feeling pretty washed out and tired sitting there after a few restless hours of sleep.

'Must be the light of love I can see – lucky fellow.' For a split second as he said these words Douglas appeared vulnerable.

'You don't have anyone?'

He gave an odd laugh, somehow apologetic. 'Me? Good heavens no.'

Unsure what to say next I felt I ought to leave. I stood up, suddenly reluctant to go. As we shook hands I smiled, and Douglas made a rueful attempt to do the same. 'Well, good luck. Don't risk too much for your reporting will you?'

He said goodbye with a strange solemnity. I turned at the door as I left, half pretending I was just glancing round the ward, and saw he was still watching me. I raised my hand in a wave. As I walked downstairs from the ward I mused over the fact that I had told him far more about myself than I had imagined possible, and that about him I knew almost nothing.

Chapter 13

Olivia stopped writing to me in any meaningful way in November 1940. After sending a letter faithfully once or twice a week, she scarcely wrote now from one month to the next, and when she did, it was a note on a single sheet, brief and frothy, as if suddenly for a few seconds she had remembered me. At first I was baffled. She'd been home on leave for a week back in the summer and we'd had a very jolly time together, laughing almost as much as when we were children. It was an escape from the war, looking at the light side of things and finding the jokes.

Livy had looked healthy and full of life, showing off her uniform – 'It's definitely the smartest in the women's services. Not like that awful drab ATS garb!' – playing the piano, and we'd gone out dancing . . . And suddenly this oddness.

'Dearest Katie,' she wrote in December that year,

> Guess what – I've been reposted! More responsibility, or so they tell me, though it doesn't feel too arduous as yet. All in all though a new, big adventure.
>
> How are things in grim old Birmingham? Life here is such a lark – as I'm sure I've said. I can't think why I didn't join up at the earliest opportunity! My life before the war seems deathly when I think back on it now. Of course we're working fearfully hard as well, but I

scarcely have a night in, except when we have to – dreary domestic nights which are a rule of the service. But at least it's a chance to reset my hair!

I do hope you're not overworking and burning yourself out with all your duties. Do remember to let up sometimes won't you?!

Just dashing this off – must finish now. There'll be a lot of disappointed faces at the dance tonight if I don't turn up!

All love for now. Olivia.

After several letters like this I felt pretty browned off with her, and not just because her writing to me was so rare when I'd been making an effort to write regularly, but because the tone of them was always similar to this one. It didn't strike me then that anything was wrong: I was just irritated by their shallowness. She felt so distant and it was as if we could no longer communicate about anything important.

Angus spent the Christmas of 1940 at home.

'Oh, look at you!' I greeted him, fingering the embroidered wings on his blue uniform. 'A real airman!'

While he was home we announced to our families that we planned to marry.

'We don't feel we can plan a date,' Angus explained to his mum and dad. 'Not with things as they are. But as soon as I know I'm going to be back home . . .'

'I can't pretend I'm surprised,' Ruth Harvey said, embracing me enthusiastically. 'And I couldn't be more delighted.'

Christmas slipped by far too quickly. Angus and I treated ourselves to one night away together, deciding not to worry what anyone thought. My parents couldn't bring themselves to comment and Peter Harvey lent us his car. When we signed ourselves into a small country inn it was as Mr and Mrs Harvey. No doubt couples were doing something similar all over the country.

In the small restaurant we had a magnificent meal considering the time of year and strictures of rationing.

'That's the great thing about being in the country.' I stared in wonder at the pheasant and generous helpings of vegetables on my plate. 'And she said there'd be eggs for breakfast!'

'Didn't you see the chickens out at the back when we arrived?' Angus said, smiling at my enthusiasm. 'That's what you really came for, wasn't it – the food!'

'Don't be silly.' I took his hand across the table. 'But it's all lovely.'

'We don't do badly for food. I think they give the services all the best.'

'Well I'm glad they're looking after you.'

We ordered a half bottle of wine and sat for a long time near the comforting fire in the inglenook, enjoying being with each other. Because my thoughts were often sad and questioning I didn't want to voice them, and I sensed there were a lot of things that Angus was not saying, was keeping at bay. We sat quietly holding hands across the table, and when we did talk it was often about the past because it was safer.

'D'you remember that day when your granny stripped off just as your mum was expecting all those parish bods round?'

I smiled back. That afternoon: Granny's graphic display of her frustrations, Olivia's strange mood – the start of so many more.

'I thought your mother would burst she was so angry.'

'Oh no. That'd be far too self-indulgent. She's prepared to permit herself some emotions, provided they're all brisk, positive ones.'

'You're very hard on her.'

'I've had to live with her. Your mother's so relaxed and warm compared with mine.'

Angus nodded, unable to contradict me. He watched me, head on one side. 'How's Livy getting on?'

'Oh, like a house on fire apparently.' I couldn't help the bitter edge to my voice. 'Taking the Wrens by storm, one long party, all marvellous ...' I spoke mocking the tone of those breezy notes which made me feel so cut off from her in their twittering, persuasive brightness.

'So what's wrong?'

'I don't know who she is any more. As if we can't ever tell each other anything. It used not to be like this.'

'Don't let it upset you.' He squeezed my hands, his own cupped warm and comforting around them. 'Everyone has different ways of getting through all this. Maybe that's hers.'

I was staring down at the cloth. 'It just feels as if I'm losing everyone – the people who really matter, anyway. Still – ' I loosed one hand to take a sip from my glass, looking at the flames through the deep red liquid. 'Mustn't start feeling sorry for myself.'

'Oh, go on – I was rather enjoying it,' Angus teased.

'At least you're here – that's the main thing.'

He shook his head slowly. His hair was so short now, clipped very precisely round his ears. 'I'm not certain for how much longer.' He spoke reluctantly.

'What does that mean?'

He leaned forward and whispered, very close to my ear: 'Strong possibility of an overseas posting coming up.'

'Oh, Angus, no!' I put my glass down, catching the

base on the ashtray. Red wine bled slowly across the white cloth. I sprinkled salt on the stain and it turned a sickly pink. I felt tears rising in me. Angus going away, no home leaves, never seeing him. I cursed myself for being so self-centred.

'Look – we haven't actually heard anything yet.'

I looked across at him in silence. He took my hand and squeezed it. 'Come on, Katie. Let's go up.'

He teased me out of my despondency on the way up the dark staircase, trying to lift me up, sweeping me off my feet.

'I wouldn't have even attempted this a few years ago,' he said, pretending to stagger across the landing. 'You're not quite such a lump nowadays.'

I kicked and protested, and high on the wine we found ourselves tangled, giggling on the bed in our little room. The fire was still alight, and we left the light off and settled in front of it. The playful mood lasted. Together we laid the eiderdown and a scratchy rug on the floor by the grate, then knelt opposite each other.

'The first person to laugh has to forfeit one article of clothing,' I said, immediately erupting into giggles.

'Right,' Angus said. 'That's you for a start. And the second rule is that the other person has to take it off for them.'

We didn't hold back on our laughter, struggling slightly hysterically with buttons and fastenings until Angus said, 'The only thing you've got left now is your specs.'

He lifted them slowly from my face, serious now, his grey eyes close to mine. His excitement was evident and I felt suddenly awed by it, by the responsibility each of us had for the other's happiness.

'I've missed you. I've wanted you so much.'

Our lovemaking that night was the least reserved I ever remember it. A fierce combination of need, fear and passion, not mindful of what was proper or permissible, only what was strong and right. He stayed out of me for a long time, not wanting to give himself up to it too soon, and we knelt together in the firelight, fingers on each other's skin. The tautness of his mood excited me, his eyes closed, breathing me in, touching every part of me.

We lay together, then, on the blanket as the fire faded. I could see only the closest things: Angus's face, his dark hair, chest pink in the light and the shape of my breasts falling heavily to one side as I lay beside him. He ran his hand very softly along my side, again and again, thigh, hips, waist, ribs, following the deep curves. He closed his eyes. Eventually we moved to make ourselves comfortable on the bed, lying tucked tightly together.

I woke later in the night to find him moving beside me, slight shifting movements of his head and limbs too controlled and conscious for sleep.

'Angus?'

Silence at first, then his voice: 'I think I'm going to die.'

Swiftly I turned over. 'Don't. Please don't.' I could see only the faint outline of his face. I held him close to me.

'We don't talk about it – none of us. Best not to. It's not the done thing. You can't function if you think about it, so we joke about collecting scores, flying aces and all that. None of my squadron have seen much in the way of real action of course, but we've heard enough.'

Silently I listened, my arm crooked across his flat

stomach. He spoke quietly into the darkness, in an even voice.

'You can't say the obvious, can't share it. I'm shit scared. I don't want to die. I don't want to leave you, Katie.'

Our arms tightened round each other.

'My darling, I love you,' I told him helplessly. 'I love you so much.' We slept, clinging as if afraid that the other might slip away.

That room has stayed with me always. Waking the next morning: the white bowl and pitcher on the chest of drawers, powder-blue wallpaper with trailing pink roses, the pink eiderdown with satin finish, sun through that window overlooking fields. And the shadows of the place round us the evening before, the firelight: Angus's face.

They embarked from Liverpool in early January 1941, on the *Empress of Australia* for Freetown, Mombasa, the Arabian Sea. At Bombay, the squadrons joined the *Aquitania* with its draft of a thousand service personnel bound for the nutmeg smell of Rangoon. In March the squadrons formed at Kallang Airport to aid the defence of Singapore, with their cumbersome Buffalo fighter planes.

Two days before he left, Angus sent me a postcard.

> Thank you for a wonderful leave, my love. Something to carry with me in the darker days ahead.
>
> Guess who I ran into last night – Olivia! At one of the local Naafis. We had quite a jolly time together. Good to see a familiar face in all this. Keep your spirits up, my darling. Thinking of you constantly. Love, Angus.

*

I ran into Elizabeth Kemp, forced the meeting, though I'm sure she would have preferred a pretence of not seeing me. Even her appearance grated on me. It was the spring of 1941, and the air raids were at last beginning to let up, but it had been a hard, heartbreaking winter for so many people. The city was peppered with bomb sites and we were all pale-faced, haggard from nerves and lack of sleep. But there was Elizabeth, sauntering along New Street dressed in what must have been a very expensive navy coat, stylish high-heeled shoes and an extravagant, wide-brimmed hat. So few people looked glamorous in the city. I couldn't help thinking how typical it was of her, this inability to confront even the reality of the war.

'Good morning, Mrs Kemp.' I wouldn't call her Elizabeth. I stood square in front of her in my flat nursing shoes and blue serge coat.

'Oh! Katie!' She recoiled slightly. 'I didn't see you.'

'How odd. I could have sworn you were looking straight at me.' I gave her a broad smile so that she was left unsure whether I was being sarcastic or not. I could feel her thinking what a frump I looked.

'How's Olivia? I don't hear all that much from her.'

Elizabeth's hands fiddled with the clasp of her glossy blue handbag. 'To tell you the truth, neither do we.' She looked down, watching the drab feet passing us. She had aged even since I last saw her. Her face was thinner, more lined. 'I gather she's getting along fine. Well settled in. Doing her bit – you know. To tell you the truth we thought she might soon find she'd had enough, but not a bit of it.' She forced a laugh, still unable to meet my eye.

When she looked up again it was over my shoulder at the grand frontage of the bank behind me. 'And how are you, Kate?'

We exchanged a few more pleasantries. As we said our goodbyes she looked at me directly for the first time, eyes slightly narrowed.

'Was it you that put her up to joining up?'

'Good heavens, no.' I began to turn away. 'Actually, I had the impression that it was your influence. Both of you.'

I didn't see Olivia all that year and only heard from her occasionally. My letter telling her of Angus's departure and our plans to marry provoked a brief note of congratulation. The year sped past. We were all so taken up by the war and all I could do was to hope she was safe. It wasn't until November 1941 that I knew she was home. A freezing, windy day, the breath clouding back from her face as she stood on the step in Chantry Road.

'Olivia?' My face must have shown blankness or astonishment.

'That's not much of a greeting.' She gave me a self-conscious smile. 'Didn't your mother tell you I'd called yesterday?'

She must have forgotten. Typical of her, to have let something so important to me slip her mind. Both my parents were, as usual, busy.

'No. I'm sorry, Livy.' I laughed, suddenly full of delight, and tried to hug her. 'It's so amazingly good to see you – it's been such a long time. Are you on leave?'

'Not exactly,' she said abruptly.

I was full of questions, but Olivia stood stiffly in my embrace, and as she walked in past me I took in her extreme thinness and the exhausted sag of her face. Her black coat made her skin look very white and she coughed as her lungs met the warmer air of the house.

We sat in the living-room drinking tea. Livy toyed with the spoon on her saucer.

'You look terrible. Have you been ill?'

She crossed one bony leg over the other, a tight gesture. 'Yes – a touch of pneumonia.' She spoke lightly. 'The dear old navy took pity on me and sent me home to recuperate for a couple of weeks. I think I was really on the mend by the time I got here, though. Mummy and Daddy have been clucking over me of course, poor darlings.'

'Why poor?' I said tersely. 'It's not them who've been ill.'

'Oh, they seem to be missing me rather a lot. The centre of their lives taken away by the war and all that . . . Actually – ' She looked warily at me, then shifted her gaze down to her lap. 'They were asking after you. They wondered if you'd come round some time, just for tea or something. It's been a long time, Katie. It'd be so nice to have you in the house again.'

'You could have let me know you were ill.' My voice softened. 'I'd have come to see you before.'

'Oh – ' she brushed this aside. 'They were told to keep me very quiet and rested. Of course they always follow doctors' orders to the letter. Anyway, darling – tell me what you've been doing, won't you?'

'I'm doing my Health Visitor's training. I've written that to you, if you remember.' Clearly she didn't. I poured more tea, putting plenty of sugar in Olivia's. 'That's since September. Before that I did my midwifery experience.'

Olivia sat watching me, her pinched face arranged in attentive lines. Somehow I felt I was being interviewed.

'I adored doing that. I was very tempted to stay on, but I've been set on doing Health Visiting for so long.'

I had been totally absorbed by my experience of the beginning of life: the extraordinary miracle of it, the price of it. I laughed. 'I think I cried at every birth I attended. The other midwives thought I was completely cuckoo. They kept saying, "You'll soon get hardened to it. Seen one, seen 'em all."'

'How very interesting,' Olivia said brightly. 'I always knew you were a soppy old thing really.'

'The first time I was allowed to deliver one myself, I was so afraid I wouldn't be able to manage it. I laid my hand on the top of its head and guided it as it came out. I thought his mother would crack apart, you know, giving him life – ' I found myself making gestures with my hands, remembering it all. 'And he looked so cross, as if it was all a shock with the light suddenly all round him. I couldn't see a thing, my eyes were so full of tears! Livy – oh, don't!'

I leapt up and went to put my arms round her. 'I'm so sorry. I didn't mean to upset you.'

Her shoulders were shaking, the sobs breaking into coughs. I could tell even through her layers of clothes how little flesh she had now on her bones.

'I'm sorry,' she said in a broken voice. 'I just feel so very low at the moment. The slightest thing makes me go all weepy.'

'Of course. It's always like that after you've had a bad illness. I got carried away, talking like that. I'm so sorry. Poor Livy, you must have been very ill. You feel so thin.'

I sat on the arm of the chair, my arm round her and her head resting just above my waist. Here we were, back to normal, all the awkwardness and brittleness gone in these moments. I could forgive Livy anything. All my feelings of love and protectiveness washed through me. It was a relief to feel warm towards her again.

'I know I've been silly.' She turned to look up at me, brown eyes still full of tears.

'Have you? Why? You didn't write much. I haven't much idea what you've been up to.' I couldn't help the resentment showing a little in my voice.

'It was the freedom – being away . . .' She started crying again in a helpless, broken way which disturbed me.

'Livy, don't. Please don't be so unhappy. You really must rest and get yourself better.'

She didn't speak, but just cried herself out until she sat jerking and gulping like a child, wiping her eyes.

'Have you heard from Angus?' she asked eventually.

'Yes. He's well so far as I know.' I felt close to tears myself. It was so long since I'd seen him and I ached to hold him, to be held, just to feel him near me. 'I gather you met him?'

'I was in London, briefly,' she said flatly. 'He was passing through. It was good to see someone from home.'

'That's what he said. Oh, I so wish it was all over. I just want him back here with me.'

'Will you come – to the house?'

'I've only got tomorrow. Then I'm back at work.'

'Tomorrow then.'

'Katie – how marvellous to see you.' Alec actually kissed my hand when I arrived. He raised his head and looked into my eyes and I felt his charm turned on me fully. Anything that had gone before was apparently to be forgotten. My ungracious meeting with Elizabeth might never have happened. She was once again the smiling hostess, perfect in every detail, each syllable of speech and every gesture exuding the correct measure of friendliness and pleasure in my company.

How I longed to be beguiled again after my long absence. I had seen pictures of Alec, of course, but the grainy quality of newspaper print concealed just how much he had aged. It only added to his looks. The lines round his eyes and mouth gave him a kind of vulnerability. I wanted to admire, to be wooed. But I knew, as he took my hand, that I was keeping myself closed, not letting him in the way I had as a child when I blushed at anything he said.

'It's been so long since we've seen you,' he said smoothly. It was a moment before he let go my hand. 'We mustn't let that happen again.'

They had lit a fire in the drawing room, and the wind moaned outside and buffeted the window. Over the fireplace hung the De Loutherbourg painting of the furnaces of Ironbridge in a thick gold frame. We drank China tea and ate sponge and delicate *langue de chat* biscuits.

'Is business going well?' I asked Alec. I heard an abruptness in my voice. I was determined not to play along with this new situation. He must want something from me.

'Oh, not bad,' he said. 'Not bad at all.' He sat back casually in the cream chair, one leg crossed over the other. His hair was slicked back and his suit perfectly cut. The dainty tea plate and knife rested foolishly on the palm of one hand. 'It wouldn't be right to say the war's done you a favour, would it?' He chuckled uneasily.

'But it has?' I questioned him, not joining with his laughter.

'Well, let's say it hasn't been the end of the world where business is concerned.' He gave me that smile of his, its suddenness designed to dazzle.

Elizabeth leaned forward. 'Alec is thinking of standing as an MP,' she said in her soft, whispery voice. 'Isn't it marvellous? He'll have the backing of so many people. Of course there might be quite a wait, until the end of the war, but I think he'd be absolutely marvellous, don't you?'

I stared incredulously at the two of them. Was there no limit to their self-promotion, their obliviousness to whatever else was going on? Olivia was gazing at the fire, cut off from the conversation, her face so sad that I wanted to go to her and put my arms round her.

'Oh, marvellous,' I said abstractedly to Elizabeth. She saw me watching Olivia and stood up quickly.

'More tea, Katie? Let me give you another drop. It's very good, isn't it? Lapsang souchong.' As she poured from the slim spout, she said, 'Do tell us about your exciting work.' I felt her eyes boring into me as she sat down again.

Briefly I filled them in.

'How very brave of you to work during the raids!' she exclaimed. 'It must have been simply dreadful. We're so proud of both of you – Olivia working so hard in the Wrens as well. It makes me feel quite useless.'

'Oh, I'm sure you could find something to do if you were to look around,' I said unctuously.

'Well – of course Alec wouldn't hear of me working,' she said. 'Would you, darling? Not unless there was some really catastrophic reason.'

I was wondering how much more catastrophic a reason she needed than this war, when she said, 'And of course, Olivia has been so ill, I've been needed here at home. Poor darling. We were really frightened for her at one stage.'

This confused me. Olivia had said she had only been home convalescing for ten days or so. I saw her turn to fix her eyes on her father's.

'It was a bad do she's had, no doubt about that,' Alec said. 'Double pneumonia, the doctor told us. Should have been in hospital really, but we all felt the best place for her was at home. Nowhere like home when you're ill.' He chuckled. 'I bet your patients are keen to see the back of the hospital, aren't they?'

'That rather depends on the state of the homes they have to go back to,' I said. 'Of course you'd understand, with all the interest you've taken in housing, why some of them seem to find the hospital rather restful.'

Alec laughed extra loudly. 'Well, yes – I'd never thought of it like that. We're the lucky ones, of course.'

'And it's been so lovely having Olivia home again, hasn't it darling?' Elizabeth leaned over and stroked Olivia's hair. Livy accepted the caress passively.

'Proper family again.' Alec sliced more cake. 'Come on, Katie, have another go at this. You're looking a bit peaky. Not the girl you used to be.'

Not the fat, ugly one, you mean, I thought bitterly.

'Lovely to be home, isn't it, Olivia?' he went on.

Olivia nodded meekly, fingers crumbling the uneaten cake on her plate.

'Eat up, my lovely. You need some flesh back on those bones. Don't want the Wrens to think we've been starving you, do we?'

'You're going back then?' I asked, surprised. She didn't seem herself at all yet.

'Next week,' she said quietly.

'Are you sure you're well enough? You do seem pretty run-down still.'

'Absolutely,' Olivia said in a tight voice. 'I don't do physical work, you know. I'm a typist. And they need all hands on deck, as they say.'

'You're a secretary, not just a typist,' Elizabeth corrected her. 'And a very good one, I'm sure.' She glanced anxiously at me. 'Do you think she should be going back? You're a nurse – what's your opinion? Of course we'd be much happier if she'd throw in the towel and stay at home.'

Olivia stared at me with unmistakable appeal. There was a desperate look in her eyes.

'I'm sure Olivia knows whether she feels well enough,' I said carefully.

I stayed talking with them for a time, and it was polite if not relaxed. I had hoped for a few words with Olivia alone, but when I stood up ready to leave, Alec followed us out into the hall.

'D'you like these?' he asked, guiding me by the elbow to the wall opposite the stairs, almost as if anxious to delay me. 'Bought them a few weeks ago.'

He was looking up at a set of five prints. I moved closer and stared at them carefully. They were all black and white engravings of the sort you might have come across in an old half-crown gift book. One showed a couple walking through woodland, she with the hem of her high-necked dress brushing the grass, the strings of her bonnet between her fingers; a young man, casually dressed, was leaning protectively towards her, one arm round her shoulders. Underneath, the caption read *Shall we fix the wedding day?*.

Some were scenes of Victorian families with rosy-cheeked children at the fireside: *A romp with the children* and *Love is a mighty power.* There was one slightly bigger than the other four which he had arranged in the middle. It showed a bearded man with an austere expression standing in a dark street lit only by a dim gas lamp. In the background a church spire was just visible. Kneeling at his feet was a young girl, her long hair over her shoulders and her hands outstretched to him, begging for assistance or for money, it was not clear. Much more apparent was the expression of desperation on her face. Underneath the title read, *The Supplicant.*

'Marvellous, aren't they?' Alec said softly. He pointed at *The Supplicant.* 'Especially that one. Don't you agree?'

He was clearly moved by the pictures. There was even a slight break in his voice as he spoke. I turned to look at him carefully. We were standing close together and I couldn't fail to notice the magnetism of the man. I realized suddenly how exhausted he looked, the dark patches under his eyes. He adored Olivia. Her illness had evidently taken a lot from him.

I could find nothing honestly polite to say about the pictures, but he didn't seem to expect a reply. I actually saw tears in his eyes as he stood staring at the engravings. For a second I found myself moved, an instinct to comfort welling in me. Then I wondered if this was not a theatrical ploy, the kind of thing he used to approach other women, luring them to pity.

'I must be off,' I said.

'Of course. Of course. It was good of you to come.' He was flustered, eager to please.

As I left, he and Elizabeth were full of wide smiles and good wishes. Olivia and I finally got away from them, and we held each other out on the cold of the steps. Her arms were almost convulsively tight round me.

'Look – are you really sure you're all right?' I asked. 'You don't look it at all.'

'Perfectly. I'll be better when I'm back to work.' There was an unflinching braveness in her voice.

I could see she wasn't prepared to say any more. I kissed her. 'Keep well, Livy. See you soon. Try and write more often, eh?' I spoke half jokingly and didn't receive any promise in reply.

She stood waving by the door, a tiny wisp of a thing, her belt pulling in all the loose tucks of material at her waist. The sight of her frightened me. I could see she wasn't well, but it was more than that. It was as if something in her had frozen, and she couldn't help it or explain. I wanted to stay, to try and help her.

But she vanished from me again as if swallowed up by the navy and her letters were as sparse and infrequent as ever. It was a long time before I saw her again.

Chapter 14

Birmingham, 1942

I remember that morning in small details: frosted windows between the criss-crossed tape, the slightly knobbly cotton of my old nightie, my blurred impression of the sepia and white wallpaper. It was February, freezing, and I was still in bed, reluctant to face the chill room. I was making the most of the fact that it was Saturday and that I didn't have to go in for lectures: Acts of parliament affecting health and social welfare, hygiene, breastfeeding. I lay half awake, wishing Simmons was still around to come and build a fire in the bedroom, though I was ashamed of this wish. The war gave us a new awareness of the old order of things. Why should Simmons be my lackey?

Then feet hammering urgently up the stairs.

'Kate – come down quickly!' My mother's face was pale and taut.

'What's happened?'

She couldn't face saying any more. My numbness began even then. I put on my dressing gown, fastening the buttons with extreme care, delaying going down. Icy air gusted up the stairs. I could see out to the garden. Dry leaves scratched in over the step and the laurels shuddered in the wind. Only as she saw me did my mother regain the presence of mind to close the front door.

Ruth Harvey stared up at me, her face very still and white. She was holding a creamy sheet of paper.

'No!' I shrieked, as if at a torturer. 'Oh no no no. Please no!' I sank down in the middle of the staircase.

'Kate,' Mummy said sternly. 'Control yourself, for heaven's sake.'

Ruth climbed up and sat on the step beside me, taking me in her arms. When I looked at her face she seemed to have aged and shrunk.

'It says he's missing.' She held out the telegram to me. 'There may be hope. It could just be . . .'

'What?' I couldn't think at all, or make sense of anything.

'Perhaps he landed somewhere – or parachuted, and they haven't found him yet. We can make inquiries. There's a special section of the Red Cross . . .'

I only half heard what she said, but I knew then already like a doom drum beating in my mind and I could only think, Angus is dead, Angus is dead. Ruth Harvey had shiny black buttons on her cardigan and leaves stuck to her shoes. My mother stood very still, hand on the banisters, looking up at us.

'Katie?' Ruth gripped my shoulders powerfully with her arm. 'We've got to be strong – for him. We can't give up hope. He could be making contact with them even now.'

I thought Ruth was not a woman to spin me false optimism. I turned and looked up into her eyes. 'D'you really think so?'

'I have to. I can't do anything else for now.' Only then did she begin to sob, her body jerking, though no tears fell from her eyes. Her mouth pulled to one side. 'Oh my God,' she whispered. 'I can't bear it.'

I put my arms round her, noticing how much grey

there was among her brown hairs. My mother disappeared along the hall to the kitchen and I heard her rattling cups and saucers.

We drank our cups of tea almost in silence before Ruth left, folding her arms tightly across her chest. I saw her rally herself.

'I'll go and take this off,' she said, touching the black cardigan. 'It seems to indicate a lack of faith, doesn't it?'

If it had not been for Ruth and Peter Harvey I would have despaired during those months. There was no one else I could turn to. We all tried to get on with the business of our lives as the war reached its gloomiest. The fall of Singapore to the Japanese, the Battle of the Atlantic, people demonstrating on the streets for a second front to be opened in Europe. The Harveys spent months in correspondence with the Red Cross Wounded and Missing Relatives Department.

'I just feel sure there must be hope,' Ruth said to me one day after another ICRC missive had arrived saying that they had so far drawn a blank but would try to pursue inquiries further. 'He could be in hospital. Or lost in the countryside. If your plane lands in the middle of nowhere, how are you supposed to find your way out? It could be months, couldn't it?' Her voice rose high, full of tears. Peter came and put his arm round her, his gnarled hand stroking her shoulder. He had lost weight since the news about Angus, and his cheeks were gaunt, showing deeper shadows. He had not been a fleshy man before.

'All we can do is hope and pray,' he said. 'If Angus is alive, we know we'll hear eventually. Of course we will.'

'Suppose he's lost his memory or something like

that?' Ruth said wildly. 'I keep picturing the most dreadful things.' She put her hands over her face. Peter guided her to a seat.

I was prepared for the worst. Though I couldn't help a rush of hope at the infrequent communications from the Red Cross, I forced the feelings away each time their searches yielded nothing. Angus was dead. I could sense it. A terrible knowledge like a light going out somewhere across the world that I couldn't see, yet sensed it growing darker. I didn't voice this to the Harveys, but I could at least share other feelings about Angus with them. We remembered him together.

Confiding feelings was something I had given up trying to do with my parents. Even when I made the mildest attempts to open up to my mother, everything, down to the sharp, defensive angles of her elbows conveyed to me that she did not want to listen. Could not endure it.

One weekend during that summer, just before I started my first post as Health Visitor, I was working out in the garden. It was a humid morning. My hands were clammy. And it was sunny, poignant in the illusion of tranquillity. The hearts of the lettuces were washed in dew, and we had good crops of spinach, carrots, beetroot and onions. At one end my mother had set up bean-sticks and the plants snaked up them, mingled at one end with the bright tendrils of flowering sweet peas, her favourites. I stood looking at them, at the pinks, mauves and whites, which had always represented summer and friendship and a kind of innocence. I had not cried much over Angus. The feelings crouched inside, hurting me. I bent over and began to weed for victory between the carrots and onions.

My mother came out with a basket of handwashing

for the line. We were silent together among the buzzing insects. Then I realized she was standing at the edge of the vegetable patch next to me. She must have sensed I was close to tears.

She cleared her throat, awkwardly. 'It's been a great help having you back at home.'

I straightened up and looked at her. In the bright sunlight her sharp-featured face looked weary and lined. Her hair was still long and pinned up carelessly behind so that bits of it were always coming loose. Seeing the pain in my eyes, her face crumpled suddenly and she burst into tears.

'Mummy – what's the matter?' I stepped across the onions to stand on the grass beside her. I didn't know what to do with my hands and wished it could have felt natural to embrace her.

'I'm sorry,' she said. 'I just don't know how to be of comfort to you.' She couldn't meet my eyes. She looked down at the ground. 'I know how unhappy you are – and Ruth. I just ...' She paused with a helpless shrug. 'In some ways it would be better if you and Angus had never got so ... closely involved. Then you could just get on with your life.' She shook her head. 'I'm sorry. I shouldn't be talking like this. Not now.' Pulling a hanky from her sleeve she blew her nose on it resolutely. 'Oh, this dreadful war!' She picked up the wicker basket and quickly crossed the lawn to the house.

Watching her go, I felt a heaving sensation from inside me and thought for a moment I was going to be sick. But then instead, the tears came. I sat down on the grass, head on my knees, and cried and cried. Then I dried my tears alone.

*

'Here – you gas or 'lectric?'

'Come to read the meter, 'ave yer?'

Two scruffy boys dashed sniggering away from me down the entry into number eight court Stanley Street, their bare legs splashed with muddy water from the recent rain. Wearily I pushed my bicycle along the wet blue bricks of the entry and propped it against the wall near the yard tap, opposite the back houses. There were children playing round the gas lamp in the middle of the yard, and a woman stood mangling her washing.

She eyed me up, throwing the garment she had been about to mangle back into the maiding tub. 'They won't 'alf be glad to see you!' she called out to me, disappearing into one of the houses.

It was September, and early days in my job as a Health Visitor. It had not been a good morning. I'd already found one baby with chronic diarrhoea. Her mother was feeding her condensed milk from an old Daddy's Sauce bottle with a couple of inches of decayed rubber tubing. Another woman had called me an 'interfering cow' when I suggested she might spoil her baby when feeding it whenever it demanded and carrying it round all over the place. A feed every four hours, we were taught, and not too much cuddling and stimulation. 'I didn't ask you to come forcing your ideas on me, did I?' the woman said aggressively. The Welfare. Snoopers. That's how we were seen, though not many came out with it as bluntly as that. The majority listened politely and probably ignored a large percentage of what I said. Sometimes I looked back with longing for the hospital and its controlled environment.

Still, Mrs Callaghan, the young mother I had come to visit, was gentle enough and had a thriving week-old baby. I was just gathering up my bag with the leaflets on breastfeeding and brushing down my blue serge skirt when a voice behind me shrieked, 'Thank God you're 'ere – come on, quick, or we'll be too late!'

A young woman in a worn grey dress, with sandy-coloured hair, was hopping agitatedly from foot to foot, her pasty face taut with anxiety. 'Hurry up – Margaret's up there on 'er own with 'er.'

'You mean . . .? But I'm not the midwife.'

'I know you're not the flaming midwife. We can't find 'er anywhere. The babby's come on fast and the doctor's not 'ere yet neither.'

She made as if to take hold of my arm, but I said, 'All right, I'm coming,' and we hurried across the wet yard. As we passed through the front door, though it was much like any of the other houses, I had a strong sense of having been here before. In the gloomy downstairs room an elderly man was sitting smoking, stretched out in an armchair in a stained singlet and trousers with the fly unbuttoned. At the tinny fender sat a young boy intent on a comic, and two other tiny children cruised round what remained of the floor space. In those few seconds passing through the room, I took in that the dark shape taking up most of the centre of the room was a coffin.

God Almighty, I thought. But I was on the stairs with my heart thumping. Let this one be normal, please, I prayed as we clattered up the bare treads. And let the doctor get here soon.

'About time,' said a voice from the top of the stairs. 'Thought I'd 'ave to deliver it meself.'

A hefty middle-aged woman with a black plait coiled above each ear and a round fleshy face ushered us into the room. Our feet crackled on the floor which was strewn with newspaper. There was a pungent smell of sweat in the room.

'I'm Margaret and this is Sandy,' the older woman said. 'We're neighbours of 'ers.' She seemed very capable and had evidently helped organize the room. 'I've 'ad a good few meself,' she went on. 'But I draw the line at delivering 'em. Still – got the place sorted out too. Not too bright about keeping house this one.'

I took off my hat, glancing round. There were two narrow beds in the room. Clothes were hanging from oddly distributed hooks round the walls.

'I'll need to wash my hands.' I glanced at the silent woman on the bed. She hadn't even bothered to look round when I came in. She was lying curled on her left side, covered only by a stained sheet. Apart from one hard chair the beds were the only furniture in the room. 'Is she all right?'

'She's grand,' Margaret said. ''Ere you are – ' She presented me with piping hot water in a bucket. As I hurriedly covered my hands with the carbolic soap and rinsed them off, the woman on the bed gave a low moan.

'Awright,' Margaret said, going to her. 'Not long now.' I realized the sweaty smell came from under the arms of the tight, crimson dress she was wearing. 'Don't fret, bab.'

Tied to the end of the bed was an old strip of towelling. The woman's hands tightened on it, her whole body tensing as she panted through the pains, the veins standing out on her neck. She was a strong-looking woman, about my own age I realized, with straight brown hair.

'You're going to be absolutely fine,' I said in my

firmest nurse's voice, hoping to God it was true. The woman didn't reply except with a long sigh as the pain subsided, her eyes closed.

'You're getting close, aren't you?' I said.

She opened her eyes and nodded. Then her face contorted. 'Oh, not again.'

She showed the immense control that I'd seen in so many women giving birth at home, their children waiting downstairs, even though she was obviously in agony. She pulled herself up on to her knees. At the height of the pain she pushed her head into the pillow and groaned into it before lying still again.

'Least it's quiet out now,' Margaret remarked, jerking a thumb towards the window. 'We 'ad one or two come on in the bombing and oh my, what a to-do. Cissy Taylor's babby arrived in the shelter.'

'I've got scissors,' I interrupted as the contractions began again. They were very close together. Sandy was kneeling by the bed saying, 'It's all right, Lisa – you're nearly there.'

'Have you any string?'

Margaret calmly held up a twist of white twine. 'We're all prepared. All we need now's the babby.'

The woman suddenly hauled herself up from the bed on to her knees, her teeth clenched.

'Oh, lor' – 'ere we go,' Margaret said. I found her stolid calmness reassuring. 'Here, Sandy – cop 'old of 'er other arm. We can 'old her up between the pair of us.'

Once the baby started to come down it was very quick.

'It's 'er fourth,' Sandy said. 'So she ain't no beginner.'

As the two women held her in a half-sitting position, her knees up, I guided the baby's head out. I saw the strength of her body, the self-control, even in that crisis, of not crying out. The little sticky body slithered into my hands. I looked up at her mother who shimmered in front of me through my tears. She craned her head up to see.

'You've got a little girl,' I told her as the child roared in healthy protest between my hands.

'Oh, a little girl – at last!' Weakly she sank back on to the pillow.

'Eh – ' Sandy was at the window. 'Looks as if the doctor's got 'isself 'ere at last.'

I had wrapped the baby in a strip of sheet, and was tying off the umbilical cord as the footsteps grew louder up the stairs. Seconds later I found myself face to face with my father.

'Katie!' he exclaimed. 'What are you doing here?'

Margaret and Sandy stared from one to the other of us, bewildered.

'Delivering a baby,' I said briskly.

He watched as I deftly knotted the string tight round the quivering cord and cut the child's lifeline from her mother.

'Placenta?'

'Not yet.'

As she began to moan a little, I went and massaged her stomach. Minutes later the birth was complete, and Margaret and Sandy washed her down and covered her up again. As they tended to her I noticed that the soles of her feet were black with grime.

She saw the direction of my gaze. 'I went down to the shops just before,' she said apologetically. 'That's what must've set it off.'

'Tea,' Margaret said. 'That's what we all need. You got time for one, doctor? Even if it was your daughter done all the work.'

'Nothing I'd like better,' Daddy said courteously.

Stately, Margaret clumped off downstairs.

I looked round shyly at Daddy, who was watching the new mother suckle her baby.

'A miracle every time, isn't it?' he said quietly to me. And to the baby's mother: 'She's a fine child. Another, I should say.'

She smiled, her face softer now. I knew there was something familiar about her, as I had about the house when we first arrived.

'I'm sorry,' I said. 'In the heat of the moment I didn't think to ask your name.'

'You don't remember each other, do you?' Daddy said. 'Katie, this is Lisa Turnbull, now she's married. She was Lisa Blakeley before. D'you not recall taking her little brother Sid home with us for a few days once?'

Sid Blakeley, the grimy baby I had ridden home with in the car that day. And Lisa, his skinny sister whose father had 'buggered off'.

'I knew there was something I recognized as soon as I walked into the house,' I said. 'Now I look at you I can see ...' She was much more robust-looking now, and her hair had grown thicker, but I could remember her in the pale grey eyes and high cheekbones.

'You've changed a bit, too,' she said, her eyes leaving the baby's face for a second. She smiled again. 'Your dad's been ever so good to us over the years.'

There was a sudden bustling around us as Margaret arrived, panting from the stairs and making a great to-do with cups of tea for us all, milky and loaded with what must have been most of their sugar ration for the week.

'You're out of stera so I got Agnes to borrow us

some,' she remarked. 'And Lisa, you ought to apologize for the coffin downstairs. It ain't nice with people coming in.'

'Oh, sorry.' Lisa looked at my father. 'Auntie Glad. Dr Williamson came out to 'er, more's the pity. Funeral's tomorrow.'

'No need to apologize at all,' Daddy said. 'Now, may I give the child a quick look over before you bath her? And then I must be on my way.'

I watched him handle the tiny baby, her limbs still clenched tight, feeling her soft fontanelle, checking her hips and eyes.

'I've got a scale with me today,' I remembered, pulling the spring balance out of my bag.

The baby squalled resentfully as we popped her into the weighing sack and she hung dangling as if from a stork's bill.

'Six pounds four,' I said to Lisa. 'She's a good weight. And you're going to carry on breastfeeding?'

She nodded. 'Oh yes – can't be doing with bottles and all that.'

'Much the best thing.' I closed up my bag. 'Much less chance of her picking up germs.'

'The Health Visitor approves,' Daddy joked.

'What're you going to call 'er then?' Sandy had evidently been bursting to ask.

'Daisy,' Lisa said. 'After my mom.'

My father and I said our goodbyes. 'I'll see you in a few days after the midwife's been in,' I told her.

Downstairs, Sid was sitting looking blankly out of the window, absently tapping one foot on the coffin lid.

'Stop that.' The older man cuffed him. ''Ave a bit of respect.' Neither of them seemed to have taken in the arrival of Daisy upstairs.

Daddy stood with me in the shadowy light outside. The sun had sunk behind the houses. Lines of washing were draped across the court, blocking the light even further and giving off a faint whiff of Hudson's soap. More pungently I could smell the drains.

'What happened to Lisa's mother?' I asked.

'She died. Never came out of hospital after that time we had Sid. Puerperal infection. One of the worst I've seen. Sadly we lost the baby too. Lisa's relied on neighbours all her life really, and they've been marvellous to her. And that uncle of hers – the old fellow. He's a man of few words but he's kept up the rent for her until she could manage it herself.'

'Was that his wife – in the coffin?'

'No, his sister. She's been living with them for the past year or so. She had a bad chest. Lisa looked after her – she's got a kind heart. She'd look after anyone, I think.'

We stood in silence for a few seconds.

'Well, I'd better pop into Mrs Callaghan,' I said.

Daddy started feeling in his jacket pockets as he did sometimes when he had something on his mind. 'You did very well today, Katie,' he told me awkwardly. 'I was proud of you. You'll be a very good addition to the team in this area.' He paused. 'You're looking very peaky. You won't overdo it will you?'

It was only later, when I was alone in my bedroom and found tears running down my cheeks, that I realized fully how much his words had meant to me.

Chapter 15

Daisy Turnbull was asleep, tucked in a deep drawer, taking quick, snuffly breaths.

'She's beautiful,' I told Lisa. She was sitting, dressed, but still wearing a pair of ancient slippers, a cigarette in one hand. The coffin was gone and the table now occupied the centre of the room. 'Feeding all right, is she?'

'Oh yes – loves 'er food. Can't get enough of me. Bit of a nuisance at times, of course, but it keeps 'em quiet, don't it?'

'You are sticking to the four-hourly feeds though? You know that's considered best for the child?'

Lisa cocked her head to one side so that her hair tumbled over one shoulder of her milk-stained blouse. 'You aren't married, are you? No kids?'

'No, of course not.'

'That's the trouble with you people, if you don't mind my saying so. You're full of instructions about what to do when you ain't had a go at it yourself. All this about doing it by the clock – for a start I ain't got a clock. It's broke. And even if I 'ad, if my babby starts screaming, it's not a clock I need to tell me to see to 'er, is it?'

'But we're trying to introduce the baby to regular habits – see her in good stead for the future . . .'

Lisa made a dismissive sound. 'She'll grow out of this. Then she'll be eating what there is, regular with the rest of us. Won't be any choice about that. The way I look at it, Miss Munro, this is 'er one chance in life to get as much grub into 'er as 'er wants. Won't be like that for long, will it?'

I could see I was on a losing wicket with Lisa. I may have been fresh out of training with all the ideals and regimens of Truby King fresh in my mind, but in the end I couldn't force anyone. I had more luck with my middle-class ladies who'd read the childcare books and took it all very seriously, but then some of them got rather over-concerned and nervy about it all.

'Cuppa tea?' Lisa asked, jumping up. 'While I've still got my 'ands free?' I was warmed by her hospitable ways, the enthusiasm with which she had greeted me when I arrived. My delivering her baby had formed a bond between us.

'That would be lovely. I've got a few minutes to spare,' I said. 'And I missed my morning break today.'

Several mornings of the week we Health Visitors made our way into the middle of town to attend to our patient records which were housed in the majestic Town Hall. As often as not we'd stay on for coffee and cakes afterwards, but I hadn't been this morning.

Lisa shuffled round in her slippers on the grimy brick floor, then planted her round behind on the chair across the table from me, much as we had sat when we first met as children. She stirred her tea and looked anxiously round the room. There were unwashed plates and cutlery on the table, a pile of dirty washing in one corner and a bucket of nappies with a stick poking out from it. On the range stood two badly stained pans.

'Sorry the place is in such a mess,' she said. 'Usually is, I'm afraid.'

As she took a sip of tea a high mewling sound came

from the drawer. Lisa rolled her eyes towards the ceiling. 'Wouldn't you know it?'

'What a plaintive noise.'

'Just like a little cat, int she?' She picked up the baby, whose face wore an expression of outrage, and lifted the edge of her blouse just enough to attach the baby to her swollen breast. The child's body was so small she could cradle it on one arm. She drank, making tiny squeaking noises. Lisa was one of those mothers who made me feel redundant. Despite the chaotic look to her house she exuded an air of competence. Nothing I might say would make much difference to her. I watched her with admiration, sipping her tea with one hand, cigarette burning on a saucer, the baby balanced on the other arm and a patch of damp darkening the material of her blouse over her other breast. There was something comforting about her.

'Where are your other three?' I asked.

'Two. Asleep.'

'But that woman – Sandy – said Daisy was your fourth.'

'We lost the first one.' Her voice was clipped 'Stillborn. 'E were a lad and all. Terrible it was. Don took it even worse than me. 'E cried. Never seen 'im cry other than that.'

'I'm sorry, Lisa.' I hesitated. 'Where is Don – the army?'

'Yes, with the Warwicks. God alone knows where. I've 'eard from 'im of course but I 'aven't seen 'im for months. She – ' she jerked her head towards Daisy – 'she was the last time. 'E'll be like a kid when I've writ 'im about 'er. Always wanted a little girl.' She smiled directly at me, and I was startled by the transformation of her face. She had widely spaced front teeth, and her large mouth dominated her face. The pale eyes were full of life. I warmed to her further, to that smile. It lifted me and I smiled back.

'You got a fella?' She lifted Daisy and transferred her to her other breast, stroking her little head.

'I don't . . . know,' I said hesitantly. I never usually discussed my private life when I was working and few people would have been bold enough to ask. But Lisa was different. 'I think he's dead.'

The smile dropped from her lips. 'Oh, Kate – you poor thing.'

Her calling me by my name like that, like a friend, brought tears to my eyes. I cried so easily at that time.

'We had a letter saying he was missing. He's – he was – in the RAF. His parents have been in touch with the Red Cross for months, of course. We heard nothing for ages. But I've been sure, well, almost sure, that he's dead. I could feel it. Last week they had some more information. He was almost certainly shot down over the sea. They won't be able to recover his body.'

'But was it 'im? Are they sure?'

'No one's entirely sure. It seems it's the only thing that could have happened. But his parents can't accept it – especially his mother. They don't know whether to hold a service for him or to carry on hoping he might be alive. They've aged twenty years, both of them.' Tears ran down my face which I wiped away hastily. 'If we had his body we could mourn him properly.'

Lisa watched me in silence, her eyes sad.

'I'm sorry,' I said, blowing my nose. 'I shouldn't be doing this. Very unprofessional. I'm supposed to be here to help you, not carry on like this.'

'It doesn't matter,' Lisa replied straightforwardly. 'I don't think I need any 'elp really.'

I smiled, still sniffing. Daisy looked the picture of contentment. 'No, you don't, do you?' Pushing my unneeded leaflets back into my capacious blue bag, I went to the door. 'I'll come back and see you, though. Find out how you're both doing.'

'Come whenever you like,' Lisa said, standing up to open the door. I gestured at her to sit down again. 'Any time you want a natter, Kate. I'll be glad to see you. I like a bit of company. And we go back a long way don't we – sort of?'

In the spring of 1943 Mummy ran into the mother of one of my old school friends, Marjorie Mantel, which of course set them exchanging news about their daughters. Marjorie was soon expected home on leave from the WAAF. A fortnight later I got back from work one evening to find a note waiting for me.

> Home for a spot of leave and Roly too, so we're planning to hold a hop next weekend and would be chuffed if you could make it. It'll be a kind of reunion! A song and dance to cheer the Home Front troops! It'd be marvellous to see you. Do bring a friend if you can. Hope you can make it. RSVP, Marjorie Mantel.

I hadn't seen her in years and only dimly remembered that she had a brother called Roland. Marjorie was always rather 'jolly hockey sticks' when we were at school, and I was intrigued by the thought of seeing her. I found myself smiling, missing Livy. The old Livy. We would have laughed together about this invitation.

It was such a long time since Livy and I had met, let alone laughed together. Once again she had been reposted, and I wasn't sure where. I wrote several times asking if she was recovered, was anything wrong? She assured me in a tight sort of way that she was better. But there was another change in the letters: they were no longer bright and over-excited; they were determinedly factual, flat – actually dull – something which would have been unheard of before. But I kept writing. When the war's over, I thought, we'll sort this out. We'll talk properly and everything will be all right.

I took Brenda Forbes along to Marjorie's with me.

'Hello,' Marjorie brayed, swinging her front door wide open to the dark evening. 'Kate Munro – how absolutely marvellous to see you! It must be how long? And who's this?'

I introduced Brenda '. . . we did our nursing together.' Brenda said a curt 'Evening', in her rather graceless way.

Marjorie had grown from a buxom girl into a sizeable woman. She had a wide face with a large, beak-like nose and very thick dark eyebrows, and her black hair was curled and piled round her head. She wore a bright pink dress and a leafy brooch which put me in mind of a Christmas decoration. Brenda, who was short and stocky, was dwarfed by her.

'Nursing!' Marjorie boomed at me. 'How heroic. I simply couldn't do it.' An elderly black Labrador stood panting at us. 'Don't mind Wally,' she went on distractedly. 'He wouldn't dream of hurting you, would you darling?' As she patted his gaunt head the doorbell rang again. 'Oh – someone else! No rest for the wicked. Do dispose of coats . . .' She shimmered towards the front door again.

Brenda shot me a look of amazement.

'She's very good-hearted,' I reassured her.

The Mantels had a very large drawing-room at the front of the house with a smooth olive-green carpet and green curtains to match covering the blackout blinds.

The chairs had been pulled back round the edges of the long room and a row of tall red candles were burning in front of a huge gilt-edged mirror above the fireplace. The effect was a blaze of warm light adding to the more discreet table lights arranged round the room on the piano, a sofa table, a chest of drawers.

'I expect she hoped you'd bring a bloke,' Brenda said in a low voice, 'since they're probably in short supply. I expect you'll find half your school here.'

'God forbid,' I murmured. 'I must say I did get the impression we were asked to make up numbers . . .'

We must have been almost the last to arrive. The room was well filled by a throng of people all talking loudly, and it felt very warm. A shout of laughter met us from one corner as we walked in. There were plenty of men there, too – a few in uniform, most not.

'Yanks, a lot of them,' Brenda observed. 'Seem to look bigger than our lot, don't they?' Brenda, who wasn't much interested in men, often talked about them as if they were some queer breed of squirrel.

The two of us stood looking round the room, at a loss.

One man – small, English – peeled away from the crowd. 'Hello, you look lost,' he said amiably. He had a thatch of dark hair like Marjorie's and a chubby pink face. 'I'm Roly, Marjorie's brother. Come and have some punch? It's fearfully good. Made by her own fair hands. In fact there's homemade wine, too. We're disreputable soaks in the Mantel family, I'm afraid. Make it out of anything that's going. This is a brew from back in '38. Those fair, halcyon days . . .'

For a moment I thought he was going to break into poetry. More usefully he poured us some of the fruit cup.

'The fruit's a bit limited, of course. Nearly all apples and pears from the garden.'

'It's very nice,' I said politely. 'Marjorie said you're both home on leave?'

'Yes, bang on. I'm army and she's a WAAF. Marvellous spot of luck being able to take leave at the same time. Not often we coincide. I'm due to be posted soon, so I'm making the most of home.'

Looking at Roly's face, I realized he was much younger than he seemed. His manner was already so middle-aged.

'I say – it's Katie, isn't it? Kate Munro?'

A face swam towards me which I recognized instantly. The sight of her brought back the classrooms, the very smell of school.

'Celia Oakley!'

As I stood reminiscing with Celia, Marjorie appeared and pounced on Brenda, saying there was someone she 'must meet'.

'And what's happened to Olivia Kemp?' Celia wanted to know. She had a very pale face and almost white blond hair and lashes. 'You were always such friends. I found her a bit, well, odd myself. Rather stand-offish. I always presumed it was because she got fed up with people carrying on about her father. It surprised us all when you two teamed up.'

'Livy's in the Wrens,' I said. Celia made impressed sounds. 'I haven't seen much of her, of course, though she was home for a stint of sick leave – ages ago now – end of '41 it must have been. Went down with pneumonia. I think she's quite taken to service life apart from that.'

'She always did look delicate,' Celia said. 'Though as I say, I didn't have a great deal to do with her. Kept out of her way really.'

'Now everyone!' Marjorie hooted suddenly in her huge voice. 'Shall we have some music? Does anyone fancy a dance?'

'Let's have a singsong,' someone called out. 'Cheer us all up. And then we can carry on drinking!'

There was a flutter of agreement round the room. 'Come on, Marj – play us a song!'

'She's very staunch, isn't she?' Celia said, mouth near my ear. 'You know the other brother's missing?'

'I had no idea.'

'Oh yes – air force. They're all worried stiff, poor things. But Marjorie's got such guts – look at her. You'd never guess.'

Marjorie advanced on the piano, looking serene.

As people began to move towards the edge of the room to claim chairs, I suddenly saw someone sitting in the corner next to the mantelpiece, who had been hidden before by all the chattering bodies. I squinted, pushing my specs further up my nose to see more clearly.

'Excuse me,' I said distractedly to Celia.

As I walked across he looked up at me. That face with the prominent cheekbones, vivid eyes, a scar worming down his left cheek.

'Douglas Craven?'

He frowned, taking his cigarette from his mouth. 'Yes, officer?' Looking at me more closely, his face broke into a smile which seemed to take it by surprise, pulling the pink scar tissue tight across his cheek.

'Florence?' he called out loudly. Marjorie had started playing 'Hands, knees and Boomps-a-Daisy' with heavy-handed enthusiasm, and a group were bottom-bumping in the middle of the room.

'Kate,' I corrected him. 'Florence Nightingale is dead. As is Queen Victoria.' Already, before we'd exchanged more than a few words, I felt the same combination of prickliness and attraction towards him that I had when we first met.

He smiled cautiously. 'Are you always so tart with everyone?'

'Not everyone.'

'So it's my fault. Listen – take a seat. Forgive me for not getting up.' He spoke with the odd, ironic tone which I remembered.

I looked round at him, using an examination of the healed wound as an excuse to take in his appearance now his face was free of dressings. He had wiry-looking blond hair, long compared with the clipped styles of the servicemen which we were growing used to. His eyes were less blue than I remembered in the soft light from the candles above his head. The scar curved round from one high cheekbone towards his fair moustache. He obviously found the candour of my gaze disconcerting and looked down. I thought he was blushing.

'It's healed well. You're jolly lucky it missed your eye.'

'Yes,' he said sardonically. 'Jolly.' He turned and grinned at me suddenly, looking into my eyes so that it was I who felt compelled to look away.

'Not in a dancing mood?' I was glad to see Brenda across the room jigging about and laughing with a woman I didn't know. This was more her cup of tea than polite chit-chat over glasses of punch.

'Dancing?' Douglas said. 'No, most definitely not.'

Marjorie started on 'A Nightingale Sang in Berkeley Square', her hands kneading at the keys, and most people were joining in singing the lines they knew.

'Have you known Marjorie long?' I asked.

'I don't know her at all. I came with Pete over there to swell the numbers, of course.'

'We had the definite impression that we were padding as well.'

'What you're too polite to ask, of course,' Douglas said, his tone oddly aggressive, 'is why I'm not fighting with the boys in blue, khaki or any other colour? What a young male is doing here unable to make the claim that he is "on leave" from defending the nation.'

'I was wondering.'

'Of course you were.'

Awkwardly he pulled himself to his feet. I realized that I had never seen him other than lying or sitting before. His right leg was skewed at the hip, the knee bending inwards so that he had to bear its weight on the ball of his foot.

He sat down again abruptly and looked at me very directly, as if challenging me for a reaction.

'Cripple, you see. Born like it. I can get around on it like the clappers as a matter of fact, but I'm not seen as being up to the old one-two, one-two, which apparently is what matters in the services. Not that I didn't try. The army recruiting wallahs looked at me as if I was mad. Of course I only imagined they might sit me at a desk somewhere, but apparently that wasn't on either. So it was decided that since newspapers are nourishment for the nation I should be allowed to lurch around the *Mail* offices doing my job – or what we're allowed to print nowadays – as usual.'

'I'm sorry,' I said. At a time when young men felt they were proving themselves all over the country, Douglas apparently felt himself stuck like a frustrated Rumpelstiltskin, one foot trapped in the floorboards.

'Oh, don't be.' He sank back in the chair. 'After all,

I have a war wound to show for my intrepid reportage.'

'D'you always talk like that? So sarcastically?'

'You're very direct. Yes, often. It's a defence I've established. If there's something amiss with your body you have to learn to keep your end up somehow, don't you? After all, it's not everyone I allow to see me howling because I've got a lump of Christ knows what sticking out of the side of my face.'

'You don't even need to think of that. It's my job.'

He looked into my face with his disturbing gaze. 'You were wonderful, I have to say. Especially coming back to see me like that.'

I felt myself blushing. I was alarmed by the unexpected impulse I felt to put my arms round him. His eyes were extraordinary: appealing, penetrating. For a second it would have felt natural to rest my head on his shoulder. I looked away, ashamed.

But Douglas seemed to relax suddenly, as if he trusted my acceptance of him, and I found myself talking to him, animated in a way I had not been for months. He asked about my work and how I knew Marjorie and we laughed together. Then I felt caught out, laughing like that. Confused, I turned my attention to the music, thoughts churning in my head. How would I ever know if Angus was alive somewhere? Our last night together seemed such an age away. I ached to see him, for us to hold one another, yet at the same time, if that was never going to be possible, I needed to know that too. Would we have to wait until the war was over, and even then would we know for certain? And here was I, enjoying myself at a party and wishing that this man beside me, who I barely knew, would take me in his arms.

A group was standing round Marjorie, who had her back to us at the piano, all well into the swing of singing.

'I'll never smile again, until I smile at you,' they belted out with incongruous jollity. The song cut through me. Should I never smile again? Had I to wait for a homecoming that might or might not happen? And how could I feel so damn sorry for myself just having to wait when for all I knew Angus might be going through the most appalling suffering? A lump grew in my throat. It all felt so hopeless, all these months of waiting and praying when I knew in my heart that Angus was dead.

'Grim little number, isn't it?' Douglas leaned forward and spoke gently. 'I say – you're not crying, are you?'

'No, I'm not,' I said in a determined voice.

'You are – nearly, aren't you?' he persisted with ungentlemanly intrusiveness. 'Is it that – fiancé of yours?'

Dry-eyed now, I told Douglas about our correspondence with the Red Cross.

'The open grave,' he said. 'You poor girl.'

'Don't be nice, I really shall start, else.'

'I shouldn't mind.' His tone was kind.

'But I should. This is supposed to be a party.'

Fortunately Marjorie decided to move on to the ENSA tune, 'Let the People Sing', at this point, which got some of them dancing again.

'Good job it wasn't "We'll meet again",' Douglas said. 'Or the floodgates would have opened.'

I laughed. 'You're terrible.'

'Am I?' He directed an uncertain smile at me.

'Actually, no. In a funny way you've cheered me up.'

'The feeling is mutual. Most girls, once they've found out about my gammy leg, start treating me like some sort of damned invalid with only half a brain.'

He sounded so bitter that without thinking I laid my hand on his arm as I would have done with a patient, then quickly withdrew it.

We spent most of the evening talking and I found myself forgetting about everything else in a way that I only normally did when we were exceptionally busy at work. Again I found that Douglas was more ready to ask questions and learn about me than he was to disclose anything about himself. The shreds I managed to glean from him were that he had a fierce satisfaction in his job and that he was an only child whose parents lived near Gloucester.

Towards the end of the evening, Marjorie came breezing over and said to me, 'Ah, Katie, darling – I see you've been looking after poor Douglas.'

'Oh yes,' Douglas said in a mock pitiful voice. 'She's a proper little Florence Nightingale.'

Marjorie couldn't work out what we were both laughing about.

As we were leaving I moved towards the door with Douglas. I could tell he was painfully conscious that I was seeing his rocking, distorted walk for the first time. With an effort, and taking refuge in his tone of self-mockery, he said, 'I don't suppose you'd consider seeing me again?'

I knew I couldn't hold back from saying yes and giving my address for his sake. But I knew I was doing it as much for my own. As we parted, shaking hands, our eyes met and Douglas smiled, his face transformed from the sad, rather uncertain expression to one that was warm and hopeful.

After I'd thanked Marjorie I said, 'I'm so sorry to hear about your brother.'

She reddened, her only hint of emotion. 'These things are sent to try us, I suppose.'

Brenda joined me outside, glowing from the warmth of the room and her dancing. 'That Susan's a good laugh – we're going to Ivy Benson's tea dance next week if my duty hours fit in with it.' She did a little twirl on the pavement. 'That was the best evening I've had in ages,' she said as we made our way carefully along the blacked-out street.

'Yes,' I said, surprising myself. 'Me too.'

Chapter 16

Birmingham, 1944

'Dr Williamson?'

I can't say I'd have been pleased to see him at the best of times, and his presence on our doorstep in the early evening foretold trouble. He walked in brusquely with barely a glance at me, saying, 'Is your mother in?'

I showed him into the front room. Mummy was at the back with Gladys Peck and the children. Gladys, a young mother with skin the colour of curdled milk, had come to us from South London to escape the flying bombs.

'Winifred,' Dr Williamson said, stroking his little moustache uneasily, 'you'd better sit down.'

Mummy wasn't keen on Dr Williamson either. 'I don't wish to sit down,' she said. 'What's the trouble?'

'Very bad news, I'm afraid. It's Bill. He collapsed at the surgery – his heart.' He paused, looking down at the floor. 'I'm afraid he died in the ambulance. I got here as soon as I could.' My first thought was how much better Daddy would have handled this, his gift with his patients.

My mother stood rigid. She said nothing. Her knees buckled and I helped her to a chair.

Dr Williamson looked monstrously uncomfortable. 'Is there anything I can do?'

Mummy stared ahead of her as if hypnotized. Then she came to herself and without turning her head said, 'No. Thank you.'

Dr Williamson cleared his throat. 'He would have been proud to die in harness,' he offered.

I showed him the door.

Gladys Peck was a pleasant, anxious woman who was perpetually grateful. Although she had to care for her five-year-old, Eric, and Lizzie who was not yet two, she seemed to think that because she had been sent to live with us in a house which resembled the one in which she had first gone into service, she ought in return to act as our maid. We took a lot of trouble to stop her.

But now Gladys came into her own.

'What you need at a time like this,' she declared, 'is help.' She plonked fair, curly-haired Lizzie down on the floor as if trying to root her to the ground. 'Good job I'm here now, isn't it?'

And for several days, with impressive capability, she completely took over the running of our house. While Lizzie slept in our wooden cot upstairs, she scrubbed floors. She settled Eric at the table with crayons, copies of the *Eagle* and *Beano* which he was too young to be able to read properly but enjoyed the pictures, and an old toffee tin full of William's cars and soldiers. He was a quiet, pallid child with cropped, mousy hair. Gladys donned an apron, tied back her thin hair in a pink scarf and set to, humming and singing like someone who had finally found a purpose in life. Then she'd stop, tactfully, remembering that we didn't have much to sing about. I didn't mind. I liked to hear her. Mostly she sang hymns: 'The Old Rugged Cross' and 'Great is Thy Faithfulness', adding her own warbles and fragments of melody.

What was most striking was that Mummy let her do it all. She surrendered control of the house while we made arrangements, sitting in miserable silence in the sombre offices of funeral directors or in the sitting-room at home. She was like a person winded, unable to gather herself up to protest or move into action.

'Gladys is wonderful, isn't she?' I ventured one day. Mummy was sitting with Lizzie on her lap, occupying the child with a string of coloured wooden beads. Her hair was scraped back and she looked exhausted.

'She's a great comfort,' Mummy said, to my surprise. 'Hearing her singing sometimes I feel . . .' She trailed off, stroking the little girl's curls and her soft, spongy limbs.

'What?' I asked softly. So far we had said almost nothing to each other about Daddy's death. We had been to see him, hands across his chest, his face relaxed and strange to us. But the house felt as usual. He had been there so little when he was alive.

'It's as if she's a kind of messenger,' Mummy said.

'From Daddy, you mean?'

'No. I don't believe that sort of thing. You know I don't. I meant from God.'

'I hope so,' I said grimly. I got little else out of Mummy. We moved round one another, each guarding our own pain.

I wrote and told Livy about Daddy's death and she wrote me a sweet note in reply, but her letters were still rare. If she was having leave from the navy, she was no longer taking it at home.

The war was turning: Paris had been liberated in August. But it all felt so sad and futile. Life was empty of the people I cared about. The one thing which warmed me at this time was that Lisa told me she was going to have Daisy baptized.

'I wanted to ask you,' she said shyly, 'if you'd be her godmother?'

In the middle of all this came a telephone call from Douglas. Although I'd given him my address at Marjorie's party he had never got in touch, and he had slipped again from the forefront of my mind though I had quite often noticed his name in the *Mail*. In a way I was relieved. I didn't want my feelings complicated further.

My mother took the message. Would I meet him after work later that week, at Snow Hill Station?

Work was a distraction at that time, being able to go out and immerse myself in it. I didn't feel like going out socially and making an effort with someone I barely knew, but I felt that telephoning him to refuse might prove even more awkward and would hurt his feelings.

I waited for him under the clock in Snow Hill Station as arranged, nervously tapping my umbrella against my legs. Above the cluster of people standing there, the huge hands of the clock jerked the minutes round. I was wishing like mad that I hadn't agreed to meet him, that I could be at home, able to think quietly on my own. But as the big hand clicked over the twelve – seven o'clock – I saw Douglas come limping across the station forecourt, his camera over one shoulder, held close to his body. When he caught sight of me his smile lit his face with a warmth that lifted me.

'Katie, my dear – I'm so sorry.' He took my hand and his voice was the gentlest I'd ever heard it. I had left him a note at his office in Corporation Street, agreeing to meet him for a short time and telling him about Daddy. 'You poor girl. You've had enough knocks already. I mean look at you – you're a shadow of that bustling nurse who came along and swore at me.'

I smiled wryly. It was true. My clothes were hanging on me. I'd had to put a tuck in the waist of my blue uniform skirt and my face was pale, shadowed under the eyes, and too gaunt for my bone structure.

'Oh, well' – I made a Douglas-like quip – 'I always did want to be a beanpole.' Pointing at the camera, I said, 'D'you take that everywhere with you?'

'Yes, pretty much. Just in case.' He looked at me, concerned. 'I'll bet you haven't eaten yet. Come on, let's find somewhere to go.'

The thought of intimate conversation across a table suddenly filled me with panic. 'D'you know what I really feel like?' I said quickly. 'Fish and chips.'

Douglas laughed. 'There was I thinking of something really sophisticated. Oh well – fish and chips, then. At least we don't need our ration books for that.'

We crossed the busy station forecourt, both starting to talk at once and trailing off into embarrassed laughter.

'You first,' I said.

'Look – ' His handsome face grew serious and rather rueful. 'I'm sorry for not looking you up before. I've thought a lot about you since I saw you. It was a bit of a failure of courage on my part, I'm afraid.'

I was disarmed by this admission. 'I'm so glad you did get in touch. It's very good to see you again.' And I meant it, had forgotten how attractive he was, his combination of wit and vulnerability.

'Your father – ' Douglas turned to look at me. 'It must have been a terrible blow to you. What happened?'

'His heart gave out. Overwork, I suppose. He's always had quite good health actually but he worked so hard, and since the war started he's not let up at all.'

'I'm so sorry,' Douglas said again. As we stepped

outside he laid a hand gently on my shoulder to guide me through the crowds at the door.

We carried our warm newspaper parcels, strolling down through what remained of the Bull Ring. It was a melancholy sight in the half light, quieter than it would ever have been in peacetime, the bombed shells of buildings round us filled with queer shadows. Droves of starlings circled the wreckage of St Martin's, shrieking sadly.

A couple of boys appeared out of the gloom, tearing past us.

'Peg-a-leg!' they shouted at Douglas. 'Cripple!' They disappeared behind us.

'D'you want to catch the bus?' Douglas asked ruefully.

I felt embarrassed for him. 'I was rather enjoying walking – that's if it's not difficult for you. Does it hurt to walk?'

'Oh, no – no pain,' he said, his sardonic voice back again. 'I just look like an inebriated clown as soon as I set foot, that's all. In present company I'd enjoy a walk too. That's if you don't mind being seen out with me?'

'Of course I don't mind. You mustn't think that.'

'I get a fair bit of what we've just heard.' He jerked his thumb in the direction the boys had gone.

'It must be ghastly.'

'Oh, don't you start!' he protested cheerfully. 'I can stand the abuse, but for heaven's sake don't pity me.'

'OK. Subject closed.'

We cut up along Cheapside, climbing the steep slope up to Camp Hill. Douglas chatted about work, performing such comical impersonations of his colleagues that they came alive in front of me, and soon I was laughing as I'd begun to think I'd never laugh again. I felt warmed by the thick chips and crisp battered fish, and temporarily uplifted. It was a still evening, with the last waning light of summer. The factories throbbed on either side of us, their high grimy sides towering over us, half muffled by sandbags. A truck reversed out from a gate in front of us and roared off up the road.

'"One has no great hope of Birmingham,"' Douglas quoted lugubriously. '"I always say there is something direful in the sound."'

'Who said that?' I was still recovering from his last bout of clowning. 'D'you always mimic people? You must get yourself into frightful trouble.'

'Yes, I'm afraid I do. And in answer to your question it was Jane Austen.'

'Well, it may have been, but it's still nonsense,' I argued. 'Just listen to this place – all these people round us working away day and night. Up there and down under the ground. Listen – it's as if the city's alive. There must be more coming out of Birmingham for the war effort than anywhere else in the country.'

'All right, all right. I didn't say I agreed with her, did I? Can't say I'd want to settle here for life, though.'

'I wonder how much longer it'll all be needed.'

'I did a piece today on the Fire Guard, now they're standing them all down. The Home Guard'll be the next to go, I suppose.'

It was getting really dark as we walked down the Moseley Road. I shivered. Now we had both thrown away our greasy newspapers holding the food, it had created an awkwardness. We had nothing to do with our hands. Douglas walked with his clasped behind his back. I folded my arms, pulling my cardigan closer round me.

'I should have brought a coat,' I said. 'I keep thinking it's still summer.'

Pain washed through me suddenly. Angus. If Angus had been here we would be walking arm in arm, easy with each other, our knowledge of each other so long, deep and familiar. For a moment I felt insanely angry with Douglas for being who he was, for lurching along beside me and for not being Angus. I was bewildered. My moods seemed to switch so quickly.

I was silent for so long that Douglas said, 'Is there anything wrong?'

'It's been a very difficult week,' I said in a tight voice. 'As you can imagine.'

'Oh Lord, I'm so sorry. How clumsy of me.' He sounded quite distressed. 'You seemed in such good form back there that I'd almost forgotten. Were you very close to your father?'

I sighed. 'No. Not really. Only – it's been different recently. Since I started working on the district. We worked in the same area you see and I sometimes met him. It was the first time we've found anything in common. He was the sort of person who was happiest and most himself when he was working. We all used to feel terribly neglected at home really. Poor Mummy ... But he told me, a while ago – I delivered someone's baby you see ...' I felt myself growing incoherent, trying to hold back my tears. It felt too intimate to cry in front of Douglas. 'He told me he was proud of me.'

Douglas stopped me gently and turned me round to face him. Then, realizing his hands were on my shoulders, he hastily removed them.

'When's the funeral?'

'On Friday.'

'Would you like me to come?'

Startled, I looked up at him. 'I don't know. It's just – my mother's rather difficult, and my brother's coming home, I think. It could be a bit – it won't be much fun for you.'

'Fun?' Douglas exploded. 'What d'you think I am, made of wood or something? It doesn't matter about your family. Of course it'll be difficult. It's a bloody awful business. I'd come because I care about you, you silly thing.'

The scarred left cheek was twitching slightly and his eyes were full of an emotion which I couldn't read. It only dawned on me then that his feelings for me were much stronger than I had imagined.

'All right. That would be very good of you, thank you.'

I was very weary and wrung out. I knew if I stayed with him much longer it would end with me stepping into his arms and crying myself out. My feelings were confused and painful and could only be eased, I felt, by my getting away from him.

'Look, I'm very sorry. This hasn't been much of an outing, I know. But I'm very tired. I'd like to go home.'

Douglas was all courtesy. We waited in silence at the bus stop. All I could feel was my acute need to be out of his company. Saying nothing, we sat together on the slow-moving bus. I got off first at Moseley.

'Thank you,' I said, standing up quickly. 'See you soon . . .' I tried to smile at him.

As the bus passed me I saw him looking out, searching for me with his eyes.

*

At Daddy's funeral he kept well in the background. I was glad he was there, though my mind was mostly on other things. I wished Olivia could be there and that I could turn to her, but I had to be content with her brief letter.

A bewildering number of people did attend the service, though. I looked round the church seeing faces I had never set eyes on before: many must have been patients, but there were also a rather oddly dressed crew in mismatched clothes and squashed felt hats, some of whom I guessed were his Christian Socialist friends. The organ let out a bleak sound and it was raining outside so the lights had to be on in the church. The tribute all these people were making to Daddy by being there made me feel wretched and powerless, as if circumstances had cheated me. Why had I known him so little? All these people for and with whom he had worked so hard, had in fact given his life for, and I had barely known of their existence.

Mummy was dignified and calm. She was well used to buttoning up her emotions. She wore her usual brown coat since she didn't possess a black one, and a black hat with a wide brim against which her pale features looked sharp and severe. She sat beside me on the front pew, her back very straight.

William had two days' leave from his Intelligence – hush hush – work for the army. He looked older, thinner, with his cropped hair, and as ever, self-important. We were civil to each other, if not warm. I could see by the strained look of his face that he was cut up by Daddy's death.

'How's Mother?' he asked afterwards. He no longer said 'Mummy' of course.

'Oh – you know. Hard to tell. Gladys has been a gem. She's taken everything on.'

I was holding one of the plates of fish-paste sandwiches which Gladys Peck and I were handing round to the throng who were all trying to squeeze into the drawing-room. We had to spread them into the back room as well and the hall was lined with damp raincoats and umbrellas.

Gladys smiled and blushed, making her way past us. 'I'm just glad to have been here at the right time,' she said. 'Eric, don't take any more! There won't be enough to go round.' She darted off after him.

'Extraordinary,' William said, his eyes following her compact figure. 'And Mummy doesn't mind?'

'No. She's really hit it off with Gladys, odd as it may seem. I heard her crying the other day, and it was Gladys she allowed to see her. I found her with her arm round Mummy's shoulders. She's a godsend. We'd never have coped otherwise.'

I moved off to distribute sandwiches. People kept stopping to talk to me, all assuming that I knew who they were. A tiny, childlike woman in a murky green shawl seized my elbow and fixed me with watery eyes. 'Your father was a saint my dear, a saint.'

'Thank you,' I said, at a loss. 'I don't think we've met.'

'I'm Edie Webster.' She held out her hand and I could feel the raised blue veins of her wrist against my finger tips. '*Christian Health Quarterly*. Your father wrote some inspirational papers.'

A familiar face came towards me through the crowd and I excused myself from Edie's skeletal grasp. 'Lisa!' I was delighted to see her. 'How are you – and Daisy?'

'Oh, we're all right – going along.' She was wearing a patched black dress. 'Daisy's running around now. You'll pay us a call soon, won't you? I 'ad to come today – ' She took my arm in her direct way. 'Terrible, your Dad going like that. 'E were a good man. We'll all miss him.'

'Yes,' I said, still feeling overcome. 'So it seems. I've never seen most of these people before.'

'Ah well,' Lisa said. She touched my shoulder. 'You can't know everything, can you?'

This was the most comforting thing anyone had said all day. 'It means a lot that you're here,' I said. 'I'll come and see you very soon, I promise.'

'Please,' she said. 'We miss you.'

Douglas stayed until the last guests were leaving. Gladys had finally sat down with Lizzie on her lap and was gulping down a cup of tea. There was nothing on any of the plates but crumbs. Eric was dabbing at them with a wet finger which travelled urgently back and forth to his mouth.

I walked to the gate with Douglas. The rain had eased off and the ground was scattered with bright yellow leaves.

'Thank you for coming,' I said. 'I'm sorry I've barely even had the chance to say hello to you.' I had, in fact, almost forgotten he was there. The strain was telling in my voice though I was trying to sound light and cheerful.

'You've got tears in your eyes,' he observed. He had a strange, detached manner sometimes. He moved his gaze to the laurel bushes behind me, avoiding my eyes.

'Well, it's been that kind of day.'

I could think of nothing to say and felt dog-tired. I

backed away from him over the wet leaves. 'Look, I'll see you soon,' I said formally. 'It was good of you to come.'

'Kate – ' Clumsily he moved towards me and pulled me into his arms. I felt his lips, startling against mine, the pale moustache prickling against my skin. It was a hard, desperate kiss, one which I didn't have the time to return, nor the inclination.

He stepped back. 'Sorry – oh, God.' He half turned away from me. 'I just – wanted to touch you. I'm sorry . . .'

Before I could say anything he was moving off at surprising speed down the road.

Chapter 17

Evening had set in as I cycled to my last call that day, and it was all the later as I had been delayed by a punctured tyre. It was January. Fog thickened between the walls of the narrow alleys, mingling with smoke from the chimneys of houses and factories to form a smelly, sludge-coloured haze. The muffled light from my bicycle made little impression on it as I pedalled cautiously along, its frame shuddering as the wheels moved over the slippery cobbles. After a time I dismounted, tired and impatient, and walked instead.

'Damn fog,' I cursed to myself. 'Damn bicycle. Damn flaming war.'

Coughing. I wheeled my bike irritably into number eight court, Stanley Street. I wiped my damp face with my hanky. It would be good to see Lisa. She always gave me strength. Despite the cold, the alleys and yards were full of the sounds of children playing out until bedtime. A gaggle of them were shouting shrilly and from somewhere came the sound of dustbin lids being clanged together. At least now the blackout had been lifted to 'dim out', more light filtered into the yard through the thin curtains in the houses.

When Lisa opened the door she looked fraught and exhausted. She had on a washed-out fawn-coloured dress, tight across her breasts, with what looked like fat stains down the front. Her hair was unbrushed and she looked set to jump right down my throat.

'Oh – it's you,' she said unceremoniously. 'Come in.'

'Have I caught you at a bad time?' I asked, stepping into the chaotic room. I'd seldom seen her so brusque before.

'No – you're all right. It's just them little buggers out there've been banging on my door on and off all evening and it's driving me mad.' She seemed close to tears. Her two older children were fighting over the fire-tongs by the grate.

'Pack it in the pair of yer!' she yelled. 'I've 'ad enough of it!'

'What's wrong?' I asked gently. Then I caught sight of Daisy, propped in one of the old armchairs. She had grown into a rather quaint-looking two-year-old with straight brown hair and a round face. She suffered badly from eczema and was always on the move, trying to scratch at some part of her arms or legs. She was at ease with people, and normally came to me, chattering. But now she lay against the greyish pillow with her eyes closed, taking quick, fluttery breaths. Clearly she had a high fever.

'How long's she been like this?' I knelt beside her.

'A couple of days. She's not been so bad in the daytime. It comes on worse of an evening.'

'She's coughing?'

As I spoke Daisy began to give out harsh, dry-sounding coughs.

'It looks like bronchitis, Lisa.' I looked round at her. She was frowning and biting the end of one finger. 'Why haven't you called the doctor?'

With a pang I realized that for a moment I had been thinking of Daddy.

'I hoped she'd get better without it,' Lisa gabbled tearfully. 'I've been sponging her down. I give 'er a bath earlier with the oatmeal in for 'er skin. Thought it'd cool 'er down. The thing is, Kate – I can't abide that Dr Williamson. It's not been the same since your dad passed on. She will be all right, won't she?'

Daisy stirred again and started trying to scratch, pulling at the cotton eczema cuffs on her arms. Her movements started off the coughing again and her face puckered with pain.

'Look, if it's the money you're worried about I'll help you out. She is my goddaughter, after all.' I patted Lisa's arm. 'I'll go and see if Dr Williamson's still there – he often stops late, especially now he's on his own. It won't take long.'

I had never seen Lisa so upset before. It was usually her who had a calming effect on me. I felt anxious for her, and for Daisy, and angry with Dr Williamson. There was enough to feel helpless about nowadays without having to be terrified of your own doctor. Twenty minutes later Dr Williamson and I were on our way to Lisa's house. He had not been pleased to see me or to be asked out on another call. As I explained the situation he nodded impatiently.

'It's very foolish to bath a child in this condition,' were almost his first words as he set foot through Lisa's door. He threw his hat on the table. I saw that while I was away she had been trying to tidy up.

Dr Williamson bent over Daisy, breathing his tobacco breath loudly at her. His balding crown was shiny with sweat. He looked into the little girl's mouth, felt the glands in her neck with his pink, stubby fingers, listened to her chest with his stethoscope. Daisy coughed as he did so, barely able to open her eyes.

'Say ahhh,' he instructed her. There was silence. I could see Lisa biting her nails.

'Say ahhh, child,' he repeated, loudly.

'She's only two years old,' I pointed out. 'And she's almost asleep.' My usual irritation with him was turning to anger.

'She'll be much too hot in these,' he said briskly, unfastening the eczema cuffs from her elbows. 'I should have thought that was obvious.'

The two of us stood in silence. I could tell Lisa was close to tears and my breathing was growing shallower with fury.

'I think Mrs Turnbull would like some assurance that Daisy is going to be all right,' I translated for her.

He stood up. 'Oh, I dare say she will if she's looked after properly. Here – ' He wrote out a prescription and handed it to her abruptly. 'Go to the dispensary in the morning. In the meantime she needs warmth, fresh air and plenty of fluids. Think you can manage that?'

He walked straight out without another word and I was after him. I had seen doctors be monumentally rude to patients in hospital on occasion, but it seemed so much worse in people's homes.

'D'you always speak to your patients like that?' I demanded.

Dr Williamson jerked to a standstill, bristling. 'I beg your pardon?' I expect he still regarded me as a child.

'I thought our job was to try and make people feel better – to alleviate suffering. Not to go out of our way to make them feel small and inadequate and imply that they can't even look after their own children.'

He breathed in sharply. 'I'll thank you to keep your views to yourself,' he said in a low, furious voice. 'And when I need advice on how to do my job after thirty years' experience I'll find someone qualified to dispense it.'

He strode away, quickly disappearing from view. Inside Lisa was in tears.

'I only did what I thought was right,' she sobbed miserably. ''E's an 'orrible man, he is. I'd like to see 'im try and get fresh air and warmth at the same time in here, 'cause it's bloody harder than it sounds.'

I persuaded her to finish getting the other children to bed.

'Daisy's asleep now, look,' I told her. 'Why don't you get yourself something to eat and try and get some rest yourself. I'll call by tomorrow, all right?'

She smiled faintly. 'Thanks, Kate. You know – you're very like 'im.'

'Who?'

'Your dad, of course.' She added miserably, 'I wish Don was here.'

When I visited the next evening I found Lisa standing outside her door with her apron on. In her hand was a bowl and I could see steam rising from it in the light through the front door.

'Chicken soup,' she told me. 'For Daisy.' Her face looked more relaxed, though she was sagging with exhaustion.

Daisy's eyes were open and Lisa was altogether more buoyant.

'I'm absolutely wiped out,' she told me. 'We 'ad an 'ell of a night. She was burning up – got me in a right state. Thought I was going to lose 'er. But come this morning she perked up again. Look at 'er. Don't you think she's better?'

Relieved, I smiled at Daisy. 'Hello, darling – are you

on the mend?' I went to sit by her and felt her forehead. 'She's a bit warm, but as you say, her temperature's settling, isn't it? That must've been the worst of it yesterday.'

'Let's see if she'll have some soup.' Lisa settled the other two children at the table and then went to the door.

'Sid!' she yelled into the dark yard. 'Get 'ere!'

We heard running feet outside and Sid Blakeley tore into the room, his cheeks raw from the cold. He was ten now, his brown hair cropped very short, face pinched, with not a trace left of his baby chubbiness. He had on grey shorts and a jumper and *Birmingham Mail* charity boots which looked weighty on the end of his bony legs.

'Say summat to Miss Munro,' Lisa ordered.

''Ullo,' Sid said, eyes on his bowl. He sat perched on the side of the armchair which was pulled up to the table. He was dunking bread into the soup and cramming it into his mouth.

'Oh,' Lisa groaned, 'I give up.'

'Leave him.' I smiled. 'He's hungry. Looks a healthy lad.'

Automatically Lisa handed me a cup of her tea which was as unpleasant as ever, but I drank it, standing by the range, waving away Lisa's apology at the shortage of chairs.

'This should do 'er good, shouldn't it?' Lisa spooned soup into Daisy's mouth. 'Albert,' she snapped suddenly at one of the small boys. 'Get your spoon off Danny's 'ead.'

'Albert? Is that after your father?'

Lisa gave a mirthless chuckle. 'No fear. No cowing use to anyone 'e wasn't – 'scuse my language. No –

Prince Albert. I always liked the pictures of 'im. Thought 'e were ever so 'andsome.'

For a few moments there was silence as she concentrated on the little girl. The boys were intent on their soup. She got up to give them more bread and a minute scraping of jam. I looked round the room. Clothes were hanging drying in every conceivable place – chairbacks, picture frames – and the atmosphere was steamy.

Lisa's house was hardly a model home, but I could detect a certain personal order among the chaos. She had after all had to run her family home from a young age and brought up her brother and her own children.

She smiled as Daisy finally pursed her lips and turned her head away from the spoon. 'She's 'ad a good go at it.'

'Marvellous,' I said, smiling slightly as I caught myself sounding like Marjorie Mantel. 'That's a good sign. She'll soon be up and under your feet again.'

Lisa yawned, then laughed. 'Sorry – it's not the company.'

'You must be exhausted.'

'Thanks for looking in,' Lisa said. She gestured to the boys to get down from the table and they disappeared outside. Then she looked carefully at me. 'You all right? You look a darn sight better than the last time I saw you.'

'I'm well, apart from this cold.' I sat down opposite her, amid the remains of the boys' tea.

Lisa put her head on one side. 'Who was that bloke I saw at your dad's funeral? The one with the gammy leg. I was watching 'im – 'andsome, isn't 'e? 'Ardly took his eyes off you all afternoon.'

'Oh, that's just Douglas,' I said.

'That's just Douglas,' Lisa mimicked me, her spirits returned. 'Come on Kate – 'e'd put bonfire night in the shade the flame 'e's got lit for you.' She leaned towards me. ''Asn't 'e?' I knew Lisa took pride in her directness, her knowing that she could make me open up.

I nodded. 'I suppose he has.'

'And what about you?'

'I've been trying not to have.'

Throughout the previous months Douglas and I had grown closer, though the progression was awkward. He apologized repeatedly for his behaviour after Daddy's funeral, and since then had been only charming and good-natured. We had very little physical contact, and though Douglas was very tender towards me, he behaved with nothing but restraint and tact. I was the problem, confused and guilty as I was about Angus. But Douglas was very patient and he had a gift for making you confide in him. I poured out my feelings about Angus.

One day when I was telling him about our childhood he said, 'You'd known him since you were quite small then?'

'Oh, yes. The Harveys moved in when I was seven. I thought I'd told you?'

'I see,' Douglas said, as if he had suddenly got to grips with something. 'So he was really a childhood friend?'

'Well – yes,' I said, puzzled. 'We'd obviously known each other a long time.'

Since the afternoon of the funeral he had not tried to kiss me. Sometimes the way he looked at me I thought he was about to, but he held back. The only exceptions to this were times when I cried. He held me then, with a gentleness which touched me. I didn't know whether I wanted more. I didn't encourage it. It would have made me feel disloyal to Angus. I felt safe with Douglas, restored by his sheer physical presence near me, and knowing that he was not going to be sent away. And increasingly I knew how attractive I found him. But I resisted showing too much affection. It would have been unfair to him.

Gradually, Douglas began to tell me about his own family. Evidently he did not find them an easy subject to discuss.

'I wanted to get a long way away from them,' he said. We were sitting by the lake in Cannon Hill Park, wrapped in coats and scarves. 'That's why I came to look for a job up here. Birmingham's not a place they'd be all that keen to visit.'

'Not even to see you?'

'No. My father's in the Home Guard now. He's a schoolmaster in civvy street. It should suit him. Used to giving orders.'

'And your mother?'

'A waxwork.' He stared at the grey sky. Straight-necked mallards whirred above us. 'Actually, more of a plaster saint. Never talks back to the Colonel. He never was a colonel, by the way, but that's the way he behaves at home. I had to get away – it was stifling. I couldn't breathe in that house. My mother wanted to wrap me in lint and keep me there, muzzled, because of my leg. She tried to do that pretty much all through my childhood. I had to prove to myself that I had a brain even if my leg was a joke. I loved writing and I wanted to do something active, not be some dried-up academic. They didn't even send me to school, you see – because of the way I looked. I suppose they were worried about me being teased – I'd be no good at games and so on. So my father taught me when he had time, and I had a man who came to the house. Mr Lovely his name was – ' Douglas chuckled. 'Not a bad sort. Actually it was his idea that I look for a job on a paper.'

'How very grim,' I said. 'It must have been so lonely.'

'I lived through it,' he said lightly.

Sometimes I sensed Douglas wanted to touch me, or kiss me. I found him watching me with a kind of hunger in his face. He would look away quickly when our eyes met. I often wished he could just hold me and that I could respond without fear or guilt, that it could all be more simple.

'Go on,' Lisa urged me. 'You can tell me. You've fallen for him, haven't you, Kate?'

'Maybe – a bit,' I admitted.

'So what's wrong with that?'

'I'm afraid I'll allow myself this – that I'll let my feelings for him grow and then suddenly one day Angus will come home and I'll have hurt everyone. It would be terrible. What I really wish is that he'd come back and things could be as they were before.'

'They'll never be that,' Lisa said drily. 'Never are, are they? You said 'e was dead.'

'He almost certainly is. The latest from the Red Cross is that he was shot down over the sea. I know there's no real hope.'

'And you reckon this other feller's worth it?'

I hesitated so that Lisa put her head on one side quizzically. 'Yes – I think so.'

'There you are, then.'

When I left Lisa's that evening the fog had intensified, and hung dark and choking along the streets. Even though the road was no longer completely blacked out, it was very hard to see anything. I clicked on my ineffective cycle lamp and decided I would be safer walking until I reached the main road where the kerbs were painted in black and white stripes to make them easier to see. I set off up Stanley Street. Muffled figures passed me in the fog, a few saying 'Evening' as they faded out of view again. After a while I decided I'd be better off without the lamp as it seemed only to reflect off the fog.

The man approached me almost silently and I ran my bike straight into him.

'Christ,' the voice said furiously. He bent down, rubbing his leg. I think the wheel nut must have caught his shin. 'For heaven's sake, if you can't ride the thing, at least walk it along the kerb so you don't do anyone else an injury.'

He had his collar turned up against the damp air and his face was in shadow, but I knew that voice immediately. Not wanting him to recognize me, I murmured 'Sorry' and quickly wheeled past him, my heart pounding.

'I should damn well think so!' he shouted after me.

I wanted to get away from him as fast as I could. As I pressed on up the street I had a strong, horrible instinct as to what he was doing there. Kemp's stood among a collection of factories several streets away. Alec Kemp always travelled there by car, and Stanley Street was not, by any stretch of the imagination, on his way home.

Part Three

Chapter 18

KATE

At dawn it was quiet, except for the dripping trees. And then the bells: church bells so long silent, the sound of them ringing across the city all the more jubilant when unheard for so long. 8 May 1945. In the night there had been a storm, thunder and lightning like the nudge of something supernatural, ending the war just as they had begun it.

The day before we had spent waiting, confused. In the morning there was a news blackout and it wasn't until three in the afternoon that they announced Germany's surrender. War in Europe was over.

I went to church that morning with Mummy and Gladys and the children. The building was packed and they were promising to put on extra services. Between us we kept the children amused and reasonably still.

'Now thank we all our God.' Gladys's clear voice rose and fell beside me as it had when she was scrubbing our floors. I knew, sadly, that she wouldn't be with us much longer. During the prayers Mummy knelt with her eyes closed. I assumed she was thinking of Daddy and giving thanks that William would be coming home safely. But thoughts of what we had lost came more forcefully to me. I tried to bring Angus's face before me, feeling panic and shame when I could barely picture him.

'Whatever's happened to you, I love you,' I told him silently. 'If you are alive, come back to me, please, my darling. And if you're not, rest peacefully knowing I'll love you always. Always.'

Many of us were in tears, especially when we stood to sing the last hymn, 'Jerusalem', the combination of joy and loss too much for us.

Afterwards, everyone was on the street, hugging, shaking hands. There was a dazed look to people, euphoria and disbelief combined with a residual irritation at the confused way in which the news of the final surrender had been relayed to us. 'They could at least have let us know what was happening . . .' But now it didn't matter. It was over.

I went through the motions of greeting the neighbours, of laughing and exclaiming, but all the time I wanted desperately to be alone. My thoughts during the service had been so close to Angus, and this had left a knot of tension tightening in me like a physical ache.

It was a showery day, the sky busy with cloud. I just wanted to walk and walk and have time to think by myself.

'Where are you going?' Mummy called after me as I took off along the road with my umbrella.

'I'm just going to have a look round for a bit,' I called back over my shoulder.

'But that nice Mr Craven said he'd come round to the house . . .' Gladys's voice wafted to me along the pavement.

I knew this perfectly well, and it was another reason I had to take off. I turned and waved vaguely as if I hadn't heard properly, calling, 'Back soon!' I knew Mummy and Gladys would be all right together listening to all that was going on on the wireless.

Without really deciding where to go I turned automatically towards the centre of Birmingham, walking fast, needing to let off steam and exhaust myself. As I did so I looked down the side streets and could see all the hurried preparations going on for street parties, the trestle tables draped with sheets and people bustling around, some already wearing coloured paper hats. Miles of bunting was going up, rippling above the tables in the side streets, and Union Jacks brightened the grimy fronts of the houses, and everywhere movement of people, shouting, laughing.

Down one street in Balsall Heath a pair of trousers adorned the middle of one of the lines of bunting. I found myself smiling as I heard Douglas's voice in my head: 'Still hanging out the washing on the Siegfried Line!' and I was startled by the way I was becoming used to his jokes, to him.

It started raining and I put up my umbrella, but the rain didn't chase anyone from the streets for long. I walked down into our battered city, hearing bursts of cheering and bands playing as I moved into the crowded streets in the heart of Birmingham. I felt a rush of loneliness at being there alone on this day, but at the same time it was fitting. It was a day of turmoil for everyone, in its way, and I could not have stood company just then, such was the tension of mixed feelings inside me. But I wanted to be out here amid the frenzied activity of the city, to be part of it on a day when we all stood poised on the rim of the future. I suppose here in all this communal uncertainty I was longing to find the way to orientate myself in my own life. To work out what direction I should take next.

Around me pasty, tired faces smiled along the streets, chattered and shrieked with excitement under the ripple of flags. People were breaking into singing and dancing. A group of women cavorted across New Street with their arms linked singing 'Knees up Mother Brown' and pushing their legs up high, and I heard 'Roll Out the Barrel' clashing with it from further down the road, and whistles and cheers and shouts of laughter.

I made my way slowly towards Victoria Square, smelling the wet pavement mingled with cigarette smoke. People were shouting at each other, someone's voice behind me, 'Edna – Edna – over 'ere!' and a woman with curlers round her head, not caring. Dare-devils in uniform and out of it scrambled up lamp-posts and on to high window-sills and stood laughing and waving: another group, some of whom were still dressed for the Land Army, sang 'Auld Lang Syne' with their arms round each other. Worries were put aside, every-one throwing themselves into this uplifting, long, long-awaited morning. This was enough: today. I saw a few people crying and Churchill's words, relayed to us through loudspeakers in the streets, moved more people to tears: 'God bless you all. This is your victory. It is the victory of the cause of freedom in every land . . .'

I didn't cry, not then. But perversely, after such a strong impulse to be alone, what I did feel was an overpowering need to turn to someone close to me to share these moments. Angus. And he wasn't there. He never would be. Standing amid the jostling crowd and seeing this glimpse of what might have been gave me my most extreme moments of distilled pain in all the time since Angus was reported missing. I felt a physical sensation like an incision, too sharp and deep for tears. Yet once I had passed through it it left me lightened and relieved as if I had wept for a long time.

I bought a cup of tea from a mobile canteen on the street and stood quietly sipping it next to a lamp-post, hands tight round the enamel cup, soothed and easier in myself.

'Awright, love?' a gravelly voice asked next to me. A dapper man with a thin black moustache like Peter Lorre. 'What a day, eh?'

I smiled. 'Yes, isn't it?'

There was something in the man's stance and chirpy way of talking that Douglas would have loved to mimic, and I would have liked to see him do it. I stored the encounter in my mind as something to tell him. After handing the cup back I eased my way out of the crowds, away from the centre of the city, and began to walk home.

I experienced a sense of anticlimax, yet also of understanding. It was over – for us. I'd never imagined it like this, with war still raging on the other side of the world. It thought this day, when it came, would be a key to something. Angus would come home, somehow decisions would be made for me. But if the Red Cross were right, Angus lay in a sea grave. He was not missing. Not a Prisoner of War. Angus was dead. I had to accept the truth of that. I had to turn and carry on with the living.

Douglas didn't arrive at our house until late afternoon, so I hadn't been much missed.

'They gave me the rest of the afternoon off,' he told us. 'So I came round straight away.'

Gladys, charmed by him, actually simpered. She thought Douglas wonderful. 'It's a pity about his, well, you know, his leg,' she'd say. 'But he's ever so handsome, isn't he?'

Douglas was looking very spruce. Smart clothes were

important to him, and I often teased him, saying he didn't look seedy enough to be a reporter. His camera was, as ever, slung over one shoulder.

'I'm so glad you were in,' he said. 'I thought you might have taken off somewhere for the day.' Taking me by the shoulders he kissed me quickly on the cheek, and I felt myself blush. We so seldom touched each other or kissed. Covering his own uncertainty, he said, 'Well – this is quite a day, isn't it?'

We spent the evening pleasantly with Mummy and Gladys, Douglas and I telling them what we'd seen while we were out. Douglas went out to fetch an evening edition of the paper and we laughed together at the *Mail*'s assessment of Birmingham's VE Day celebrations: 'We are not much given to mass gaiety. We are gardeners, family men, artificers and very individualistic at that.'

'Rather austere,' I said. 'Is that what you'd have written? I thought they were having a pretty jolly time out there myself.'

'Yes, and I expect it'll hot up tonight,' Douglas said. 'Perhaps I'll go back in for a while . . . Would you think of coming too? We could take a tram in – they've got some of them dolled up.'

'I think I've had enough for today,' I said. 'But thanks for the offer.'

I sensed from Douglas's increasing silence as the evening wore on that he had something on his mind and that he would rather have been alone with me. The chance didn't arise until he was leaving. We stood outside on the doorstep and he seemed reluctant to go.

'Were you woken by the thunder last night?' he asked.

'Yes, of course. But it was nice to lie awake and think and take in the news.'

'What were you thinking about?' Sometimes he asked questions in a disconcertingly clinical way.

'Oh, just the rest of my life.' I tried to speak lightly.

'Freedom!' Douglas said exultantly. 'A chance to move on at last. Get on to one of the nationals.' He was silent for a moment, hands in his pockets, looking down at the ground. 'That's if I stand a chance, competing with all our heroes returning from the front.' I felt sorry for him, for his bitter sense of separateness, of not measuring up.

'Look.' He turned to me, speaking fast and awkwardly. 'I can't carry on like this – not telling you how I feel about you.'

I pulled the front door closed behind me and stood against it.

'I need to know whether you could ever feel anything for me. Sometimes it seems you do, and then . . .' He hesitated. 'You've got to face it, Katie. He's not going to come back.'

A lump rose in my throat and for a moment I couldn't speak. Douglas read his own meaning into this. With a frustrated sound he turned away from me. I reached out and put my hand on his shoulder. He jerked loose from me fiercely. 'Don't, for God's sake.'

'What?'

'Feel bloody sorry for me.'

'I don't feel sorry for you,' I said. 'Actually I was feeling quite sorry for myself. Why do you have to take it that anyone who shows you any sort of affection must be feeling sorry for you?'

'Well, why else do you keep on seeing me?' he burst out. 'You're clearly still in love with – him. There's nothing I can do about that.' He looked into my eyes and I was rocked by the strength of emotion in his. 'I feel helpless. That's what drives me mad. I've spent months watching you mourn for someone else, feeling I should keep my distance from you, when it's all I can do to hold myself back from touching you. Because I don't want you to think I'm . . .' He made another frustrated gesture.

'What?'

'I don't want you to think I'm a crass idiot coming crashing in when you see me as nothing more than a second-best companion.'

'That's not how I see you.' I looked away, down at the brick floor of the porch. In a flat voice I said, 'I can't tell you I didn't – don't – love Angus. And in some ways that hasn't been finished properly. But that doesn't mean I don't have feelings for you. I'm just so afraid – '

He waited for me to finish. I couldn't look at him as I spoke.

'I'm afraid of him coming back. And I'm afraid of him not coming back. It's utterly unfair on you, I know. And you've been so good to me. I'm very grateful.'

'He's not going to come back, Katie,' he repeated gently.

'I know that really. In fact today, when I was in town, I really saw properly that I have to try and put it all behind me.' I moved closer and laid my hands on Douglas's shoulders.

'Katie – ' He sounded wretched. 'Please don't do this if you don't really mean it.'

'I do.' I wanted to mean it, wanted things to be resolved and clear. I reached up and stroked his face. 'Thank you for being so patient.'

He pulled me hard into his arms. 'Katie. Katie ...' His lips pressed hard on mine. I felt firstly the comfort of being held. As I kissed him back, the desire for him I had fought against for so long lit at his touch.

On a beautiful, tranquil Sunday in July we sat together on the grass at the far end of our garden, beyond the vegetable patch and bean-sticks. Douglas often spent part of the weekend at our house now, rather than in his spartan digs, the garden of which had space for nothing but vegetables. My mother was civil to him, if not exactly warm, but he apparently saw no lack in her then, and even seemed to be quite fond of her.

Douglas was sitting up with a newspaper spread over his legs. He usually read a whole range of papers at the weekend: *Times*, *Express*, *Daily Worker*, some of them several days old. Work: always work. I lay back contentedly with my head on my bent arm. All I could see was the branches of our apple tree and the pale blue sky.

'It's so quiet without Eric and Lizzie,' I said. Gladys had departed tearfully soon after the war ended, begging us to keep in touch. 'Mummy really misses Gladys, I think. She's invited them to come back for holidays if they want to.'

Douglas looked up. 'That's good. She's a staunch character, isn't she?'

I watched a tiny curl of cloud unfold itself slowly across the sky. Only now it was over, the images of the war seemed to bombard me, a delayed realization of what we had all been through. 'Even now I keep expecting something to appear – I'm always looking out for planes.'

Douglas folded his newspaper untidily and flung it on the grass, then lay back beside me. 'You don't throw off habits like that in five minutes. I dreamt the other night that there was an air raid on, and I was all set to get out of bed and down to the shelter.'

I laughed, and we lay together looking up into the blue. Though I was happy, I had an odd feeling of disconnectedness now we had peace. It was as if we could not pick up the threads of our life before the war, that we were cut off at the roots. And now the war was not our main preoccupation I found myself missing Olivia far more acutely. She belonged to the peace. She should be here. I also missed my father.

I rolled over and looked down at Douglas. 'What about your family? Don't you think you should contact them?'

Douglas had mentioned to me only recently that his mother wrote to him without fail every week and had done all through the war. 'She knows I'm all right,' he said in the dismissive tone he always used when talking of his parents. 'I've dropped her a line here and there.'

'But shouldn't you go and see them?'

'What you should do is not always the question, is it?' he said, surprising me with his harshness. 'And besides, I don't think we've got a lot to say to each other.' He sat up and held the camera to his face, altering the focus. 'Lie still.' I waited patiently as he took yet another photograph.

'I don't understand you,' I said. 'What is it about your parents that's so terrible?'

'Don't let's talk about them.' He moved closer and we sat leaning against the high garden wall, Douglas putting his arm round me. I saw his pale, flecked lashes. As we began to kiss, sitting side by side, I ran one hand over his strong hair, then down his back, stroking the raised muscles each side of his spine. He kissed me strongly, hungrily, arms tight around me. I was beginning to respond to him, when suddenly his hand was on my breast, grasping me clumsily and hard. I gasped, drawing back. Douglas snatched his hand away again.

'Darling,' I said gently. 'You've never touched a woman much before, have you?'

His face turned red. He was twenty-five, a year older than me, and innocent. 'No,' he said very quietly, as if ashamed. 'Never had the courage – or the chance much. Not many girls go for cripples, you see.'

'And men don't make passes at girls who wear glasses,' I said, trying to joke him out of his embarrassment. But he was solemn and unsure of himself.

'I'm sorry.' He couldn't look me in the eyes. 'You're different, Katie. You're so very special. I love you.'

I leaned to him and kissed him again. I longed to show him the joy of it, to let him touch me. It would be all right here, where it was so secluded. He began to unfasten my blouse, fumbling with the top button. He looked me in the eyes as if waiting for permission.

'You don't mind? I've never – I'd like to see you . . .'

When he had undone the buttons and slowly parted the two sides of white cotton, he slid his fingers inside the lacy edge of my bra. As he touched me I let out a slight sound, wanting him to continue. I could hear his breath coming fast and his hands were not steady.

When my clothes were undone he stared, childlike suddenly. 'Oh, Kate – they're so beautiful.'

I waited for him to touch me, eyes closed and crying out with the pleasure of it as his hands reached my flesh. His breathing was fast and excited. A sudden sound startled me, a whisper of foliage, and I sat back from Douglas in time to pull the front of my blouse together as my mother advanced on us down the garden, her hands gigantic in gardening gloves. We sat feeling utterly foolish, but to her credit she gave us as wide a berth as possible and kept her eyes fixed on the vegetable patch beyond us. Passing back in front of us moments later with a garden fork she'd come to retrieve she said casually, 'By the way, there's tea . . .'

Douglas's cheeks were burning red. Silently I buttoned my blouse.

'Look,' Douglas said eventually, 'if we really care for one another, we ought to be able to wait for all that, don't you think? As a mark of respect. It should really be for after marriage, shouldn't it?'

I kept my gaze turned away from his, blushing now myself as I realized Douglas assumed I was innocent.

He misinterpreted my heightened colour. 'And I should be very happy if we didn't have to wait very long.'

Olivia didn't come home until shortly before the Japanese surrender in August 1945.

'My darling, darling!' I cried, when she first arrived to see us, all my niggles about her letters forgotten. I held her tight, tears on my face. 'It feels like a lifetime since I've seen you.'

'To me too,' she said, returning my embrace.

She smiled and kissed me, but even in my happiness I could hardly conceal my shock. She was skin and bone, her hair limp and straggly and her eyes dull.

'Livy – you look so ill,' I said gently to her, feeling I had to cajole her. She seemed so knotted up in herself.

'Well, you don't exactly look like Doris Day yourself,' she replied, evasive and teasing.

It was true. Like so many other women we were shrunken and worn down by the war. I assumed that the exacting hours the Wrens had demanded from her had taken their toll, compounded by her bout of pneumonia. But I couldn't imagine what they had done to her emotions.

One evening I went round to Park Hill to spend some time with her. I felt slightly nervous as I walked down under the trees. She was so unpredictable nowadays.

Alec and Elizabeth were evidently frantic about the state of her. They trod around her as if she might detonate at any second, while being on the other hand ferociously jolly towards me in an attempt to pretend that all was well, that 'poor Olivia' was just a little worn down after all her war work.

'What she needs is a good holiday,' Alec said. He was leaning against the polished surface of a grand piano which I dimly remembered seeing in the house on my last visit. He was leaner, his forehead lined and grey hair showing at his temples. Hearing his voice, I remembered my encounter in the fog with my bicycle, and I knew for sure that it had been him.

When Livy and I were left alone, I said, 'That's a really beautiful piano,' I hesitated. 'Look, I've barely played through the war and I'm fearfully rusty, but would you like to have a go at some duets?'

'Oh no,' she replied languidly. She seemed to find it almost too much effort to speak. She sat smoking, drawing hard on the cigarette so that her cheeks were sucked in. There was an ashtray on the little table beside her with several stubs in. 'I haven't played for months either. I don't suppose I shall. Can't think what he bought the wretched thing for.'

'But you were so good at it,' I protested. 'You mustn't just let it all go.'

She ground her cigarette stub into the ashtray. Her next words sent a chill through me, they were spoken with such flat indifference. 'What does it matter?'

'Livy – ' I went to her and knelt down carefully beside her chair and took her bony hand in mine. It felt like a starved bird. 'My dearest Livy – what's wrong? You look so thin and unwell.'

She looked into my eyes then, really stared, as if she was searching for something. But in hers I saw a kind of hard blankness so unlike the vivaciousness of the young Livy that it made me want to cry.

'What is it?' I asked softly.

She stared at me in silence and I thought she was making up her mind to say something. Then she put her head back, resting it against the chair, and closed her eyes.

'Livy?'

'I'm all right, Katie. Don't fuss. I'm just tired. I'm always so tired. It's been an exhausting war. Not just the work, you know – so much else going on.' She rallied suddenly, switching into another gear. She sat up straight, eyes open. And she was off on her old track of how marvellous the Wrens had been, the parties, all the men, the team spirit, the romance ... She talked very fast in a high, slightly childlike voice.

'I was just the belle of so many navy do's,' she giggled. She began to rock the upper part of her body back and forth. I found myself shrinking back from her. 'And when they discovered how well I could play' – she held her hand out, indicating the piano – 'well, of course I was in constant demand.'

'But I thought you said you hadn't played?'

She waved a hand at me as if I was a half-wit. 'This was earlier. And I was always top of the men's lists for dances. There were fights over me you know. One poor fellow was knocked out cold outside the Naafi one night over me. I thought it was simply terrific. So romantic!' Her laughter came out exaggerated, as if she'd been drinking.

'Livy.' I found myself speaking in a measured voice of the sort we used for patients who were confused or agitated. 'I'm glad you enjoyed it all. But it's over now, isn't it? You need to rest and settle down again. Get well properly. And you'll have to think what you're going to do. You never wanted to come back and live at home, did you?'

She sank back in the chair, suddenly limp. 'Daddy didn't get elected, did he?' She gave a malicious laugh. 'Missed the boat. He jumps on the bandwagon thinking he'll get a seat because of all dear Mr Churchill's done, and then they go and elect the Labour wallahs instead. Isn't that a joke? Don't you think it's a scream?'

'Livy – don't. Look, think about yourself. What are you going to do?'

'Oh, I don't know. What a nag you're being, Katie!' She threw herself up out of the chair and went to the piano. She lit another cigarette and offered me one. I shook my head. She sat perched on the piano stool, pulling in the smoke hard.

'I suppose I'll get some tedious little job in a tedious little company somewhere. I'll have to find a way of livening it up somehow, won't I?' Suddenly an odd, gleeful smile spread across her face. 'Come here, Katie.'

She beckoned me urgently. 'I'll tell you a secret, shall I? You must promise not to tell.'

Encouraged, I walked over to her. Putting her lips close to my ear she said, 'They think they've got me here now, all locked away. But I still do it. I do. Every week at least I do it with a man. Anywhere I can. Even once in the gazebo – like when you found me and William. I told that one he had to be a very good boy. Nice and quiet, no shouting out. A lot of them shout you see, the things I do to them. Poor fellows can't control themselves.'

I drew my head back as if from a hornet. Of course I wasn't a total innocent, but it had dawned on me only gradually as she spoke that she meant sexual intercourse. Her face wore a terrible, smug smile.

'You'll keep this all under wraps of course, won't you, Katie?'

I felt sick. I took her in my arms. 'Olivia. Oh my sweet one – whatever has happened to you?'

Chapter 19

Soon after VJ Day Douglas and I announced to our families that we were planning to marry. My mother digested this piece of information almost entirely without comment, other than to suggest that, to start with, we live with her.

'There are hardly any houses to be had and there's plenty of room here. You'd have no need to fear for your privacy.' She spoke stiffly, perhaps afraid we'd reject her.

'Are you sure you wouldn't mind?' I said doubtfully.

'I don't entirely relish the thought of living on my own. I should have to think about selling the house. And in any case,' she announced, 'I shan't be around bothering you. From the new year I shall be very busy – I've accepted a post on a children's ward at Selly Oak Hospital.'

'Mummy, that's terrific!' I said. 'Whyever didn't you tell me?'

'I just have told you,' she said, stalking off with an armful of dried washing.

Though my inclination was not to accept her offer I knew it made sense, and Douglas was delighted. 'It's such a beautiful home,' he said. 'Otherwise we'd be in some poky little place. It's very good of her to ask us.'

Douglas received a formal, tetchy note from his father, to the effect that he was glad to be informed that 'my boy' was planning to settle down, but that it was very bad form that they hadn't even been allowed the privilege of meeting his intended. It also rebuked him sharply for not visiting home. His mother had been distraught with worry. Douglas was to travel to Gloucester immediately.

'We really must go,' I insisted to an enraged Douglas. I was shaken by the impersonal tone of the letter, but also by its description of Mrs Craven's distress. 'You can hardly blame them, can you? You've barely contacted them at all and your mother's written so faithfully to you.'

'Oh yes – she's very good at giving completely the wrong impression,' Douglas snapped.

I was taken aback by his tone. 'What d'you mean?'

'Nothing.' He got up from his chair in our back room and went to the window. 'I'm not going to be summoned to Gloucester like that. I'm sorry, Katie, but I've got away from them and away is where I'm going to stay. Once you've cut ties it's better to keep it that way. That's my view of things.'

'You can be very cold.' I was upset, not wanting to begin married life with us so much on the wrong side of my in-laws. 'Look, why don't I go and see them on my own if that's how you feel?'

'No!' Douglas shouted, his face flushing a deep red. 'Don't you dare. I'm not having you going down there behind my back.'

'Don't shout at me like that.' I was furious with him for reacting like this. 'It wouldn't be behind your back, would it? I've just asked you.'

Without turning round again he said, 'Well, the answer's no.'

After a few moments he hobbled over and put his arms round me. 'I'm sorry, darling. Don't be angry – please.'

He wrote an immediate reply to them saying that we wouldn't be coming. I felt angry, guilty about treating them in such a way. Eventually I dropped them a brief note myself, trying to sound as pleasant as I could, saying I was sorry for our lack of contact, but that I hoped to meet them in the near future. By return of post I received a strange note from Mrs Craven.

> Dear Katherine,
>
> I was most relieved to receive your letter. I suppose Douglas has stopped you coming to visit us, being the stubborn boy he is. He doesn't find it easy to forgive, the poor darling. He won't change, you know, they never do. If you can persuade him to let us meet you I should be very grateful of course. I'm sure you'll look after him. I shall do all in my power to be at the wedding.
>
> Best if you don't mention to my husband that I've written.
>
> Sincerely, Julia Craven.

Soon after she heard of my engagement, Ruth Harvey came to our house. She stood on the doorstep, her bag on her arm and an odd look on her face which reminded me of the day she had come to tell me Angus was missing. I showed her into the front room. She refused to sit down.

'You're marrying someone else.'

I hadn't anticipated such directness. I nodded, not speaking.

'Oh ye of little faith.' Her voice was low, almost menacing. Her belief that Angus was not dead had reached the point of obsession. She was a thinner, stranger woman, hair now pepper-and-salt grey.

'He's dead. He's not coming back,' I said, pitying her. 'It's not that I don't love him still. I shall always love him, Ruth. But we have to face up to it. We shan't see him again, however much we still feel for him.'

'We'll see,' she said, though I thought I heard the beginnings of resignation in her voice. Opening her handbag she drew out a white envelope and handed it to me. 'You'd better have this.'

I stared at it for a few seconds, unable to give any meaning to it. I saw my name written carefully in blue ink and knew immediately that the writing was Angus's. Frowning, I looked across at her.

'He left it with me. That Christmas, when he was on embarkation leave. For me to give you if he – ' she struggled for a second to steady her voice. 'He said I was to give it to you at the right moment.'

Just managing to control myself, I said, 'And if I was not now about to marry someone else, when exactly do you think the right moment might have been?'

She turned her face away from me and looked beyond, out to the garden. 'I hoped I should never have to give it to you.'

It was all I could do to prevent myself running at her, tearing my nails across her face.

'How dare you keep it from me?' I shrieked at her. 'How could you? How dare you decide when I could read it?' I flailed my arms helplessly. 'Give it to me!'

I went to take it but she held the letter clutched to her chest. 'You gave up on him.'

'And if you carry on like this you'll be giving up on John and Mary. Now give it to me.'

'Whatever's going on?' My mother's shocked face appeared in the doorway.

I held my hand out, my eyes fixed on Ruth's. Finally

she laid the envelope in my palm. I pushed past Mummy, beyond thinking of anything, and ran to my room, shaking, bewildered at the violence I had felt towards Ruth. We who had been such a comfort to one another in the early days of Angus's disappearance had grown sharply apart when I had moved forward, able to grieve, to find the beginnings of acceptance.

Before I opened the letter I let the tears come, months' worth of grief still raw in me, compounded by my rage with Ruth. I even half suspected she had chosen this moment to give me the letter in order to blight my marriage to Douglas. What a comfort it could have been having this letter when I first knew I might not see Angus again. To have his voice through these words at a time when he still felt close and recent. I sat holding the envelope, weeping and shaking.

Only when I was spent did I open it. Seeing his writing on the paper brought a new ache. He had headed the letter Christmas 1940.

Dear Katie,

I'm sitting on my bunk writing this, only just able to see as the sky is so heavy with rain outside, and I must admit to feeling as weighed down myself by what I have to say to you.

I suppose like anyone writing a letter such as this I am praying above all that you will never come to read it. The thought of you having to do so is unbearable but I know I must write. I can't assume that I shall come through all this unscathed. Unlike some of the other chaps I don't have a supreme confidence that I am indestructible.

All I know is that with every fibre of my being I want to stay alive. I love life, and above all my darling, I love you. I am only thankful that I shall not be leaving you widowed, perhaps with our young children to bring up alone and unsupported. That would be an enormous sadness and shame to me. Sometimes I dream of our having a family together, but not now – not in the middle of all this. When I am low I think of your smile and the feel of you close to me. I want to live and live, and to be back sharing this life with you.

All I can say is that you are everything to me, and I shall love you and remember your touch through life or death. But if it comes to it that you are left alone, Katie, please don't feel you mustn't love anyone else or allow them to feel for you. You are so lovable, and above all I want to think that you will be happy. You must take whatever life can give you with my blessing.

I'll end this by saying 'until we meet again' in whatever way that is possible. Pray God that it is in life.

Goodbye, my dearest love. Yours always, Angus.

I lay on my bed for a very long time with his letter pressed to my body, while calmer, quieter tears moved down my cheeks like a benediction.

Two days later, my mother told me that Ruth Harvey had agreed to hold a memorial service for Angus.

Douglas and I were married by Mr Hughes in January 1946. I would not have felt right dolling myself up in a long white dress, and in any case I've never been the frilly type, so instead I chose a cream suit which was smart and flattering, if not ethereal and virginal. My mother approved. I'm not sure Douglas did. I think he would have loved a white angel on his arm.

The evening before the wedding there was a stream of people through the house. Olivia, who was of course to be my bridesmaid, came to try on her dress for the last time. It was made of a vivid blue shantung, in a straight, elegant style which suited her. But I couldn't help noticing the painful boniness of her back as she undressed, facing the mirror. Her face looked washed out and strained and there were dark shadows under her eyes.

She was excited, nervous, and barely stopped talking. 'I so terribly want to get everything just right for you.' She chattered on, looking at herself in the long mirror. She had on a pair of high, slim-heeled court shoes in cream, and twisted herself this way and that on the balls of her feet as I sat watching from the bed. 'This is so exciting, Katie, and Douglas is an absolute love. It's got to be a perfect day. Nothing else will do for you.'

I smiled at her extravagance, happy to see her so animated. 'Livy – it's wonderful to have you around again.' I stood up and went to kiss her. 'Thanks for being such a brick.'

Peter Harvey came to see me. I found it very difficult to communicate with Ruth, despite the service for Angus which had been held just before Christmas. But Peter had been kinder and more resigned from the beginning.

He held both my hands and kissed me. 'We shall be at the service, but I wanted to see you properly while you've got the chance to talk. The actual day is such a bustle. Now, now,' he said, seeing my eyes filling. 'You deserve a bit of happiness. Ruth wishes you well really, you know. It's just taken her a long time to come to terms with it all.'

I kissed his worn face. 'It's all right. I understand. You do know if I still thought there was a chance of Angus coming home, that I'd never – '

'Oh, now – that's no way to go into your marriage.' He gave his chesty laugh. 'You're marrying Douglas. You be happy, girl. That's an order!'

Mummy helped me with my simple preparations for

the wedding dutifully, but without obvious enthusiasm. She had shown more vivacity when, shortly after coming home, William announced he was going to abandon Oxford and embark on a career in banking. She felt it would stand him in far better stead. Clearly he had no desire to return home, and had taken off to London acclaimed by Mummy as being very clever and sensible. I had thought Mummy and I had grown marginally closer during the war years, but as soon as William arrived home I had sensed the distance growing between us again.

'You always did prefer him to me, didn't you?' I said to her sadly, the night before the wedding.

She had taken to wearing little pince-nez for reading and close work, and she peered up at me over them, fingers still busy stitching the hem of her dress.

'It's not a matter of preference,' she said, apparently scandalized by the idea.

'What then?' I was feeling emotional, and in need of support and reassurance.

She stopped sewing for a moment, the needle poised. 'Boys are so much easier somehow. Their lives are more direct. And William's always been so clever. Not that you're not,' she said unexpectedly, shooting a glance at me. 'It's just that normally, with boys, their lives go in a straighter line. The war's made a difference to that, of course. But I knew I shouldn't have to watch William grow up, get an education and then throw himself away on a man.'

I gasped. I knew she had found aspects of her marriage frustrating, however good a man Daddy had been. I'd had no idea her thoughts were so bleak.

'Health Visitors can still work when they're married,' I ventured. 'They started allowing it during the war.'

Mummy looked severely at me. 'You think you've got all the answers, don't you? Well, you just wait. It's never how you think. You'll find you're expecting and you'll have all that on your plate. And who d'you think'll be doing all the work and worrying about the children and the house? It won't be Douglas, take that from me, whether you're in a job or out of it. Once you're married it's curtains to any ideas you might have for yourself.'

Accompanied by these cheering words I faced my wedding day.

Olivia looked stunning the next day in her dress of rich blue. She was well made up so her face wore a healthier colour. I had chosen roses for our bouquets as I loved their scent of summer and childhood – mine yellow, Olivia's white. They were hard to come by and expensive because of the time of year.

'Good luck, darling,' Livy whispered, smoothing the shoulders of my dress before I stepped into the church on William's arm. How I missed Daddy then! And I found my legs shaking unexpectedly. But I was collected enough to be able to take in whose faces were turned to watch me arrive. My mother in sky blue with white flowers on her hat, peering anxiously along the aisle at me; Lisa holding Daisy up to get a better view, the little girl's hair scraped up into tiny bunches, and Don's freckled face beside them. Just as I was taking in how smart Douglas looked waiting at the front of the church, I noticed the couple standing opposite Mummy, and realized with a shock that they must be Douglas's parents.

I had felt very uneasy in the weeks before the wedding about the fact that we hadn't been down to visit them, partly because it seemed so odd but also because I was afraid of offending them and of their having a bad opinion of me. Now, though, I felt a new sense of foreboding. If the sight of Douglas's parents was so strange and puzzling, what did this say about how much I knew of Douglas and where he came from?

His description of his mother as a plaster saint could not have been more inaccurate. I assumed this had been his ironic sense of humour. Julia Craven was a small, very curvaceous woman, dressed today in a suit of shimmering candyfloss-coloured silk. Her hair was a more vivid blond than Douglas's, and I could see from where he had inherited his eyes, his full lips and high cheekbones. She was extraordinary rather than beautiful. As I passed her, her gaze fixed frankly on me. I noticed a pungently perfumed smell.

The incongruity of her husband beside her almost made me turn my head to stare back at them. He towered over her, hugely tall and bony with wide, stooped shoulders giving him the look of a bird of prey. He fitted the part of a crusty schoolmaster: the chalky-skinned, lined face, heavy spectacles, the dull tweed suit. His mouth had a bitter slant to it and I felt immediately that I should find him hard to like.

We were married standing as it was difficult for Douglas to kneel. For the first hymn we had chosen 'My Song is Love Unknown'. Singing the beautiful melody I tried to calm my mind. The sight of Douglas's people had really thrown me. I panicked, suddenly breathless, and had to stop singing. I was glad to be facing the front so that no one except Mr Hughes could see my face as my mind raced through a whole assortment of questions.

Who was this man beside me, and what did I really

feel for him? Were those feelings strong enough to bind myself to him for the rest of my life?

'Love to the loveless shown that they might lovely be,' they sang behind me. The words pierced me. Was it pity after all that I felt for Douglas? A powerful combination of pity and desire? What about the kind of love I had felt for Angus, a steadiness between friendship and passion. That knowledge that I could not conceive of the future spent without him. Yet this was precisely what I had been forced to face up to. And now I was giving that future to Douglas.

It's too late now, I said in my thoughts. Please forgive me, Angus.

'Are you all right?' Mr Hughes whispered. I saw Douglas glance anxiously at me.

'Yes,' I replied. 'Thank you.'

I began singing again: 'Here might I stay and sing, no story so divine ...'

Yet suddenly I had an ominous feeling that ours was not a marriage made in heaven.

Chapter 20

After our reception at a modest hotel, we travelled by train to Malvern, having decided that mid-January was no time to head for the coast. I had changed into a new wool dress in a soft mulberry colour and packed warm clothes, imagining wind sweeping the pointed hills and log fires in the hotel. The railway carriage still had its wartime feel of dinginess and lack of attention, and stank of stale smoke. My seat cover was torn and the floor was dirty. By late afternoon a fine rain had begun to fall, obscuring the first, uplifting sight of the Malvern Hills and leaving outside little to see but a grey murk.

Instead of the new relaxation into certainty I had expected once the nerves of the ceremony were over and the marriage an irrevocable thing, I found my mind jittering around, alive with troubling images.

My mother's ambivalent expression as I finally said goodbye to her: was that simply a mother's mixed feelings at her daughter's wedding? Or was she thinking of her own marriage, or of my father's death, his absence at this occasion? I knew she would never explain such a commotion of feelings to me, but I felt a perplexed need to understand.

When I managed to banish these thoughts from my mind, Olivia slid into it instead. Trotting out after William in the vivid blue shantung dress from a side corridor of the hotel, he walking with urgent speed, slipping between other guests as if trying to throw her off. She wore a tense, fixed smile. There was the exaggerated way she embraced Douglas, throwing her body close against his until he protested, 'Steady on, old girl – I'm not as firm on my feet as I might be, you know.' Even when standing still, performing in ordinary conversation, I noticed the way she held her body in the close-fitting dress. She looked posed, self-conscious, like someone fearful of being startled by a camera at any time.

From her, my mind flitted to Douglas's parents. Having no alternative, he had introduced them to Mummy and me as we arrived at the reception on the Hagley Road. Mummy, I have to say, rose to the occasion and was charming, conveying just the right balance of warmth, welcome and regret at their not having made each other's acquaintance before. In a quiet moment afterwards she murmured to me, with a subtle nod in the Cravens' direction, 'What a very odd couple. I hope you know what you're letting yourself in for.'

When I met her properly, Douglas's cameo of his mother as a 'plaster saint' did not seem quite so wild after all. Close up, the age difference between the two of them was hugely evident. Bernard Craven must have been at least twenty years his wife's senior. His hair, once presumably black like his eyebrows, was storm-cloud grey, his face lined, eyes deep-set behind the thick glasses and his manner unapproachable.

I shook his hand, saying, 'I'm so glad to meet you at last,' and received in reply a nod and a slightly absent-minded 'How do you do,' like an acquaintance in a baker's shop, while his wife watched him with wide eyes as if willing him to expand on it.

Seeing her face close up, I realized it was at odds

with the over-bright, predatory-looking clothes she was wearing. She had, like Douglas, a sensuous face, but there was more sweetness to it, and she looked as young for her years as her husband appeared old for his.

'Katie, my dear – ' She reached up to kiss me. Her skin was flawless. I had expected a heavy, brassy voice, but instead it was small and hesitant. She kept glancing anxiously at her husband as if inviting his permission to open her mouth.

'We're so delighted. We've worried so about Douglas – we have, darling.' She took his arm playfully and kissed him, standing on tiptoe. Douglas, who up until now had been smiling and affable with all the other guests, was now blushing and obviously uncomfortable, but didn't resist her kiss. 'He's such a naughty boy about keeping in touch, but we're terribly proud of him. And we're so happy to be here and meet you – aren't we, Bernard?'

Bernard Craven coughed and gave an almost imperceptible nod. Douglas stared at the ground. I saw Julia Craven watching her husband as if gauging whether he was about to speak, in which case she would desist from doing so, his words counting for more than hers. As he didn't, she continued, trying to draw both husband and son into the conversation. I sensed this was an old pattern. She addressed first one, then the other and drew so little response from them that she was left to turn to me in desperation. In her childlike way she appealed, 'I do hope we shall be able to see something of you both?'

'I hope so too,' I said. I found that I meant it.

That evening we ate beef and drank wine in the pale coffee-coloured dining room of our hotel, one of many elegant buildings in the spa town which straggled its way across the smoke-grey hills.

'Douglas,' I said. 'Tell me about your parents – properly, I mean.' Their strangeness made me feel unsure of him.

'Why? What do they matter?' he asked flippantly.

'Don't be ridiculous – of course they matter. They're who you come from – and you haven't managed to prevent me meeting them. But I'd at least like to know why you tried so hard to keep them away.'

At last he told me more, words spilling fast from his lips as if he had them all prepared.

'My father was a postmaster's son in a small town outside Gloucester. He was bright and he became a schoolmaster, even though I'm not at all sure he liked children very much. They met when she was sixteen and he was already thirty-eight. All rather a cliché really: the shy, graceless schoolmaster sinking into bachelorhood – no one interested in him. He wasn't handsome. He's the kind of man no one normally notices very much. But she noticed him – she's like that . . .' His voice softened. 'She sees things in people that others miss and brings them out. She's very compassionate, would do anything for people.' He paused and looked across the room as if stopped by a painful thought. 'She was lovely to look at then, perfect really. Pretty, innocent, very vivacious. You can see it all in the photographs. He was forever having portraits done of her. He was completely taken over by her. I suppose his life began again when he met her. She saved him, and he knows it. But she adored him as well. She was an only child, and I think her parents were reasonable enough people, but she had a great store of affection to give away. They married two years later. When she was nineteen, the next year, reality crashed in on them. I arrived, wonky leg and all. Imperfect. A disappointment. She was very good to me, of course – defensive of me. But she was so protective, she wouldn't let me breathe – give me a chance to get out and cope.

'She's always been dominated totally by my father. It was his age, his manner, and I think she felt guilty for not giving him a proper son. It was he who ruled they must have no more children because the first pot was cracked, so to speak.' Douglas gave a self-mocking laugh. 'If this one's like this, think what the next one might be like, was his attitude. He's an arrogant man, and cold. I suppose their courtship was the one aberration in his life. And she still loves him. Heaven knows why. She was so young when she married him and in some ways she still is. Didn't she strike you as girlish?'

'In a way.' I thought of her letter to me. 'She must be strong, though.'

The cheeseboard arrived at our table and we cut slices of Leicester and Wensleydale to eat with water biscuits, luxurious in this austere time.

'Your father looks so bitter,' I said, thinking back to the man's sour features. 'Why would that be? Not because of you, surely? He ought to be proud of all you've achieved.'

'Things built up over the years,' Douglas said evasively. He reached out and took one of my hands in his. 'Can we change the subject now? I'd really prefer to leave them out of tonight.'

My curiosity was still unsatisfied, but I agreed.

'You must miss your father,' Douglas said kindly. 'Especially today. It seems tragic to die so near the end of the war.'

I nodded slowly. 'He was a pacifist – I expect I've told you. When the war ended and those pictures of Bergen-Belsen and the other camps were all coming out, it was the only time my mother allowed me to see her cry for him. She was crying partly about the terrible things in the pictures, of course, but she said to me, "Thank God your father didn't live to see this." And I understood exactly what she meant. Although he had worked with so many people in all walks of life, and seen some awful things, he still had such strong beliefs in the sanctity of people. There was a kind of innocence about him.'

Douglas squeezed my hand. 'I'm sorry I didn't meet him.'

We sat talking over our coffee, well fed, warmed by the cosy room and suddenly intimate. I relaxed, unburdened of the painful thoughts that had marred the train journey. We ordered more coffee, delaying the moment of going upstairs, luxuriating in the sense of anticipation.

As soon as we were in our room our hands were pulling at each other's clothes. Our lips opened up to each other's, and I pulled his body in close to mine. He seemed startled at my passionate response to him, drew back and looked at me, and I could see the urgency in his eyes.

'Stand still,' he ordered. 'I want to undress you.'

I realized only afterwards how prominent in his mind was the thought that he was the first person to do this. I waited, my legs unsteady with longing for him. Both of us were breathing fast, shallow breaths. Douglas's physical presence had always had a strong effect on me and now I could allow those feelings to be satisfied. He slipped off my wool dress, slip, stockings, camisole and the rest of my underwear, his hands trembling as he loosed my breasts. Without giving me the chance to do the same for him, he began to tear off his own clothes, struggling impatiently with his tie and collar studs. He turned his back to me as he removed the last of his clothes. I had never seen him naked before. Shivering, I looked at the broad top half of his body, the strong straight back. His legs were very white, the bad one slightly thinner than the other. He turned, very bashful suddenly, braving both the exposure of his leg and his obvious arousal. At first he couldn't look at me, as if he was afraid that having seen, I would reject him.

But I wanted him for everything he was. 'Come here,' I said. 'Please.'

His hands flickered over my body, lightly, then with more firmness and confidence. He stood back from me a little, not allowing the lower part of his body to touch me. His hands moved over my breasts, waist, back, and then, as if he could no longer resist, his fingers stroked quickly between my legs. I responded, moving my hips forward, eyes closed.

'My God,' he cried. His voice was harsh and loud.

I opened my eyes. 'Sssh. People will hear you. Whatever's the matter?'

His face wore an incensed, cheated expression, lips tightening. 'You know exactly what you're doing! You're not a virgin are you?'

Half stunned, I looked into his livid face. 'No.'

He turned abruptly and limped towards the window. 'You've made a proper fool of me. I should have seen it that day in the garden. You'd have had all your clothes off if I'd let you. I might have known – just like her.' There was a bitter conviction in his voice.

'Who?' I was bewildered. I folded my arms across my goosepimpled breasts, shivering now from the cold.

'My dear sweet mother.' He was silent for a moment, then spoke very fast, his back to me.

'Go with anything she would. Almost, anyway. D'you really think she was faithful to my exhumed mummy of a father? There were a number of them on and off as I grew up. After all, she was lovely, wasn't she? Sympathy and intimacy were what she wanted. And the young men with their tight skin and vigorous bodies wanted her for her hips and breasts, those eyes, for the sparkling life she gave off. And they made her laugh and stay young. I had to lie for her sometimes and I found out how easily it comes. He always knew, of course. But they didn't stop needing each other. That's the power they've always had over one another – the dependence – each afraid of losing the other's love. The more he withdrew, the harder she tried for him. It was poison – the house was full of unspoken rage all the time. And I moved between them like a symbol of their warped marriage.' His voice began to break up. 'She doesn't know who she is. She's a child, a butterfly, a whore...' He controlled himself. I stood waiting, frozen.

'You went with...?'

'Angus. Yes.'

'I thought your relationship with him was innocent.' He seemed to force out the words.

'Douglas – ' I went closer to him, finding it unbearable talking in this distant way. 'You didn't ask. It's not something I could just come out with easily. I loved Angus. And of course, the war ... We lived from day to day. Every time he came home on leave we knew we might never see each other again. And the last time we happened to be right. If it hadn't been for the war it would have been different.'

'You'd be married to him, wouldn't you?' Douglas asked miserably.

'Most likely.' I kept my voice gentle. 'But there's no point in thinking like that. Angus is dead, Douglas. It's you I'm married to. You can't go through our marriage being jealous of a ghost. It's absurd.'

'A woman should be a virgin on her wedding night,' he said peevishly. 'It's what a man expects.'

'I'm sorry.' I put out my hand and touched the top of his arm. He didn't shake me off. 'There's nothing can be done now. All I can say is, it's you I want.'

He turned and looked at me hard then, his blue eyes searching mine with frightening intensity. 'How do I know I can trust you?'

The question grated on me. 'You can't know. That's what trust is about. I shan't be unfaithful to you.'

We were both very cold and I took his hand and led him to the bed where we got in under the covers. The shock of the sheets made us shudder. I put my arms round him. This was someone I wasn't used to, this weak, exposed Douglas, deeply insecure. After a moment he laid his head on my chest and I moved my body closer to him.

'That's right,' he said, his sarcasm less wholehearted now. 'Throw yourself at me.'

Silently I stroked him with my hand until we were both warmer. He began to move his face against my skin.

'Katie – I want us to be together so much.'

And he began touching me very fast, almost perfunctorily; breasts, stomach, thighs and momentarily between my legs, removing his hand with a jerk as if I'd bitten him. His face was tense.

'It's all right,' I reassured him. I raised my head and

pulled him to me, kissing him, trying to inject some warmth into our lovemaking when all I could find was a hurried kind of desperation as if he wanted it over.

His movements became urgent suddenly. He tried to climb on top of me but got caught up in the sheet and had to kneel up to free himself.

'Lie back,' he ordered abruptly.

He flung himself on me. 'Quickly – for God's sake.' He was too high, against my stomach and I arched my body under him. But he lay very still suddenly. His face creased, agonized, hands gripping the pillow behind my head.

'No.' Now he was almost sobbing. 'No, no.' He sank his head down beside me and gave a sigh which I felt right through his body. Gradually I felt the wetness between us. He began to shake and I knew he was crying.

Eventually, raising his head a little he said, 'I couldn't have deflowered you anyway, could I?'

We lay there for a long time and I stroked him like a child. He was too deep in his own feelings to notice the tears on my face.

'Don't worry, darling,' I whispered. 'We've got the rest of our lives for this, haven't we? It'll get better.'

Chapter 21

It might have got better had things been different. Had it not been for Olivia.

In May, the Kemps sent her away.

'So where is she?' I demanded of Elizabeth.

'She's having a spell in hospital.' She had invited me in, but we remained standing in that bleached, fussy drawing-room. She fiddled with a silver cigarette case, turning it round and round in her hands.

I had re-established more contact with the Kemps over the past months, especially seeing the state Livy was in. I felt for them, disturbed as they were by her depressed listlessness interspersed with loud, over-excited behaviour But now I could feel my civility slipping fast.

'Where?' I asked. 'I'll go and see her.'

'It's not that kind of hospital.'

'What d'you mean?' I was afraid of her answer.

She couldn't meet my eyes. 'She's in All Saints.'

All Saints, the mental hospital on the north side of the city. Part of an old, forbidding complex of institutions: asylum, prison, workhouse, shoulder to shoulder, only separated from each other by high brick walls.

'My God!' I was horrified. 'Why? I mean I know she's seemed very overwrought at times, but surely things weren't that bad?'

Speaking in a whisper, Elizabeth said, 'We didn't

know what else to do. You've only seen a little of what she's been like. Her behaviour has been horrible. I can hardly bear to think of it. She's been going with men like a . . .' She wrung her hands. 'Alec felt he'd lost control of her. Just a little spell in there, he said, to bring her back to her senses.' She began to sob quietly, her shoulders heaving.

'Alec says, Alec says,' I stormed at her. 'Don't you ever think or say anything for yourself, you pathetic woman? Or at least for your own daughter? He's not God, he's just a man, and a pretty unprincipled one at that.'

'It's not his fault,' she cried, gulping and sobbing. 'It's all my fault. I am a pathetic woman. I am!'

'What is the *matter* with you?' I was inflamed, unable to see anything but my fury. 'Don't you realize how difficult it is to get someone released from a mental institution once you've had them certified? And you have, I take it?'

Elizabeth crumpled. I found myself looking down on the pins in her blond pleat of hair as she knelt in front of me. 'I don't know,' she said. 'I don't even know that. Help me, Katie. You're so strong. As strong as he is. Help me. I don't know what to do.'

'Help you?' I blazed at her. 'Why should I help *you*? But I'll do whatever it takes to help Olivia. And damn the pair of you – damn you!'

I turned and left her kneeling with her beautifully coiffured head pressed to the floor, weeping with harsh, broken sounds. My feeling at the time was that it served her right.

But I also shared with her a terrible sense of guilt. I'd seen for myself that things were not right with Livy and had done nothing. I was preoccupied with my own concerns, and also I simply didn't know what to do. She had needed help – perhaps for a lot longer than I realized – and I hadn't responded. What sort of friend could I call myself?

* * *

OLIVIA

Other people can love. Katie loves, but I have not learned how. She cries when babies are born. I think that's a kind of love. She cares for other people's children. But I have never been able to make things turn out right. Everything I touch curdles. I am like brown spots on apples or the monster skulking under the stairs.

My initial training in the WRNS is at Mill Hill. The Wren officer who interviews me looks as if she is in the wrong place, as if she has just stepped out of her kitchen fresh from bottling fruit.

She asks, 'What were you up to before the war?'

'I was a pianist.' The words stride out of my mouth. I want it to be true. It ought to be true.

She frowns at my forms. 'It says here you have secretarial qualifications.'

We all hear this regulation: we are to 'be amenable to naval discipline and put service before family ties'. To me this is beautiful, a kind of psalm. I want it in embossed silver letters across my wall. It makes my life feel narrow and simplified like a nun's. I am free.

I hope freedom will make me clean. I can be a child and begin again. Like any child I need love.

My first job is at Southampton. I am Personal Assistant and shorthand typist for —. I don't want to give his rank or write his full name. People can make things out of anything. His wife lives inland in Hampshire. He is Peter. Just Peter. He is strong and lean with a face lined beyond his years, possibly by sea and weather. His nose is large, with character and authority. He has strong, square nails and I watch his hands move over paper, reach for pens, lift the telephone receiver. After days, only, alone in that small square office I know his eyes are on my hands, on my curved body, his eyes piercing me when he believes my attention is away from him. We match each other in our dark blue uniforms. I know we must touch, skin on skin.

I wait a long time because this is different. It hurts me, is fish hooks under my skin. With others it is I who decide, who take charge, because it is nothing. With Peter I am paralysed, cannot flaunt, at times can barely speak. I watch him work so hard. He is very tired and I want to comfort him. The air takes on life between us.

We are forever working late. When it happens he pushes his chair back in a rush and stands behind mine. My hands move like machines on the typewriter until I am trembling too much. My breaths are thin as wafers. My body feels scraped raw, waiting for his touch. I have never felt this before, so tilted and falling.

He says, 'I can't get through another day without touching you.'

It is not skin on skin because there's no time. It's buttons and layers of clothes and a hard floor. I no longer know what I am doing. I have not known I could want a man, that my body could cry out and hurt until it's losing me, leaving me behind. I hear myself moaning and my teeth are biting into stiff cloth and flesh and hair and the room is rocking and my head crashes back and forth and more words spill out of my mouth as he does it to me and I am there and not there.

When everything slows and the room is still he's climbing away from my body, fast. He says 'Christ', and his voice is small and frightened. When our clothes are straightened out he is giving me looks across the room from the sides of his eyes. My face is bleeding.

He has me moved to another office. I know it's his way of showing remorse because of that cold wife. He never talks about her but I know she's cold like cod on a slab. I don't take it personally. Liaisons of that kind are naturally frowned on in the forces. I leave some time before seeking him out. Then I think he needs encouraging, that he might be afraid he's hurt my feelings.

I telephone then, every day. Of course the new secretary answers. She says, 'Peter' (she doesn't actually say Peter of course) 'is not able to speak to you at present.'

And I say, in my best Wren voice, 'Perhaps you could tell him it's a matter of the utmost urgency?'

I try to see him, but he is never alone, and is colder than the winter sea. The nose takes on a look of cruelty. I write. I wait outside his quarters. His face looms in my sleep. Eventually I go to his office, in tears, though I haven't meant to cry. The secretary is still there, blond, trim and impassable as a shield for him. Following that they move me away from Southampton.

Since that I have been with men a lot. Anyone's. Everyone's. Other Wrens won't speak to me. Officers' groundsheet, and not just officers. It's something I can do well, when I don't care for them at all. There's a comfort in a man's body, but I am playing it, I never lose myself. I am supreme for those moments. I'm queen, jewelled with ice and thorns.

They never come back to me. They're coated in a thick rime of disgust. I don't allow myself disgust.

* * *

As days, then weeks passed, I became almost savage with anxiety about Olivia. At that time I was taken over by it and it felt as if nothing and nobody else mattered. Just as when Alec had imprisoned her in her bedroom all those years ago, my energy was all directed into thinking how I could help her and release her.

It was not a good start to our marriage. We stayed at the house in Chantry Road, which was an arrangement Douglas was happy with, but made me feel I had not yet graduated fully from being a child, and I was restless and perverse. Douglas was working very hard as ever, pushing himself on, conscientious to the point of obsession, and I suppose lonely. He found it difficult to talk to men his own age, all returning now with their stories of war. Now and then he talked about moving on, finding a job in London. Each of us seemed shut away in our own thoughts and concerns.

We lived chiefly on the top floor of the house, which in itself was equivalent to a spacious flat. We had an arrangement whereby we only ate with Mummy at weekends, if she was not working. In fact she had few weekends off and we did not see a lot of her. Mostly I prepared meals for Douglas and myself after work, chatting often with Mrs Drysdale who still came in daily, carrying them up to our living room which looked out over the garden. Douglas often worked odd hours too, covering evening meetings, and then I ate alone. Sometimes recently it had been a relief to do so.

'You're not here with me at all, are you?' he said one

evening as we ate mutton chops and vegetables. 'In your head, I mean.'

I looked across at him guiltily. He was eating fast, his tie off, shirt unbuttoned at the neck, keeping his eyes on his plate as he spoke. Our clock on the mantelpiece seemed to tick too loudly.

'I'm sorry. I'm just so worried about Livy.'

Douglas helped himself to more carrots. 'It's a shame, of course,' he said with his horrible journalistic detachment which sometimes made my blood boil. 'Terrible, those places, from what I gather. But I can't understand why it is you're so attached to her. Nice girl of course, but she is off-centre you know. She was even flirting with me at our wedding. I don't see what she's done to merit such blind devotion.' The tone of his last words was edged with sarcasm. I chose to ignore it.

'It's very hard to put it into words.' I was trying to explain it to him and to myself. 'You never saw her as she used to be. We've been friends for so long – I just can't help loving her.' My voice became high and tearful. 'And I can't bear to think of her locked away in that place.'

Seeing me cry, Douglas was immediately full of concern. He pushed his chair back and came and leaned over me, an arm round my shoulders. 'Don't cry, my darling. I hate to see it.' He stood stroking me with the immense gentleness he could sometimes summon, as I wept, feeling angry and helpless.

When I'd had a cry, I said, 'You finish your meal. I'm all right.' I polished my specs on my napkin. Sniffing, I tried to smile at him.

Douglas beamed at me across the table. 'My darling, I do love you.'

I was gradually learning that when I came to Douglas

tearful and needy was when he could best cope with me. He always did love me most in my weakness.

I went to the hospital. The walls were very high and the iron gates locked. All that could be seen of the inside was the tops of the trees. It took me some time to find the entrance, walking round the wide perimeter of the hospital grounds.

On Lodge Road I heard voices calling desperately to the unseen world. They were men's voices. One was shouting, 'Hello? Hello? Is anyone there? Can you hear me? Hello?' On and on. Another voice, high and strangely sexless, was insisting, 'Tell her. Tell Doris I'm coming, Friday. Tell Doris I'm coming.'

It was a beautiful spring day. I couldn't associate my sweet friend with this place. Nor, of course, could I get in.

I wouldn't leave the Kemps alone. I went round to the house almost daily.

At first Alec was jovial and defensive. 'She's all right,' he assured me on a day after they'd been to visit. 'A little better, we thought, didn't we, Elizabeth?' His wife nodded dumbly. 'I don't think there's any need for you to feel so crusading about all this, Kate. She's where she needs to be at the moment. None of us like it.' He gave me a challenging look. 'Her being in there isn't a fact we want broadcast, of course.'

'I bet it isn't.'

Alec stepped over to me, leaning down to put his face close to mine. I remembered for a second how I used to dream of him leaning over to kiss me. 'Look here,' he hissed. 'If you let anyone know about this . . .'

I met his gaze, steadily.

'Don't come here again,' he finished in a low voice. He left the room.

Elizabeth began to cry. 'She told us they'd put her in one of those – those things where you can't move your arms.'

'You mean a straitjacket,' I said brutally. I felt like screaming. 'What did you expect? It's a mental hospital. That's what they do.'

'But I thought – being who she is – that they'd be kinder. You know, treat her a bit differently. She's in there with all nature of people.'

'Since when has madness distinguished between classes?'

Elizabeth put her hand to her head in a gesture of despair.

'Who can get her out? Just him?'

She nodded slowly. Her hands were never still as she talked. 'It's not that he wants her in there – you have to understand that. He loves her very dearly. He wouldn't let you see it, of course, but he's so afraid and ashamed of what's happening to her. Of how she is. Things in our family haven't always been – ' She stopped, silenced herself. 'We've been at our wits' end.'

Speaking more gently, I said, 'I'll go and see her. When are visitors allowed?'

Elizabeth looked up at me. 'I don't think they'll let you. They said close family only.' I saw an unusual look of determination enter her face. 'Perhaps if I were to write you a note. You might have to pretend to be her sister. If it had Alec's signature . . .'

'Being who he is,' I quipped. 'But he's hardly going to sign anything for me now, is he?'

Elizabeth looked at me with surprising calm. 'Don't you think I'm familiar with my husband's handwriting by now?'

I stared at her, only grasping slowly what she was saying.

'I daren't write it while he's here. I'll bring it round to your house later.'

As I was leaving, Alec appeared out of his study and I realized he had been waiting for me. His expression was very stern. 'You'd better keep your mouth shut, Katie.'

I was exhilarated suddenly. This man's true colours were showing under the strain and I could be free of him.

'I'll keep it shut,' I said. 'For as long as it helps Olivia.'

That evening an envelope was delivered at our house. The note inside explained that I was Olivia's friend, that we were very close and that it would be beneficial for me to visit. The likeness of the handwriting to Alec Kemp's was so extraordinary that I thought at first Elizabeth had persuaded him to put pen to paper himself. But there was a separate sheet on which Elizabeth had written, 'I'm sure this will do it. Please believe better of me. E. K.'

The following Sunday I took the note to All Saints and was let in through the gate. The hospital was a huge, stately building like a country house, with stained-glass windows above the entrance and sunlight pouring on to its soft-coloured stone.

They wouldn't let me see her. Not because I wasn't a close relative, but because she wasn't, they considered, in a fit state.

In June they had her moved to Arden.

'Alec wanted to get her out of the city,' Elizabeth told me. I always tried to visit the house when she was there alone. 'He's very much afraid it will get out somehow that his daughter's in an institution. He's still hoping to stand at the next election.'

I knew I had a kind of ally in Elizabeth, but I was wary of her. She had clearly decided that for the moment her feelings for Olivia must override her loyalty to her husband. But I saw I had never really known her at all, and she was so conditioned to giving nothing away. I was growing more suspicious about the whole situation. Clearly there was something more seriously wrong with Olivia than the odd outburst of emotion and anxiety she had shown before the war. And all these things were now beginning to build into a sequence of events that I hadn't identified before. I wanted to get to the bottom of it: her unhappiness before the war, her withdrawal from me over those years, and what it was that had tilted her so far over that she had to be speedily put away out of sight.

I knew, though, that I'd never get the answers direct from Elizabeth. Sometimes when she looked at me with those childlike blue eyes and gave her automatic smiles, I wondered what it would take truly to break her into honesty.

Olivia had been in Arden for two weeks when, with Elizabeth, I managed to get into the place for the first time. I had gone alone the week before, carrying with me Elizabeth's forged letter, but they turned me away.

We went together on the sort of day which normally makes you feel glad to be alive. The sky was almost unmarked by cloud and there was a feeling of expectancy in the strong sunlight that I always associate with early summer. But sitting in the cab in which we travelled from Leamington Spa I was churned up inside with apprehension. As we passed under the stone archway at the entrance to the drive I felt as if my heart was going to explode. Even being a nurse, like most people I regarded places like Arden with a kind of flesh-creeping horror. The surface of the curving drive was so rough I was thrown from side to side on the back seat. I watched the place move nearer, a vast brick building, the edge of its roof sculpted into points, looking dark and impersonal.

The grounds at Arden were in a shocking state. The hospital had been used for wounded servicemen during the war and it was only just in the process of adapting back to its normal use. This decrepitude only increased its grimness. It looked terrible. The grass was long and full of dandelions and thistles. The drive itself had clumps of grass growing between the wheel tracks and the flowerbeds were only just identifiable, so choked were they with weeds and branches from the overgrown bushes behind them. The wide view across the front looked more like a cattle field than the grounds of a hospital.

The brickwork of the building itself was stained in places, and the roof, half covered with moss, showed dark gaps where slates had slid off and smashed on the ground where they still lay. The windows were grimy, some of the panes broken, and I wondered if these were in windows of dormitories. The building must have been cold enough in the winter as it was. I could hardly bear to think of Olivia inside there. Already, I felt I had stepped out of the world into a terrible, removed place.

When we told the porter, a leathery-cheeked man, who we had come to visit, he said, 'Crikey – we don't get many visitors coming to see this lot.'

He led us into a large hall and told us to wait. The hall must have been very grand before the war. Its ceiling was high and decorated with ornately carved wood. There were long windows along one side with iron radiators beneath them, which I found a reassuring sight. There was a platform at one end of the room. But once again everything looked dirty and worn. The grain of the wooden floor was obscured by grime and hundreds of round black indentations showed where rows of metal bedsteads had stood.

We waited in silence, not looking at each other, as if we were both ashamed to be there.

I was prepared for Olivia looking different, but when they brought her in, her arm grasped by a muscular nurse, I actually gasped. Her removal from the world outside seemed to have become a physical reality. Everything that had made her beautiful had in a few weeks altered or faded. They had dressed her in someone's green gingham dress of a ludicrously large size which sat limp on her like a sack. Her hair, normally so glossy and curling, hung in flat, lank sheets each side of her face; her cheeks were pale and blemished. She barely raised her gaze from the floor, and when she did, her eyes were empty of expression.

'Livy?' I bent my head to intercept her gaze. I saw myself, guiltily, as I must have seemed to her: larger somehow than this place would allow, face blooming from the air outside, healthy and free in a blue dirndl dress and light coat. She continued to stare at the floor.

The nurse, with cheeks the colour of boiled ham, led her to a chair. When she made no effort to sit on it the nurse pushed her down. The woman's masculine-looking arms bulged out from the sleeves of her tight blue uniform dress and she smelled pungently of sweat. I pulled a chair round to face Livy. The nurse stood over her. 'Could you leave us, please?' I said sharply.

'I've got to stay in the room.' Her voice reinforced

the impression she gave of a man dressed as a woman. She ambled over to another chair by the door. 'You've got fifteen minutes,' she shouted across to us.

Olivia sat quite still, hands clasped in her lap, head down. The top button of the dress was missing and it was so loose that it gaped open, showing her dark, naked nipples. I leaned over and softly pulled it together and pressed it against her body.

After a moment she looked up at her mother and the tears came straight away. 'Mummy, oh Mummy.' She flung herself sideways and buried her face in her mother's shoulder, grasping on to her, knuckles white.

With surprise I watched Elizabeth's steely calm. She held Livy for a few moments, then made her sit up again, almost pushing her away. 'Listen, darling. *Listen* to me. You're not going to be here for long, we hope, but you've got to try and get better.'

'But people don't come out of here.' Livy's eyes were bulging. 'Some of them have been here years and years.'

'You won't be,' Elizabeth said firmly. 'You won't.' I felt they had forgotten I was there.

'Isn't this enough?' Olivia whispered. I watched her white, strained face. 'Haven't I done enough for him? Isn't he satisfied?'

I saw a look of panic flash across Elizabeth's face. She actually shook Olivia slightly. 'What are you talking about? This isn't a punishment. Don't be so stupid. You're here because you're ill and you need help.'

'She died,' Livy said suddenly, her eyes still stretched wide. She perched on the edge of the chair, kneading the fingers of one hand with the other ceaselessly as she talked.

'Who died?' Elizabeth asked sharply.

'Eileen.' She spoke very fast, her voice like that of a

little girl. 'They put her in the side room next to the ward when she went off. They call it going up the stick, the nurses. Eileen went up the stick. Right up – up to the top and she fell off. She shouted and shouted. All day for hours and hours. They went in and tried to stop her – men as well. Crowds of them. But they couldn't and she carried on. Then she went quiet suddenly. They tried to stop us seeing, but we saw anyway when they carried her out. They're always dying. The man comes round every day and asks if they've got any for him. His thinks we don't know what he means, but we do. And Mary says she'll be next because it's waiting for her, always there waiting for her because of what she did years and years ago. Like me . . .'

Elizabeth made a convulsive gesture towards Livy as if to silence her, but she stopped abruptly of her own accord.

'Livy?' I took her hands. Trying to speak calmly, I said, 'You do know who I am, don't you?'

She nodded, and in a tiny voice said, 'Katie.'

'Are all the nurses like her?' I asked, inclining my head a fraction towards the woman who had planted herself over by the door.

Olivia followed my glance, fearfully. 'She's not a nurse,' she whispered. 'She's a miner's wife. Her husband works in the men's side. He couldn't get a job. They're from Cannock.' She added as if incidentally, 'Everybody shouts here.'

Then the little girl voice came back. 'I think I've had some sort of breakdown. That's what Daddy says, and the doctor says so. I can't seem to – manage any more. And they give me things. I don't know what they give me.'

'Give you things?'

'Medicine. White stuff. They don't tell you.'

'It's probably to help you keep calm,' I told her.

'My tummy hurts. I think there's something wrong with my insides.'

'Did you tell the doctor?'

'He said I was imagining it.' She began rocking the upper half of her body quickly back and forth. I saw the nurse's eyes swivel towards her.

'Livy,' I whispered. 'Try and keep still or she'll make you go back now.'

To my shame I found myself half wishing the nurse would take her away from us, out of my sight. I felt utterly helpless. What could I say? It was impossible to talk about anything: the past, the future were meaningless here. Everything was foreshortened into these minutes, here between these walls.

'What day is it?' Olivia asked.

'Sunday,' Elizabeth told her gently. 'It'll always be Sunday when we come, darling.'

'The thing is,' she said, suddenly speaking calmly and firmly. 'They say I'm not well.' She directed a look of piercing malevolence at her mother. 'Nurse Tucker says she thinks I have good reason.'

Suddenly there were tears pouring down her face again. She had a terrible grip on my hands, and appealed to me, not her mother. 'I don't want people to see me like this. Help me, Katie. Help me – please.'

I was filled with panic, choking with it. 'What can I do? I don't know what to do.' I pulled my hands away and took her tightly in my arms as she cried, making loud, jarring sounds which reached higher into shrieks. The nurse was upon us immediately.

'Come on, now,' she said 'That's enough. You come with me.' With rough skill she seized Olivia and pinned her arms to her sides. She was more than a match for her in size and strength.

'I can't go back up there!' Livy screamed. 'Not through all those doors. Don't take me back!'

'We'll come again,' we told her, but she wasn't hearing us.

The last sounds I heard were her screams echoing along the dark corridor, and the sound of a large key being turned. My legs were shaking so I could barely stand.

As our taxi moved down Arden's curving drive, taking us back to the station, I said to Elizabeth, 'What d'you think she meant – about having good reason? What is all this about?'

There was a long silence. I could tell the woman next to me was struggling hard with herself, her eyes glassy with tears. But with an enormous effort she regained control. Wiping her eyes, she looked down and straightened the front of her blouse.

Finally, turning her gaze to the half-open window she said, 'I really don't have any idea.'

'Oh, so you're back at last are you?' Douglas burst out when I walked into the house. The train to Birmingham had been delayed and then I'd refused Alec's offer of a lift and had a long wait for the bus. Douglas was seething with resentment, so much so that he had come downstairs to confront me. Seeing the advent of trouble between us, my mother, with the expression of a prophet whose words have come true, disappeared towards the other end of the house.

In a peevish tone which I had been hearing from him more and more lately, he said, 'I suppose it's too much to expect that you might spend Sunday with your husband?'

I was too tired and upset to point out that often when I did spend Sunday with Douglas, a good part of it consisted of hearing the sound of his typewriter coming from the small study next to our bedroom.

'You know where I've been.' I wanted him to hold me, for something to feel normal and right.

'Do I?' he hurled the words at me. His blue eyes were hard with fury. 'Why should I believe you?'

'Oh for goodness' sake, stop being so melodramatic,' I said. 'D'you really think I'd be making up some story about carting all the way to a mental hospital half way across Warwickshire for my own entertainment?'

'That depends.' He limped badly towards me, accentuating his disability. He did this to goad me, had been doing so increasingly lately. At first it had made me feel guilty, as if I was failing him in some way. Now I was beginning to resent it. I'd certainly had enough of everything for one day.

'It all depends who you were really going to see, doesn't it?'

I stared at him coldly. 'What are you talking about?'

He stood silently for a moment, looking hard into my eyes and I met his stare, angry now.

'Oh, forget I spoke,' he said in a disgusted voice. I wasn't certain whether the emotion was directed towards me or himself.

'I went with Elizabeth Kemp. You know that.'

Ignoring this he moved towards the stairs. 'I suppose there'll be something to eat this evening.'

'Yes,' I agreed flatly. 'I suppose there will.'

When he'd gone upstairs, my mother came back in.

She'd obviously been listening. She walked across the room with a vase of flowers, not looking at me.

'It's no good.' Her tone was brisk and neutral. 'You'll have to put him first. He's not going to be the sort to play second fiddle to anyone.'

'But he's not having to,' I cried, tearful now. 'I'm doing my best. I can't help it if Olivia's ill, can I?'

Mopping a ring of water from the table, she said, 'Perhaps you should think of giving up work.'

'I'd have thought you'd be the last person to suggest that.' But I wondered wearily whether if she wasn't right. Douglas had been so demanding recently, expecting so much from me and never seeming satisfied with what I did. I kept wondering what had happened to the kind, charming man I had married. I felt tired and pulled in too many directions at once.

I told my mother that Douglas and I would eat upstairs that night, given the bad atmosphere between us. We ate our meal in silence, but by bedtime he was repentant.

'I don't know what I said all that for, darling.' He was lying with his head on my breast. 'Don't take any notice of me when I'm like that, will you? I've been alone so long I don't know how to behave with someone. You know I'm only like this because I love you and I need you so much.'

I need you. I need you. Douglas's constant refrain nowadays. He looked round at me, his expression contrite, and I was filled with sudden tenderness for him.

'Can we try it again. Please, darling?'

I'd had to be very careful, very patient with him as a lover. One hint of my own, usually unsatisfied desires, and he built mountains of resentment and insecurity. Almost as soon as he was aroused he had to be in me. Sometimes he left it just too late, and came with agonized embarrassment almost at the first contact of our flesh. When he did manage to hold back until he was inside me it was over in seconds, but he was jubilant with himself.

We did have times of great affection and tenderness, but the frustrations of the bedroom seeped out to affect everything else. It was a huge obstacle to him, something he felt he had to work at, be good at. It was equally frustrating to me, except that I learned this was something he must never be made aware of. I found I was learning to tread very carefully with his moods, tiptoeing round him fearfully.

I turned to him, and we held one another. Half my mind was still occupied with Olivia and I tried to keep it that way. I still found Douglas attractive but I tried to avoid becoming aroused by him because he seemed so incapable of giving me anything sexually. I had begun to think of our love life very much as my wifely duty, more painful in its frustrated expectations than a complete absence of lovemaking would have been.

Douglas began to take his pleasure, running his hands over my body as if testing himself. I was ready for him as he plunged into me, panting with anxiety. He thrust into me once and it was over. He laid his head next to mine as if with relief, then raised it to smile at me, searching my face with his eyes.

'That was good, wasn't it, Katie? I think it's getting better.'

* * *

Things I remember about Arden

Arden is deep in the countryside, ringed by stagnant fields and petrified trees. I thought when they took me there that I was going to my death. They would have absolute control over me. They proposed to bury me alive behind all those doors. Every ten yards along the corridors, doors and more doors, unlocking, slamming, relocking. When they visit me, Mummy and Kate, I come up to them as if from a well, hauled up, up, door after door. From where they sit they can never see the bottom of it nor understand that this is where I have come from. I don't want them to see me like this. And I don't know whether it's yesterday that I saw them or last month because the days run into each other and never change.

I can't tell them. Since I've been here I learn that what we say here is twisted into nonsense to those outside and whatever words I use make them frown, further convinced of my instability. I don't try to speak about the way the staff slam and shout, treating even the doors with hatred, how they edge round the room, their backs to the walls of the ward which are the colour of dead skin, their eyes never leaving us. They are afraid of us. In my opinion they are very odd.

We have reason after all, for being here: that's what I know. Bridget has reason; she's perhaps sixty, gave birth to a dead baby all those years ago. Agnes won't eat the food. She feeds only from the pig bin outside the kitchen. She is heavy and slow like a cow. She lived among cows because she is a farmer's wife. I don't know why she thinks real food is too good for her, but she does have a reason, I know. So many of the others sit and stare, or if they talk I can't make it out; it comes in odd waves and jerks like a jumper unravelling. But I hold this tightly in my head: no one's here without a reason. I know that. The staff, however, choose to be here. What sort of reason is that?

Other things I never tell them
How it feels to wear a shroud of canvas, layers thick, stitched across and re-stitched, and to sleep in sheets of layered and cross-sewn calico, made so strong to stop us hurting ourselves with them. It chafes my skin red. Our ward is twenty strong. Like animals we rise with the light and are in bed at four-thirty, laid out under the high, blistered ceiling, our beds crammed in only a few inches apart. We breathe each other's sour air, smell all of each other's most intimate smells. I sleep between Gladys, a skeleton who wears the sweat perfume of death, and Mary who soils her bed and flies somewhere every night with massive wings and a chatter in her throat. I have never known this class of women before. They don't worry about such distinctions, each wrapped in her own cocoon. It's only the nurses who can't hear my voice and learn about my family without goading me. 'Posh cow.' 'Your Highness.' 'Lady Muck.'

It's a farm here, inside and out. On Sunday mornings they make us bath, all three hundred women, eight at a time, our shrouds in a stinking heap on the floor. The bath nudges sharply against my bones. Women scream and whip the water with their hands. The outlet pipes are four inches thick and I wonder if I could fit down them and be sucked away into the black womb of the sewer. The nurses parade among us shouting and eyeing our bodies.

At mealtimes they are forever counting. No knives

are allowed in the place. The prongs of the forks are an eighth of an inch long. They count them out, count them in. When they shout 'Tables!' we fight for a place at the benches round the pine tables even though we are always, in the end, sitting in the same place. At first I am numb and don't know how to survive. As the days pass I am too hungry and wrangle and cram my mouth with the rest, for one hesitation and the food is down another's throat. Food is all our pleasure here: warmth, comfort, a loving touch.

Am I a Certified Lunatic? I don't even know. No one tells me what Daddy has said to them to make them seal me in. Every morning the man comes to take away the bodies on his covered trolley. The old ladies stay in bed and die, dropping like bugs from the walls. With half-obvious relish he says, 'Any for me today?' He gets 7/6d for each corpse and he gathers them like a bunch of flowers. Will I leave here like that? Perhaps this is the beginning of it, knowing this: that within these dark walls there is another behind which I stand. It is so close it fits my skin, and behind it I am too chilled to feel even despair. The doctor said I might be schizophrenic because I'm thin. I watch others and wonder if I am already as bad. I feel lost.

Some things I don't do

I don't stand for hours in impenetrable silence. The crust of my silence can still be broken.

I don't touch myself intimately when other people can see.

I don't relieve myself in my bed, except during treatment.

When we are outside for our morning shuffle round and round the scabby paths of the airing court, I do not look for leaves, shreds of groundsel, human waste, sycamore seeds to eat, nor do I chew my shoes, the hardest of leather (no laces) which can eventually be devoured after hours of sucking.

But nor do I – their mark of a degree of trustworthiness – get led out to work in the kitchen, garden or laundry.

What I do

When I am allowed near my bed, I find myself standing there for many minutes at a time, not knowing why I am there.

I sit in the dayroom and time must be passing but I can't tell how long, nor can I solve the problem of how to lift and move an arm or leg even when there are alarms and fights on all sides. I look at the shiny wood of the floor and find patterns.

I can't sleep at night. I listen to hours of coughing and muttering and Mary's airborne chatter and women relieving themselves in the privy in the corner. I stretch my eyes open wide to see if there is any hint of light in the sky between the bars of the windows even though there is no reason to hope for tomorrow. I talk to myself as there is no one else. I summon Mozart and Brahms in my head but they refuse to be roused. I call on my Daddy dream.

On first arriving here I am energetic with fright. I charge to the walls and hammer myself against them while high sounds come out of my mouth. 'Up the stick,' they say. 'Side room for her – that'll teach her.'

I am in a room with thick Rexine walls and a curved floor so my mess slides to the gutters at the edges. I am covered by a hard canvas jacket, my arms strapped round me so that I can only buffet my sides and shoulders and head against the yielding wall until I fall. I find myself in here several times, hardly knowing how I got here. When they come to retrieve me I hear spring-loaded bolts snap back. The first time, they bring nurses from the men's wing to help. They charge in clumsily together like fat beetles and there are blue sleeves with white chevroned cuffs round me and a stench of male sweat.

'You could've managed this one, surely?' they bellow. 'She's only a little tiddler!'

After several afternoons in there and the stunning doses of peraldehyde, I sit quiet.

Nurse Tucker knows why I'm here. I haven't told her, but she knows.

* * *

Chapter 22

'Darling, whatever's the matter?'

Douglas followed me, hovering anxiously at the bathroom door as I rushed from our bedroom, still holding the empty cup from my morning tea.

'Are you ill?' He stood at a loss, toes on the edge of the lino in his pale blue pyjamas, as I retched. The tea had brought on instant rebellion from my stomach. I felt better immediately and drank a glass of water, doing fast calculations in my head once more to make sure. I'd missed my last period, I must have conceived during the first half of August, which made me about five weeks pregnant now.

'D'you think you've caught a chill?' Douglas asked, still standing back from me as if I might explode. He rubbed his hand through his unbrushed hair. 'What? What're you laughing at?'

I felt a strong sense of relief. Something I could do for him, and do right. I went and put my arms round him. 'Definitely not a chill,' I said happily, looking up into his perturbed face. 'Darling – we're going to have a baby.'

'A what?' He was so flabbergasted that I laughed even more.

'You do know the facts of life don't you? This has happened the past couple of mornings except you didn't notice. And my period's very late.'

A flush spread across Douglas's face, and I watched his expression break into a bashful kind of wonder. I realized he had scarcely thought himself capable of producing a child.

'Oh, my love.' He sounded awed. His scarred cheek twitched slightly as it did when he felt strong emotion. He held me close. Then he turned brisk, deciding to take charge. 'We must take very, very good care of you. You must give up your job straight away, of course.'

'Nonsense.' I went to the basin and splashed water over my face. 'I've got heaps to do and I can't just give it up now. Exercise in pregnancy is supposed to be good for you. Don't fuss, Douglas.'

But he did fuss. Fuss would be a gentle word for it. That Sunday I was due to visit Olivia. The hospital had agreed to me visiting on my own, and I was anxious to go as often as possible without Elizabeth. We were settling into a pattern of seeing her once a fortnight, on alternate weeks. Elizabeth was occasionally accompanied by Alec. Douglas already resented this. Now it became a symbol, an issue on which to focus his lack of trust and his need to control me in order to feel safe.

'You're not to go,' he ordered on the Saturday afternoon. I was sitting with my feet up looking through a box of books. I realized, as I looked at the old, forgotten titles, that Angus had given me several of them.

'Douglas,' I said quietly. 'Please don't start giving me orders. I'm going to Arden tomorrow. I'm sorry it means not being with you all day, but you did say you had work to do, and I simply have to go.'

'But you need to rest, not keep gallivanting about all over the place. Don't you care about our child?'

'Oh don't be so ridiculous,' I flared at him. I was

really needled by him lecturing me on a subject about which I knew far more than he did. 'I've been out shopping all morning carrying heavy baskets of food for your dinner, which is far more exhausting than sitting on a train to Leamington. But it doesn't even cross your mind to stop me doing that, does it?' I stood up, still holding one of the books, intending to leave the room, but Douglas seized my arm, gripping me tightly.

'Don't raise your voice at me,' he said in an aggressive voice. 'I've provided you with a child. What more do you want?'

I looked up at him coldly. 'Let go of me.'

Douglas loosed my arm and I stood before him, turning the book over in my hands. The soft, leather cover of Angus's gift to me made me feel choked with bitterness. What did I want? To be with someone who I didn't have to tread round so carefully, who didn't want to keep me in a box with a few holes punched in the lid. Someone who could love me properly and let me be.

'I'll tell you what I don't want,' I said, keeping my voice low. I was always conscious of my mother overhearing if she was in. 'I don't want to be treated like a Victorian wife, nor like a member of the regiment. If you want me to respect you then you're going to have to stop being so mistrustful and childish about it. I'm not your mother, so there's no need to behave like your father. I'm going to visit Olivia tomorrow. If you're not happy about that, then I'm sorry, but she's my friend and she needs me.'

Douglas's face had gone tight with fury. 'Everybody needs you, don't they?' he sneered. 'You'll run round after anyone except me.'

He slammed out of the room. Feeling immediately sorry, I ran down after him to the front door, but he was already off down the street, lighting a cigarette. I saw him bend his pale head to the lighted match, watched his painful gait, his jerking angry manner, and thought how much he felt like a stranger to me.

In the railway station, among the unpredictable, jolting movements of the crowds, I felt already that I wanted to protect my unborn child. To warn off anyone who moved too quickly or advanced too close, shielding my stomach fiercely with one hand. It was a feeling I knew Lisa would understand and I longed suddenly to tell her about the baby.

On the journey, rattling through the freshly ploughed Warwickshire fields, I sat sucking peppermints, wondering in what state I should find Olivia. I had observed no change in her during the summer. She remained withdrawn, frozen, and I seldom got her to speak about anything other than the immediate facts of her state or occasionally an event on the ward. I realized suddenly that Olivia and I had never discussed having children or how we might feel about them, and thinking back on that, it seemed a strange lack. I wondered what sort of parents Douglas and I would make. Surely he would see this child as a sign of my commitment to him, make him more able to trust? But I was already beginning to see how quickly communication could break down between us. I had to admit to myself that I was becoming miserable in my marriage.

Olivia was brought in to see me not by the bacon-cheeked nurse this time, but a younger, less buxom woman with a gentle air and a very straight brown fringe between her eyes and her starched white cap. She seemed apologetic and didn't impose a time limit on us, sitting herself quietly by the door as if trying to pretend she wasn't there.

There was something different about Olivia, a slowness, as if to move at all was unbearable for her. Most striking of all was the fact that her hair was now short, lopped in a rough pageboy level with her earlobes.

I loathed asking her how she was. It seemed such an obviously foolish question, almost an insult. Instead I said, 'I like your hair.' In fact, had it been more expertly cut and more often washed, it would have suited her delicate features very well. 'Did you ask them to do it?'

She lifted one hand slowly to the back of her head and stroked her hair vaguely, as if wondering what I meant, and then shook her head. I looked round the room, already feeling desperate for something to say. I had a familiar feeling of wanting to shake her, to force her to talk to me but we had been so long out of the habit of talking, even if she were capable of it now.

'Was there a show or something on yesterday evening?' I asked eventually.

Her eyes rolled up towards the ceiling, before she looked dully down at the floor again, frowning. 'I can't remember.'

I was frightened at the way she spoke. I had tried to hold on to her, believing she would somehow revert to the person she was supposed to be. That with rest and encouragement she would surface again, break through this blankness which was all she seemed able to present to us now. But she was becoming unrecognizable as the person I had known before. I didn't know what to believe about her any more. I began to wonder whether she was really losing her mind, and whether she was, after all, in the right place.

We sat in silence for a moment. Feeling nauseous, I fished a peppermint out of my bag and offered Livy one. She refused the sweet, but suddenly grabbed my wrist, gripping me tightly. Moving closer to her, I smelled a stale, sweaty odour coming from her. Her eyes were stretched wide, terrified.

'You've got to help me.' She spoke in an urgent whisper. 'They're doing things to my head. They took me to a room downstairs and put pads on me, here – ' She let go of me then and pressed her fingers to her temples. 'And electricity went through my head. It hurt worse than anything I've ever known and I couldn't control my body. They held me down . . .' She started to cry, not sobbing, but making high, mewling noises. 'They're going to do it again. They said every day. I can't – I can't – they'll kill me.' She was panting now, seeming beyond tears. 'They can do anything they want.'

I had heard of the new treatment, though never seen it. Electroconvulsive Therapy. The textbook definition: an attempt to stimulate the brain by passing an electric current through it.

'Daddy must have told them to do it.' She seized my arm again as if she thought I wasn't hearing her, or that I might get up and run away. I held her hands, despair sinking deep into me. What could I do when she was in this state? There was silence.

Then Olivia whispered, 'They're going to kill me. I shall never come out of here.'

'I don't understand.' I took her other arm with my free hand, so that we sat locked together. I wanted to keep her from moving about and attracting the nurse's attention. 'Livy, my dearest, dearest friend.' Tears ran down my face. 'Just hang on, please – please, darling. It won't be much longer now . . .'

For a few seconds she sat motionless, her cheeks very white. Her eyes moved across my face, as if searching me for solidity. But her gaze was so strange.

The nurse walked across to us with apparent reluctance. She spoke calmly, with sympathy. 'I'd better take her back.'

Olivia sagged, exhausted. I wanted to make promises to her, but could think of none I could offer honestly. Instead I kissed her as she stood passively in my arms.

As she left me, I said, 'I'll do something Livy . . .' She didn't look back as she was led away.

Outside I took deep breaths of the cooling air, leaning against the wall trying to control my rising nausea. I failed, and vomited wretchedly into a tangle of shrubbery at one end of the building.

I knew Douglas would be timing my journey back from Arden that day and, in spite of himself, adding each moment of what he considered my lateness to his catalogue of my wrongs. But I felt defiantly that his needs in this case were less important. I had to talk to someone. I also needed one of Lisa's cups of sweet tea. I got off the bus early and walked through to Stanley Street.

The light was going and in the narrow entry it seemed darker. I found the court unusually quiet. The children must have been inside eating. I could hear the sound of a wireless through an open window and cutlery clattering and voices.

'Surprise surprise,' Lisa said, opening the door to me. She was more relaxed now Don was home. She turned to him. 'Look who's come to pay us a call.'

Don nodded at me as I peeled my coat off, raising his round, freckled face for a second from the job he was absorbed in at the table. He was dismantling the clock which had long sat silently on the mantelshelf. He was a quiet man with an easy manner and I never felt awkward in his presence.

'We've just finished tea,' Lisa said. She was in her apron still and the old slippers which by a miracle were still surviving. 'Here – ' she pulled a chair out from the table, 'sit yourself down.' She chased the boys outside but allowed Daisy to stay. I gave her a peppermint. 'You look terrible,' Lisa remarked, pouring tea.

'I'm pregnant.'

Lisa stopped half way to the table with Don's teacup. 'You're not! 'Ere – d'you 'ear that, Don?'

'Course I 'eard – not deaf am I? Congratulations,' he said, giving me a shy smile.

''Appy about it, are you?' Lisa asked, sitting down wearily. She saw my face. 'Course you are. Lovely.' She looked across at her husband. 'Shall we tell 'er, Don?'

He gave her a mischievous grin across the table. 'Tell 'er what?'

Lisa tutted. 'Tek no notice of 'im, Kate. I'm expecting as well.'

We both laughed and exclaimed and compared dates. Lisa's baby was due a couple of weeks earlier than mine.

'A baby brother or sister for you, Daisy,' I said to the little girl, who was standing beside me.

'If it's a girl I'm going to call 'er Alice,' she said, cheek bulging with the sweet.

Lisa shrugged. 'Don't ask me. She's just taken a fancy to it.'

Don got up and lit the gas before carrying on with his job. It hissed quietly behind Lisa's head. She sat with her teacup in one hand and a cigarette in the other. After a time I started to tell her about Olivia.

Lisa listened, frowning. 'Olivia Kemp?' she interrupted. 'You mean . . .?'

'Councillor Kemp's daughter, yes.'

'You never said you was friendly with 'er!'

'She was away most of the war. I didn't see her.'

Lisa let out her loud laugh. 'Bit different from the likes of us, I'll bet!'

I was trying to protest at this when I saw Don looking up at us, frowning.

'Kemp.' He turned to Lisa. 'Isn't that – ?' He gave a jerk with his head, eyebrows raised meaningfully.

'You mean Kemp's,' I said. 'His factory's on Birch Street.'

Don shook his head impatiently. 'Anyone knows that. No, I mean that Joyce, up in nine court – you know.'

Understanding spread across Lisa's face in the form of a blush. 'The one with the babby?'

Don's face reddened as well and he looked down again, realizing the full implications of what he'd said.

Lisa's eyes widened. 'Come to think of it, I've even seen 'im round 'ere once or twice. Course, I didn't put two and two together at the time.'

My heart began beating faster. That foggy night towards the end of the war came back to me clearly.

Lisa and Don both looked very awkward. 'Sorry,' Lisa said. 'We shouldn't be saying all this.'

I put my cup down and sat forwards. 'Are you saying that this woman – Joyce – has carried a child by Councillor Kemp?'

Lisa grew flustered, her cheeks red. 'Look, we don't want to make any trouble It was just 'earing the name

... I believe 'e gives 'er money – takes care of 'er a bit. 'E puts 'isself about a bit round 'ere like ... Only in 'er case there was summat to show for it. I s'pose 'er 'usband thinks it's 'is.'

'I see,' I said grimly. I sat back and automatically stroked Daisy's hair, my mind lurching from question to question. 'Look, this is very important. Can you be sure that Alec Kemp is the father of this child?'

'Well, no one can tell you that for sure, except Joyce, of course. But she ain't normally one for – you know, you wouldn't call 'er fast. And she used to work at Kemp's before the babby.'

Thinking aloud, I said, 'I wonder how I can find out.'

Lisa looked at me doubtfully. 'If it was me I wouldn't thank you for asking, but I s'pose you could go and see 'er.'

I lifted Daisy on to my lap. 'Oh, I will,' I said with such determination that Lisa looked puzzled. 'I shall be round there like a dose of salts.'

By the time I got home it was after seven o'clock. I was two hours later than usual. My mother was waiting for me.

'He's out,' she said drily. 'I gave him a meal, and he's gone to have a drink with someone from the paper.'

I felt myself breathe easier.

'Thank you, Mummy. I'm very grateful.'

She looked sternly at me. 'Why are you so late?'

'I called in to see Lisa Turnbull on the way back.' I tried to enlist Mummy's support. 'I needed to talk to her. Was Douglas getting very impatient?'

'I think for your sake it's a good job he went out. He was very short with me.' She relented for a moment.

'You look tired. It's a lot, all this back and forth to see Olivia. I've got some soup over – would you like some?'

I could have wept with gratitude. She sat with me in the kitchen as I ate.

'How is Olivia?'

'They're giving her electric shock treatment.'

Mummy winced. 'What a terrible thing.'

I nodded, my eyes filling. I looked down into my soup bowl, not finding it easy to show emotion in front of Mummy.

Suddenly, not looking at me, she said resolutely, 'It's no good. If you don't put Douglas and your marriage first you're soon going to be in trouble. You can't neglect him. He needs your attention . . .'

'Look – I do want to put it first,' I protested. 'I do. But I love Olivia too. And Douglas – ' I broke off, the frustrations of the past months welling up in me. Cheeks hot and red, I tried to talk. 'He's so possessive you see, and insecure. And it's partly because – ' I stumbled over the words. 'We have – there are some difficulties . . .'

My mother held up her hand abruptly. 'Problems in the bedroom are between you and him. It's your marriage. None of that's anyone else's concern. And anyway,' she added, 'he's managed to get you pregnant at least.'

I remembered Joyce Salter quite well. I had called to see her after the baby was born about a month before VJ Day. She lived with her mother in court nine, Stanley Street, and had told me that her husband had been called up for National Service. Thinking back to her delicate, pretty features, I could see what Alec Kemp would have found attractive about her.

Nervously I waited at her door, trying to prepare what I might say. I understood how she'd feel about me barging in to ask the identity of her baby's father. She would most likely find my questions odd and insulting.

Fortunately she was alone with the child, so I didn't have to contend with her mother, a mean woman whose features must once have resembled Joyce's, but had since spread and roughened.

For a few seconds Joyce looked very perturbed at seeing me. Then her face cleared. 'Miss Munro, isn't it?' I didn't bother to correct her. 'Couldn't think who you were for a minute then. Come in. Take no notice of the mess. It's our Maureen.' She indicated the crawling baby. 'Shocker for mess she is.'

I smiled. The small amount of confusion in the room was not such as could have been caused by the baby, who was in any case settled to play in an orange crate. Sitting down, I asked after Joyce's health and had a good look over Maureen. She was a well-covered, healthy-looking baby, bar the catarrh which dogged just about everyone in the area. She gazed at me with interested dark eyes. I had a sudden instinct that she looked very much as Olivia must have done as a baby.

'Joyce – I'll tell you why I'm here,' I said. 'I need to ask you something which I'm sure you'll think very strange and probably even rude, and I wouldn't dream of coming here like this if it wasn't very important. I'd like to assure you that I'll keep anything you tell me in confidence.'

Joyce looked very anxious at my serious tone, and took refuge in wiping Maureen's face with a cloth. 'Whatever did you want to know?'

'I need to know the name of Maureen's father.'

Blood rushed across Joyce's face. She pulled a hanky

from her sleeve and stood worrying it between her hands. 'My 'usband's away in the army. I told you . . .' She was a timid woman, not the sort to throw me out like some would have. She had a persecuted look, conscious of having done wrong. Trying to stand up for herself, she dared to say, 'What's it to you, anyway?'

'Look,' I assured her. 'Strange as this may sound, the reason I'm asking you this actually has nothing to do with you and I shan't want to trouble you again. I'll explain to you in a moment. What I need to know is – is Maureen's father Alec Kemp?'

Joyce grew very flustered, wringing the hanky, starting to cry. 'My 'usband mustn't find out.' She looked into my eyes, her face stricken. 'Who told you? No one was to know. I've never breathed a word. 'E said if I told a soul, 'e'd stop the money.'

I stood up and walked round the table to her. 'Joyce – I'm afraid people have a way of working things out. Look, please, I don't want to upset you.' Shyly I touched her shoulder and she gazed up at me, eyes wide, pleading for reassurance. 'I can guarantee your husband will never hear anything from me. I'll tell you what this is all about. Let's sit down, shall we?'

While Joyce listened, wiping her eyes, I explained briefly about Olivia. 'I'm sure you can understand why I'm desperate to get her out of there. The only way I can think of is to force him into it. My knowing will make no difference to your position. He won't stop the payments to you. You see, he's well aware that my husband's a journalist. We could make things rather awkward for him.'

Joyce was watching me in bewilderment. 'His poor daughter,' she said. 'What a thing.'

'Do you know of any others?' I asked her.

She paused. 'I know of others 'e's bin with.' She rolled her eyes to the ceiling with a hard laugh. 'Thought I was the one and only, didn' I? Jackie Flint – up at eight court. Lost a baby a month ago.'

'And she said it was his?'

Joyce looked at the floor, blushing. 'She's a pal of mine. We was both on the line at Kemp's.' She raised her eyes to me and they were red and filling with tears again. 'I never meant for it to 'appen. 'E's not like the others, you see. I can't say 'e forced 'isself on me or anything like that. 'E just has a way of making you feel sort of special – like the only person in the world. I can't explain it to you. I s'pose I were in love with 'im. I'd 'ave done anything 'e wanted.'

'I know,' I told her gently. 'Don't worry – I believe you. I haven't come here to judge you, Joyce. But I would like you to tell me one more thing. D'you know when I'm likely to find him around here?'

Chapter 23

Silence began to take root between Douglas and me. Silence which I began to imagine might never be broken. There were days when almost the only times we spoke were in response to my mother. That was when Douglas was there at all. He worked every possible hour, late into the evenings. Isolation and work were familiar havens for him.

I began to panic. I was being punished and I felt I deserved no punishment. I imagined bringing up a child in this silence.

In October it was Douglas's birthday.

'Will you be free tomorrow night?' I asked the morning before. We were both dressing, Douglas careful and immaculate as ever. 'I thought I'd book a table at the Midland. It'd be nice to celebrate properly.'

I'd caught Douglas's morning mood, brisk, already with the aura of the newsroom about him, not welcoming intimacy. 'I can be. I'll check.' He fastened his tie. 'Good idea of yours.'

I moved forward to embrace him but he kept me at a distance, allowing only a light kiss on the cheek. 'Breakfast. I need to be off.'

The next evening I put on the soft wool dress I had worn after our wedding. I wanted Douglas to remember it; the dress, the day. He was late arriving, but not enough for me to have become edgy. I waited in the bar, self-consciously a woman alone. When he finally came limping across the smooth carpet I met his eyes and smiled. We had spent too many days avoiding each other's glance. Douglas could see I was making a special effort, and with an intensity of relief which surprised me, I realized he was going to respond.

'Sorry I'm late.' He returned my smile and kissed my cheek. There was a glow about him, some pent-up excitement. 'Just fetch a drink. Another for you?'

We sat in the bar for a time, Douglas smoking and talking over the day with what felt like exaggerated courtesy. Once we had settled in the softly lit dining room and ordered some food, Douglas sat back, looking into my face 'I've got some news.' I had not imagined the excitement. 'I was talking to a chap on the *Express* today – '

'The *Daily*?'

He nodded, lighting another cigarette. 'He said there's nothing doing so far as jobs are concerned at the moment. Too many demobbed and would-be journalists. But he said he knew I'd been on the job all through the war and he's read some of my pieces – he liked the bits I did on the blitz. So he said I can send stuff in on a freelance basis, and as soon as there's a job going, he'll be in touch.'

'Douglas, how marvellous for you!' I cried. 'Well done – you thoroughly deserve it.'

Douglas leaned back and took a satisfied drag on the cigarette. 'So, we'll be heading for the big city. Not before time, I'd say. I mean Birmingham's all right, but it just doesn't have London's – ' he waved his arms expansively, 'atmosphere, excitement. Does it? Even the Hun couldn't knock the stuffing out of London.'

I watched him, trying to keep my own feelings at

bay. I couldn't leave here now. Birmingham was home. I didn't want to go to a strange place to have my baby, and above all, there was Olivia.

'How long d'you think you'll have to wait?' I asked, forcing myself to sound bright and enthusiastic.

'Anyone's guess. Weeks, months, who knows, darling. But the main thing is' – he gave a gleeful smile – 'I feel sure I'll be in there before long.'

This was not the moment to argue. Douglas, of course, took it for granted that I would do whatever suited him. After our food had been laid in front of us, I raised my glass. 'Happy birthday, darling. And I hope it turns out to be a very successful year for you.'

We ate in silence for a few minutes. Douglas's cigarette sent up a thin thread of smoke from the ashtray.

'I wanted to try and clear the air a bit,' I said eventually. 'Things have been so awkward between us recently, and – Douglas, we shouldn't be like this with each other. It's no good, especially with the baby coming. It's wretched, it really is.'

'Oh, look, I'm sorry.' Douglas reached for my hand across the table. 'I know I've seemed rather preoccupied the last few days. It's just my way of ... Sometimes I find it difficult. Things don't feel quite right. Not how I think they should be.'

'What d'you mean?' For a moment I was encouraged. I shared this feeling. I wanted to take apart the whole puzzle of our marriage, to examine and restore it. But there were areas of it we could never reach with words. What happened between us in bed was something we could never even begin to discuss, even if this had been the place to do it. It was too fraught, too embarrassing. And the fact that I was now pregnant had apparently convinced Douglas that all was well in that department.

But there were all the other uneasinesses between us. I hoped that Douglas, too, wanted to face and alter them.

'Well, for one thing,' he began, 'I think we should move out of your mother's house.'

I was taken aback. 'But you were the one who wanted to live there!' Having chafed at our living there when we were first married, I was now resigned to it. I was looking forward to our baby being there too, to her growing up in the ample space, the garden . . .

But he was already slamming something else at me. 'And really, Kate, it's time you stopped working.'

'I am going to stop. I've only a few months to go!'

'So why not give up now? I don't like the idea of my wife working. And all those slummy houses around St Joseph's. A married woman shouldn't be out doing things like that. You should be at home, not out hobnobbing with all those rough women. I'm sure it can't be good for the baby. Heaven knows what you might pick up there.'

I could feel a harsh outburst of temper rising. I did have feelings of guilt about being out at work, because most married women I knew were at home. My mother had already taken me to task several times on the subject. I resented this pressure to give up a job I enjoyed so much. But I knew I must keep my temper under control. If I lashed out at him now for his pompous preoccupation with his own needs the conversation would be scuppered.

'I can't see that a few more months will make any difference.' I spoke softly, squeezing his hand. 'And then the baby'll be here, and I'll be at home just how you want.'

'Then why can't you give up now?'

'I've agreed to work until February.'

'They'll find someone else. Please, my darling.' He looked imploringly at me. I saw his cheek twitch slightly. 'All I've ever wanted was a proper family. Mother at home, children. Coming home to you at the end of the day. Doing what families are supposed to do, not like mine. More like yours.'

'Mine? A father who we hardly ever saw, a mother who was mostly bored stiff, resenting every moment her talents were being wasted, and a brother and sister who despise each other? It's true that we held together and my parents respected, probably loved, each other. But that was the truth of it. The only person I could ever really communicate with in my family was my grandmother.'

I took a mouthful of wine, felt it fingering warm down into my stomach. Douglas examined my face closely in silence as if trying to find something there.

'You know, sometimes I wonder who on earth you really are, Kate.'

A wave of exhaustion swept through me. Sometimes I felt Douglas was trying to wring me dry. It was as if he could bear me to have no private thoughts: he needed total possession of me to feel safe.

There was a silence. Then he said, 'It is my child?'

I could have hit him. 'What else do I have to say to you?' I said wearily. 'Yes. It's your child.'

As we finished our meal in silence, I reflected over fruit tart and coffee that I would never have believed it possible to be married and to feel so utterly lonely.

The next Sunday when I went to visit Olivia it already felt like winter. The sun barely seemed to rise and mist hung thick over the fields, merging with the grey clouds. The train moved like a needle of light through this shadowy landscape, windows running with damp, the lights still on in the compartments even at midday.

My thoughts that morning were no less sombre than the view outside. When Douglas and I had returned home after our meal he made love to me with cold self-absorption. He was no longer apologetic about his inadequacies in bed. He just took what he wanted. I had to get used to preparing myself the way he wanted me; ready for him, on my back. He liked to test himself, leave it until the last moment. He knelt between my legs playing with my breasts like someone tuning a wireless, touching me until he was fully aroused (I wasn't to touch him), then came into me hurriedly.

I watched him that night. His heavy body lay along mine, the lion-coloured hair in childlike disarray. For a long time he didn't look into my face. I felt I might just as well not have been there. But suddenly he glanced up and saw me watching him. I don't know whether he expected my eyes to be closed. I was just lying there, looking. He brought his hand up and slapped me across the face, hard, so that I cried out, the tears stinging my eyes. Then he took his pleasure. Though his orgasm was soon over it affected him like an acute pain, his body convulsing, face puckered. He lay still, recovering. Afterwards he needed comfort. Afterwards, so did I.

During that week he had also announced from behind his newspaper, 'I'm looking for a house to rent. Somewhere we can have more privacy.'

'I don't understand you,' I said. 'One minute you say we're going to London, and the next you want a new house here.'

He lowered the paper and looked coldly at me. 'Why do you have to question everything I decide? I think it's time we moved away from your mother and got a place of our own. She can take in lodgers if she needs to and listen in on their conversations instead.'

'She doesn't.' I felt unusually defensive of her. In her way she had been good to us. Though I wasn't quite sure that she didn't sometimes stand on the stairs trying to hear what we were saying. 'Anyway, she's hardly here now she's working again.'

But Douglas wasn't going to put up with me disagreeing. 'There are a couple of houses I've seen up for rent in Kings Heath and it's no good waiting around. I'm going to see them today.'

He came back that evening saying he'd taken out the lease on one of them. I felt disappointed for myself and my mother. She was looking forward to a baby in the house. And, though I could barely admit it to myself, I was afraid of being completely alone with Douglas. With my mother there at least we had to speak.

I took a small flask of coffee from my bag, and poured it carefully against the motion of the train. It tasted nastily of the Thermos, but after it I felt a little restored. My thoughts returned to Olivia. I dreaded what I was going to find. I wanted to give her some reassurance that I could help her.

Joyce Salter had told me that though Alec Kemp did not come to see her very regularly, when he did it was always on a Tuesday evening. Lisa confirmed for me that this had also been the case with Jackie Flint.

'I'm going to have to come here on Tuesdays,' I said to Lisa. I had no clear idea in my mind of how I was going to find Alec Kemp even, let alone confront him. But it had to be there. I wanted as strong a hold on him as possible: first Olivia, and now this.

'It's like something out of the pictures, isn't it?' Lisa giggled, suddenly girlish, even with Daisy in her arms. Then she frowned. 'You can come when you like, you know that. But you know where 'e lives. Why don't you just go up to the 'ouse if you've got summat to say to 'im?'

'Because he could say anything then, couldn't he? He'd laugh and tell me the girls are making it all up. I need to be here – to see him here.'

'Catch 'im with 'is trousers down, you mean?'

'Perhaps not literally.' I laughed, holding out my arms to take Daisy. 'Come on, my lovely.' The little girl came to my arms, gripping me with her strong fingers.

'Jackie Flint was ever so bad after losing that babby. Couldn't go out to work or nothing for weeks. She's 'opping mad with 'im. Come to think of it, she's got bits of family all over the place round 'ere who could keep an eye out. I'll 'ave a word if you like, Kate.'

'Would you? That would be terrific!'

Lisa stood my me, buckling one of Daisy's little boots. 'What you need is one of them private detectives.'

I smiled. 'I seem to be fast turning into one myself!'

Three Tuesdays had passed and I'd had no luck, and none of this was helping Olivia. Although I tried to sound certain about what I was doing in front of Lisa, I was in an agony of doubt all through those weeks. Would this work, and even if it did, was I actually doing the right thing for Olivia? When I did see her, I felt I would do anything to get her out of there, away from the horror of those electric shocks. And how could I face her month after month if I was achieving nothing?

As my taxi drove away from Leamington, once more between sodden fields and bushes hanging with glassy drops of water, my nervousness grew and the sense of dread on approaching the hospital was even stronger than usual. We wound our way along the drive and Arden's angular outline cleared through the mist. The barred upper windows were dark, though I could see some lights on downstairs. Outside it was very quiet once the car engine was switched off. I could hear not a voice or a bird. I pulled my coat round me in the freezing air, trying to imagine how cold it must be inside there, and walked up the steps and through the ornate doorway.

I waited for her for longer than usual, in the weak light from the hall's high windows and the faint smell of polish. Those long radiators could not have been working, as I could see my breath on the air. I heard occasional footsteps echoing on the stone floors outside and, once or twice, the rattle of keys in the inner door. Eventually there came the sound of the door being unlocked again, the key being turned and hurried footsteps.

They came quickly into the hall, Olivia on the arm of the young nurse with the fringe who had brought her in the last time. She seemed agitated, bundling Olivia through the door at a pace with which Livy could hardly keep up. Part of my mind registered that as the nurse came in she turned to take a last anxious glance down the corridor. But my attention turned immediately to Olivia, to the ghastly whiteness of her face, her eyes enormous against the sunken cheeks, to her short hair straggly and unbrushed, and to her right arm which was bent at a protective angle across her body and encased in a fresh white plaster cast.

I was beside her in an instant. 'What's happened? What have they done?'

Automatically I found myself addressing the nurse. Olivia looked so absent. The nurse was apparently suffering such anxiety that she was unable to keep still and kept up a shuffling movement with her feet. 'There may not be very much time,' she whispered. 'I think we'd better sit down.'

I was already feeling so overwrought that for a second I thought she was telling me Livy was dying. 'What d'you mean?' My breathing had gone jagged. 'Why's her arm in plaster?'

The nurse positioned Olivia in a chair, manipulating her like a doll, then turned to face me. Her features had a certain sweetness that I remembered. 'It happened during the treatment. It does sometimes. When they give them the electric shock it makes the body seize up. All the muscles go into a kind of spasm – like a fit. They have to be restrained to stop them hurting themselves.'

I sat down. I felt as if my lungs were constricting. 'You hold them down?'

She nodded silently. I took in several deep breaths. 'Can't it be stopped? The treatment, I mean?'

The nurse made a helpless gesture. 'The doctors . . .'

'Livy?' I stood up and approached her, feeling an irrational wariness as if she were charged and I might be electrocuted if I touched her.

'She's at the end of the treatment now,' the nurse was saying. 'She's had two courses. There won't be any more – not for a while.' Her eyes flickered back and forth to the door.

I drew up a chair and placed it next to Olivia's. She sat staring ahead of her with no expression, looking completely exhausted. I reached out and took her undamaged hand. 'Darling? It's Katie.'

I felt I could not reach her. She looked so strange, so impassive and resigned. They could do to her what they wished.

'You do know who I am, don't you?' I asked, frightened.

She gave a very slight nod.

'She's ever so tired,' the nurse said. 'She'll get better.

It can affect their memory for a little while.' I knew the nurse had a special bond with Olivia and felt protective towards her. She gave me a sudden smile, sympathetic and wistful.

'Livy,' I implored, almost sobbing. 'What is all this about? It's been so long now – can't you tell me why you're so sad?'

I thought there was going to be no response. She was shivering in the huge, echoing room, wearing the gingham dress again, and so far as I could see she had no other garments. I embraced her bony shoulders. 'Oh Livy, I love you.' Helplessly I sat and cried, and she remained like stone in my arms.

But she turned to me then, gave me that strange, searching look of hers and said, 'The baby.' And went limp as if the words had been a rod in her spine. She folded her arms across her and began to rock, her voice tiny and plaintive.

'My baby, my baby. My little baby.' She was cradling the plaster cast as if it was a child, and this looked such a classic pose of madness that for a moment I wanted to seize hold of her and make her sit still. I glanced anxiously at the nurse. She met my eyes for a second, then moved her gaze deliberately to the high windows, light falling on her face.

'He was mine for one night,' Olivia was saying. 'Mine. He drank my milk and I held his little hands. In the morning they took him away from me.'

I struggled to make sense of what she was saying, wondering if all this was some kind of delusion. 'When?' I asked softly.

'He was born on October 15th, 1941. On October 16th they took him away from me.' She recited this woodenly, staring away from me across the room.

Things started to make terrible sense. 'But they said you had pneumonia!'

'Of course. They wouldn't tell you the truth, would they? My bastard baby. And now he's punishing me.' The high, babyish voice came back. 'It was my fault. It always was my fault. I'm filthy. I asked for it.'

Her tears came then. As she cried she made retching sounds, her whole body jerking. All I could do was hold her, feeling the grief cutting her inside. My own tears fell on her chopped hair.

I was barely aware of the footsteps in the corridor. The nurse fled across the room in a second. The heavy wooden door swept open and I heard a deep, angry woman's voice. 'Get her out of there . . .' It fizzled out to a furious whisper. There was a fierce exchange by the door, then the young woman came back to us, watched from the door by the other nurse, with oily looking skin and thick black eyebrows, who I had never seen before.

'She'll have to go back now,' our nurse said. Her cheeks were burning red, but she had an air of defiance.

'Nurse Tucker deliberately flouted my instructions,' the other woman's voice boomed from the door.

I was so shocked I didn't even have the wits to kiss Olivia goodbye before Nurse Tucker pulled her to her feet by her good arm and led her away. Olivia went without protest. But as they left, the young nurse turned to me a last time, her eyes expressing both sorrow and a kind of appeal.

'Thank you,' I mouthed at her before they disappeared.

I sat down again, listening to them, the older nurse haranguing the other in the corridor, the noises of keys, lock, door. A slam, then all but the faintest of sounds was gone. I would have liked to sit there. Just sit and try to pull my thoughts together, but I felt compelled to go out to the taxi.

Outside the clouds had not thinned and a fine rain was falling. As I stepped out of the front entrance of Arden I saw the handcarts. They were moving closer, very slowly, from across the field to my right. Three heavy wooden carts joined together by ropes. As they came closer I could see the carts were piled high with weeds and grass. At the front, two long thick ropes extended forward pulled by lines of men. There were about fifty of them, I calculated, all dressed in dark overcoats, some far too long, others obviously too tight, sleeves ending somewhere between elbow and wrist, and most of them had their collars turned up against the wet. They shambled along over the hummocky grass, stumbling in their boots and pulling on the ropes, the lines ragged and uncoordinated. They were of a wide variety of height and build but somehow all the same, the cropped hair taking a segment of identity. Some moved with an unnatural slow stiffness, others quicker, more jerky. They trudged along in silence except for someone near the back giving out panting sounds, almost sobs, as they moved across in front of me. Their breath left unearthly-looking sworls of mist behind them.

* * *

OLIVIA

The nurses who have been giving insulin therapy can be seen afterwards on the ward with a white silt of glucose down the front of their blue uniforms. Their charges are pushed down into the flabby-walled darkness of coma and then, at the given time, hauled back up through its narrow neck.

When Nurse Tucker has been helping administer ECT her eyes are wide and her hands tremble. This is her very first job and she is in shock herself. She has not been in the army or the mines. She has too much will and imagination left for this.

I believe my treatment is twice a week, but the days are so thin-edged I may be mistaken. The fear of it seeps into every moment of the week.

The treatment is performed in the basement where there are tiny cells along the dark corridor. At one end are the isolation cells, but the doors are iron-clad and so thick that any sounds from inside are tiny and muffled.

We are herded, unfed, down the steps, about thirty of us, where we meet with an icy draft of air when we are already frozen with dread. The walls have a lick of ancient whitewash and above our heads snake the metallic intestines of the hospital, pipes stretching off into the gloom of the passage. There are no windows down here. We are alive, but already entombed under the soundproof earth, in the smell of rubber and urine and the sour stench of fear.

We stand in a line hearing the animal distress of those who go before us. I am already mute with fear. What we feel does not matter to them and I have learned it is not worth protesting. Once I appealed to the doctor, put on my best voice: 'I'm afraid of what it'll do to my mind.'

He gave a half smile, actually sincere. 'Don't worry. I don't suppose you'll be needing it.'

In the cell I lie on a trolley. Their faces are a ring round me, quiet, as if they're waiting for a seance to begin. Then one jokes into the silence. 'We'll break our record this morning,' he says, rushing the machine to my head. I wish I had something to hold on to: a bead, a stone, a strand of hair, anything to call mine.

In seconds I taste rubber, still saliva-coated from the last mouth. The gag is thick and hard and punctured with holes for our sharp breaths to hiss through. There is cold jelly on my temples and immediately they are across my body, three of them lying on me as the current is applied and everything of me is seized by it, burns and blackens and I am no longer conscious to know of the wet coursing from my body adding to the vapour of urine in the room.

Return to the seeping grey light is a process of despair, in a recovery room filling with thirty bodies writhing in the incalculable dread of consciousness.

Will this be my life now, waiting for this to be done to me?

It is during the second course of treatment, while my body is in spasm, that they break my arm forcing me down.

* * *

By the time I climbed into a compartment of the train at Leamington Spa after my visit to Arden, I felt completely wrung out. My legs were weak and I was unsteady with shock at what Olivia had told me. It was as if a window had opened on a whirlwind. I understood. A baby. Olivia had had a baby. Finally I knew what it was the Kemps had kept strapped down tight all this time. A tiny, new person, the explanation for all this.

I took off my damp hat, sat down and closed my eyes. Even in my state of shock I realized that part of my shakiness was hunger and I was longing for a drink.

If I had taken the time to buy one I would have missed the train, and to keep the peace I had told Douglas very specifically what time I would be home.

As the whistle blew outside, there was a flurry of movement beside me. The compartment door slid across and there was a sound of a bag being rather frantically pulled inside. For a moment I resented anyone else's presence and then, contrarily, was grateful for the diversion. I opened my eyes to see a short man reaching up to stow his case on the luggage rack. He made a to-do of shaking water from his hat and gloves and took off his overcoat.

'So sorry,' he said, turning to me. 'I hope I didn't give you a shower?'

I shook my head. We looked closely at each other.

'I do know you, don't I – from somewhere?' he said. I shared the feeling of recognition.

He snapped his fingers. 'That's it. You're a friend of Marjorie's, aren't you?'

I managed a smile. Of course. 'Roland Mantel. Yes, I'm Kate – Munro before I was married.'

Roland darted across and shook my hand with enthusiasm, still clutching his gloves in his other hand. 'I remember you well now. How are you?'

We exchanged pleasantries and I felt myself relaxing through the sheer obligation to behave normally and make conversation. Marjorie had married a wartime sweetheart and was happily settled in Portsmouth. Roland seemed genuinely pleased to see me, and to have found a companion for the journey. I couldn't help warming to him, once I'd grown used to the quaint elderliness of his manner.

'Have a sandwich?' he offered suddenly. 'You look all in.'

'I'd absolutely love one.' I felt an absurd impulse to burst into tears and realized it was caused by hunger.

Roland stood up again. He was wearing a pair of crumpled tweed plus-fours and a jacket. I smiled to myself, watching him.

'Been anywhere nice?' he asked.

'Just visiting a friend.'

'I've just been to stay with my Auntie Sylvia out at Turnham's Farm,' Roland said, reaching up to fumble in his bag. 'She always feeds me up like a turkey cock, the old dear.' He gave a grunt of exertion. 'Where are they? Ah, here we are.' He brought down a package, firmly wrapped in layers of greaseproof and a final covering of what looked like a page from an artist's sketchpad. He sat down beside me. 'Now, these are ham, and I believe she said there's some pheasant in these. I've a flask of tea, too, and some plum cake.' He looked up and saw tears in my eyes. 'Gracious, are you all right? You're not against killing fowls and all that, are you?'

I laughed then, at the sight of his good-natured, anxious face, laughed and laughed so that he looked rather alarmed. 'It's all right,' I gasped, trying to control myself. 'I'm just very hungry. It takes me that way sometimes. I'm expecting a baby, you see.'

'Oh,' he cried, pink cheeks bunching into a smile. 'How simply marvellous! So you're – Is it...? Who's...?' He stopped, all confused. 'I'm sorry. I remember. When we saw you at the party, your – intended was missing, wasn't he? Did he...?'

I looked down at my lap. The pain of Angus's death sliced through me so suddenly, so overwhelmingly sometimes. For a moment I could barely speak. Then I managed to say, 'No. I'm married to someone else. Douglas Craven. He was at your party too.'

Roland frowned.

'Journalist. The one with the gammy leg.'

'Ah yes. I think I recall. I didn't know him at all actually, but one couldn't help noticing. But he can work all right?'

'On the *Mail*.'

'Marvellous. Well, congratulations all round then. Here, tuck in – do.'

He poured tea into the Thermos cup, and I found something reassuring, comforting even, about the way he lifted the flask, the cups – one big, one smaller – so carefully with his immaculate, white-nailed fingers. 'You go first.'

After a few sips I handed it back. 'Roland, your brother was missing too, wasn't he?'

The chubby face folded immediately into lines of misery. It was like watching a clown, except the emotion was real.

'We lost Edward as well, I'm afraid. He was RAF, of course. We're still not sure precisely what happened. It was all during the fiasco in Singapore. Don't suppose we ever shall know exactly now.'

'It was the same with Angus,' I said. 'They think he was shot down over the sea near Sumatra. That's the most information we ever had. His mother pursued it for months.' I watched Roland. He seemed so bereft that I touched his hand for a second. 'I'm so sorry. It's absolutely awful, isn't it?'

Roland nodded silently.

'When Angus was missing I felt as if everything ought to stop. That I couldn't go on until I knew for sure. But you just had to go on, didn't you? No choice in the matter. It was very brave of you both to have that party then. I admired you for that.'

'Did you?' He turned to look directly at me. 'It was the last blasted thing I felt like doing, I can tell you. Excuse me, Kate.' I waved aside the apology. 'My family is very that way you know, stiff upper lip, keep the home fires burning and all that. Edward was as well. Not me I'm afraid. Never been very good at it.' He gave a half smile. 'I adored Edward. He was five years older than me and I knew from when I was a tiny child that I could never possibly be like him. He was all the things I'd have liked to be. But he was very good to me – sort of looked out for me.' He stopped. 'I'm boring you, or worse, embarrassing you?'

'Not at all. Please go on.'

'No one talks any more, I find. Not about things like that. I suppose it's their way of putting it behind them.'

'I feel the same. And I can hardly bring it up now, not while I'm married to someone else.'

'Quite, I see that. You poor girl.'

Roland didn't question my need or see it as disloyal to Douglas. We shared his refreshments and talked all the way to Birmingham about Edward, Angus and our lives now.

'I'm with PEL,' Roland told me. 'Practical Equipment Ltd. Furniture design, though I'm more on the admin side. It's all quite exciting. Fashions are changing fast, of course, and we need new designs, a change of direction. There's a great deal to do.' He spoke of his work with infectious enthusiasm. As the train slowed, clanking into the great arching space of New Street, he took my hand suddenly. 'It's been marvellous meeting you again, Kate. You've so cheered me up.'

'Probably not as much as you have me.' I laughed. 'And thank you for the much needed food.'

'Ah – thank Auntie Sylvia for that,' Roland said, gathering up his things.

As we walked out from the platform together I explained that we were still living with my mother.

'You won't be going my way then,' Roland said. 'I've a little place in Edgbaston now.' He produced an address card. 'Keep in touch, won't you?'

'I will.' I looked into his sympathetic face and reached out to touch his shoulder. He leaned forward and quickly kissed me on the cheek. 'Goodbye then, Katie.'

Smiling, I watched him walk away out of the station. The smile locked on my face when I saw that standing a few yards away, watching me with a terrible expression in his eyes, was Douglas.

I walked slowly over, trying to turn the smile on him. 'It was very good of you to come and meet me.'

'Was it?' His voice was hard with fury, the emotion barely controlled. After only a few seconds he burst out, 'I knew it. Was that him then?'

'Who?'

'The father of that – ' He pointed towards my stomach. 'That baby.'

I lost my cool completely then, not caring who could hear us. 'For God's sake, Douglas,' I shouted. 'Don't be so bloody ridiculous.'

Chapter 24

I went to Elizabeth Kemp. I wasn't going to let on that I knew about Olivia's baby. I was saving that for the right moment. But I wanted to confirm the information I had about Alec. I also wanted to goad her. My anger with Elizabeth now was like something chiselled thin and hard. We stood, a few feet apart. She watched me warily, her face cold, aloof.

'What evenings does Alec go out regularly?'

'And what business is that of yours?'

'Tuesdays. Does he go out on Tuesdays?'

'Quite often.'

'Any other night?'

'This is extraordinary – coming here and interrogating me.'

'When did you last see Olivia?'

She couldn't meet my eye. 'Three weeks ago.'

'Not since?'

'I thought it might be better if I kept away. She looked so ill. She barely responded to me at all.'

'If she stays in there much longer I'm not sure she'll be able to tolerate it.'

Elizabeth raised her eyes with a closed, defensive expression. 'Surely you're exaggerating?'

'Do you know about the treatment they're giving her?' I experienced my habitual feeling with Elizabeth of wanting to go and shake her with enormous force. I didn't know whether electric shock treatment was effective or not, but something in my very being revolted at the idea of it. 'What are you doing to get her out of there?'

Her voice was strained thin as broth. 'I've asked him – I've begged him. I don't know what else to do. He says we have to wait for them to make her better.'

'Is Tuesday the only night he always goes out?'

She made as if to think about it, smoothing her hand round the pleat of her hair. 'He does have a regular social arrangement on a Tuesday. They meet for a drink – business, you know.'

'Oh yes?' I kept my voice neutral.

Elizabeth looked at me very directly. 'Yes. It's been a long-standing arrangement.'

'Hasn't it just?'

Without changing her expression, she said, 'Please leave my house.'

'I thought you wanted my help.'

Abruptly she turned her back to me and leaned on the mantelpiece in a cringing pose. 'I don't want it at the expense of . . . of everything else.'

I was silent for a moment. 'You know just where he goes most Tuesdays, don't you?'

She lowered her head as if I was whipping her. When she spoke I heard the break in her voice. 'He is whatever I have made him.'

When I got home that evening I felt weighed down and filled with a kind of disgust at myself. Everything felt so strange, at odds. Even this house of mine would not be so for much longer. In each room there were packing cases, some already full for our move in a few days' time.

Douglas was out, working as usual. I sat for a long time in front of my dressing table, staring at my face.

I had felt like a torturer with Elizabeth Kemp. I remembered how I used to stare so often at my reflection, wishing I looked different; like Olivia. My face was thin now, severe, with my hair pinned up at the back, my oval, steel-rimmed specs. As a girl I had looked so much sweeter. Then I had dreamed of Alec Kemp, kissed my reflection in the glass, fancying it was him. I had wanted to look beautiful and alluring. I gave myself an ironic smile. Twenty years on, nearly, and I was still being goaded by the thought of Alec Kemp. Except that now my pursuit was driven by revenge; for Olivia but also – though I could barely admit it – for myself, for the bitter person I felt that night.

Now I knew about Olivia's baby I was certain in a way I had not been up until now that she was being wronged by her confinement in Arden. Through the summer I had been beset by doubts, waiting for some improvement in her that might give me hope: a grain of light through the black screen of her depression. An explanation. Instead it had grown worse until she was almost unreachable and I no longer knew who or what to believe.

But now I had reasons for the changes in her: grief, loss, anger. And now, by waiting, I had more to hold against Alec Kemp. Soon, very soon, I was going to catch him at his most vulnerable.

* * *

OLIVIA

I have only one thing left and I keep it in my head, calling upon it like a rosary or a lucky stone. It's real and not real. That is, it never happened exactly like this. It's a summing up, a kind of poem. I call it up at night when I am once more lying awake and often in the day. It makes me ache with happiness and sometimes I cry. It's my only doorway to feeling, even if it is an illusion.

I am five years old. I live in our beautiful house in Moseley. It is a smooth, pure house, for I do not yet know its drawers and cupboards are full of squirming secrets. As the years pass the drawers are topped up until the pressure becomes unbearable.

But I am five. I am playing in the garden on velvet grass, the sun like warm hands on my face, and I am wearing a pretty white frock. Mummy likes me to wear white. I have a hoop which I am using for skipping. I twirl the smooth wood round over my head and down for my feet to jump over as it passes at the right moment in perfect rhythm. Step, twirl, step, twirl.

Suddenly I stop. I am happy, full of a deep, thrumming joy, but there is one thing missing. What I need to fill me right up to the top is indoors. I like to see my feet moving neatly one in front of the other. My white sandals clack on the path as I trot into the blue shadow of the house. Through the glass door, along the hall, clack clack still on the grey, white, orange tiles.

I know that all I need is here. Searching, I go to the back room, our refuge with its bulging sofa, for the family only. He is sitting with white shirtsleeves rolled in the heat, his strong, dark hands gripping the newspaper, legs stretched out and comfortable.

'Daddy!' Running to his arms. 'Daddy!'

The newspaper is laid down immediately. The arms are always open, as hungry for me as I for him.

'Angel! Hello there, princess!' His lips are on my cheek and I am in his smell, the best in life: crisp shirt, whiff of sweat, tobacco, man.

I lie against his body, warm, overflowing, tearful with contentment.

* * *

My chance with Alec came in November, the week after Douglas and I moved house. The night I found Alec Kemp was also the first time I saw Jackie Flint and one of his other women.

'Lisa!' We heard Jackie hammering at the door. It was about eight o'clock on a Tuesday evening. Don was at the pub, Douglas, as usual, at a meeting. When Jackie came in from the darkness, panting, I started to wonder whether Kemp's employees were selected purely on looks. She was lovely; a soft, rounded figure, long fair hair, big blue eyes and square, widely spaced teeth. In one hand she had a cigarette. Catching sight of me, she said, startled, 'Oh, it's you! I remember you from when Doris 'ad 'er babby.'

I had no recollection of her, but held out my hand to introduce myself. She ignored it, taking a puff on the cigarette. ''E's 'ere again. Me sister just saw him – up Catherine Street. 'E's after some kid at number twenty-eight. You'll 'ave to get a move on. They won't be stopping up there long.'

I was all of a dither, heart going like mad and suddenly no idea what I was doing.

'Where do I go?' I asked, breathlessly.

'After 'im of course,' Lisa said, poised as if to throw me bodily out of the door.

'Round the back of Kemp's,' Jackie told me. I could tell she was enjoying this, being in the know, and the prospect of revenge. 'That's where 'e takes 'em. We'll come with you.'

'No!' I was trying to pull on my coat, arm catching in the sleeve. 'It'll mean waiting around. I'll need to be absolutely quiet.'

'She's right, you know,' Lisa said. 'Be like a cowing 'en 'ouse with us tagging along.'

'Right,' I said, trying to sound as if I had any idea what I was going to do. 'I'll be back later – I hope.'

'Bring us 'is 'ead back!' Lisa called.

'Or summat else!' Jackie shouted brazenly, and their ragged trail of laughter followed me out through the door into the smoky air.

I turned into Catherine Street and began to walk up the sloping brick pavement. I was so wound up that every sound – a dog barking, the slam of a front door – made me jump. There weren't many people about and I certainly couldn't see Alec Kemp. Nearing number 28, a house fronting on to the street near the top of the road, I stopped. I could hardly hang about here: I might run straight into them.

A short distance away was an entry to one of the back courts, so I slipped just inside and waited, moving from one foot to the other, unable to keep still for nerves.

It was a freezing night and very still, a half moon shining clear-edged in the sky. Children were playing out despite the cold. The entry was dark, smelled of urine, and the high walls muffled sounds so that I was constantly straining my ears to hear voices or footsteps.

They went past so quickly that I only glimpsed them and for a few seconds I was paralysed and couldn't think what to do. Then I rushed after them, seeming to fly down the dimly lit slope of Catherine Street. A gaggle of children were shivering round the steps of the Catherine Arms, and as I passed there came a waft of warm, beer-fed air and a wave of noise from inside the cosily lit windows, voices singing above the talk. Otherwise the street was quiet.

They went right down to the bottom, towards Kemp's, and I slowed down, frightened that they might turn and see me. At the corner they turned down into Vaughan Street and I hurried to keep them in view.

The two figures in front of me were walking side by side but not touching. I knew the man was Alec Kemp by the height, his walk. The woman beside him looked small and slight. Now and then they appeared to exchange a word, but they were brisk and purposeful. He seemed to be urging her on. Once I saw her stop and turn to look up at him, saying something. Alec appeared to speak softly, touching her shoulder for a second. I froze, seeing him glance back up the street. I should have kept walking, looked more normal. But he can't have seen me. I saw he had his hat pulled down well over his face. They walked on.

As we neared Kemp's, I realized the factory was still running. I had not given any thought to whether Kemp's worked a night shift and had imagined him going to a place closed and deserted. Instead there were lights on, the front gates open, the hum of machines inside.

Surely to God he can't be taking her in, I thought. Round the back, Jackie had said, but so far as I could see there was only the main gate. They were going past it. There must be another entrance behind.

Walking on the opposite side of the road from the

factory, they skirted it and turned swiftly into the next street. I saw Alec putting his arm round behind her, urging her on.

Looks as if this is it, I thought. My heart was going like the clappers.

But when I turned the corner, they'd vanished. Damn and blast it! I stopped.

The street was a short one, linking Vaughan Street to the main road at the bottom. At a glance it appeared to present a uniform frontage of two-storey houses, but a short way down there was a break, a narrow alley barely wider than the entries to the back courts. The alley was pitch black and I didn't much like the look of it but I didn't see there was anywhere else they could have gone. I couldn't miss this opportunity now. I stepped into the black slit between the houses.

The first part was very dark, hemmed in by the walls of the houses on each side. I couldn't see the moon in the ribbon of sky, though I sensed the blackness thinning out ahead of me and becoming less intense. I felt my way along, moving my hands over the rough bricks, trying to tread absolutely silently. I heard a slight crunch as my foot pressed on broken glass. I stopped immediately and waited, taking in a deep breath and straining my ears to interpret the small sounds around me: the murmur of conversation from inside the houses, a distant rumble from Kemp's and, surely, a faint voice from along the alley in front of me.

I reached the end of the houses and the walls of their yards on each side and I could see fractionally better, as if hands had been lifted from over my eyes. The moon gave my surroundings a dim outline. The ground underfoot was rough and unpaved and I felt my way carefully into each step. On the right I could make out that there was now an iron fence, but not low enough to see over; behind it a silent warehouse. I realized I was soon going to be level with the back of Kemp's to my left. The high wall tapered down roughly level with my head, and over it came a faint glow of light. The yard of Kemp's was quiet, but I wondered just what sort of thrill it gave Alec Kemp to be in this particular place with a woman, so close to his daily role as grand panjandrum overseeing his laboratory and the works below it.

I heard his voice before I could see them and stood absolutely still. His tone was soft, persuasive, and they were closer than I'd realized. They were standing against the back wall of Kemp's. I made out their shapes, sensed them by the sound of their voices.

In a tiny voice, the girl said, 'Oh, Mr Kemp – it's so dark.'

'It's all right, Dolly.' That voice came back so soothingly. 'I'm sorry it has to be like this, but it's only for now. I'll find somewhere better for us to go. If I hadn't wanted you so badly ... You can see I'm in a very difficult position, can't you?'

I heard nothing. The woman must have nodded.

'That's my girl. You've no idea how I feel about you, have you? How long I've wanted to – to touch you like this. It's just – ' There was a pause. 'Sometimes I get very lonely, you see. My wife's not – well, she's not like you. She won't let me touch her, and . . .' Another pause, as if he was taking in a long breath. 'I can't live without this. Without having someone to hold.'

My eyes widened in the darkness. As he began speaking I had readied myself to hear the line being spun, the Kemp magnetism knowingly at work. What I was not prepared for was the sincerity of his distress. I felt shame wash through me at being here, hearing this.

'When you first came to work for me I saw something special in you immediately. I saw you were someone I could trust, who might give me a bit of . . . loving.'

The girl made a small 'oohh' sound, of tenderness and arousal. He'd got her well and truly. Had he spoken those words to me, my arms would have been round him as well. Clenching my teeth, I dragged an image of Olivia into my mind. I could see the faintest outline of Alec and the girl fastened together by a kiss.

I let out a cough, loud and deliberate. The sound broke into that black, tense space with all the force of an explosion.

'Who the – ? What the bloody hell d'you think you're doing?' The panic was plain in his voice. 'Come back here!'

I started to run. He was soon right behind me, grabbing at my back. I had no intention of trying to escape him completely but I wanted to get to the street so that he could see me and I could face him properly, see the look in his eyes.

'Stop right now or I'll call the police!' he shouted irrationally.

In a few seconds we were out on Vaughan Street. His hand came down hard on my shoulder.

'Don't touch me, Mr Kemp.'

He released me more in surprise than anything, standing back to look at me. 'Kate? Little Katie? What on earth?'

I suppose he was relieved for a moment when he saw me. His voice was soft again, full of that persuasiveness. I gritted my teeth against it, the way that tone could even at this moment make me want to run into his arms.

'A few things have happened since you called me Little Katie.' I injected venom into my voice.

He gave me his charming smile, gesturing with his hand back towards the alley. There was no sign of the woman Dolly. 'For goodness' sake, Katie. That didn't mean anything.'

'So what does mean something to you? Does anything mean more than getting a seat at the next election?' I took a step closer to him. 'Do I really have to spell this out? Your daughter is in a lunatic asylum. You creep around the streets at night to have – relations – with your employees and you have at least one illegitimate child to show for it.'

He was silent. I saw shock freeze into his face.

'I'm well acquainted with both Joyce Salter and Jackie Flint who – God alone knows why – have been remarkably loyal to you up until now.' I paused for a moment, watching his expression. 'I'll go to anyone I have to, you know. My husband knows all the right people to tell.'

Alec gave a kind of laugh, containing no mirth, merely an enormous tiredness. 'Oh, I see. I see.' He leaned his head back, looking to the sky for a moment, then his eyes met mine, direct again, and prepared. 'What do you want? D'you want money like all of them? How much do I have to pay you to keep you quiet?'

'Money?' I was enraged, the sensation coming as a relief. 'Is that always the first thing that enters your head?'

'What then?'

'What the hell d'you think? I want Olivia. You're the only person who can get her out. You can say the word, and – ' I snapped my fingers.

'She's not well. You've seen it – the way she talks . . . I can't tell them to let her loose. I won't take responsibility for her. She's not my Olivia any more.'

'She's not well because you snatched her baby away from her against her wishes.' I was having to hold on tight to myself so as not to become incoherent. 'It's enough to make anyone ill. Can't you see she's sick with grief? But no. All you care about is what people will think – your career at the expense of everything else.'

He put his hands over his face, slightly bent forward as if I'd kicked him in the stomach. He was distraught. 'She told you. She wasn't supposed to tell anyone. She was my girl. Mine.'

Words spilled out of my mouth like thick green slime, cleansing me. 'I don't know what you've done to her between you. You had a beautiful, talented daughter and together you've crushed and warped her and you're too much of a cowardly bastard even to go to her and see with your eyes what you've done. You sicken me, Alec. You're despicable.' I stopped, finding I was shaking.

Lowering his hands, Alec stared at me. 'I never thought I'd hear you talk like that, Katie. You used to be so innocent. So charming.'

Tears blurred my eyes. I felt the sadness of his words.

'Look,' he said quietly. 'I know what you think – how this looks to you. I can't – ' He took in a long, shuddering breath. 'I can't bear it that she's in there. It's killing me. I can't stand to see it. But she is ill, Kate. You didn't live with her. For weeks after she came home it was unbearable, the way she was. It was like a bad dream. We didn't feel we could leave her . . . her moods. And then I found out she was . . . was . . .' He shook his head, unable to go on.

'Going with all those men?'

He expelled his breath with a sound that was half

sigh, half sob. I stood with my arms straight down by my sides, clenching my fists. He put his hand into his coat and pulled out a handkerchief. 'We've been at our wits' end.'

After recovering himself for a moment, he said, 'You'd do all this for her?'

I nodded, somehow unable to look into his eyes. 'I want her out. I'll take her. I'll look after her.'

'I'll have to think about it,' he said.

'You do that. You've got two days.'

He turned from me and began to walk off down the street.

'I'll be round!' I called after him.

Walking back to Lisa's house I felt not in the least jubilant. I was heavy-hearted and disgusted with myself at what I had felt forced to do.

When I went in I was startled to find four women waiting for me, their eyes darting in my direction as soon as I appeared. Lisa and Jackie, but also Joyce Salter and another woman I'd never seen before with red hair.

'This is Sarah,' Jackie said. 'She works at Kemp's.' A thick blush spread across the woman's pale skin.

They were waiting.

'Well,' I said flatly, 'I've done it.'

They must have seen the shamed lines of my face, and I didn't see in them any of the triumph I had expected: raucous, perhaps a little sadistic. Instead there was sadness, and shame in them, too. They had egged each other on, brazenly, to the idea of revenge, women drawing together against the vile seducer, all bravado. But now, seeing their faces, I knew it was not just for money that they had kept faith with Alec Kemp. He had aroused feelings in each of them which, whatever the cost to themselves, had bound them to their silence with a kind of tenderness.

* * *

OLIVIA

Once the WRNS have released me, six months pregnant, with my little suitcase, and once Daddy has stopped shouting and abusing me, he tells me, all sorrowful, 'The only thing that matters is that no one finds out.' He says, 'My girl, my little girl. How could you? You're spoilt now. There's no going back.'

They keep me inside for nearly three months. Sometimes in the evenings I walk in the garden at dusk, feeling the new weight of my body.

They polish up my story about pneumonia and, fortunately, at the right time, when they are ready to let me out, my chest is bad. Mummy, of course, manages to believe the story at least half.

I am so afraid. I say to her, 'What will it be like? What will happen to me?' And, 'I'm frightened Mummy, the baby's getting so big. It'll never come out, I'm so small.'

She fusses about me. 'Darling, you must rest. Have a cushion. Eat this liver, drink that milk.' She pours concern over me like cream, but cannot be with me in the place where I am. The word baby barely escapes through her lips. They keep me there, almost motionless, in the dark like a white puffball, feeding me, waiting for me to spill my terrible seed. Threads of feeling string themselves between the three of us, always tangling and knotted, never direct and spoken. Had they pulled straight they would have snapped, spraying blood metallic red.

They buy me a new piano. I refuse to play it. I sit staring at the world outside, forbidden me. More than anything I want Katie to comfort me.

They call Dr Penn when my pains begin and Mummy leaves the house as he enters it. I am terrified and there are no women at my delivery to lead or hold me. Dr Penn strolls in and out, often leaving me on my damp sheets, the pain crushing me.

'I'm too small,' I cry to him. 'I'll bleed to death.'

'Your pelvis is perfectly adequate,' he tells me over his spectacles. He is not unkind, but he's a man and he doesn't know.

After twelve hours he is born, my son. Daddy weeps when he sees him. He has always wanted a son for the business. My body is drenched and stretched and when I look down I don't recognize it.

Dr Penn washes him and instructs me how to feed him. They leave my baby in a drawer by my bed with a thin pillow lining the base and soft squares of blanket. There is no cradle, of course, because this is not to be his home.

Before he hurries away I hear Dr Penn's murmur beyond my door, 'I'll be round tomorrow – early.'

Mummy does not come home all night.

He lies in the drawer that evening, like the poor babies do. Daddy brings me food and is soft-spoken and kind which makes me cry. He holds me and strokes me. I sit in sheets which were once those of childhood.

When he has gone I don't sleep as he tells me to. I keep the light on, just a small sidelight, like I've always done. I see the little bedclothes twitching up and down. Then he works one arm loose, although I've wrapped him well. There is his hand, so small, jerking back and forth. I watch. I can't stop looking at him. He's getting ready to cry. Then his voice, a high, sad sound, all alone in there after the warmth of me. I pick him up and put him to one breast then the other, he pulling sharply on me, full of astonishing, separate life. I keep him beside me all night though they told me I wasn't to. The house is so quiet around us. Sometimes he opens his eyes for a few seconds and looks at me. I know he sees me.

I unwrap him and take in every part of his body, every shadow of his bone and muscle, the delicate, puckered skin. He has a long strong back and a birth mark like a wild strawberry at the bottom of his spine. I feel each bit of him, arms, legs, each rib, ears, cheeks, his soft skull. I hold his head against my cheek. By the morning I know him. I want my life to be his. And they take him away, then, at first light.

* * *

Chapter 25

I was watching out for her. The ambulance arrived on a December day threatening snow, and against the grey clouds it looked very white and clean. Turning into Springfield Road it seemed to be moving in slow motion, stopping outside our door with a final shudder of the engine.

'She's here!' I cried. Aflutter with nerves, I forgot I was alone in the house, calling out only to myself.

A man wearing a blue cap jumped down from the driver's seat and scuttled round to the back of the vehicle. He opened the door at the back and I saw him reach out a hand.

Olivia was dressed in a black sable coat and black boots. Elizabeth must have seen to that. She was carrying a small overnight bag. I saw immediately that they had already removed the plaster cast from her arm. As she stepped out of the ambulance she hesitated, her face screwing up as if in pain after the darkness inside, even though it was not a bright day. She looked down for a moment, chopped hair falling forward round her cheeks, in a gesture of surrender. It was only once they had stepped inside the gate that she looked up again in bewilderment, taking in our new house, part of a long red-brick terrace, with Russian vine spiralling up the drainpipe, the green front door and wide bay window in which I stood with my hand raised to greet her. She stared at me without responding, as if she could make no sense of who I was. Her face looked so white, so haggard.

'Here you are,' the young man said as I opened the door. He handed Olivia over to me as if she were a bolt of cloth, and he was gone, striding back along the short path.

I closed the door and stood leaning against it long enough to let out a long, long sigh. I felt I hadn't been able to breathe like that for months. She was here, safe, with me.

She was still standing where I had taken her in the front room, not having moved except to stand the little case beside her on the floor. I burst into tears and went and took her in my arms. 'Livy, Livy . . .' I could say nothing but her name, over and over, holding on to her so tightly.

She stood quite still, impassively letting me hold her and cry over her. But I did hear her whisper, very quietly, 'Thank you.'

When Douglas had finally decided to move us out of my mother's house, she treated the situation with indifference, whether real or not was impossible to say. What with the hospital, the church and the British Housewives League she was scarcely in anyway. Douglas seemed to think it would be the answer to everything. He was still pursuing some abstract ideal of 'family life' which, among other things, involved having your own home. I think he hoped he would have more control over me.

In fact this short, sweetish time was the best in our marriage. A lull, when I saw glimpses of the Douglas who had charmed me into believing I loved him.

That day Douglas had seen me with Roland we had

rowed terribly. Once we'd travelled home, mute with fury, we attacked each other across our bedroom with words whose viciousness frightened both of us. I was already overwrought about Olivia, and Douglas held me guilty of wild, bizarre things, the unreasonableness of which shocked me more than the accusations themselves. He'd got it into his head that I was having an affair with the new doctor at the clinic, when I'd barely even got a grasp on the man's name. He called me filthy things, turning on me all his icy verbal power.

'You're not a real woman at all are you? You can't just stay at home where you should be. You have to be working like a man or gadding about with your friends and heaven only knows who else.' His eyes bored into me. 'You don't even respond to me properly in bed. It's like making love to a bloody corpse.'

At this I finally burst into tears, overcome by the injustice of it. 'I can't respond to you in bed,' I wailed, 'because you're so hopeless at it. You don't make me feel anything at all. It's humiliating. Can't you see that?'

The first time we'd ever broached the subject and it had to come out so harshly. Douglas was silenced. I saw the pain in his face.

'Can't you see,' I went on, 'that you're making my life miserable, spying on me and not trusting me? I don't want another man. Coping with you is too much already. I can't stand much more of it, Douglas. I'd almost rather be alone.'

'Don't say that.' He crumpled then, sinking on to the bed, his shoulders shaking. I sat beside him. He put his hands over his face. 'I can't help it. All I need is for you to want just me.'

'I do want you,' I said. I tried to believe it.

He began to kiss me, laid me back on the bed, his

eyes watching my face anxiously as he jerked my clothes off.

'I do want you,' I repeated softly.

He came to me then and made love quickly, desperately, in much the way he had always done. I felt nothing except resignation. At the time I was exhausted enough not to mind.

Strangely, the new extremes to which this row had taken us cleared something from the air between us for a time. We had been trying harder with each other since then. I had given in to Douglas and told him I'd give up my job at the end of November. And the house was a symbol of our new carefulness.

It was a three-storey terrace, reaching back from the road with rooms off a corridor from front to back and quite dark inside, but with a strip of garden ending in a row of poplars. The bedrooms let in a little more light than downstairs. I decorated one as a nursery, painting it pale yellow. I hung curtains sprigged with flowers. Douglas wanted a boy. I hoped my child was a girl.

We enjoyed the novelty of the house and discovered new skills in each other. One day I watched Douglas building a small cupboard for the kitchen, impressed with the deftness of his hands.

'I didn't know you were good at that sort of thing.'

He looked round, squatting on the floor of the back room, and grinned. 'My hands have never been the problem.' His face grew serious. 'You look lovely – with the baby I mean.'

I smiled, stroking my stomach. My pregnancy was showing by then and I was proud, excited. Except that now, knowing about Olivia's baby, I could not enjoy these feelings without a sense of ambiguity.

'You do look different, though.' Douglas lurched to

his feet and came over to me, lifting and stroking my hair which was hanging loose. 'Your face is – softer somehow. More womanly.' He took me in his arms. 'I love you, Kate. Things'll be better now we're here, won't they? New and different.'

I looked over his shoulder across our new room. I thought of Olivia. I could smell the curled wood-shavings on the floor. 'I hope so.'

I wouldn't want to deny that there was fault on my side where Douglas was concerned. I was so caught up in my feelings for Olivia, and bringing her to our house seemed the natural, the only thing to do.

'Don't make me go to Mummy and Daddy,' she'd pleaded with me on my final visit to Arden. 'Please don't.'

'I'm not going to make you do anything,' I told her. 'Livy – when you get out of here people aren't going to be able to make you do things any more.' When I told her she could come to live with us it seemed to settle her mind, and especially as it was no longer to Chantry Road, which was so near the Kemps and all the associations with childhood.

I made the promise before I told Douglas. But he was all right about it. He felt safer with me then, knowing I was going to give up work, to the regret of my colleagues, and would be constantly at home.

'It'll be nice for you to have some female company, won't it?' he said. 'And both of you will need to rest. You should be good for each other.' It let him off the hook for working so hard, of course – I would not be relying only on his company. And I was relieved – I would no longer have to be alone with Douglas in the loneliness of our marriage. I would have Olivia.

Before she left the hospital, I knew I had to tell her about the baby. It was becoming so obvious and she was going to have to know.

'I'm worried for you,' I said. 'That it'll be upsetting for you living with me when I'm pregnant. I would have told you about it before, only then you'd just told me about . . .' I trailed off.

'About my baby?' Determinedly she said, 'My baby. I had a baby. He was mine.' She spoke with more energy than I had seen in her for a long time, turning to me with a kind of fierceness. 'I can't hold it in my head. It's like a dream that keeps floating away. When I try and touch him, he's gone. But I don't think it matters about your baby. That's different. Your baby is yours. It might make mine seem real when I see it.'

I was encouraged by this. It was her longest speech for a long time, and she hadn't sounded like someone trying to be brave. There was sense in it and I'm sure she believed it then. That all she needed was to be able to feel properly, to remember, and to have a period of grieving for her child.

So far as I was concerned at that time, Livy's state of health and her odd behaviour immediately before being sent to hospital were all connected with the loss of her baby. My mind carefully threaded everything into that weave, discounting things that had happened before, much earlier. Of course she'd been highly strung and moody, but nothing more. And I had a clear, substantial explanation for the state she was in now.

Douglas greeted her with surprising warmth. The sight of her in the limp new clothes Elizabeth had sent to the hospital and which did nothing to hide her emaciation was pitiful in itself. Both of us were moved in those early days, wanting to protect and indulge her.

In a strange way, for a short time, Olivia helped to bring Douglas and me closer, united in our care for her.

'It's appalling,' Douglas exploded at me soon after her arrival. 'What the hell have they done to her? When I think how she used to look! Those places must be a law unto themselves.'

I hadn't told him about Alec Kemp, though. I didn't want to do it to Olivia, nor even to Elizabeth Kemp. Alec had been worried enough about his public image – and presumably about Olivia – to keep his side of the bargain. That was all that mattered. They could go to hell apart from that.

The silence that had come over Olivia in Arden was still wrapped around her in her waking hours. It was a silence, though, that held no calm. Her mouth was full of ulcers which made it difficult for her to speak or to eat. She was slow in her movements, as if she found it hard to do anything voluntarily, was unused to making choices for herself. She ate very little, wincing at the pain in her mouth. Mostly she sat still and barely spoke.

In the beginning, she slept for hours of each day. I had prepared a room for her with a comfortable chair close to the bed. It was not a very bright room, but she could sit looking out at the garden and the changing light on the poplars. She sat swathed in blankets and extra layers of clothing, often seeming to want to be alone up there. Everything was in shortage that winter. There was barely any fuel to be had and I couldn't light a fire in her room. Often I came in to find her sleeping in the grey daylight, her head propped on a pillow tucked against the arm of the old maroon chair. Sometimes one of her almost weightless hands might be outside the blankets, and I'd cover her again, watching her face, the translucent blue like bruising under her eyes, her hair lying against her cheek.

Her dreams came to her at night. Often I heard her before she had woken herself with her screaming and sobbing. At first came the tiny mewling sounds: small signals of a distress beyond words. I came to recognize it and left my bed to be beside her when it all broke over her, the terrible cries, her eyes opening finally, bulging in her head. Every part of her would shake with extraordinary force.

I held her, night after night, saying, 'Livy, my Livy. It's all right, my love. It's all right now, Katie's here,' over and over until she could hear me. I felt so full of tenderness towards her in those days that it was like a physical ache in me. I devoted myself to this feeling.

When the snow came that winter, falling for days and lying thick, permanent-looking, we stayed in almost all the time, the muffling whiteness like a seal around the house. The city was silenced by it. Factories were being laid off for lack of fuel. I felt my energy concentrate in that house, for my friend and my child.

Livy's silence concerned me, but I felt there was activity in it, not absence. I waited for it to end.

Then one Sunday, after the snow had fallen, the Kemps arrived. Fortunately Douglas was in and answered the door.

'We've come to see Olivia,' I heard Alec say, his voice brisk and businesslike.

Olivia and I were in our sitting-room, chairs pulled close to the meagre fire. The sound of her father's voice seemed to pass through her like a physical force.

'No!' She was on her feet immediately, shaking with agitation. She ran out of the room before they had even got through the front door and took refuge in the kitchen, stumbling down the step. I followed.

'I don't want to see them. I can't. Never. I don't want to see them . . .' Her eyes were stretched open, flecked with distress.

'Livy, Livy – stop.' I took her firmly by the shoulders. 'Listen to me. What matters now is what you want. They don't matter. If you don't want to see them I'll send them away.'

She watched me mutely, disbelieving.

'I promise. You don't have to do anything you don't want to do.'

She said she'd go upstairs and I led her out, repeating what I'd said, trying to soothe her.

'Olivia!' Alec's voice cut harshly across the tiled hall. Douglas had had little choice but to let them in.

Olivia made a convulsive movement, as if the word had struck her like a bullet, and dashed to the stairs. 'No. No!' She ran up, her voice higher than a child's.

'Olivia?' her father cried after her, this time his voice containing a hurt, wheedling tone. 'Darling, come down. We've only come to see you.'

I found myself noticing small details: the smart line of his black coat collar, the white hairs beginning to outnumber his dark ones, the tiny lines like cracks round his mouth. Behind him Elizabeth, wearing a fur hat, was weeping quietly.

'She doesn't want to see you,' I told him. 'You can see that. It's not me trying to stop her, so you needn't accuse me of that.'

I knew Douglas was watching me, taken aback by the bitter tone of my voice.

'But I've come to see her. She's got to see me. We've

had quite a job getting here in this.' He waved an arm towards the door and the white light outside. 'I'm not having this nonsense.' He moved as if to go to the stairs. Elizabeth suddenly reached out, clutching the back of his coat. 'Darling, no. Don't – '

'Let go of me, Elizabeth,' he said quietly. 'I've come to see my daughter and I'm damned if these people are going to stop me.'

'No.' Douglas moved to stand across the foot of the stairs. 'You heard her. She doesn't want to see you.'

I watched Douglas's face, his powerful eyes boring coldly into Alec Kemp. Elizabeth was sobbing, no longer trying to hide the fact.

'Get out of my way.' The ugliness of Alec's tone took even me by surprise. 'Just get out of my way. I'm not putting up with this. I've come to visit my daughter. I'm not being ordered around by some jumped up cripple.'

Blood rushed to Douglas's face. He looked so broad and strong standing there. For a second I thought he was going to punch Alec Kemp but, keeping control, he blazed at him: 'Your daughter doesn't want to see you, and having seen the way you behave I'm not at all surprised. Now take yourself out of my house and don't come back until you're invited here.'

Perhaps that was the first time Alec noticed Douglas's size and strength instead of only seeing his leg. After staring at him for a few seconds, he turned silently and walked back to the front door.

Before Elizabeth could disappear I caught her arm. 'It's not been long,' I said. 'She's not ready yet.' Elizabeth nodded, face half covered by a lace handkerchief. I moved closer and whispered, 'Come on your own another day.' She gave a tiny nod before following her husband out into the flurry of flakes.

Douglas slammed the door behind them. 'What a complete bastard,' he said. He turned to me, embarrassed, needing my approval. 'Sorry.'

I went and put my arms round him. 'Nothing to be sorry for. That just about sums him up. Thank you for what you did.' We kissed, briefly. Then I pulled away from him. 'I'd better go and see what state she's in.'

The tears which followed this went on for days, and I could give her no comfort. It had punctured the great reservoir of feeling in her and she cried and cried, clinging to me in a storm of grief, '*Katie, oh Katie . . .*' her body racked with it. She wept when alone, and when I saw her afterwards her face was puffy and distorted. Sometimes when I looked in on her when she was sleeping there were tears slipping out from beneath her closed lids, rolling down the angle of her cheek towards her hair and the pillow. She couldn't eat. She cried herself sick.

At first I was relieved by this outbreak of emotion. Then I began to panic. I didn't know who to turn to. I wondered if her weakened body could stand such an onslaught of pain. Alone with her, the silence of the snow around us, I feared she might die and I would be responsible for having kept her here without looking for help. I held her tightly, sometimes for an hour or more, making soothing sounds, caressing her and pouring my own emotion into her.

'I can't bear it,' she cried to me. 'My baby. My tiny, tiny boy. I feel as if they've torn my heart out of me.'

Sometimes she took a pillow in her arms and rocked it with her body, trying to find some comfort. I couldn't bear to see it. I could feel the movements of my own child so clearly now. Sometimes I cried with her.

After the thaw came her tears slowed, then stopped. She began to talk. I realize now just how little she really talked about. She had schooled into herself an inability to confide about her home life and her parents. She talked instead, on and on, about her lost baby.

We ventured out at last, walking slowly round the sodden ground of the parks. I revelled in the sensation of the cold air on my face, of using my limbs, feeling I was convalescing after a winter illness. As the days passed, bulbs pushed up through the ground, bursting colour into our grey, sad world. It felt a long time that I had been confined with Olivia. My feelings had been so exhaustingly twisted up with hers. And because of the weather I had seen scarcely anyone else, neither my mother nor Lisa. I longed suddenly to see Lisa, or someone like Brenda Forbes, someone with whom I could have a good, careless laugh. I reflected that the months of my pregnancy had been sad ones, and hoped my child would not be downcast as a result.

One day we were standing by the pond in the middle of Highbury Park, the water flooding over the lip of its normal bed after the thaw. A woman walked past us with three children, two of whom ran boisterously on ahead. The last and youngest, a little girl with straight, brown hair, sidled past us slowly, her eyes never leaving our faces until her mother called her, a sharp note of impatience in her voice.

Watching her, Olivia said, 'You know, by now he must be running around like her – talking – everything. He would be calling me Mummy, wouldn't he?'

I nodded, helplessly. Olivia turned and stared at the ducks, skirmishing on the unusually wide expanse of water. The collar of her black fur coat covered the lower part of her face. I wondered how this wound would ever heal. She had talked endlessly of his birth, every detail of what she remembered of her first and only night with him.

Standing now on the mush of leaves by the bright water, she said, 'I wonder what they've called him?'

'What was your name for him?'

'James. James Robert.'

'Good names,' I said. 'You know Angus's second name was James?'

For a second a smile touched her lips as she stared ahead. 'I remember.'

Those early months of 1947 come to my memory so poignantly. As the spring came, my body blossomed with the season. Douglas was admiring and careful. He understood it was his role to make fewer demands on me in bed and this was a relief.

Olivia's mood shifted gradually. After her time of intense preoccupation with the baby she stopped talking about him. I tried to encourage her to discuss other things: her family, the Wrens, but she was reticent about both. She grew quieter again, calmer, I thought. She did like to talk about our childhood. My mother allowed us to have the piano from her house and Olivia began to work on her music again. Her hair and skin began to show signs of life. She even encouraged Douglas and me to go out together.

'You've had a hard winter, what with the weather and looking after poor old me.' She tried to make it into a joke. 'You should go out together, before the baby comes.'

When she suggested it, it seemed very appealing.

Douglas and I decided to go and see a show, eating out beforehand.

'I do feel rather guilty about leaving her on her own,' I said to him as we were getting ready. 'After all, she's had the hardest time of us all this year.'

'It was her idea, though,' Douglas said. 'And we have had next to no time together.'

Brushing out my hair, I said, 'You've been so patient, darling. Thank you for that.' My voice sounded very polite. I often seemed to find myself being studiously polite to Douglas.

He cleared his throat. 'Well, it won't be for too much longer now, will it?'

I stopped brushing and spoke to his image in the long glass. 'Have you heard more from London?'

'Nothing definite yet.' He was knotting his tie. 'But it won't be long I don't think. And then we'll be on our own again, won't we?'

I tried to sound lighthearted. 'There will be the small matter of a baby!' But I felt desolate at the thought of being alone with Douglas, in a place where I knew no one, and with no Olivia.

Life without her here was becoming unimaginable. Sometimes, when Douglas came in from work, he would find us sitting together having already prepared a meal. Livy might be playing the piano while I rested or sat stitching frocks and coatees for the baby in soft white cotton. Now and then I'd look up at her back, loving the sight of her, absorbed in the music, her hair now gradually inching its way back to its original length and curling a little at the ends.

'Your hair's growing fast,' I'd tell her sometimes, and she'd just shake her head, sending it frisking across her shoulders. She didn't seem to care whether it was or not. I felt a warm, filling happiness at our being together there like that. Other times we sat on the couch talking or reading, Olivia resting her head on my shoulder, her hair soft against my cheek, our feet stretched across the rug towards the fire. And Douglas, walking into this scene, carrying the evening paper, hanging his coat while I fetched him a drink, would say, 'Hello, girls. What sort of day've you had?'

And while he drank down a glass of Scotch, he'd tell us how his had been, bringing some of the outside world in to us. And I knew that in this routine, his finding me always here like this, he felt safe. He had me in the place where he wanted me: an ordered household, female and domestic.

That evening, as we left to go out together, Olivia was cooking poached eggs for herself.

'I'll eat by the fire,' she said lightly. 'It'll be cosy.' She turned, as if inspecting us, and came to straighten the neckline of my frock as if I were a schoolgirl. I kissed her.

Douglas and I stood arm in arm. My coat was tight at the front, but did cover me. 'I shan't be able to do it up soon.' I laughed. Douglas put his arm round me in a show of protectiveness. And I felt very aware of us as a couple, how we must look an exclusive unit, shutting Olivia out. Her face became closed suddenly. She looked at us with a strange, frozen expression.

'Livy?' I stepped aside from Douglas, concerned. 'Are you sure you'll be all right?' I almost felt compelled to call it off, say I'd stay. But she forced a wan smile to her face. 'Yes, of course. Go along now, do. Have a lovely evening, won't you?'

I didn't have a lovely evening. Though I tried to pretend otherwise to Douglas, I felt very uneasy. There was the strangeness of being alone with him, of feeling we had so little to say. And I was worried. That look of Olivia's, something in it hard and realized, which lingered in my mind. By the time we arrived home I was taut with anxiety. I rushed through the house as fast as I could manage in my condition. There was no sign of her downstairs. I climbed the stairs and stood panting at her bedroom door, feeling so foolish when I found her settled in bed. She was sleeping with the little lamp still on, her face severe. I knew that tonight was a warning, though small, that all was not yet well, despite the warm moments with her when I might be lulled into thinking her recovered.

Chapter 26

'What d'you think?'

Olivia burst into our sitting-room which was full of April sunshine and curving tulips. She stood in front of me twirling this way and that.

'What on earth?' I gaped in astonishment at the silky, sea-green material, the close-fitting bodice and abundant, flowing skirt. The dress was everything we had longed for during the scrimping years of the war. Most of us were still longing.

'Isn't it a dream?' Olivia said, still turning in front of me so I could see its effect from all angles. 'A real Dior dress – it's the New Look. I just couldn't resist something with a bit of go in it.' On her feet were a pair of matching green shoes with high, slim heels.

'It's beautiful,' I said, lolling back wearily in my chair. The sight of her looking so thin and elegant made me feel ungainly. The baby was due in three weeks and I was huge and sluggish. 'Are you going anywhere in particular?'

She was jittery with excitement. 'Not yet. But I was thinking, it's about time I started putting myself about a bit more.' She twitched at the skirt, taking a fold between finger and thumb to pull it wide, and dancing round on our worn square of carpet, singing 'I'm gonna meet, a certain party at the station...' She danced too long and hard and stumbled, nearly falling, so that she had to save herself by grasping on to the other armchair.

I watched uneasily, trying to smile at her delight. There was that brittleness, the over-excitement I had seen in her in the weeks before Arden. I was not comfortable examining each of her moves for signs of unbalance, like her warder, but I was worried. Things had begun to niggle at me. I had been concentrating so hard on the thought that if she could grieve for her baby she could find a degree of healing and calm. But now the other memories, which had been pushed out during our time of intense closeness when Livy was childlike, dependent solely on me, needled my mind. Some of the difficult aspects of her behaviour even before the war forced themselves on me.

I could feel things sliding. We had been so close, so tranquil for a few weeks. Unknown to us, we had been inching along a balance, and now the ground was beginning to tilt under us.

Livy had started seeing more of her mother.

'*Darling!*' Elizabeth would say when she flurried into our house, putting on her sparkling social face and a relentless cheerfulness with Livy. 'Look what I've brought you,' she'd cry. She came with new clothes, money, flowers, even sweets, as if pacifying an infant. Elizabeth showed more vivacity than I had seen in her for years. Sometimes the two of them went out shopping together.

On the previous visit, though, it had been damp outside, and they sat in with me. The house felt cosy, smudged light coming from outside through steamed-up windows. I made tea and sat listening to them, taking refuge in knitting to avoid being drawn into the conversation.

'So how are you, darling?' Elizabeth gushed over Livy. She sat close to her, fondling her hand. 'You look so much better,' she went on without giving Olivia time to reply. 'Quite my girl again. Dear Katie must be looking after you so well.' She darted a smile in my direction, her face immaculately masked by powder and lipstick. 'We owe you such a debt, Katie.'

I managed a smile. I didn't want Olivia to know what had passed between me and her parents while she was in Arden, or quite what it had taken to get her out.

'Katie's so marvellous,' Olivia said. Her voice had gone small again: that of a six-year-old. 'I'm really feeling much much better.' I thought of her dreams, the tremor of her body, most nights still.

Elizabeth reached down for a parcel which she had been carrying when she arrived. 'Look, darling – I've brought you something to give you a bit of a lift. Nothing like something new to raise your spirits, is there?'

Olivia took the gift and unwrapped it, sliding out from the layers of paper a handbag in soft brown calfskin. She gave her mother a brilliant smile and leaned over to kiss her cheek, giggling a little breathlessly as she did so.

'It's gorgeous, Mummy, thank you. A lovely thing to have.'

Elizabeth took it from her and unfastened the catch. 'I thought these would come in handy too.' Inside she had put three Arden lipsticks, missing the irony of this completely. She could at least have chosen Helena Rubenstein.

The two of them tittered away together, trying the rich, waxy shades on the backs of their hands.

'That one's more your colour, Mummy,' Olivia said, handing her one of them. 'It's a bit pale for me. Why don't you have it?'

'Oh no, darling!' Elizabeth pronounced the 'darling' each time in an exaggerated, caressing way. 'I bought it for you. It'll look lovely. And listen, I thought after the time you've had' – this her only reference during the visit to the state Livy was in – 'you could do with a nice smart outfit for the spring. We'll go out again and I'll treat you, shall I?'

'That would be lovely,' Olivia said, though perhaps in a flatter voice than Elizabeth had hoped.

Elizabeth kissed her again. 'I'm so glad.' She glanced at me. 'I don't know if Katie would like to come? I suppose now is not the time for you to be laying out money on new clothes for yourself, is it? It'll be all matinée coats and napkins for a time . . . all such a bother at that stage.' She gave a tinkly laugh, smoothing down her crisp fawn skirt. 'Believe me, you'll be glad to have your body back to yourself.'

She took her leave finally, giving me, as she did so, a look of strange coyness as if it were I, not Olivia, who was off-centre and needed humouring. Then she brought out the smile with which she had learned to embellish so many occasions of her married life.

'She does look so much better, doesn't she?' she hissed at me. 'Marvellous, really. And Katie – ' The face was carefully arranged now in lines of solemn gratitude. 'It's you we have to thank.'

I watched her walk down the path to the wet pavement, so elegant and fragile. That woman, I thought, skates round the edges of her life and never dares to reach into the middle of it.

*

When Olivia stayed out all night for the first time, I sat up in bed through the small hours, taut with worry. It was a week before my baby was due to be born.

'This is absurd!' Douglas raged beside me, after both of us had tried and failed to sleep. It was two o'clock in the morning. 'She shouldn't be depriving you of your rest like this, thoughtless little minx.'

'She's not thoughtless,' I said. 'She's off balance. She doesn't know whether she's coming or going – like grass in the wind. I really don't think she can help it.'

'Why d'you always defend her?' Douglas flung back the bedclothes and went for the umpteenth time to the window. He peered each way up and down the street, then gave a loud, impatient sigh. 'No sign. Look, shouldn't we get the police or something?'

'No!' I cried out so vigorously that I felt a kick of protest from the baby inside me. 'I don't want anyone getting hold of her like that. They'd have her back in there . . .'

Douglas limped back over to the bed. 'You think there are grounds, then?'

'Do you?'

'She's not – well – normal, is she?'

'She just needs time.' It was my turn to pull myself out of bed and hold back the curtain. 'Oh, Livy, where are you?' I stood there for a long time, willing her to appear along the road. 'At least it's not as cold as it was.'

'Come back to bed,' Douglas ordered. 'You're not responsible for her. She's an adult.'

'But I am. I feel I am, at the moment. That's the trouble.'

Douglas lay beside me, eyes narrowed. 'Where d'you think she is?'

I hesitated, hardly even wanting to admit it to myself. 'With a man, most probably.'

'But who?'

I sighed. 'I've absolutely no idea.'

'I don't think we can put up with much more of her.'

'Don't start,' I said, trying to find a comfortable position for myself. 'Not now.'

The night crawled past. I made watery cocoa at three. Douglas brewed tea at four-thirty. We lay dozing uneasily. I was sleeping badly at that time anyway because of the pregnancy. I dreamt repeatedly of Olivia, and once I was so certain that she was banging on the front door that I went down to open it and saw only moonlight whitening the houses opposite. By the time morning came, we were exhausted and full of nervous irritability.

At ten o'clock, long after Douglas had left, she came sailing in, wearing an expression of smug satisfaction, of victory almost. There was mud on her coat and her stockings were laddered. She also seemed more than slightly drunk. I felt like strangling her.

'Where've you been?' I snarled. 'We've been awake all night waiting for you.'

'Oh, how quaint – thank you,' she said, walking unsteadily to the kitchen table and sitting down. She gave an enormous yawn. 'I must say, I'm all in.'

'Where have you been?' I found myself shouting, tearful, my voice sliding up to a wail. 'Have you any idea how much worry you've caused? I'm supposed to be looking after you.'

She put on a startled look. 'Katie darling, you musn't worry about me any more. You've got quite enough on your plate with the baby coming and everything.' She stood up again and put her arms round me as I sobbed, the tension of the night releasing itself. 'I want to give you all the help in the world.'

'You smell of booze,' I told her brutally. 'And sex.'

She put on her baby voice, then, that she usually reserved for Elizabeth, and which made me feel wild with rage. 'I was just having one tiny night out,' she wheedled. 'Just for a little change. Don't be cross with me, Katie.'

I pushed her off me impatiently. 'Olivia, come to your senses. You're behaving like a blithering idiot. What d'you think you're doing? You're like a dog on heat.'

'I just wanted a little bit of fun,' she carried on, in the same silly voice.

I lost my temper completely then. 'If you go on like this you'll end up getting pregnant again. Or you'll get VD. Or both.'

She looked at me smugly. 'I'm not that stupid, Katie.'

In a hard, clear voice, I said, 'One more night like last night and you're out of my house. Understand? Out. I'm not going to put up with it.'

The tears came then, hers and mine again. She stood bereft in my arms. 'No, Katie, please. I can't manage without you. I promise I won't do it again. I love you – I've got no one else. Please don't send me away.'

And I stroked her and soothed her, my anger bleached to tenderness, and told her, as I knew I should eventually, that she could stay with me as long as she liked.

Anna. You were born in Selly Oak Hospital into a beautiful April dawn. Your birth was short and harsh, and even in my release of you I felt your energy. You wanted to be born, thrusting towards it urgently. The midwife in the hospital said, 'That's one of the best first births I've ever seen.' And you screamed with all your force, all eight pounds of you, your hair wet and smooth on your head.

I might have had you at home, but I decided not to for Olivia's sake. She was with me when the first pains began and she was the first to see you, even before Douglas, who came after work.

They had brought you for me to feed when she came in that afternoon. I was still in that exhausted, dreamlike state after giving birth, suddenly both empty and joyful, watching your face, letting your existence flow through me.

And there she was, standing in the doorway, dressed smartly in a coat and wide-brimmed hat, both of which would need shedding in the warmth of the hospital. In her hand was a generous spray of freesias. There was a look on her face which was the most genuine and naked she had allowed herself in a long time. It was both hungry and profoundly anxious. I saw that her eyes were fixed not on me, but on the tiny child at my breast.

She smiled suddenly and half ran forward. 'Katie, oh Katie, you're marvellous!' She kissed me, laying the flowers beside my bed. 'They told me it's a girl. How was it, darling? Was it terrible?'

'Not for long.' I smiled. The experience was so close to me still, yet suddenly utterly irrelevant.

Olivia's moment of exposure had passed. From then on she was the model visitor, listening, concerned. When the feed was finished there was a nurse hovering to take you away again.

'Would you like to hold her for a moment, before she has to go?' I asked.

She held you with awe, partly afraid, I could tell, gazing into your tiny, squashed face, her dark eyes wide and tender. She looked across at me and smiled. 'She's wonderful, Kate. She's a miracle. Does she have a name yet?'

'Anna.'

'Just Anna?'

'One name's enough, I think.'

'Of course it is. Little Anna.' She raised you so gently and kissed your forehead before handing you to the nurse. You let out a roar and Olivia looked taken aback and then laughed. 'Be happy,' she said. 'Little Anna.'

Later the nurse said to me, 'She's a lovely-looking girl, that friend of yours. I thought I recognized her – or was it just my imagination?'

If only Douglas could have seemed so lovely. He disliked seeing signs of human frailty and was very ill at ease in the hospital. I had hoped for him to be loving and awestruck, reaching out to his child. Instead, he was deeply uncomfortable in this public place of the ward, unable to expose any softer feelings he may have had.

His progress along the wooden floor to my bed was rather like walking across a stage. I was so used to the sight of him that I barely thought of it, but I knew he sensed the eyes of the other women on his contorted leg, the terrible graceless walk.

He said, 'Hello,' leaning over to give me a busines-like peck on the cheek, for which for a second I hated him.

'Did they tell you we have a little girl?'

'Yes.' He sat down on the chair by the bed. 'They told me. Are you all right, Katie?'

The question came awkwardly. I suppose the act of giving birth was so foreign to him, so personal.

'I feel better than I expected.' There was a silence. 'I thought we'd call her Anna.'

Douglas nodded. 'Whatever you like. Is she . . . she's healthy and all that?'

He was afraid, of course, that you'd be like him: not whole. That he would have marred you in some way.

'She's beautiful.' I reached out to take his hand, which rested stiffly in mine. 'Don't worry. She's a lovely baby. I'll ask them to bring her, shall I? She'll need feeding soon.'

He was so awkward with you, Anna, right from the beginning. He watched your little form approaching in the nurse's arms with a solemn face.

'I'll give her a little bit of a feed,' I said. 'Then she'll be happy when you hold her.'

The moment I started to feed you he was on his feet. 'Look – I'll go and have a cigarette outside. I'll come back when you've finished.' And he was off again along the ward as if he couldn't get out fast enough.

When he did come back and hold you, there was no engagement in it. He held you in the stiff way I have seen some other fathers put on with infants, not wanting to expose their tenderness, not knowing how. He rocked you too hard and made you cry. He never looked into your face deeply the way a mother would. To him you were my realm, something abstract, 'a child' for which he was in some way responsible.

When I got home I was so grateful for Olivia being there. Douglas seemed to have nothing to give us. My mother called a few times, admired you in a professional sort of way, and made comments like, 'I hope you're not overfeeding her,' but seemed unable to cope with being at a remove from you, so that she could not just take over. Her visits soon dwindled. But Olivia, for the first month, was as loving and helpful as I could ever have wished.

At that time her devotion to us was so warming. I needed someone to rely on and she was always there offering to hold you, there for me to talk to. She was comfort, while Douglas was more absent than ever.

'She's an absolute darling,' she'd say, rocking you on her lap, her eyes fixed on your face. I can see her now, her hair curling on her shoulders, her look of adoration which made me ache for her. Once I said to her, 'Doesn't it make you feel sad, seeing her and holding her?'

Without taking her eyes from your face, she said, 'No, it's marvellous. I could sit and hold her all day.' She smiled, running her finger down your cheek. 'That'd be heaven, wouldn't it, little Anna?' Then she looked up at me. 'She's ours, isn't she?'

I should have taken note of the strange intensity of this, but I was happy then, feeling we shared you. She showed far more interest and feeling than Douglas, and I confided in her completely.

'It's so silly. Douglas is so jealous of the baby. He just can't seem to adjust to it all. I feel so much for her and he just . . .' My voice trailed off.

'He does seem rather stiff with her,' Livy said smoothly. She was busy now, knitting for me as we sat looking down the long garden, pansies flattening open in the sun. Now that I was a bit unsteady in myself and relying on her, she looked better, calm and secure.

She reached out one hand to jiggle the pram slightly. 'Never mind, little angel Anna. You've got two people here who love you. There's nothing to worry about. Oh Kate – can I just give her another cuddle?'

'Leave her!' I protested impatiently. 'I've only just this minute got her to sleep.'

Olivia pouted. 'All right. Better let her get her rest.' She went back to her knitting, curling soft white wool round her fingers. After a moment she gave me a quizzical look, tilting her head. 'Is everything all right with Douglas . . . otherwise, I mean?'

I knew what she was asking. 'The doctor advised us that there should be no intercourse for at least six weeks. You'll know that, of course. I think Douglas feels pushed out. He doesn't like to see me feeding her. I know that's not an especially unusual reaction, but it's still hurtful.' I found myself unexpectedly in tears.

'Poor Katie,' Olivia said, coming over to put her arm round me. 'And poor old Douglas. But still, you must do as they tell you,' she went on in a silky voice. 'You need time for your body to recover. Don't let him push you into it, will you, before you're ready?'

'Don't worry.' I was laughing now. I was supposed to be the Health Visitor. I leaned against Olivia. 'I'm sorry to be so soggy – and I'm so glad you're here. This would all have been very lonely without you.' We smiled, our eyes meeting, and I thought Livy looked happy.

'D'you feel better?' I asked.

'I think so.' She shrugged. 'I don't want to keep examining it. I just want to be here, with Anna – and you.'

I remember that month, its fractured nights, its intensity and blossoming of new feelings, only as a blur now, like a kind of illusion. There was sunshine, bright green leaves on the trees, walks pushing you in the huge, heavy pram in which I myself had lain as a child and which my mother produced in magnificent condition from where it had been stored, swathed in canvas, in the cellar. There were quiet times sitting in the park, light shimmering on the water; there was watching Olivia's face at the sight of you and feeling that you were healing her; and my own contentment: your eyes wide over the top of a white sheet, reflecting sky.

But there was also Douglas's discomfort with our new state, his absence and immersion in work, always his resort. There was my mother's stiff detachment from us. And then there was the day when I heard you screaming downstairs while I was resting, leaving you in Olivia's care. On coming down I found you beside yourself with frustration, and Olivia's face all red, her hands grabbing at the front of her blouse which was open to reveal her breasts. I stood staring with an icy fury of which I barely knew I was capable.

'I just thought I might be able to do it,' she said, in that stupid, childlike voice again. 'To save you the trouble while I'm looking after her.'

Trembling, I snatched you from her without a word, and ran upstairs, holding you close, so tight and close to me.

Chapter 27

'We thought you'd gone off us,' Lisa said, when I arrived that Sunday afternoon, baby in arms. Don and the boys were out.

'I'm sorry. I've been dying to see you.' As I spoke I realized just how true that was, how Olivia's company weighed on me. I had had to get out, to have a rest from her. I'd managed to be away from home most of the day by going to church in the morning.

Lisa and I sat side by side with cups of tea on the table and babies on our laps. Lisa had her little girl, Alice, who looked small at the side of my Anna, but whose face was full of character, her nose cheeky and snub. Daisy, a quaint, fussing little thing now in a dress at least a size too big, hovered around us.

'She's mad about babbies,' Lisa said, after we had been admiring the little girls together. Daisy slid from one to the other, kissing them and stroking their heads until Lisa had to say, 'Go easy now, Daze, eh?' The babies followed her with their eyes, giving gummy smiles.

Lisa looked robust and content. 'She was the easiest of the lot,' she told me. 'She got 'ere in a couple of hours.'

'I'll have to get more practice, obviously.' I laughed.

'You're looking all right on it, though.'

I played with Daisy for a while, giving her a Ladybird

book I'd brought with some pictures and simple words in. Daisy pointed and said, 'Dog. Flower. S'easy, this is.'

''Ow's your friend coming on?' Lisa asked.

'Bit by bit, I think. It's a slow business, though. Have you seen anything of Joyce, or Jackie?'

Lisa shook her head. 'Not really, now you mention it. Funny thing is, they said 'ardly a word about it after. I thought they'd be full of it, you making a fool of him like that. But they all just went.'

'They were ashamed.'

Lisa's brow crinkled into lines of surprise. 'Ashamed?'

'When it came to facing him like that. I was ashamed too. Wouldn't you have been?'

'Me?' Lisa hoiked Alice further up in her arms. 'Nah. There's a lot of men around'll use you for anything – wipe the floor with you if it suits 'em. Don't see why we should spend our lives kowtowing to 'em.' With her free hand she topped up my cup of tea. Then, as if a connection had been made in her mind, she said, 'How's your 'usband?'

I longed to be honest, to say, he's a detached stranger who I don't know how to be with any longer and I'm not sure I even like. But who is ever so honest?

'He's well,' I said. 'Thank you.' But I found myself adding, 'Lisa – has Don ever minded, when you're feeding Alice?'

'You mean is he jealous?' She thought about it. 'Can't say as I've ever asked 'im. 'E just 'as to put up with it. Why, is your old man?'

'It is rather difficult at the moment,' I told her stiffly. I found it so hard to confide about my marriage. Lisa was much more matter-of-fact about the subject of hers. But I had been brought up to regard this subject as the proverbial closed book. It was only Granny Munro who had let me into her feelings, shown me that her marriage had survived despite so many things.

'Course, I know some do carry on a bit. Come to think of it, Agnes over there' – she jerked her head in the direction of a house along the court – ''as some right ding-dongs with 'er old man. On and on 'e goes, and it's always worse when 'e thinks the babbies're getting 'is share of 'er titties.'

I laughed. 'That reminds me of Marj Redmond, an old Health Visitor I used to work with. She said they only ought to allow people to get married if the wife spoke only French and the husband only German.'

Lisa gave an explosive chuckle. 'That's about it though, in't it? That's marriage all over for you.'

But I could tell from her tone and from the look of her that Don and she were far happier together than Douglas and I.

'Lisa,' I told her, 'it's unbelievably good to see you.'

I would have liked a longer journey home. As the bus ground its slow way along the Alcester Road towards Kings Heath I sat with you, warm and sleepy on my lap. I wished I could just stay there and follow the route right out of the city to anywhere, in order to sit there and have some peace.

The week before there had been a scene with Douglas. After I came home from hospital I had, as promised, sent a line to Roland Mantel. He had been kind and interested that time on the train, and I hoped he'd pass on the news to Marjorie.

Roland arrived one afternoon when Olivia was out shopping. I was taken aback by the rush of pleasure I felt at seeing him.

'Got the opportunity of a little bit of time off,' he said in apologetic tones from the doormat. He rotated the brim of an old panama hat nervously between his fingers, his round face looking red and moist. 'I expect you're busy. Am I an awful bother?'

'Not at all, Roland.' I found I was smiling broadly. 'I've just put the baby out in the garden. Do come through and have a drink, won't you?'

'Well, if that's really all right.' He followed me down the hall, every gesture of his body self-effacing. He made admiring noises about the house. 'You've got it looking so nice, haven't you? I'm afraid I've been rather lazy with mine – the people before left it in reasonable repair and I've done next to nothing on it. Not one of my skills in any case.' He laughed.

In the garden he said, 'I thought I must come and see the baby before she's off to school – you know how the time goes!' He gave another little chuckle and I waited for him to relax. His nervous nature could make him sound so silly. Once relaxed out of that, the kind, sympathetic person could emerge.

He beamed with pleasure bending over to look into the pram. You were asleep, your face round and relaxed, arms flung out beside your head, hands clenched into plump fists. 'Oh, isn't she a poppet!' he exclaimed. 'Oh, Katie, I do envy you, you know. There's nothing I'd like more than a family of my own.'

I smiled gratefully at him. 'I'm sure you will have one one day. And you'll make a lovely, devoted father.'

He sat with me for a while. He declined beer, so I fetched tea and an ashtray and he sat, his short legs encased in grey flannel, smoking and chatting to me, gradually losing his twitchy demeanour. Marjorie was expecting her first child and sent her love. We spent an unruffled half hour, refreshing to me for its lack of angles or tension.

'I'd love to come again,' Roland said. He lingered by the pram before leaving. 'And perhaps she'll be awake next time?' I assured him of a welcome.

Douglas found the ashtray, forgotten between the chairs in the garden, when he came home from work. He went outside for a smoke in the summer evening air and came crashing back in again, holding the ashtray away from him like a half-decayed bird.

'Who's been here?' he demanded, in the self-righteous voice that I was coming to loathe.

Olivia sat very still watching us, the baby on her lap.

'Oh, just Roland,' I said casually. I was shelling peas in the kitchen, refusing to be ruffled by this ridiculousness.

'Roland? That's him, isn't it – the one I saw you with at the station?'

He advanced into the kitchen, his face ugly, and slung the glass ashtray down on the draining board, pettishly and too hard.

'D'you mind?' I protested. I dried my hands on my apron, preparing to walk away before I really let rip with my temper and announced that Roland had been the most pleasant and normal company I had had for weeks.

'Why didn't you tell me he was coming?'

I clenched my teeth. 'Because I didn't know. He was just on his way from somewhere I think. I didn't ask.'

'How many times has he been here before?' He leaned up against the sink, menacingly close to me. It was so silly and alienating. I felt impatience choking me.

Just controlling my voice, I said, 'That was the first time. And I don't really see it's any business of yours.

He was passing and he wanted to see Anna. Some men actually like babies,' I finished bitterly.

'It is my business.' He pushed his face too close to mine and the expression in his eyes was very cold. 'This is my house and you are my wife. I won't have you entertaining other men under my roof.'

I always felt at my most strong and perverse when he was like this. I knew I didn't have the attitude of subservience apparently expected of a 'good' wife. Even trying to have it would have suffocated me. I could hear Granny Munro saying, 'Don't let anyone take your life away from you. It's not worth it in the end. It's only convention.'

I stared Douglas in the face and said something that I am still ashamed of now for its cruelty. 'You're useless to me, Douglas. Completely useless.'

He picked up the pan into which I had been shelling peas and smashed it as hard as he could through the kitchen window, peas and all. Glass tinkled down on to the flower pots outside. I heard you, Anna, begin howling in the adjoining room, startled by the noise. At the time I felt most annoyed about the peas going out after I'd spent all that time shelling them.

Douglas stood for a second looking stunned and foolish. Then, as if it was his masterstroke, he brought out the announcement, 'What I came home to tell you is that I've got the job. We're leaving for London.'

He went out of the house then, leaving this ultimatum dumped like a tin trunk in the middle of the front room. Olivia came to me and we managed somehow to put our arms round each other, you pink and distraught between us.

Sitting on the bus that afternoon, I thought about Douglas and about how he always seemed to get it wrong. How he could never see that my feelings for my child and for Olivia were far more of a threat to him than Roland Mantel or anyone else was. I knew already that my going to London with him was inconceivable. I dared myself to imagine, for a second, what it would be like without him at home: just me and Anna and Olivia. I knew that part of this breakdown between us was my fault. But I also knew that I was inextricably tied both to this place and to Olivia.

I walked slowly along the road back to our house. Though still small, you felt heavy in my arms and were beginning to clamour for a feed. I took in the smell of flowers on the warm air, the sensation of milk aching in my breasts. I walked faster. Inside, I expected to find the house quiet, Douglas sheltering behind his newspapers, Olivia busy with her knitting or napping.

But he was upon me before I'd even shut the door. 'She's got to go!' At first I thought he was angry, but it was something a few degrees away from that. He was distraught.

'Whatever's happened? Look, I'll have to feed Anna or I can't hear you.' I unfastened my dress and Douglas waited impatiently until the room grew quiet. 'Where's Olivia?'

'Out. I sent her out. Kate, she's got to leave here as soon as possible. Tell her to go – tonight.'

I stared at him, feeling mutinous already. Douglas turned round, looking into the fireplace as he spoke to me. 'She started on me this afternoon.'

I couldn't take this in. 'What are you talking about?'

With injured dignity he said, 'She tried to seduce me.'

I fought back a wild desire to laugh. The first words which rushed into my mind were, 'Well, that must have been a disappointment for her.' Fortunately, instead I managed to say, 'Heavens, how dreadful!' Then I added, 'Are you all right?' before realizing what an absurd question that was. The awfulness of the situation began to sink in.

'Of course I'm all right,' he snapped, pacing up and down. 'But we can't very well carry on having her here. She's outstayed her welcome by a long time as it is. And she's not right, is she?' He turned to face me. 'Don't you mind that she's tried it on with me?'

'I can't quite take it in.'

Douglas came and sat down beside me, suddenly vulnerable. 'The thing was – it wasn't so much that she tried it on that worried me. I mean I know she's always been a bit, well – fast like that. I could have laughed about it, or told her to leave off. But it was her look. She was like a snake, and the things she was saying, it was frightening. I felt what she really wanted to do was to torture me. That was how she looked, absolutely intent and venomous, as if she ought to have had a red-hot poker in one hand.'

I listened, chilled. That thread of something corrupt in Olivia which kept lashing out like a poisoned tongue.

In the end I said, 'I'm truly sorry, Douglas. That's unforgivable, of course. It's just – where's she going to go? If you could just put up with her a while longer . . .'

There was a silence before he said, 'She'll have to leave anyway when we go to London.'

I couldn't tackle that one. Not now.

'It won't happen again,' I said. 'Not now she's tried it once.'

I didn't confront Olivia. I found myself unexpectedly embarrassed by the thought of it. I had been lulled, since giving birth, by her apparent steadiness, her adoration of my baby, my need of her when I would otherwise have felt so low and alone. Now, though, I was bristling and alert, on guard once more. The evening Douglas had sent her out of the house she stayed out all night again and came back with the same air of repletion and triumph. I didn't even speak to her when she came in next morning.

'Aren't you dying to know where I've been?' she goaded me. 'I do hope you haven't been waiting up?'

'I was up anyway,' I said curtly. 'Anna's been restless with this cold.' I was still pacing up and down with you fretting in my arms. By that time I was tired enough to be almost beyond feeling.

'Here, give her to me,' Olivia said, reaching out to take you. 'I'll get her settled down.'

'We're getting on all right, thank you,' I said shortly. 'She's been like this for hours, on and off.'

Olivia held out her arms again, commandingly. 'Then you need a rest. Come on, hand her over to Auntie Livy.'

'No. She's my child, not yours – especially not the state you're in. She wants her mother.'

Olivia's arms dropped to her sides. She said nothing and turned to go out of the room. As she did so she twirled round and whipped her skirt up high, showing her suspenders. On one leg the stocking was held up by only one fastening. The others were broken and the stocking was laddered down the back of her leg. With a terrible smile on her face she said, 'They can't resist me.'

We couldn't be normal with each other now. I found myself thinking of ways to get her out. I couldn't send her back to the Kemps. At that point I wouldn't have been so cruel. I still wanted to do it kindly, to ease her out, with our move to London as the excuse. My thoughts of staying here with her now seemed grotesque. But I couldn't think of anywhere she could go. I even considered asking my mother if Olivia could lodge with her, but I knew instinctively that this would be a disaster. Besides, my mother had held herself at such a distance from us over the months that I couldn't even have asked. Olivia was just going to have to find digs for herself.

I didn't want her looking after you any more, Anna. Before, I had pushed away any feelings of resentment at her swamping possessiveness of you. I had thought her feelings for you would help her heal, her holding you like that, staring into your face so long that sometimes I had almost to fight her to make her hand you over to me. At times I had wanted to shout, 'Give her to me – she's my baby, not yours!' like a child with a toy. I had been ashamed then. But now I allowed myself those feelings: a new instinct of protectiveness in me, a premonition that I did not yet understand.

Neither she nor Douglas ever told me directly how far her attempts to seduce him had gone, but that final week Olivia started making remarks, taunting me deliberately, eyes wide and brazen, and I realized it had gone further than Douglas had felt able to admit. Far enough for her to learn of his inadequacy.

'Are you sure Anna is Douglas's?' she giggled to me one evening when we were alone. She was on the gin. 'I'm surprised he could keep going long enough to hit the target!'

I no longer knew what to do with her. I could feel far more sympathy now for the Kemps and what they'd been through. All the warmth had gone. Mostly I ignored her, moving round her as if she wasn't there, preparing myself to eject her. As a last resort I knew I should have to call a doctor, and the thought played on my conscience.

Then, that one morning, I gave in to her. I felt so harassed. Your cold was no better and you were almost constantly in my arms, since I could find no other way of pacifying you. I had a huge pile of washing to do and a host of other jobs. And Livy seemed calmer that day.

'I just can't get on with anything,' I cried, tearful with frustration. 'If only she'd settle. I'm doing all the things I used to advise my mothers not to do!'

'Let me take her,' Olivia said. She spoke so smoothly, her face soft and smiling. 'We've hardly seen each other this week, have we, darling?' This last word was said in just the tones Elizabeth used with her.

Livy was wearing a cornflower-blue frock that morning. She was looking very beautiful and I relented, almost wanting to kiss her. When I handed you to her, a soft cotton sheet wrapped round you, she stood for a moment with you clasped in her arms like a madonna, her face radiant and smiling.

She turned the smile on me. I've never been able to forget the look of worship for you in her face. 'Come on, little Anna,' she said. 'We'll just go and have a play upstairs and let Katie get on with all her chores.' She left the room, humming lightly as she climbed the stairs.

I was seized with the urgency I always felt when you were sleeping or taken off my hands. I already had all the clothes heaped on the kitchen floor, napkins soaking in a pail. I spent some time sorting them, dividing whites from coloureds while the wide sink filled slowly. When I'd finished with the clothes, it still wasn't ready and I sprinkled Hudson's into the water, impatiently turning on the tap as far as it would go. The water had slowed to a trickle and I tutted in exasperation, staring at the dull metal of the tap, willing it to force out more water. Before the sink was even full I pushed in a bundle of clothes and began pummelling at it, trying to wet everything in the inadequate depth of water. Suddenly the water came on again with a rush. I frowned, turning the tap down again. Bubbles rose softly round my wrists.

A few moments later I remembered our nightclothes and ran upstairs for my nightdress and Douglas's pyjamas. On my way down, I paused at the top of the stairs. It was very quiet up there, except for a sound, a tiny sound I couldn't place but which alerted me. Puzzled, I looked into Olivia's room. I thought perhaps she might be lying on the bed, trying to settle you down beside her.

She was standing with her back to me, the blue frock vivid in front of our dark furniture. My mind struggled – for such a long, slow time it seemed – to make sense of this. The chest of drawers in front of her had been cleared, the toilet mirror now standing at a queer angle on the bed, along with her perfume, powder, lotions. I could see each end of the enamel baby bath, its bright, bluish white; Olivia's elbows looking creamy against it. Her arms were held straight, taut. And there was silence. Then a movement of water. A tiny splash in the quiet. It was this sound, its restrained smallness which I had registered as odd and which now sliced across my mind.

You were never silent in the bath: you gurgled or screamed.

I was there in a second, my body tight and violent. Half turning, Olivia glared at me with a hard, determined expression. One of her hands was spread over your face, pushing you under the water, the other holding your body down. She had filled the bath deep. Your arms and legs were moving madly, but barely managing to agitate the water's surface.

I grabbed Olivia by the neck and flung her across the room with all my strength. She fell and hit her head on the bedside cabinet, and I was pulling my baby up into my arms, completely possessed by panic, water saturating the front of my dress. I held you upside down, banging on your back, and a small gush of water came from your nose and mouth, then your choking, anguished cries reaching higher and higher. As I held you you thrust your head back, so beside yourself that there were seconds of silence between each cry, your spine bowing, rigid. I snatched up the little sheet and wrapped you in it and held you close to me, hearing distressed, animal sounds of comfort coming from me as I rocked you.

After a moment, hands shaking, I unfastened my dress and tried to let you suck to calm you, gulping and trembling as I did so, and your little body twitched convulsively as you began to latch on to me, too agitated to do so at first. I was oblivious to Olivia. I didn't care if I'd killed her.

It was only as I was beginning to come to my senses that I realized she was laughing. Sitting on the floor rubbing her head and giving off high peals of laughter. Too stunned to think, I sat staring at her, still crying, stroking my little Anna again and again.

Olivia got to her feet. 'Sorry, old girl. I've not had much practice bathing babies. Never even got to bath my own.'

She walked over to the window, standing with her

back to me, a scrawny silhouette against the light. She lit a cigarette and stood smoking it in silence.

Then she said, 'You want me to leave.' There was amusement in her voice, as if she found me ridiculous.

I didn't answer, couldn't.

She blew out a trail of smoke. 'By the way, there's one more thing I haven't told you.' The voice floated over to me, to wherever I was.

'I'd have spared you this, but truth does have a way of finding us, doesn't it?'

I waited. There was nothing worse she could do.

'That child of mine. My baby. I did know who the father was, you know.'

Indifferent to this information, I sat in silence.

'I was in London – that January – for the Wrens. Pretty beastly it was too. Then who should I run into, fresh back from embarkation leave, but an old friend from home . . .'

I was on my feet. 'No. No!'

'Dents your image rather, doesn't it? Pure, loyal old Angus. Actually, he was in a bit of a state, I thought. Terrified about the posting. And of course by the end of the night he was worse. Full of remorse, disloyal to you and all that. Katie his love, how could he have . . .' She mocked me. 'Of course I said he must think of it as something that meant nothing. I expect he wrote to you, didn't he? "Ran into Olivia. We had such a nice cosy chat."'

'I don't believe you.'

'I knew it was his, Katie. I was unusually busy that month. Very little time to spare for any hanky-panky . . .'

'You're lying to me!' I screamed at her, so that you released me and started yelling as well, Anna. 'Angus would never have done something like that.' The words fell awkwardly from my mouth. 'As a matter of fact he didn't even like you all that much.'

Olivia laughed again, head flung back. 'Oh, darling – they don't have to *like* you!'

'You're lying.' I could hardly breathe, was growing incoherent. 'Why are you doing this? I've done everything for you . . . Tell me it's a lie, just a story.'

But she was silent, turned to watch me, the cigarette held at a jaunty angle in her hand, her face exultant.

We stood like that in silence for a few seconds before I found my voice again. 'Get out of my house. I want you out by midday. Otherwise you'll be back in Arden tonight.'

I left her, holding you close to my body. I couldn't let go of you. I wrapped you up and walked to the park, carrying you round and round in the strong sunshine, hardly knowing what I was doing. When finally I returned home, the house was empty.

Chapter 28

It was Lisa I turned to, then. I was in a terrible state. I couldn't bear to be parted from my baby for a second out of fear something would happen. Night after night I woke sweating, my hands grasping for you, sometimes screaming. I moved out of my bed with Douglas so that I could sleep with you, guard you. It was as if the odour of Olivia had not passed from the house and she could still harm you. And in my fear of losing you I couldn't bear to try and imagine how Olivia must have felt in parting with her child. It was too much – such thoughts sent my emotions into too great a conflict. I pushed them out of my mind.

Douglas was very impatient and thought me hysterical. 'She's all right – none the worse for it.' At least it had meant me getting shot of Olivia. That's what he was bothered about. But I couldn't have cared less about him. You were the only person who mattered to me, Anna. I saw everyone else close to me as a source of betrayal and I curled in on myself. I had a wall round me. I suppose now they would say I was traumatized and depressed

Lisa was different, of course. She was full of common sense and free of illusions.

'Look,' she suggested, when to the fascination of her neighbours I had turned up again, weeping and distraught at her door. 'When you're ready, leave the littl'un with me. She can be with Alice for a bit and Daisy'll help look after 'em. You know what she's like with babbies. Even five minutes. It's a start. You can't go on like this. You're making yourself bad with it.'

I needed help and I took her advice. I had an instinctive trust in her that I felt for no one else. Sick with anxiety the first time, I left you lying there on the blanket next to Alice. Daisy was shaking an old tin with a few dried peas in for you. For ten minutes I paced with weak legs, up and down Stanley Street and Catherine Street. When I had decided to return to you I had to hold myself back from running down the road. I dashed the final few yards across the court and went in to find you laughing.

'See?' Lisa said. Then added, 'That Kemp girl needs locking up. You should've called the police. You've spared that family too much.'

'Perhaps it was partly my fault,' I said, holding you close to me, my legs still trembling. 'And I don't want them on my conscience. I want them right out of my life – all of them.'

'But she might try it with someone else's?'

I sat down, frowning. 'I don't think so.'

'Where's she gone?'

I shrugged. 'I've no idea. Away from me, that's the main thing.'

Lisa gradually weaned me off my terror. When I could leave you with her for an hour, I knew I was overcoming it. But often during that time I would arrive at her house and dissolve into tears. And she was always welcoming, sitting me down amidst all the chaos of her life and letting me be there, whatever was going on at the time.

'You're so good to me,' I told her. 'There's just no one else.'

'We're friends, aren't we?' was all she said.

My mother would be no good, I knew that. I was in a thoroughly distraught state, but couldn't have admitted it to her. And anyway, other people's nerves usually got thoroughly on hers. I knew also that she was not the person to consult about the other decision which faced me more pressingly as each day passed. If I didn't go to London with Douglas, I knew it would be the end of my marriage.

'What would you do?' I asked Lisa one day.

Lisa eased Alice up over her shoulder, the child's head resting against her cheek. Her skin looked grey and tired.

'In your shoes?' She frowned. 'I dunno. I s'pose 'e is your 'usband when all's said and done. But 'e's making you uproot yourself . . . 'Ow d'you feel about 'im?'

After a silence broken only by small sounds from the babies, I finally admitted, 'I can't stand him.'

'Well then,' Lisa said. 'You can earn a good wage on your own, can't you?'

When Douglas left we moved into our small terraced house in Florence Road in which you grew up until we moved to Drayton Road when you were eleven.

I didn't find the courage to tell him until he insisted on us beginning to pack. We were speaking so little anyway. He said, 'You've betrayed me. I always knew you would.'

I sat on our bed and replied, 'Then why marry me?'

The communication between us remained thin and stretched through those days of practicalities. I found myself looking at him in such a detached way sometimes, wondering what, in those disturbed days of the war, I had thought I felt for him and what had kept me believing it. I was weary and indifferent. You were asleep when he left and he, your father, didn't even go to your room to look at you. We didn't speak. I watched him walk down the road from the house with his cases and his camera round his neck and thought that I still hadn't been to see his parents. He didn't write. I never pursued him for money. I could, as Lisa had remarked, earn my own. Occasionally I saw signs of his career developing in newspaper bylines and felt some shame at how little I missed him.

I was happy with you, Anna, and happy to devote my life only to us.

It was Lisa who had prepared me for my separation from you. When I went back to work I found dear old Mrs Busby. I suppose she wasn't so old, when you were still a baby, but she was grandmotherly even in her late forties. The first time she opened the door to me and saw me standing there with you in my arms, she said, in real tones of appreciation, 'Oh, what a beautiful baby.' I trusted her immediately. Whenever I came to collect you you were always clean, fed and occupied, and you had Reni James, company which you wouldn't have had at home. I owed such a debt to Edith Busby. I loved my work. Life settled and didn't feel lacking. I had you, my job, Roland. Dear Roland – he has always been such a good friend to us.

I saw Olivia one more time, in the summer of 1962. She was back up here for a time then. Alec Kemp more or less paid to keep her out of the way, like a wayward son being packed off to be shameful somewhere distant like Africa. Except she chose London.

My morning's list of calls included a visit to a Mrs Kemp, with a new baby. The name registered, of course, but it never occurred to me it would be her, not here in Birmingham, nor with 'Mrs' as the handle on the name. She was living in Moseley in one of those enormous Victorian houses that had already been sliced up inside for flats. I had to climb a flight of stairs – grand ones once, though dirty and communal now – to find the chipped door marked '3'.

She was holding him as she answered the door, her small frame wrapped in a turquoise silk robe, hair loose and falling all over the place. The child was very tiny and startlingly dark. I realized immediately that the father must have been from India or similar. His eyes were huge, brown and alert.

We never spoke. As soon as I'd realized who it was I was on my way back down those grimy stairs and out to the car. When I sat down in the seat I was shaking. I managed to drive back to the clinic, and handed Olivia's notes over to another Health Visitor. I wasn't having anything of that. Not after all this time.

For Anna

May 1981

My dear one,

I suppose I should have written this a long time ago and got it out of my system. It's our story: Olivia's and mine. You used to ask me about Olivia so often when you were a little girl, and what I used to feed your curiosity was a lie, or at least such a selective version of the truth as to amount to one.

You will see from her letter enclosed with this that Olivia didn't die during the war. In a way it was simpler for me to let you think she was dead all this time, and the fact was that for me she might just as well have died. I wanted her out of my life as cleanly as death would have taken her. She'd done such damage and I couldn't stand any more.

But I couldn't resist telling you my happy memories. When you were young and fierce with affection for your friends it made me think of her so often and how we were together. We did have those good, happy times, Anna. I shouldn't want you to think I had invented those. I always wanted you to know about Olivia as I knew her then, because I have loved very few people as I loved Livy.

I've tried to be frank with you about all aspects of my life. I've always admired your straightness and I know this is what you would want. Some of it you'll already know, but there's much that you don't. I seem to have ended up telling you my life story – but then there's not much from that period of my life which is not somehow bound up with Olivia.

I hoped to tell you all this at some point. I didn't, though, expect you to hear any of it from Olivia herself. But in 1976 Alec Kemp died, and not long after that she began writing to me. They had gone very quiet, the Kemps. He stayed on the Council for a time, but he certainly never made it as an MP. I don't recall him ever standing for Parliament again – a fact which has somehow made it easier for me to forgive him. What relations were like between Olivia and her parents all those years, I've no idea. But the letters started coming. She begged me to see her. She sent me bits and pieces which she must have written in London after she left Arden Mental Hospital. Some of these were rather disconnected, but the ones I have included for you speak clearly. They tell of things I barely guessed at the time: the hidden side of her life at home of which I felt the vibrations, but for many years knew nothing of the causes. Her father's death must have prompted her to reach back into the past and try to explain it. These fragments are, though, I have to add, stamped with Olivia's hallmark: a complete lack of remorse for her actions.

I didn't respond. Even now I couldn't bear to see her.

I hope, Anna, that I have also given you enough of a sense of who your father was. Even had things been different, I don't think we would have lasted in the end. He wanted to keep me like a cupboard full of starched white napkins and bring one out now and then to wipe his face on. Your generation would put up with that even less well than I did.

I'm sorry I couldn't just tell you this face to face, but it goes too deep, and I find I am more like my own mother in some ways than I've always hoped. I'm even glad you won't be able to question me about it. I know how ill I am, whatever they say to humour me, and that my life now measures in weeks.

But if you were to decide you needed to see Olivia, I should understand. Of course I haven't seen her properly for over thirty years and I no longer know her. I'm sure she would wish you only good – really she always did – but I still can't help feeling I want to pull you close in my arms and protect you from her as if you were still my tiny baby. This is quite irrational I realize. Even so, I would give you one warning: caution.

Now I have finished with all this I feel only sadness about the Kemps. About all of it. I'm sorry if you feel I cut Olivia's truth in half and chose to give you only the more palatable slice. It was all I could do. And now all I want is peace for the remains of my life. I want to remember the loving parts. What is forgivable by me, I forgive. Anything else is probably God's department.

I'm so very proud of you, my Anna. I hope you know that in all you have done you've been the greatest joy of my life. Go well, my darling.

Part Four

Chapter 29

ANNA

Warwickshire, 7 August 1981

'You're not going *in* there, surely?'

The ivy leaves snaking round the stone gateway were such a dark green that in the stormy light they looked almost black. Between them she could make out some of the carved letters: *Arden Mental Hospital*, and in Roman numerals, 1848.

The black cab growled rhythmically, wipers swishing away rain which was hammering on to the windscreen. The driver had spoken with his nose buried in his hanky.

'Yes – I need you to wait please,' Anna said, more sharply than she had intended. 'I shan't be long. 'Specially not in this.' She pulled a navy beret over her straw-coloured hair.

So this was the place. They had driven for some time, winding between cornfields, seeing its gaunt shape growing nearer on the rise, until they reached the entrance further round the flank of the hill among the trees.

Arden.

Trying to control her nervousness, she asked, 'When was the fire?'

'Can't remember exactly.' The driver gave a sneeze which ended in a groan. 'Late seventies sometime.'

'Anyone hurt?'

'Oh, crikey, yes. Killed twenty or more of 'em – terrible thing it was. They moved the rest out, didn't think it was worth the cost of rebuilding. What the hell d'you want to go there for? Place gives me the creeps.' He blew his nose again.

Her fingers were round the cold lever, poised to get out. 'Just give me a few minutes.'

As she turned to slam the door he called nasally, 'They're all set to knock it down soon anyway.'

Anna strode away from the taxi, glad of a rest from him and his hayfever and lamenting nature. She cursed not having an umbrella. The days before had been so intensely hot it had been hard to imagine the possibility of rain like this. She was lightly dressed – black cotton jeans and a denim jacket – and the rain was falling steadily and hard. The sound of it was all around her and in minutes she was soaked. But she was relieved to be walking.

The main building was no longer visible from here, and the drive curved up and round to the right, disappearing into what looked like a soft wall of green until she moved close up to it and saw the path straighten out again in front of her. Its surface was fractured and heaved up by quitch-grass and dandelions, puddles collecting in the cracks. Foxgloves and brambles held sway in what had evidently once been tended beds at its edges and the branches of the trees on each side were overgrown and meshed together, creating a tunnel of interlocking stems filled with the smell of wet leaves, wet earth.

She followed it round the rightward curve, then to

the left. The trees thinned, then stopped, the path opening out into an area which had been concreted over for a car park, now covered in tussocks like boils. She stopped. The building was there suddenly in front of her, shockingly black even against a grey sky.

It was lower than she had imagined, but very wide, with an impressive entrance at the centre, carved scrolls of stone above the lintel. The square brick water tower in the middle of the complex had escaped the fire, although it was blackened. The decay of the place was evident in its every line. The points of tapering brick which Kate had described adorning the parapet of the roof were now all knocked off leaving jagged edges. The windows on the ground floor were boarded up behind the rusted bars and though the upper windows were uncovered there was no glass left in the frames. Through those to the right, at the eastern portion of the building, she could see only sky. At the west end, the windows were dark, looking into the one whole remaining wing of the building. As she walked nearer, a pigeon, startled from behind clumps of thistles, lifted itself to the roof with slapping wings.

On her way along the west wing she saw a large sign nailed to the front of the building warning, 'Danger, Falling Masonry'. For what seemed a long time she made her way down the side of the building, through rampant grass and thistles which sent cool shocks of water down her thighs with every step she took. There was nothing to see. No chink of the windows was left uncovered. About half way along were two wooden doors with large rusty keyholes, and she pushed against them, relieved when they refused to budge and she didn't have to go inside.

Very little remained of the hospital's east end and the

fire had worked its way round and eaten into most of the middle wing which separated the two open quadrangles, but had stopped short of the water tower. These areas were cordoned off with flagging white plastic tape. Most of the rubble must have been taken away, leaving only some charred bricks which looked as if they had come loose since the clearance. Uneven sections of walls remained as partitions between the rooms.

Anna lifted the tape and stepped over one of the sections of wall, hearing the throaty sound of other pigeons unseen in their shelter among the ruins. She was standing in what must have been a long room. Whatever it had once been used for, its character now was quite lost. Had there been beds in this part, or were the wards only upstairs? Was this a dayroom? Squatting down at one end, she could see patches where the texture of the wooden floor showed through the silt of ash and plaster. She stroked the wet grain of it with her fingers, a tiny contact with Arden's past. With Olivia.

Ignoring the tape, she scrambled over the remains of the inner wall into the quadrangle. The hospital had been arranged in two separate halves, the men's and women's sections, each with their own airing court for daily exercise. There was the remains of a circular path, now colonized by weeds and made from uneven segments of stone, a tree stump in the middle. Following the path round, she stumbled over tufts of grass and groundsel. She stood looking at the ruined walls and the slit-eyed water tower.

The airing court. Their light on the world, this enclosed rectangle of sky. Images from Olivia's strange, disconnected account of herself filled her mind. How had she felt that June morning, moving along the drive towards this hospital? Was the sun shining, sky an exuberant spring blue and the leaves new and bright? She had not mentioned these things of course. Perhaps she had seen nothing. They arrived from Birmingham by ambulance, closed in, probably dark inside, Olivia sitting or lying in the juddering, gloomy space, watched over by iron-faced orderlies. Had she been tied in: strapped? How had they restrained her frail body? Perhaps they had already tamped her down with phenobarbitone so that she knew little of the journey. Or had her brown eyes had to face, wide awake, this place of lost souls, of strange cries and wild movements?

'I thought, when they took me there' – Anna heard the words in her mind – 'that I was going to my death. They would have absolute control over me. They proposed to bury me alive . . .'

Anna began to cry, the sadness of the past days swelling in her at the sight of these remains: hundreds of square yards of stone and brick which had been the crucible of so many lives. Raindrops on her cheeks felt cold compared with her tears. She turned her face to the sky.

She had never seen Olivia, yet she had learned, through her childhood, to love her: her mother's friend, beautiful and tragic, their affection for each other passionate and sparkling as a fairy story. The mention of her brought a special light in to her mother's eyes. Kate and Olivia – best friends. Ordinary but magical. Olivia enshrined as something Anna longed for. She was more than a girl who had been a friend: she was friendship itself.

And now she was left with the legacy of their story, this telling of the other side of Olivia so long left hidden in blue shadow. This woman with whom she was so oddly linked. She had held Anna's life in her hands and almost taken it away.

But even despite the worst Olivia had done, now Anna had seen Arden she could only feel an aching empathy with her. And coming here had not finished this as she had somehow hoped it might. Her mind was alive with questions that now only Olivia could answer. She felt the past clutching at her, filling her with a need she could barely even explain.

Her tears still coming, she folded her arms across the front of her wet denim jacket and turned away. The place had made her feel jumpy, nerves stretched taut, ready to run on hearing the slightest sound. But there was only rain falling from the low, grey sky.

Wiping her face with her hands, she headed for the drive. For a moment she turned and walked backwards watching the hospital recede, then hurried to the taxi and sat shivering on the rear seat.

'Must be out of your flaming mind,' the driver commented without turning round. His bald patch was round and pale like a peppermint. The radio was on, an over-bright voice beating from it.

They drove back through the Warwickshire countryside without speaking. Anna stared out through the streaks of water on the window, badly wanting to smoke, but a large sign in the back of the cab forbade it. She watched trees and hedges passing. Some of the corn had been flattened by the rain. Arden faded behind them like a mirage.

Chapter 30

The night after the funeral, Anna hadn't been to bed until well gone four. Apart from Richard's phone call she didn't speak to anyone. She cut slices of bread and cheese to eat with Patak's pickles and sat on Kate's velour sofa, feet up, reading and reaching for cigarettes. Every hour or two she pulled herself up and stretched, shivering a little, made coffee and ate Dairy Milk until it was all gone. Once she went to the back window and saw a bright sheet of moonlight across the golf course behind the house.

When finally she put Kate's pages of writing down and went upstairs to bed, her eyes felt dry and sore, her head tight inside. But it took her a very long time to sleep, her nerves jangling from the caffeine, images from what she had just read swirling in her mind.

Late the next afternoon, as promised, she drove their dusty blue car to Coventry and let herself into their terraced house off the Kenilworth Road.

'Richard?'

How silly. Of course he wouldn't be there. It was very quiet, the air in the house stuffy, plants drooping on windowsills. A fly droned round the kitchen like a distant bomber and the tap with the dodgy washer was dripping into the quiet, down the side of the washing-up bowl. The bin smelled in the heat.

Richard had evidently worked his way through their supply of crockery for each meal without washing up any of it. Mugs waited on the draining board rimed with coffee. There were cereal bowls encrusted with muesli and two plates with grains of basmati rice congealed in grease. Saucepans with various dribbles down their sides were stacked drunkenly against the tiled wall. Richard's ideals of intellectuals taking their turn at menial work never had quite translated into cleaning up after himself.

Anna automatically started to do what she had always done: restore order. She pulled the overflowing black bag out of the bin and tied the top. The yellow washing-up bowl was almost full of water ringed with orange grease. She tipped it away, cutlery crashing across the bottom of the bowl, and turned on the tap to run hot, staring at the bright thread of water. Then she thought, sod it, turned it off and went out to the tiny garden, to sit on the rickety bench with a bottle of beer from the fridge and a cigarette.

The house was squeezed into the long curve of the terrace, its window frames a muddy green, the built-on bathroom jutting out into the garden. The sight of it made her feel sad. She had spent too much time in there feeling low. It had been only days away from Christmas when she lost the baby. She was alone of course. Term was over for her, but Richard still had to work. The miscarriage had seemed such a violent thing: pain, blood, panic. Eighteen weeks pregnant and she had thought it was safe, established. Since then she had hardly let herself think about the child as it might have been. But now, suddenly, there was a pram in front of her on the baked paving stones, old fashioned and not the sort she would actually have had. She saw it moving, jerked by vigorous kicks from inside, tiny feet bare in the heat.

And herself leaning over, lifting, holding warm flesh, a small head with hair moist in the heat. Tears stung her eyes. The house should not have been silent this summer. She thought of Olivia, what she must have felt.

After six, when she was already angry, the phone rang.

'Anns? It's me. Look, sorry, but I'm going to be late. We've got a problem here.' He had on his harassed work voice. 'Look, I know I said I'd cook and everything, but could you maybe get something going? Otherwise it'll be midnight when we eat.'

'No, it won't, actually. I shan't be here at midnight. The last train goes before then.'

'Tonight? But I thought you were back now. Staying, I mean? Come on, at least stay the night?' Anna pictured him hunched over his desk, hand running through the wild brown hair, intense frown on his face.

'No.'

'Oh – ' He sounded very put out. 'Well, look, I'll be home within a couple of hours – definitely.'

'Sure.' She put the phone down, trembling with fury.

Kate had never openly criticized Richard. They had got on civilly enough, even had things in common. But Anna remembered her once saying, 'It's no good. He'll burn out carrying on the way he does. His work's very worthwhile, of course, but you have to keep it in perspective.'

Thinking back, Anna saw that Kate had known their relationship was at odds long before she had herself. It wasn't that she'd said anything. It was more what she hadn't said: none of those encouraging signals of hope for it to last. When the two of them had moved in together four years ago, Kate had been helpful but not exactly over the moon about it.

'We're not thinking of getting married – at the moment anyway,' Anna had confided, wondering what the reaction would be. 'To tell you the truth, Richard's not too sure about marriage – as an institution I mean.'

'I think you're very wise,' Kate said unexpectedly. 'Being tangled up in buying property together is enough of a complication without rushing into marriage as well.'

She had, back then, fallen for something Richard represented as much as for himself. After she met him, her life before seemed to have been spent in slumber, wasted in some way. She had drifted from college to teaching, unsure what else to do, had barely examined what she believed about anything. And there was Richard, fresh from his degree, embarked as a mature student in sociology and politics. Old as she was, she had been impressed by someone who could bandy terms around as if they owned them: the jargon of sociology. And Richard's ideals, which he could lay out for her like a pack of cards. But of late she had begun to notice other things: all the friends she had somehow not seen for a long time because Richard had condemned them as bourgeois or just plain boring. Friends she had once valued, who'd seen her through other times, college and teaching. And she had mistaken Richard's openness about his own feelings for sensitivity to hers.

She decided to face the rest of the house. In their room the duvet lay in a strangled twist across the pine-framed bed. There were underpants and socks and shirts left lying all over the coconut matting (Richard didn't like carpet).

She sat on the side of the bed holding a photograph in a wooden frame from the dressing table. A close up of her and Richard, both grinning foolishly at the camera. It was taken a few months after they got together. She had her hair even longer then and Richard said she looked like Mary Hopkin. She had been clowning, singing, 'Those were the days my friend – la la la la la la . . .' Richard had a cigarette hanging from the side of his mouth, a lazy half smile, arm crooked round Anna's neck and smoke threading up through her hair. His shirt was a loud check, hair curling down into his neck and chunky sideburns.

Anna put the photo back and looked round at the bed. All the nights there with Richard, his intensity even in sleep. But the more recent memory was of being alone there after the miscarriage, empty and distressed. Richard had no idea of her need for him to be there. She had wanted to keep the news from Kate, until one day, unable to bear the loneliness any longer, she phoned her, and Kate came immediately, full of comfort and understanding.

Their lives had always been dictated by Richard's timing. 'I'm-so-busy-so-much-work-this-will-really-make-a-difference.' Never there when she needed him, in her own crises at work, or when the bleeding began and she had to call an ambulance, or through her mother's death.

She thought of Douglas, of Kate's strength in ending her marriage. Turning to the photo again, she stroked dust from the film of plastic covering Richard's face, as if in order to speak to him. 'No,' she said, her voice sounding loud after the hours of silence. 'No more.'

At eight-thirty the phone rang again. She ambled across to answer it. 'Look, Anns – sorry. Meeting's running on a bit. Bit of an emergency. It'll be another hour, then that's it – definite. OK?'

'As you like.'

Upstairs she packed an old suitcase which had been Kate's. Richard always used a rucksack to go away, suitcases, like carpet, apparently representing something too staid. Folding clothes into the deep expandable case, Anna felt calm, peaceful almost. These few days away from Richard had allowed parts of her, long submerged, to bob to the surface like corks.

She took only what she needed most immediately, nothing like books or cassettes. This could not be finished now. There was the joint ownership of the house to deal with for a start.

She called a taxi to take her to the station. While she was waiting, she went to the kitchen and rummaged round in the store cupboard for a tin of baked beans and left it standing out on the side, the tin-opener resting on top.

Without looking round any further she went outside with her case and sat down beside it in the coppery evening light.

The next morning she went on impulse to a hairdresser's in Kings Heath and had her hair cut very short. Her head felt strangely light and she could feel the air on her neck. In the mirror her eyes seemed bigger, the cheekbones more prominent. She looked different.

When Richard phoned she didn't tell him she'd left home for good. After her decisiveness in Coventry she found she couldn't face talking to him about it, especially not over the telephone. She found herself in a period of limbo, strung between an old life which she had to finish and a new one she barely knew how to begin.

'The thing is, I've got so much to do here,' she told

him. 'All the house to clear. And there's lots of the holiday left. I shan't be around for a while . . .'

Roland Mantel lived a street away from Kate's house, in a similar style of twenties semi. Its rectangle of front lawn was boxed in by trim privet hedges, the front door sky blue, slightly chipped and the windows huge clean panes of double-glazing with their chunky white frames.

It was a few moments before he came to the door. He was dressed in fawn cotton trousers with mud stains at the knee and gardening gloves clasped in one hand.

'Anna, my dear – how lovely!' His face lifted into a cherubic smile. 'Called in on you yesterday, but no joy.'

'Yes, I was – out,' she replied vaguely, unsure how to explain her day visiting Arden.

'I say, I do like the hair.'

'Thank you. I wanted a change.'

Reaching up, she kissed his cheek, soft and broken-veined and familiar. 'I'm very sorry it's taken me so long to get round here.' She gave a shrug, ashamed of letting the week go past since the funeral. 'Uncle Roland, I need to talk to you.'

'To me? I'd be honoured. I've missed our chats since you've been in Coventry. Come on through – I've got the kettle on. You're in luck because I've got some digestives in. Can't beat a McVitie's, can you?'

'I know I'll always get fed well when I come to see you.' Anna smiled, following Roland's plump figure into the kitchen at the back of the house, across the hall's worn brown carpet. The house had always been bare and functional, and kept in the methodical way of someone once in the armed forces. The only splashes of exuberance had been handed down from his parents' house; the standard lamp in the living-room with its huge tasselled shade, a vase shaped in deep blue glass. And the tablecloth embroidered with a riot of wild flowers which was always spread on the table when they used to come for teas of crumpets and Eccles cakes – an iced bun for Anna – all produced out of white bakery bags.

In the kitchen there were still the old wooden cupboards with blue handles which Anna knew she had run to pull open and explore when he had first moved in, some time within the memory of her childhood. He had a red and white sixties cooker with metal racks beside the grill for warming plates, an ancient Russell Hobbs kettle and a cupboard full of mismatched crockery. Coming back here after this long gap, Anna saw now only the simplicity of the house. He could have had so much more, but chose not to.

The sun was slanting through the french windows, etching a rectangle on the grey lino. Roland's cat, black and white and very hairy, was spread across its bright heat.

'Hello Maisie, old lady.' Anna squatted down and ran her hand across the inert body which just raised the energy to give a half-hearted purr.

Roland was fishing teaspoons out of a drawer, frowning with concentration. 'Yes, I suppose she'll be leaving me soon too.'

Anna looked up startled, suddenly ashamed. Roland's reserve and gentlemanly tact had kept her from appreciating how deeply he felt about her mother's death.

'I'm really sorry, Roland. You'll miss Mummy a lot, won't you?'

He paused, not meeting her eyes, a jar of Nescafé

poised in one hand. 'I don't think I can quite imagine how much yet.'

Anna wanted to go to him, give him a hug, but she held back, wondering whether she wouldn't just be piling her own emotions on him. And there was an odd feeling now, the two of them alone without Kate who had always been there.

'You were such a good friend to her – to us both.'

Roland gave her a watery smile, determinedly cheerful. He handed her a mug patterned with ears of wheat. Biscuit packet in his other hand, he said, 'Come on, let's go out. Much too good a day to be in.'

There was a covered verandah at the back of the house, where they sat on old canvas chairs, looking out over the vivid summer green of the lawn. Roland was cultivating a vine up the two supports of the verandah, its tendrils just beginning to reach across the wooden slatted roof. It was very peaceful, quiet enough to hear birds, insects even. Anna thought of the little yard at the back of the house in Coventry with its dusty slabs and tubs of bolting geraniums.

Roland sat back with a wistful sigh. 'Biscuit? Go on. Look as if you need it.'

Anna smiled, taking one. Roland always made the smallest things seem a treat, should have had a host of grandchildren to spoil. She could tell he was waiting for her to speak, clearing his throat now and then as if to do so himself but unable.

'It's so lovely just to sit still,' Anna said. 'I feel as if there are whole aspects of life I've forgotten – as if I've been underwater for a long time.'

'That's what Kate said. Work, work, work all these

years. She said when she retired she was going to make time to stand and stare.'

Anna chuckled. 'That's not how it sounded to me. She was so full of plans and projects.'

'Ah well – I expect she didn't want you to worry or think she was going to vegetate.'

'It never occurred to me she would.' Always some campaign with Kate, even in Anna's earliest memories. Getting people to see that the National Health Service was for them. 'All these women, so prolapsed that their insides were sleeping beside them on the bed. "Go and get yourself fixed up," I'd tell them. That's what it's for.' And sex education: working in schools, determined there should be openness, trying to combat the ignorance of young women. Recalling Kate's energetic, no-nonsense style, how much she loved people, Anna felt tears rise in her eyes.

'Roland,' she began. 'There were a lot of things Mummy didn't talk to me about, weren't there?'

Roland made a slight grimace and attended to brushing biscuit crumbs from the front of his shirt. 'I'm not sure about that, my dear. You mean your father?'

'No – not really.' Anna sat forward in her chair, reaching for the end of her hair, her habit of playing with a strand between her fingers, but it was gone – shorn and strange. 'She talked about him a bit. Enough so that I've never needed to be too curious about him. I always knew who he was. And she told me enough when I was younger – not in great detail of course – to make me understand why they were divorced.'

'Oh no,' Roland corrected her quickly. 'They were never divorced. Not formally.'

'They must have been!' She sat up straight again. 'I

mean it's so long ago.' Roland was shaking his head. 'I'm sure she told me . . .'

His gaze fixed on the far side of the garden, Roland said stiffly, 'Her name was still Craven, remember. If they had applied for a divorce I can only assume they would have been granted one after a certain time. But of course you don't have to be legally divorced if you are living apart unless you want to remarry. Presumably Douglas Craven never wanted to do so.'

Anna had the words 'And Mummy?' on her tongue, but bit them back, seeing how Roland suddenly turned very brisk, sipping his coffee, twisting the top of the biscuit wrapper to seal it up.

'D'you mind me asking you things?' she wondered anxiously. 'If you'd rather I didn't . . .'

'Of course you have questions, Anna,' he said, his tone gentler again. 'But I don't know that I'm going to be much help. I never met your father properly, you see. Really I saw very little of your mother while she was married. It was only afterwards we spent more time together.'

'Did you meet Angus Harvey?'

Roland startled her by suddenly closing his eyes and putting his head back for a second, giving out a long, tired-sounding sigh. 'No. I never met Angus. The first time I remember seeing your mother was after he had been reported missing.' He looked at Anna with sad eyes. 'The war. If it had not been for the damn war . . . Messed up so many of our lives. Only one who did reasonably well out of the war was my sister Marjorie, strangely enough. Never looked back. Five children, running all sorts of naval wives' do's down there.' He sounded amused.

Anna had a slight recollection of having met Marjorie, a woman on a large scale with a booming voice, rather intimidating in a child's eyes.

Hesitantly she said, 'I wondered whether Mummy ever really loved my father?'

'Well that I can't tell you. Couldn't be sure.' Roland's tone had turned stiff again. 'Rather a private person really, your mother.'

After a silence, she asked, 'What about Olivia?'

'Olivia?' His brow puckered.

'Olivia Kemp. You must have met her. She was living with Mummy after I was born.'

'Ah – Kemp. Yes, school friend of hers – the councillor's daughter. I do remember someone was staying for a bit but I never met her. Course, when I saw a lot more of you both, you were already living in Florence Road.'

'It's so strange,' Anna said slowly. 'She seems to have kept bits of her life in such separate compartments. Didn't she ever talk to you about Olivia?'

'Not that I remember. She didn't hark back to school much. No real reason to I don't think. Why?'

'I just . . .' She felt weary suddenly, ready to go and lie under a tree and sleep, rest her brain from all these thoughts. 'You think you know people, don't you? And instead you only see little glimpses of them.' She could feel herself growing tearful.

'Anna, my dear . . .'

She knelt down and was in his arms, his smell of sweat and shaving cream. Sobbing as she had done as a child after scares or bumps. 'You're such a good man,' she said into his warm, fleshy chest. 'There aren't many about like you.'

He didn't speak and she could tell that he was unable. His body gave little jerks. She didn't look up at him, knowing his shyness and that he wouldn't want her to see his tears. As he wiped his pink face with the back of his hand, she said, 'My father didn't want to know me. You've been a father to me.'

He spoke softly, in a controlled voice, holding her with great tenderness. 'Nothing would have made me happier than to have been your father.'

Chapter 31

The two of them wouldn't leave her alone: Kate and Olivia. Those days immediately after the funeral and her visit to Coventry it was as if she was paralysed. She moved round the house, tired and stunned, not achieving anything. When the phone rang she ignored it now. Often she found herself standing or sitting, just staring across the silent rooms. She might wander up and down stairs opening cupboards and drawers, looking, not certain for what, but somehow unable to begin disturbing anything.

On the window-sill of Kate's bedroom, overlooking the garden, were photographs, all of Anna at different ages. A tiny monochrome print with white edges and her serious little face looking out, all eyes. This was stuck into the lower edge of the frame of her graduation portrait, the brick Italianate tower of Birmingham University in the background. 1969. She smiled at the shortness of her dress, her hair bobbed round her ears and backcombed specially for the occasion. There were the familiar snaps Kate had had on show for years: Anna in the backyard of the Florence Road house, aged about eleven, a black and white kitten cuddled close to her face. Another at nine, on a beach, bending over a metal-tipped spade and looking up to grin delightedly into the lens, hair swept to one side by the wind. Wales, and their first-ever holiday.

Revisiting herself at these young stages she tried to relearn her mother, playing through their lives together year by year like tracks on a record.

After seeing Roland she felt spurred to make a start on the house.

Clearing Kate's wardrobe and dressing table was the worst part. All those intimately shaped garments. The one bottle of cologne, sparing amounts of powder and scantly filled jewellery box. She found a pair of clip-on earrings, fifties style, round and white, dotted with tiny pink spots. She had seen them in the shallow wooden box all her life, yet now they looked so foreign, belonging to a stranger.

She worked in as detached a way as she could, a caul of practical concentration wrapped tight round her. But sometimes it slipped, or something penetrated it, and she sat and cried among this residue of Kate's life.

There were no diaries. Apart from Kate's last effort to explain herself to Anna she had not been a writer by habit. She was not an introspective woman. Too busy out there getting on with it. Nor were there a great number of books. She did find several volumes of poetry though, arranged incongruously in with Kate's few crime novels and old copies of *Reader's Digest*. They were old books, their pages almost orange at the edges and smelling musty.

'With all my love, now and always', was written on the first page of one in small, looped handwriting. 'Angus'. It was dated 1940.

The past seemed to swoop, swallow-like, through the house those two weeks. Though she was confronted at every turn by the things which had made up Kate's life, it was Olivia's voice which kept coming to her. She imagined it soft, sweet, always edged with tears: 'By the morning I know him. I want my life to be his. And they take him away . . .'

Anna thought of that loss. Unbearable. She knew she could not let this rest. Soon, when she was ready, she would have to try and see Olivia. And after all, why would Kate have left the letters, made her explanation as she did, if she had not been deputing Anna to face Olivia for her?

The only person she could stand to be with was Roland.

The first time he called round with the opening greeting, 'I thought you might like a bit of help.' Then added quickly, 'Or company?'

She opened the door in an old pair of mauve dungarees, hair standing on end from bed, and was about to say no, she could manage, but then saw Roland had come out of his own need. She saw his emotion, coming back into Kate's house again, eyeing the bin liners stacked for Oxfam in the front room in the grey light of net curtains and looking round as if memorizing the place. He took out a handkerchief and wiped perspiration from his pink forehead, talking a little too fast, trying to cover his wretchedness. She remembered how his face registered every crease and tuck of emotion. His lips twitched as they walked into the kitchen. It was the room she was leaving until last and it still felt as if her mother might walk in any moment, put on the plastic Colman's Mustard apron and start bustling around in her brown brogue shoes.

She found jobs for Roland: he spent one afternoon clearing the garage.

'You'll put the house on the market, I suppose?' he asked when she brought out a mug of tea.

Anna shrugged. 'I really don't know what I'm going to do. You see, I've left Richard.'

'Oh, Anna – ' Roland's eyes were two pools of concern. 'I am sorry. I'd no idea. How long?'

'The day after the funeral.' She held up a hand to stem the rush of Roland's sympathy. 'It's right, I know that.' She paused. 'I've also decided to resign my job.'

Roland gaped at her. 'Anna. Why? Everything at once, so hastily like this? What are you going to do?'

She shrugged, pulling dead heads from a pink rose by the garage. 'I just want things to be different. I don't want to have to decide anything else yet. I want to take stock for a while.' She looked round at Roland. 'Mummy never thought much of Richard, did she?'

Roland's brow creased. 'I wouldn't say that. She admired his drive, I think. It's just that I think she felt you weren't – what was her phrase? – building each other into more than you would be on your own. That was her idea of what a good relationship should be. She thought Richard was dragging you down.'

'I wish she'd said.'

'You wouldn't have liked it if she had.'

'True.' After a silence, she said, 'That's how it was with my father, wasn't it? She felt he was chewing away at her, diminishing her.'

Roland looked uncomfortable again. 'I suppose that was about it.'

She had found some old photographs of Daisy Turnbull and Lisa and asked Roland about them.

'Lisa Turnbull?' He chuckled. 'Now I did meet her. Kate said she owed Lisa a lot. Not sure why, but she liked her because she was rather to the point as I remember.'

'I remember her – from when I was little. She *is* dead, isn't she?' It seemed terrible, all these years passing and not knowing now whether people were alive or dead.

'Died three or four years ago,' Roland said. 'Cancer as well. Lung I suppose. She used to smoke like a power station.' He eyed the cigarette in Anna's hand.

'I know, I know,' she said.

'Lisa went to live out at Sheldon when they did away with the slums round the Birch. Kate saw more of her towards the end again.'

She later found a few other photographs. Roland appeared in some of them, the three of them grouped together like a family. In one he was holding her, aged about three, a rather slimmer but still comical Roland, smiling at her in his arms. He must have been tickling her because she was giggling, face crinkled. Anna looked at it, frowning. Exactly what her mother had felt for Roland was something she knew she would never now find out.

*

August 27th, 1981

Dear Olivia,

I am Anna Craven, Kate Craven's daughter. I have your address from my mother and wonder if I might call in and see you some time in the next few days?

It took Anna what seemed a ridiculously long time to phrase this simple note. It was so odd to think of Olivia as a real person now, to use ordinary words. That evening she started up Kate's Metro and drove to Moseley to deliver the letter, leaving it until it was almost dark because she didn't want to be seen, to start anything then.

The house was set back from the road, one in the

row of looming Victorian mansions of that area, a jumble of gables and turrets which blocked out the light with its sheer size and its screen of mature trees. Creeping up the short drive under the arch of branches, she felt foolish and very nervous.

A tinny sound of music came from inside. Heart pounding, she pushed the paper through the metal letter-box, jumping as it snapped, and fled back to the car.

Her reply pattered on the mat with Tuesday morning's circulars and a seed catalogue. Anna took it into the kitchen, still dressed in her baggy T-shirt from bed. She looked at the ornate handwriting.

> My dear Anna,
>
> I should so love you to come. Any time is convenient for me. I'm always here.
>
> Warmest regards,
>
> Olivia Kemp.

She went that afternoon. It was a fine day, with a waning feel to the light, and piles of cloud kept blotting out the sun. She drove through the slow-moving traffic in Moseley Village, its pavements crowded with shoppers.

After parking the Metro round the corner from Olivia's, outside a boarded up house, she sat for a few moments with the engine off, the windows open. From somewhere further along the road came a heavy beat of music, turned up loud. She thought of Olivia as Kate had last seen her, in the doorway of a flat only a street away from here, dressed in bright blue, alone with her child. The child – Anna had barely given him a thought – would now be nineteen. Not much older than she was when her mother came home tight-faced from work one day, going to her room in the pretence of getting changed, then crying and crying. 1962.

She was very nervous at the thought of meeting Olivia. Her uncertainty was made worse by not knowing how to approach her and by the baggage of conflicting emotions she was bringing to this encounter. There were those she felt obliged to carry with her on Kate's behalf: anger and bitter woundedness, a spirit of confrontation. Yet the warmth of Olivia's reply had taken her by surprise. Her own feelings were of apprehension, but also curiosity and sympathy. She wanted at least to try and get on with Olivia, to attempt to understand.

She stepped out of the car into the sleepy warmth of the street. In the gutter lay a crumpled Union Jack, a remnant of the Royal Wedding.

The house was on the corner of the two roads, and horse chestnut trees grew inside the front wall on both sides, casting the place into shadow and seclusion. It was a brick building with gables and a square fairy-tale turret at one corner. In the bright afternoon the windows looked dark and dusty.

In the shady porch she found an old-fashioned metal bell-pull at the side of the door, which gave off a tinkling sound inside.

She heard no footsteps and jumped when the door suddenly opened. A young man stood there, dressed in very tight jeans with faded knees, a T-shirt and trainers. He had collar-length mousy hair and a white acne'd complexion. There was something in his manner Anna didn't take to.

'Yes. Hello?' There was no curiosity in his manner but he seemed tense, his brow furrowed, apparently unable to keep still.

'I'm Anna Craven.' Nervously she pushed her hand back through her hair wondering if this was Olivia's son, forgetting he didn't match Kate's description at all.

'You want Olivia, I suppose,' he said, apparently resentful.

'She said I could call. Is she here?'

'Yeah. She's teaching at the moment. Come through.'

As she was turning to close the door she heard footsteps slapping madly down the wide staircase and another voice called, 'It's OK – leave it – thanks.' Another young man with tight curls, round gold glasses and a file under his arm disappeared outside in flip-flops. The door slammed.

Anna scuttled after the other one and found him standing on the threshold of a huge room. Her first impressions were the glowing red and yellow light from the windows, the honey-coloured parquet floor and a huge grand piano which dominated the middle of the room.

At one end, in the bay window, was a round table. Two women sat behind it, one plump with permed grey hair and a sleeveless, square-necked frock. The other, much smaller and dark, was dressed in something vivid and orange.

'Someone for you, Olivia.'

Anna stood in front of them, bewildered.

It was only when the smaller of the two women looked over at her that she knew it was Olivia. Across the room her face looked surprisingly young and thin, the eyes dark, seemingly bottomless.

'Thank you, Sean.' Her voice was deeper than Anna expected, with a smooth beauty like a nun's. 'Would you be a love and put the kettle on?' He gave a nod and disappeared through a door at the other side of the room.

As Olivia walked towards her, Anna saw that the orange clothing was a sari. She came gliding across, wrapped in the graceful folds of silk, feet bare and silent on the coloured rugs which dotted the floor. Anna's mind struggled to make sense of what she was seeing. She felt a second of panic. How should she react?

Olivia stopped a couple of feet away and searched Anna's face with her eyes. Then she smiled, a transformation, showing small, creamy teeth and an immense vivacity which shone from her eyes. She put her hands to her own face, resting her fingers lightly against her cheeks, taking in the sight of her visitor with a childlike kind of wonder.

'Anna, you're the image of your father. What beautiful hair.'

Anna smiled shyly. In seconds any anger and hostility dissolved. She was enchanted. 'Hello,' she said foolishly. She found it hard to meet Olivia's eyes, her gaze was so intense.

'I'm so very glad you've come.' Olivia reached out to shake hands with instinctive formality, and for a second Anna held her small, smooth hand. 'Come and sit with us and take tea,' she said, gesturing towards the table. As she spoke, Anna noticed an odd sing-song quality in her voice, like many Asians sounded speaking English. 'Edith and I had almost finished. You won't mind us cutting it a bit short today, will you?'

Edith, an awkward woman in her sixties, gave a nervous giggle. 'No, we've done well today, haven't we, Olivia? I think we deserve a rest.'

'I'll just go and see if Sean's fallen asleep in the kitchen,' Olivia said. 'Sit, Anna – please.'

She took a chair, noticing a strong perfumed smell in the room. Edith was stowing books into her mock-leather bag. She had tired-looking skin even in this muted light, but large, interested grey eyes.

'Are you another of Olivia's young friends?' she asked.

Just then there came an odd sound from the kitchen, a kind of muffled outburst. Edith pretended not to notice. Distracted, Anna said, 'Er, sort of.' She began to feel she was in a dream. 'What is it Olivia teaches you?'

'Bengali,' Edith said, as if surprised that Anna didn't know. 'She's very good, you know. Very gifted woman, what with all her music and everything. I've learned to speak the language quite a bit over the years what with one thing and another. Now I've retired I thought I'd do it properly and learn to read and write better.' She gave a little giggle. 'You know – Tagore in the original . . .'

There was another slam of the front door as she spoke and in seconds a black face topped by very short hair appeared panting round the door. 'Awright?' He nodded at them both. 'Sean here?'

'In the kitchen,' Edith said. 'Shall I . . .?' She made to get up but the young man, in shorts and a sports shirt, was already across the room.

'He's going to get roasted, I tell you . . . Sean – the tournament? You were supposed to be down there an hour ago. Where's your brain, man?'

There was a gasp. 'Oh shit! – Sorry, Olivia. I forgot. Have they started?'

'Course they've started. I paired up with Rob for the first set, but we need you there.'

'Look, Theo – ' Sean ran through, shouting back over his shoulder. 'You go on. I'll be down, OK?'

He was followed by a sweating Theo, shouting, 'Don't forget your racquet,' and 'See yer,' in Anna and

Edith's direction. For an odd second Anna found herself missing Richard. She felt old, vulnerable and out of place with all these new people.

'Who are these blokes around the place?' she asked Edith.

'They're Olivia's lodgers,' Edith said, bravely accepting, but obviously not quite sure about it all. 'They have the top floor, you see. There's so much space. Sean studies engineering – I think – and Theo's doing some sort of science, chemistry . . . And there's Ben who you probably haven't met. He's a postgraduate. Something to do with languages.'

Anna frowned. 'Surely it's still the holidays?'

Edith looked perturbed. 'Yes, I suppose it is. They don't seem to go home though . . .'

Olivia came back in with a beautifully laid tray of tea, including a plate of Indian sweets, bright with the red and green of cherries and pistachio.

'A good job I took over from Sean,' she said, 'or you'd have had a teabag in a cup and a stale Rich Tea biscuit.' She offered the plate of sweets to them, telling Anna, 'These are a treat on Bengali afternoons. Edith comes to me once a week.'

Anna nibbled a square of pistachio *barfi*, feeling its thick, milky sweetness slide over her tongue.

'Mostly, you see, I make my living from teaching music – and the lodgers, of course,' Olivia said, as she poured tea with an almost exaggerated grace.

'Does your son live with you?' Anna asked.

'Krishna?' Olivia's face took on a glow. 'Yes, he's home at last. He's just done his first year at college in London and is having a simply marvellous time.' Anna noticed that the sing-song quality had gone from Olivia's voice. Instead it had become gushing. 'He's out at the moment. He has an old friend in Kings Heath who owns a very nice furniture shop. Krish has done bits of work for him sometimes and poor Jake's marriage seems to have broken up so I think Krish is company for him. Krishna would cheer anyone up, wouldn't he, Edith?'

Edith managed, ingeniously, through a mouthful of *barfi*, to adapt concerned cluckings over Jake's marriage to noises of agreement and mirth concerning Krishna.

'He's doing his degree in anthropology,' Olivia went on proudly. 'And learning Bengali. He's adoring it. Finding out about a culture that's half his, after all. His father was from Calcutta, you see. I met him when I was studying in London myself after the war. He had a visiting lectureship.' She related this in the tones of someone telling a fairy story. 'I don't make any secret of the fact that I've been a single parent – after all, it's almost the mode nowadays. At first, though, I called myself Mrs, of course. It wasn't the same at all in the early 1960s ... It's not at all easy bringing up a child by yourself – especially as my family couldn't cope with what I'd done. But Krishna's been the most wonderful child – I can hardly begin to tell you.'

Edith nodded enthusiastically. 'He's a lovely boy. And I'm sure you've been a tower of strength, Olivia.'

Olivia accepted this compliment graciously. 'He's the one who's given me all the strength in the world. We keep in touch all the time when he's away. We're so close – sometimes it's quite uncanny.'

Anna watched her, fascinated. Sitting nearer Olivia now, she could see the slackness of her skin, a truer indication of her age. But she found herself mesmerized by her vivacity, coupled with an apparent openness and vulnerability which took her quite by surprise.

When Edith had drunk her tea she departed, full of thanks, saying, 'I'll look forward to next Tuesday!'

Olivia showed her out, then glided back into the room. Still in the charming voice, she said, 'Edith used to be a missionary in Bangladesh. With the Baptists. Now she's retired I think she's a bit lost, poor soul. This gives her a purpose.'

She moved to the piano, stood against it, her back very straight. Her face altered, as if something had dropped from it. In a tight voice, she said. 'Did she want you to come?'

Half prepared, Anna said truthfully, 'I'm not sure.'

'Then why did you?'

'Because I wanted to.'

'She told you about me?'

'All the time when I was little. About your childhood together, your friendship. It made me long to have a friend like that myself. You had something very special.'

Olivia's eyes were fixed away from Anna across the room. In their expression Anna thought she glimpsed something hard and malevolent. Then, as if roused from her thoughts, she said, 'Look, I'm terribly sorry, but I've another pupil due in a few minutes – piano this time. Would you be free to come again, say tomorrow evening? I don't have any teaching late tomorrow and you could meet Krishna.' She gave Anna one of her sudden, overwhelming smiles. 'I'd so like to have a talk with you and hear about Kate after all this time. She was, as you say, my very best friend.'

Anna found herself agreeing eagerly. At the front door, Olivia took her gently by her upper arms and reached up to kiss her. Anna felt Olivia's breath on her cheek, smelled again the pungent perfume she had noticed in the room, some sort of scented hair oil.

'You will come, won't you?' Olivia stood looking tiny under the high doorway, vulnerable again now.

'Of course. Seven o'clock.' Anna waved, backing down the drive.

In the car she sat for a time once more, breathing heavily, aware of the fast beating of her heart.

What on earth's come over me? she thought. She knew that her emotion stemmed partly from the strangeness of touching the past, of beginning to close a circle. But it was more than that. It was something in Olivia herself that had stirred her in this way, and not to anger or resentment, the emotions she had felt obliged to carry with her, but to something quite unexpected. Reaching down to try and put the key in the ignition she realized her hands were shaking. She was fluttery and energized as if newly in love.

Chapter 32

Ben opened the door the next evening, still in the flip-flops.

'Hi.' He squinted out through the round spectacles like a mole, round face pressed into an anxious look, then smiled. 'You're Anna.' He stood back to let her in. The house felt cool. She had put on an old sleeveless dress made of Indian cotton in pale blue and white stripes, long unworn because Richard said it made her look like Little Bo-Peep. She carried a bunch of white roses.

'We've heard a lot about you.'

Anna turned, startled. 'From Olivia?'

'No need to look so worried. All we've gathered is that you were the most beautiful baby the world's ever seen – after Krish of course!' Ben laughed. He spoke very fast, with a nervous fussiness about him. 'That's just Olivia. She's very extravagant – things she says.'

'I see,' Anna said, rather uncertainly. She was distracted by noises from the rest of the house: voices, laughter, the pulsing of music. The hall was filled with a delicious, spicy smell.

'Krish's upstairs with Jake,' Ben told her. 'I'll take you through. Olivia's getting one of her feasts together.'

'Are we all eating together then?' Anna frowned. From what Olivia said the day before she had expected to be alone with her.

'She does this every so often,' Ben said as he showed her into the long room again. 'Family meal she calls it. It's just hard luck if we've got things on. We have to cancel or she'll be under a cloud for days.' Anna noticed the tone of indulgence in his voice. 'As it's out of term now there's not much going on anyway, luckily.'

Anna was peeved for a few seconds, feeling childishly that she wanted Olivia all to herself. But as soon as she walked into the long room she felt uplifted and found herself smiling. She had been alone so much this week: it would be good to have company.

The round table was laid with a scarlet cloth, and Theo was putting cutlery on it, jigging around to a tune that must have been going on in his head, twirling forks in the air and catching them with a flourish before setting them down. At the other end of the room where there were a sofa and easy chairs, Sean was watching TV, perched forward on the edge of his seat. He didn't look round, sat with shoulders hunched, Rizlas and lighter on the table, a skinny cigarette held close to his face. His hair looked lank and unkempt.

'This is Anna,' Ben told Theo.

Theo stepped forward and to Anna's surprise, shook hands with solemn formality. 'Good to meet you properly – saw you yesterday, didn't I?'

Anna liked Theo immediately. 'D'you need a hand with anything?'

'No – I'm getting on fine thanks.'

Theo went back to finish his juggling and table laying. Ben was just relieving Anna of the flowers when there was a soft rustling sound in the doorway.

'Don't try that with the glasses, Theo.' Olivia made her entrance carrying a small tray of pickles. This time the sari was vivid blue, catching the light in a host of parrot shades.

'Anna, my dear . . . Oh, and roses – how lovely, my favourite!' She handed the tray regally to Theo and came to embrace her as if they were the closest of friends. Anna caught herself feeling gratified, her cheeks glowing, and was struck again by the contrariness of her feelings. Shouldn't she feel more hostility and reservation, at least for Kate's sake? Who was she here for after all – Kate or herself?

'Now – you must sit down and bear with us for a few moments,' Olivia was saying. 'Ben will take care of you until it's ready.' Again Anna noticed the sing-song tone of her voice.

'Oh, I don't need looking after.' She laughed.

'Will you have a glass of wine? Or *lassi*? I've made it nice and salty.'

'Wine, please.' Anna glanced across at Sean. 'All right if I smoke too?'

'No problem,' Ben said. 'There's an ashtray on the piano somewhere.'

Anna sat on the piano stool sipping red wine, a cigarette in her other hand, looking round the room. There was a beautiful lightness about it – the pale wood of the floor and the long shelves across the room – with splashes of colour: rugs on the boards, rich silk saris at the windows and also bunched and draped across the high corners of the room. On either side of the piano were leaded fireplaces, and on the walls above them, in simple wood frames, hung batik pictures, one a brightly decorated elephant, the other a scene from an Indian village in sky blue and straw colours.

Olivia bustled in and out carrying dishes, calling orders to Ben and Theo. 'And Sean,' she called. 'You're doing littlest of all. Please come and help me with the plates.' She spoke in an imperious tone.

Sean stood up slowly, pushing down the legs of his jeans, and paused to grind out his cigarette in a saucer.

'Ben – go and fetch Krishna and Jake. It's all ready.'

Anna watched, fascinated by all this activity and by Olivia's unquestioned authority over the household.

'You're working so hard,' she commented.

'I adore cooking,' Olivia said, 'especially this food. Useless doing it for one, though. Theo – water please. We'll need a jug on the side there.'

There came a burst of sound from upstairs, rock music which Anna knew she recognized but could not place before it was switched off abruptly. Then feet on the stairs.

She was having to remind herself of Krishna's existence, that Olivia had a grown-up son. She faced the door, preparing a smile. When he appeared her smile broadened. She stood up.

'Anna?' Like Theo, he shook her hand.

'Krishna? I'm so pleased to meet you.' She was looking into a face of enormous charm. He had round, boyish cheeks, the skin flawless, huge teeth creamy as almonds and deep brown eyes. He was wearing tight black jeans and a black T-shirt, and there was a ripeness about him just short of being plump, a hint of puppy fat not yet lost. There was something immensely appealing about him and it crossed Anna's mind to wonder whether this was the Kemp charm working through the generations.

'This is my mate, Jake,' Krishna said. He indicated a tall, lean man behind him with shoulder-length brown hair, a long, serious face and eyes that were beginning to hold a smile. He said 'Hello' quietly.

'What were you listening to up there?' Anna asked. 'I know I recognized it . . .'

'Van Morrison,' Krishna said. He gave Jake a playful punch on the arm. 'He reckons he's educating my musical tastes.'

'I've nearly persuaded him to part with the Donny Osmond singles,' Jake said drily.

'Surely it's not that bad?' Anna said.

'You'd be surprised.'

'Ah, Krishna – ' Olivia emerged from the kitchen, followed by Sean. 'Come and fetch the rice for me, will you, darling? The others have been doing all the work. It's time you did something.'

Krishna made a comical face at Anna. 'I see you've already met the three stooges?'

She laughed, feeling a rush of contentment and liking for these people.

They sat round the table, blood-red napkins to match the cloth folded on white side plates. Anna was between Theo and Jake, facing Olivia across the dishes piled with food, between which Olivia had lit deep blue candles.

At the centre of the table was a casserole full of scented rice, sprigged with dark splinters of cinnamon, fat green cardamom pods, and dotted with coriander seeds like game shot. Displayed round it, in blue ceramic dishes, was spiced chicken in a rich tomato sauce, a bright, mustard-coloured dal sprinkled with fresh green coriander leaves, and other vegetable dishes, potatoes and cauliflower, aubergines, okra. On a wooden board she had piled chapatis.

The boys let out whoops and whistles of appreciation at the sight of the food.

'Hey yeah,' Theo said enthusiastically. 'Come on – let's get this wine flowing.'

'I thought you were a good, church-going boy,' Krish teased him. 'No drinking, no cinema – ' He made a poor attempt at a Jamaican accent: 'No idolatry av tings av de flesh . . . eh Titty?'

Theo gave a pained though good-natured grimace, then jabbed a finger at Krish, mock threatening. 'I'll see you afterwards.'

'Don't call him that,' Olivia said. 'It's not nice.'

'I think you ought to explain to Anna,' Ben said, seeing her puzzled face.

Theo grinned, spooning rice on to his plate. 'My name's Theophilus, right? My mom's into the Acts of the Apostles in a big way – and I mean a big way. All the family's called names from the early church. Trouble is, I've got five older brothers, so by the time she got to me the decent names like Peter and John and Stephen were all used up, so I got to be Theophilus Timothy.'

'TT,' Krish finished. 'Titty.'

'Enough!' Olivia commanded.

Like everyone else, Anna filled her plate, listening to the talk around her. Her initial feeling of rawness had passed, the strangeness of being alone again in social situations. She had been everywhere with Richard for so long. Too long. She began to feel at ease, having neither too much nor too little attention paid to her. She found she was grateful that Olivia had organized this, instead of plunging them into a private, probably nerve-racking conversation, when they barely knew each other.

She sat trying to get the measure of this new bunch of people.

Sean, sitting on Olivia's left, said almost nothing throughout the meal. He ate with his pale face bent over his plate, shovelling the food in with no grace. Once or twice, though, she noticed Olivia turn to him and their eyes met. Anna watched, puzzled, unable to read the signal being passed between them. Otherwise Sean came across as preoccupied and distant, and she didn't feel prepared to try and draw him into the conversation. There was enough talk for him not to be pressurized to speak.

Krishna began the meal by creating a deep ring of rice on his plate, heaping it hugely with the chicken and vegetables and finally laying a chapati across the top like a hat. He sat back, childishly inviting everyone to look, patting his stomach with his hands in anticipation.

'I'm sure I'm getting fat being back at home,' he said. 'Next week I'm going to join the hunger strike.' He let out a laugh. 'What do I have to do to get into the Maze?'

Ben reddened across the table. 'That's not bloody funny, Krish. Everything's a joke to you, isn't it? Ha ha bloody ha.'

Krishna held his hands up, shielding himself. 'Sorry. Sorry – very poor taste I fully admit. It's all right, Ben, you can step off your soap box now.' He gave one of his appealing grins and said to Anna, 'Ben here is our elder statesman.'

Anna felt sympathy for Ben. Krishna's crassness was already grating on her. To smooth over the difficult moment she said, 'I gather you're doing research?'

'Yep. Modern French poets.'

'How's it going?' Theo asked.

'Badly,' Ben said irritably. 'Don't know why I'm doing the wretched thesis.'

'Come, now,' Olivia said. 'You're going through a bad patch. That's how it goes sometimes with research. But you don't just give up because you reach a dead end for a bit. You have to wait to get to the next notch. I promise you it'll be worth it.' Her voice held smooth, maternal concern.

'I hope you're right.' Ben's cheeks were flaming. 'Sometimes I think I'd be a lot better out there earning some money.'

'Believe in yourself.' Olivia put her hand on his. 'Look, if it's getting you down, come and talk about it.' Her tone was caressing now, soothing him. 'You know I'm always here, don't you?'

'Yeah – thanks,' Ben said, with the reluctant gratitude of a child who feels foolish crying in front of his friends.

'Anna, you've got no pickles,' Krish said. 'You should try them. She makes them herself, you know.' He gave Anna such a sweet smile that her growing irritation with him was eased a little. She accepted some of the tangy lime pickle.

'What do you do, Anna?' he asked. 'Are you at the university too?'

'No. I'm a teacher – in Coventry. History.' Simpler not to mention that she'd just resigned.

'Oh?' Krish frowned, looking at Olivia. 'But you said you knew her when she was young?'

Olivia's voice broke in across the table, somehow claiming her. 'Anna's mother and I were very dear friends, a long time ago. We've only just got back in touch.' She beamed indulgently round the table. 'We're going to have a lot of catching up to do.'

Anna felt a strange feeling of elation, of having been singled out. A flush spread across her cheeks. She kept glancing at Olivia throughout the meal, resplendent in the glossy blue of the sari, regal, presiding over the table and her admirers. She could see now what it was that had made Kate adore her so much, something in her, a combination of charm and vulnerability which made you feel prepared to do anything for her. Anna found herself waiting for responding glances from Olivia and she was not disappointed. Often she did look over, giving her a smile both affectionate and complicit. After a time Anna began to forget the incongruity of her response. It was as if the past had nothing to do with this Olivia. Whatever her problems had been she had clearly overcome them. She was as charming and lovable as the childhood Olivia Kate had known. Anna relaxed, enjoying her.

Krish spent much of the meal clowning, Theo his foil, both of them laughing, but Krish by far the loudest. Ben talked seriously to Olivia, who occasionally turned to Sean. Once, she laid a hand on Sean's and said, 'There is more bread in the oven. Would you be a darling? They're in tin foil . . .' And Sean got up to fetch them, with the silent compliance of a dog.

'How're you finding teaching then?' a voice said. Anna, concentrating on watching Sean, turned, startled, to Jake.

'I'm sorry? Teaching? Well . . .' She had various stock answers to this question. For Richard something upbeat and idealistic; for Kate, a more straightforward assessment of the job, but not going so far as to include the truth of how draining she found it, how hardly a day passed when she didn't feel despair; for others there were the brief social replies: 'Fine,' or 'Well, it's a challenge.'

Since she didn't know Jake at all and had no time to think of anything else, the only option was to be honest. 'I think since I've been a teacher I've lost any illusions I ever had that I'm a nice, reasonable person.'

She thought he might be tediously disconcerted, as

people so often were when she said something honest. Instead, he gave a laugh of recognition, the serious face suddenly transformed. 'Very like being a parent, then.'

'I don't know. I can imagine, though.' She tried to remember what she'd been told about Jake. 'You've got kids?'

'One. A little girl, Elly. She's just four. Only she lives with my wife – ex-wife.'

Anna groped for a response. 'You must miss her.'

Jake swallowed a mouthful of wine. 'Like hell.' He jerked his head to one side to flick back the hair from his face and forced a smile. She liked the smile and knew she was going to like him. There was something open about him, and genuine.

'You live in Coventry, then?'

'I did until recently. With my boyfriend.' She managed a comical face. 'Ex-boyfriend.'

Again, the generous laugh. 'Oh dear. You'd better have some more wine!'

Olivia, seeing Jake's hand poised over Anna's glass, called across, 'You'd be welcome to stay the night. Why not? I even have toothbrushes!'

Automatically, Anna said, 'Thank you, but I think I'd better get back. I'll get a cab.' She was so used to being tied to home, to Richard, who admired spontaneity but only on his terms. But now there was only Kate's empty house and she realized too late that she needn't have refused.

Olivia accepted the refusal graciously. 'Do whatever suits you best, my dear. Actually I teach early tomorrow, so unfortunately I shouldn't have much time to see you.' She leaned forward. 'And I so want us to have a talk.' The smile she produced actually made Anna's heart beat faster.

Jake had refilled her glass. Turning to thank him, she caught him watching her and saw an expression in his eyes that she couldn't quite read – puzzled, or worried – but before she could think about it further there was a loud outburst from Krish. She watched him, his laugh high and giggling, cheeks pink. He had drunk too much, she could see. She wondered what it was he and Jake could possibly have in common.

'Does Krish work for you or something?' she asked Jake. 'Is that how you know each other?'

He nodded. 'He has done. I've got my own business in School Road. He's worked there during a couple of holidays.' He grinned at Olivia. 'She came in to buy a dresser and by the time she'd left she'd talked me into giving her son a job. Persuaded me he'd be the best thing that ever happened to me . . .'

'Which of course I was,' Krish interrupted, his voice loud and slurred.

'No more wine for you,' Olivia said sternly. She beamed at Jake. 'And wasn't I right?'

'He's pretty good at making tea,' Jake teased.

Olivia let out a loud laugh, wine loud, Anna thought, just beyond what was called for.

'He learned a lot actually,' Jake added hastily.

'So what d'you sell?'

'Furniture, mainly. Stripped-pine stuff – do a lot of it myself. It's getting very popular. I have a few other bits and bobs in to decorate the shop, but I go for the big stuff really – cupboards and dressers, that sort of thing.'

'I like shops like that.'

Jake shrugged. 'Come and see it then. It's not far.'

She found herself talking with Jake for most of the rest of the evening, through the *kulfi* – ice cream sprinkled with shavings of pistachio nuts – the slices of mango and cups of strong black coffee.

'You all need sobering up,' Olivia said. Sean volunteered for the coffee making. Anna saw Jake's eyes follow him as he disappeared unsteadily into the kitchen.

They all moved to the other end of the room, lounging in easy chairs, congratulating Olivia on the food, and she sat on the sofa covered in its bright fabrics, between Theo and Krish, arranging the end of the sari over her shoulder with an air of cream-fed satisfaction.

Sean handed round squat cups of coffee and sat on a chair to one side, scowling. He made Anna feel very uneasy, as if he was a servant, someone without equal status to the rest of them.

Theo was telling jokes about his family, making the three on the sofa laugh loudly. Ben joined in politely. And Anna and Jake talked. They talked about films and books, comparing tastes, keeping mostly off the subject of their own lives, except that Jake mentioned having moved to Birmingham at the age of ten from Staffordshire. Through the shouts of laughter from across the room she told him briefly about Kate's death and he was sympathetic and not over-effusive. There still seemed to be a lot of things to say when Olivia stood up suddenly.

'I think it's time we broke this up, pity though it is,' she declared. The boys, except Jake, all stood up immediately. Anna wondered whether this was deliberate on his part, a refusal to jump to her orders.

'Did you bring your van, Jake?' she asked.

'Yeah, but I'm not in a fit state to drive it. I'll be back for it in the morning. The walk'll sober me up.'

Ben and Theo drifted off upstairs. Sean stood hesitating, as if waiting for a signal from Olivia. Eventually, indicating the kitchen, he said, 'D'you want me to . . .?'

Olivia stared at him, silent for a moment. The look in her eyes turned suddenly icy. But she said in an even tone, 'Leave the washing up for tomorrow.'

Anna, watching Sean, was startled by Jake saying suddenly, 'Have you seen Olivia's batiks? Look – come and see this one.'

She found he had taken her hand and was leading her down towards the batik of the village at the other end of the room. His hand felt very big and warm, the skin rough.

'I have looked . . .' she began to protest.

As they turned to face the picture he said suddenly in an urgent whisper, 'Come to the shop – tomorrow?'

Finding this very strange, she said cautiously, 'Well – I'll come some time. I'm not sure about tomorrow.'

He leaned slightly closer to her. 'Don't take this the wrong way. Look – this is going to sound amazingly presumptuous of me but I'm going to say it anyway. You've been going through a difficult time recently – don't get drawn in by Olivia.'

Astonished and angry, she looked up into his eyes but they were steady, concerned. 'We should talk,' he said.

She was jolted by his seriousness, and trusted his sincerity. 'Yes, of course then. If you think . . .'

His face broke into a grin suddenly. 'Plus I'd like an excuse to show you my shop.'

'That'd be great,' she said, more reassured.

Olivia and Krish were clearing things off the table. Jake thanked them and, with a final glance at Anna, left.

'Call a taxi for Anna, will you darling?' Olivia said to

Krishna. As he went out to the telephone in the hall, Anna began to join in the work of clearing the table.

'I see those other bad boys have slunk off,' Olivia said. The two of them stacked plates and dishes next to the sink. In the big, old-fashioned kitchen Olivia chatted about practical things. 'The chicken can all go together in this dish – yes, *lassi* in the fridge, please. I'll just put a plate over this rice . . .'

She turned suddenly from the table, the rice giving off a whiff of cardamom, and gave Anna a cold, appraising look.

'You're different from her, aren't you?'

Completely taken aback, Anna said, 'Am I?'

But there was no follow-up remark. Olivia turned back to cover her rice as if the exchange hadn't happened.

'It's here!' Krish's voice came from the hall.

'Ah, go now!' Olivia said, apparently all charm again. 'Don't keep it waiting – they charge *so* much nowadays.' There was a sudden sense of hurry now the taxi had arrived.

'Do come again soon. Please.'

'I've got to pick up my car tomorrow,' Anna pointed out.

'Of course. Good.' In the hall they kissed each other, briefly, and Anna watched her glide away, the plait a slice of black down her back as the harsh blue of the sari disappeared into the long room.

Krishna was out at the front. As Anna came out he stepped over to her, took her by the shoulders and kissed her clumsily on the mouth, his lips taut and painful on hers.

He gave a foolish grin. 'Sorry. I don't know who you

are or what you're doing here. But it's lovely to see you.' And he was gone.

As the taxi took her through the dark streets she felt more and more uneasy. The odd, cold look Olivia had given her, Jake's warning, Krishna's drunken kiss – these were the things which now stood out from the evening. Caution, Kate had warned. Yet she had been so quickly beguiled. She must in future be more on her guard, even if she had no real idea against what.

On Kate's inner doormat she found a roughly folded sheet of pink paper: a note scrawled on the back of a flyer advertising cheap carpets.

'Came over to see you as you won't answer the bloody phone. What the hell are you playing at? *Call* me. Richard.'

Chapter 33

Olivia's house was quiet next morning. Sean let her in and she waited with him in the kitchen where he carried on working his way through last night's washing up, his back to her and thin elbows stuck out at angry angles.

'Have you been left to do it all?' Anna exclaimed. 'Here, let me give you a hand.'

He was turning to speak when the voice cut across from the doorway. 'No. Leave him. Sean's quite happy to do some work for me this morning, aren't you, darling?' Sean plunged a pile of bowls into the water with the force of someone trying to drown a puppy.

Turning to greet Olivia, Anna actually let out a gasp. Her hard, calculating tone accompanied another transformation so startling that she took a few seconds to manage the words 'Good morning.'

Gone were the sari, the bare feet and soft, understated make-up. Her suit was emerald green, cut in straight, sophisticated lines, the shoulders padded, the effect angular as a box, and she wore high, pointed court shoes in a matching shade. Instead of the loose plait, her hair was caught up into a perfect pleat, face immaculately made up, her lips a glistening plum red.

'Anna.' She offered a smile, but it seemed brittle and forced. Anna felt her breathing turn more shallow. Thank God she'd already decided to be more wary of this woman. 'We must spend some more time together, alone.' Olivia's heels clicked across the kitchen tiles. She leaned to touch Anna's cheek with her own and again there came a waft of perfume, this time something costly. 'I so wanted you to meet everyone last night – Krishna especially, of course. What did you think of him?'

Honesty lurked in Anna's mind: I thought he was pretty obnoxious. 'He's lovely,' she said. 'A credit to you.'

'He's my life,' Olivia breathed. Sean rattled cutlery loudly behind them and Anna stood feeling very uneasy. They were stepping too near the well of emotion. Everything was at odds this morning and she just wanted to get away from this place, back to Kate's house, and sink into a warm bath.

'I'm teaching today,' Olivia said. Her voice was clipped and precise, no trace of the rise-and-fall accent she had put on the night before. 'I like to dress up for the piano. It makes me feel professional. I really wanted to be a musician, you see. My father wouldn't hear of it until it was really too late.'

'Yes – my mother told me.'

'Did she?' There was a coldness in Olivia's eyes which brought Anna's flesh up in goosepimples. 'Come for tea,' she said abruptly. 'I've no pupils after four o'clock. We must talk. I presume you came to talk?'

The words were flung out like a challenge. Anna felt angry, suddenly, as if she was being played with, and at Olivia's assumption that she had nothing else to do but be called upon at her command.

'Yes, I came to talk,' she said stiffly. 'I presume that's what you wanted. You did write to her after all.'

The bell sounded in the hall. Sean left the sink

immediately to answer, and to Anna's relief they heard Jake's voice down the hall.

'Morning.' He smiled across at her from the doorway, so tall his head nearly reached the frame, hands in his pockets. 'Come to pick up the van. Thanks for last night, Olivia. It was a great meal.'

'Krishna's still in bed,' Olivia snapped. Anna watched her anxiously. There were stings in everything Olivia said this morning.

But Jake appeared not to notice. 'As I say, I've only come for the van. Got to get back to open up. I was wondering – ' He looked at Anna. 'Since I'm going back, d'you want a lift over, to see the place?'

'It'd suit me better to come later – elevenish? I could do with coffee and a bath first.'

Jake was flustered suddenly. 'Look – don't come if it's a bother.'

'I want to.'

'Great.' He smiled at her. 'I'll see you later, then. And Olivia – if Krish wants to drop in this afternoon, that's fine by me.'

Olivia nodded, grudgingly. 'I'll tell him.'

Anna left as soon as she could after Jake.

'Don't forget,' Olivia said. 'I'll be waiting for you this afternoon. And you can stay. I like a full house.'

It was more than a request, it was a command. Anna didn't take too easily to being ordered around.

'That should be all right,' she said coolly. 'I'll be round at four.'

Then came the smile, Olivia's disarming warmth. 'I'll so look forward to it.'

At Kate's house she lay in a deep bath and watched a silvery moth flap against the white ceiling, unable to get

Olivia out of her mind. She pictured Olivia's face, its baffling flashes of light and darkness like cloud shadows racing across a valley. She thought of the glinting malevolence she had seen in her eyes, and felt her innards turn. She imagined Olivia as she had seen her dressed that morning, malign mannequin, waiting by the bath, her hand coming down over Anna's face, the nails red and sharp, pushing her down and down.

'No,' she whispered. 'Stop. Please.' She lay in the warm water, trembling and sobbing, irrationally afraid for a time even to lie back and soak her hair.

I should go away and not get involved with her, she thought, as she dried herself. I don't need this, on top of everything else.

'What d'you want me to do, Mom?' She felt foolish talking to herself in the bathroom like that. The emptying bath inflated her words with an echo but provided no answer.

She put on clean, washed-out jeans and a white shirt and walked quickly round to Roland's house.

'Come in!' he greeted her joyfully, secateurs in hand. 'I could do with a break.'

'Roland, sorry – I can't today. I've promised to meet someone at eleven.'

'Ah. Anyone nice?' he asked, with childlike hopefulness.

'Nice?' Anna teased him. 'Yes, I think you could say nice. I just wanted to check you hadn't been round and wondered where I was.'

'No, I haven't as a matter of fact. Been to see friends then? Good for you. You don't want to be in that house alone too much, I'm sure.'

'I might be staying over in Moseley tonight. I didn't

want you to worry.' She gave him the address. 'It's off Anderton Park Road.'

'Right-o,' Roland said with his implacable cheerfulness.

'Can I pop in for a coffee tomorrow?' she asked, guilty.

'Nothing I'd like more.'

'Great. I'll see you then.'

'Anna?'

She turned back.

'Spare a kiss?'

'More than.' Hugging him tight, she gave him a big kiss on each cheek and Roland chuckled delightedly.

He stood watching her as she walked off quickly down the street amid the song of birds.

The banner across Jake's shopfront was a deep green with gold letters which read, *Jake's Pine*.

'I was looking out for you.' He appeared in the doorway, an old cloth in one hand, and came to join her in the sunshine, looking up appraisingly at the building. 'So, d'you like it? I've just cleaned the windows.'

She saw the pavement was wet and felt touched. Had he wanted her to see it at its best? The windows were still drying and behind them she could see the furniture: on one side a round table and chairs, a vase of dried teasels on the table, on the other a sturdy chest of drawers topped by a swing mirror, a rocking chair beside it.

'It looks really impressive. And I like the name. I expected something more twee.'

'Yes. Easy trap to fall into with this sort of stuff. Not

really me, though.' He talked fast and she saw he was nervous, more than she was. After all, he had asked her to come here.

'Trouble is, people keep coming in and asking me if it's getting better.'

She frowned. 'What?'

He thickened his Brummy accent. 'The pine.'

Anna exploded into laughter. Jake's dry humour confirmed why she had come. Talking to him had made her happy and uplifted after the past gloomy weeks. Such a relief after Richard.

'Come in. I'll show you round.' He stood back to let her through, his huge hands holding the door. It felt strange being suddenly alone with him, but there was a gentleness about him, about those hands, which made her trust him.

The shop was surprisingly big inside and extended up to the second floor. She followed him round, their shoes sounding on the bare boards. The downstairs was arranged carefully, without preciousness, so that items could be seen at their best. Painted wooden cats sprawled over some of the surfaces, and there were vases and stacks of wooden picture frames. Anna walked slowly among the dressers and cupboards, bedframes and chairs, touching smooth wood and admiring.

'D'you do it all up yourself?' she asked.

'A lot of it needs attention of some sort,' he said. 'Most of them are painted when I get them. Look at this – this one was in a right state when I got it.'

He showed her an elegant wardrobe with carved patterns on the doors. 'Look at the texture in that.' He stroked the smooth surface. 'It's like bringing something to life again. This was covered in brown paint, would you believe – I mean imagine painting wood like that brown . . .'

She followed him up to the second floor. 'The top's my flat, well, hardly more than a bedsit really, but it does me fine. There's space for Elly when she comes. This floor's more for storage.'

The rooms up there were crammed full of chests of drawers, bedframes packed tightly together in rows, stacked chairs, their legs in the air. A large table was roped upside down to hooks on the ceiling.

'It looks as if you're torturing it,' she said.

Jake laughed. 'I get a bit carried away with the buying. But people often choose stuff from up here. I think they enjoy it being a bit chaotic. I don't follow them around or anything.'

Downstairs, he showed her his little office which opened into a small yard at the back and had once been the kitchen. On the desk in the middle of the room were an old Adler typewriter, piles of duplicate books, a calculator and all sorts of bits and pieces, tins and nails, rubber bands and wooden drawer knobs.

'How did you get into doing this?' she asked him.

'Took a degree in philosophy.'

She wasn't certain for a second if he was serious. 'I've got a degree in history so I'm a history teacher. Bit predictable in comparison, I suppose.'

'Thing is – what do you do with a degree in philosophy? I started off selling a few oddments out of a van. Did it from home. I got hooked on it really and it grew from there. Before that,' he added lightly, 'I had a successful career selling insurance.'

'Oh, yeah? I can really imagine you doing that!'

'I see you don't believe me.'

Anna perched herself on the corner of his desk. 'Does that kettle work?'

'Has been known to. Why, d'you think you're going to get a drink as well?' His grey eyes were full of amusement. He filled the kettle. 'It'd be nicer up in the flat, but I'm afraid I can't take you up just in case anyone comes in. You haven't got to rush then?'

'No. I've no plans. I'm still cleaning Mom's house but I'm taking my time over it. Actually I've just resigned from my job.'

Jake looked at her steadily. 'Wow. Big decisions.' Again she found herself grateful to him for not overreacting.

She looked back into the shop. 'I only wish I could buy something off you, but I'm already saddled with two houses and I really need to get rid of things.'

'Two?'

'Mom's, and our house in Coventry.'

'With your boyfriend?' He leaned towards the old brown kettle to hear if it was heating.

'Ex-boyfriend.' She paused. 'How long have you been on your own?'

'Year and a half nearly. What about you?'

'I left him a month ago. But to be honest I feel as if I've been on my own a lot longer. He keeps trying to get in touch but I can't face it. I'm trying to avoid him. Cowardly, really.'

He watched her, seriously. 'That's rough.'

'Yes. But I know it's the right thing, in the end.'

His eyes searched her face for a moment and she wondered with a certain amount of panic whether disclosures were about to follow, his marriage, what had gone wrong. But he looked down, pouring milk from a carton. After he'd handed her her coffee he leaned up against the old worktop.

'What did you think of Olivia's little display last night?'

'Display?'

He watched her face for a moment as if unsure what to say next. 'How long have you known her?'

'Barely any time at all in fact. But in another way I've known about her all my life. She was a friend of my mother's until they – ' she searched for a way to describe what had happened ' – fell out. Years ago. She didn't see Olivia after that.'

'What did they fall out about?' He put his hand to his forehead. 'Sorry. I don't want to put you on the spot. Only tell me what you want to, of course. It's just, there are probably things . . . Do you know much about Olivia?'

Anna sighed. 'If you've got all day, I'll tell you.'

'I actually know almost nothing about her, except a little bit through Krish. She and your mom – were they close?'

'Very. Mom loved her.'

'And she wanted you to see her?'

'I think – yes, I'm sure she did. She said she understood that I'd want to make contact. But she told me to be careful.'

'But why didn't you see her while your mother was still alive.'

'Because she told me Olivia was dead. All my life I believed she was killed in the war.'

Jake made a sound, an outward breath, half whistle. Anna hesitated. She wanted to talk about this, to share it. And she trusted Jake.

'You have to understand that Olivia's life has been, well – difficult. But she was living with us for a time when I was born. She was in a very bad state at the time. When I was about three months old she tried to drown me in the bath.'

'My God.' Jake stood upright suddenly. 'Is that true?'

'Mom wouldn't have made it up.'

'Aren't you – I mean, what the hell d'you feel about that?'

'I don't know what to feel. I don't remember it of course, not directly. I only found out about it a few weeks ago.'

'And you only met her for the first time this week?'

She nodded. 'Now I've met her I can't work out what to think about her.' She paused, looking out through the open door into the little yard. There was a neat stack of old doors covered in chipped paint, leaning against the opposite wall. 'One minute I feel drawn in, sort of ... infatuated almost, by her. I don't know if this sounds crazy to you? Then she turns suddenly and she's frightening. I don't know why. It's something in her face. It just flashes across. Then she's charming again and I can't work out whether I've imagined it, that I'm reading things into it because I know about her past. You don't really think she's dangerous, surely?'

'Only to Krish.'

'Krish? But they're so close. Seeing them together's like the mutual admiration society.'

'This is why I said I needed to talk to you.' He put his head on one side. 'Why d'you think I hang out with someone like Krish? He's fifteen years younger than me, and in many ways he's a complete pillock.'

'I had wondered. I don't know – he worked for you. I just thought you were friends.'

Jake gave an ironic laugh, shaking his head so that his thick hair shifted on his shoulders. 'Friends? Not exactly. I think I'm Krish's – resort. Refuge. He's all over the place is poor old Krish. Olivia talked me into having him here to work, just like she more or less talked him into a place at college. Not that he's not bright, but he didn't get the right grades and it's certainly not the course he would have chosen. Science is actually his thing They turned him down and she appealed – twice. Wrote letters, went down there, crusading. Eventually they gave him a place at the last minute because someone else dropped out. That was all going on while he was working here. He was OK to have around, I must say.' Jake looked embarrassed for a moment. 'I wasn't in too good a state myself at the time, and someone else working here was welcome. Otherwise I was alone all day, and up in the flat at night. I hadn't done it up then either and it was grim. Krish can be a laugh when he's not saying something crass or ridiculous.

'Anyway, after a while he started talking, confiding in me. He found it very hard I think. It made him feel so disloyal to her. Since then I've been a sort of surrogate something-or-other to him. For some reason, I feel responsible for him, as if he's a child.'

'I suppose that's how my mother felt about Olivia.' Anna picked up an old Strepsil tin from the desk and fiddled with it. Something hard rattled inside.

'Krish needs to get away from her. She's got such a hold on him. It's hard to explain. He's terrified of her – the emotion she can work up. And the atmosphere there gets very weird at times with all her boys . . .'

'The lodgers?'

'Have you wondered why they're all still there

through the summer holidays? Olivia never has female lodgers. Always these boys. They come and go every few weeks or months, depending on how long they stay the course. Whether they react as required.'

'Meaning what?' Anna asked, not certain she wanted to hear the answer.

'Well, it varies, I think. What she wants is for them to depend on her, to take over their lives. Did you see Ben the other night? She's set herself up as mother confessor to him. The guru. From what I gather he's got the most miserable family. Doesn't want to go home. Ditto Sean. He's the one in the biggest tangle with her, poor bloke. Like someone nailed to a log. Did you see the state of him? The reason he acts like a servant in the house all the time is because he gets his rewards later – if he's been a good boy.'

Anna let out a gasp. 'No – oh no. That can't be... That's horrible.' She felt tearful. All her hopes of Olivia were sliding away so fast. 'Not that – not still?'

'Still what?'

Anna took in a long breath. 'She was – promiscuous. To put it mildly.'

'She has to control people. Theo's an interesting one, though. She made a big mistake there, I reckon. He's a really good thing in that household at the moment. Lightens the place up no end. But my guess is she'll get nowhere with him at all. He may make jokes about his family, but in the end Theo's got a strong core in him. He's got values, roots. That's no good to Olivia. She needs floaters like poor old Sean. People she can bend like straws and take over.'

'Jake, are you absolutely sure about this?'

'Absolutely. She's malignant. There's no other word. Krish knows it's happening, except he tries to blank it out most of the time. You can't warn them. They're supposed to be adults. They come because they want to. And Olivia can be a darling. All small and defenceless and tempting in silk robes. I don't know what's going to happen with Sean, but he can't go on like this much longer. I mean the house varies a lot depending on who's there, but Krish says it's never been as bad as it is at the moment.'

Anna put the tin down and went over to the door, leaning on the frame. She felt slightly queasy. 'God, I can't believe it.' She searched Jake's face, tears rising in her eyes again. 'When I saw her – so lovely-looking in her big house, with all these people around her, I really thought she'd managed to get her life together. That's the worst of it, that I know there's something really nasty in her, but I still feel it's not her fault and I want to protect her.'

'Look,' Jake said. 'I'd really like to know more about her. Properly I mean. You know Krish knows virtually nothing about her past. Why don't you come round this evening? I'll cook something.'

She saw it had cost him a certain nerve to ask. 'I'd love to, but I can't tonight. I said I'd go there at teatime. She wants me to stay the night.' She felt suddenly panicky. 'I don't know if I want to be alone with her.'

'Would it help if I came round? I can get a mate of mine to close up for me. I'll come over and see Krishna.'

She felt hugely relieved at the thought. 'It's all silly, I'm sure. But I would feel safer with you around.'

'Don't worry. I'll be there.'

Chapter 34

'There are things I need to know.' Anna found herself rehearsing in the car on the way to Olivia's house. 'Things you owe it to us to be straight about.' In this odd, contorted household, she thought, the only course she could take was honesty and directness. At least, that had seemed a good idea when she was at home. Tell me what I need to know and I'll go. We owe each other nothing. She imagined sitting opposite the icy woman she had encountered that morning, coolly asking questions.

Then she thought of the reality of those questions: *Was my mother's lover the father of your child? Why did you try to murder me when I was a baby?* And the conversation became inconceivable. Hardly questions to be tossed out over tea and cakes.

She parked the car, this time closer to Olivia's house. Her watch said four-fifteen. She should have left earlier. Walking to the house, overnight bag in one hand and a white cake box balanced on the other, it occurred to her that Olivia ought to be more nervous than herself about any conversation they might have. Perhaps she had things she needed to get off her chest. With this encouraging thought that everything might not be up to her, Anna went to the house.

Sean answered the door, looking pale and miserable.

'You're late,' he remarked.

Anna felt irritation mingled with her pity for him. 'You the butler?' she asked lightly, and immediately regretted it.

She became aware of the sound of the piano behind him. She had no idea what the piece was. It was fast and passionate and hearing it brought up her flesh in goosepimples.

'Is that her?' she whispered.

Sean's white, pitted face shifted to the nearest thing she'd seen to a smile. 'She's bloody fantastic, isn't she?'

'Should I go through?'

'Yes. She's waiting for you. Just sit down and wait till she's finished. She doesn't like being interrupted.'

Anna slipped into the long room and sat on one of the easy chairs behind Olivia, the box of cakes on her lap. The room looked beautiful, her roses in a vase on the table and the breeze wafting the coloured silks at the window. Once more, Olivia had changed. The harsh look of the morning was gone and now she had a softer, more relaxed appearance: a white blouse with a wide, frill-edged collar and a full skirt in panels of red, green and gold. The back view of her, with her hair loose, was of someone much younger. She leaned her body into the music, playing with every part of her, not just her hands. Watching, Anna saw her complete absorption and concentration and knew that the beauty of it was what Kate had seen when they were girls together. By the time Olivia drew to the end of the piece and played the long, last chords, Anna was seeing in front of her the young Olivia, before the war, before Arden, even before she began listening at doors, or being locked behind them. She saw into the sadness of Olivia's life, and the death of her friendship with Kate seemed suddenly far more terrible than the loss of any bond with a man: far worse than the end of her relationship with Richard, or Kate's with Douglas.

As the music stopped there was a discordant jangle from the doorbell which made Anna jump. She heard Jake talking to Sean and felt jarred by it. His arrival was wrong. She didn't need help. Olivia was lovely, tender, sad. Anna wanted nothing more now than to talk to her alone.

Olivia twisted round on the piano stool. 'I knew you were there. I felt you.'

'That was so good,' Anna said, wiping her eyes.

'You're crying, ' Olivia said softly. 'I used to be able to make Katie cry with my music too.'

'Oh, Olivia,' Anna cried, letting the tears run down her face. 'Why did it have to happen – you and her?'

Olivia was beside her in a second, gentle, sweet-smelling, her arms round Anna, stroking her cropped hair. The cake box slid to the floor. 'My darling Anna, my dearest.' And Anna held her too, feeling the small lightness of her, and thought she would choke with sadness.

'I've wanted to hold you for so long,' Olivia said. 'When you were a little baby I cuddled you so much. I felt as if you were mine. I knew one day you'd come to be with me whether Kate wanted you to or not.'

Anna pulled away and looked up into her face. Both their cheeks were streaked with tears. 'But I wasn't yours. And you tried to drown me.' She found her voice growing shrill. 'Why did you do that to me?'

Olivia withdrew her hands, her face stony. 'She told you.'

Anna sat in silence, waiting.

'I was – not well. You know that, don't you? She

told you that? I was destructive. It wasn't me.' She looked into Anna's eyes. 'Can you forgive me?'

'I don't know.' She thought for a moment. 'For myself, I suppose, yes. But it's my mother you really needed to ask that.'

Olivia watched her face, not saying anything.

'There are other things I want to know.'

'I know.' Olivia roused herself suddenly and stood up, becoming almost cheerful again. 'Look. We'll have a long talk. Let's go and make tea first.'

Anna stood up, offering her the box of éclairs. 'Sorry – they're probably a mess by now.'

'Oh, how sweet! What a treat,' Olivia cried.

They went into the kitchen with its huge grey stove and tiled floor. A wooden drying rack hung from the ceiling holding a row of blue and white tea-towels.

Olivia filled the kettle and then turned, taking Anna in affectionately with her eyes. 'You are so like Douglas – his eyes and that beautiful hair. How is he?'

'I've no idea,' Anna said, startled. 'I've never met him.'

Olivia stood up straight, disbelieving. 'What?'

'He left her, not long after you did. Or at least, he went to work in London and she didn't go with him. He cut off completely, never a word. That was how he was, she said. Didn't you know?'

'No.' Olivia seemed quite stunned. 'I had no idea. We had no acquaintances in common even, really. And anyway, I was in London. I only ever saw her that once . . .'

'After you'd had Krishna?'

Olivia nodded. 'She wouldn't speak to me. The look in her eyes . . . And we both brought up our children alone. We should have been able to help each other.' She hesitated, gathering her resolve. 'Anna, I need . . . Will she see me, d'you think?'

Realization rushed through Anna's mind, appalling. 'Olivia,' she said gently. 'Oh God, I'm so sorry. Look, this is partly why I came now.' She could barely get the words out. 'Mummy died on July 29th. She'd been ill for some time. I just assumed you knew.'

Something stopped her touching Olivia. A glove of complete stillness had slipped over her, something impregnable which made Anna afraid. She could think of nothing to say, nor could she read the look in Olivia's eyes.

They both stood there, very still. Then Olivia said, 'No,' softly at first. She made a swift movement and grabbed the kettle beside her full of almost boiling water, yanking it so that the flex came out and water splashed from under the lid soaking her hand, and she hurled it across the pale blue table. The lid came off and water pooled, steaming, across the table, splattering down on to the floor, and the kettle took the milk bottle with it so there was a smash of glass and a diluting white pool and the tinny bounce of the kettle on the tiles.

And Olivia's cries, her hand scalded. 'No, no, no!' she screamed. 'She can't be. She can't be!' The mugs crashed to the floor and she was opening the cupboard by her head and hurling sugar, tea, coffee across the kitchen. The cries tapered to a high scream which kept coming and coming out of her mouth like thin metal tape.

When Krish and Jake came pounding down to the kitchen, Anna was pressed against the stove, eyes stretched wide. A pile of sugar was dissolving gently into the water on the table, and tins from the next cupboard were slamming against the pantry door at the opposite end of the room.

'Get her arms,' Krish ordered Jake. 'Just hold her still a minute while I talk to her.' He began making soothing noises.

Though Jake was far bigger than Olivia, he seemed to need to use a good deal of his strength to grasp her from behind and pin her arms to her sides. As soon as he held her, though, she surrendered automatically as if by routine.

Krish stood in front of her, bending to look up into her face with big, appealing eyes. '*Ma?* Are you all right, *mamaji*?' He spoke in a babyish voice, kept repeating the same phrase, hypnotically, again and again. 'It's all right, Krishna's here, *mamaji*. Krish loves you.' Then he began saying things Anna couldn't understand, in the same soothing voice, and she realized after a moment that he was speaking Bengali, and once more it was the same phrase, over and over. Olivia had gone limp.

'It's OK, Jake, you can let go,' Krish said.

Jake withdrew his arms. Anna became aware of an unpleasant smell in the room, but couldn't work out what it was.

Krish took Olivia in his arms and held her against him. The two of them were completely absorbed in each other as if Anna and Jake weren't there. Olivia was crying in a terrible, broken way, and Krish kept saying 'Ssh,' and 'It's OK. It's OK.'

'She's dead,' Olivia told him in a tiny voice. 'Anna says she's dead.'

Jake gave Anna a questioning look and she shrugged helplessly.

'It's OK,' Krish soothed. 'Don't worry now.' Anna realized he hadn't any idea who Olivia was talking about. 'Let's go upstairs, shall we, and have some time together? We could have one of our talks, couldn't we?'

'I think she's scalded her hand,' Anna pointed out.

Krish nodded. He led Olivia towards the door, arm round her shoulders. As they passed through the long room Anna and Jake heard Olivia say tearfully, 'Krishna loved me, didn't he?' And Krish's reply, 'Yes, he did. Of course he did.'

Anna found she couldn't move. Her legs were unsteady and her hands trembling. Jake took her arm and pulled her away from the cooker, turning one of the taps.

'You've switched the gas on.' He was fanning the air with one hand.

'I thought I could smell something.'

Dazed, she watched Jake push the back door ajar and fling open the window over the sink. 'That's better,' he said, coming over to her. 'Smells foul in here. Are you all right?'

She was in shock, her knees giving way. Jake caught her as she was about to sink to the floor. She felt his arm strongly round her waist, holding her up, helping her to a chair in the long room. He let her down gently and she sat shaking. 'Sorry,' she said.

'That's all right. I'm used to humping chests of drawers around.'

He squatted down in front of her, eyes concerned. 'Anna, you look really rough. D'you want me to take you home?'

She shook her head. 'No. I'll be fine. I can't just disappear after that anyway, can I? Could you pass me my bag – I need a fag.'

He stood up, towering over her, passed it over. 'Here.'

'Want one?'

'I don't any more.' He frowned. 'What brought that on? I've never seen her as bad as that before. You've really touched a nerve somewhere.'

'She didn't know Mom was dead.' Anna dragged hard on the cigarette, elbows resting on her knees, one hand raking her hair. 'I feel so bad about it. I mean we just kept mentioning her and I took it for granted Olivia knew. She wanted to see her. It's all so stupid . . .'

'Don't blame yourself,' Jake said. 'She's had years, hasn't she? She's picked the wrong moment.'

'But it's not just a wrong moment, is it?' Anna retorted, angrily. 'It's never, now. *Finito*. Chance over.'

'Look, I'll go and get the kettle working,' Jake said, retreating into the kitchen. 'You look as if you could do with something.'

There was a pause, then Anna said, 'Poor Krishna.'

It was well over an hour before Olivia came down again. Jake kept making sweet cups of tea and Anna was grateful and felt relieved at being cared for, even though she could have done with a gin.

After some time, Sean came sidling round the door. 'I heard,' he said. 'Is she all right?'

'She's had a shock,' Jake told him. 'She'll be fine, I think. Krish's up there with her.'

Sean hovered for a time, abstractedly replying to Jake's questions about how were things, how was college. He fidgeted round the table, leafing through the newspaper, standing, as he so often did, with his weight on one foot, twitching the other up and down. Then he shambled off towards the door.

'Sean,' Jake said gently. 'You do know Olivia's not completely well?'

Sean shrugged. 'Who is?' And disappeared.

Theo and Ben came crashing in soon after, Theo with a pile of books. 'Best get packing,' he said, taking swigs from a can of Pepsi.

'You going somewhere?' Anna asked.

'Yeah. Mom wants me home in sunny Smethwick for the rest of the holiday. Doesn't make much sense when I have to sleep in a shoebox with two of my brothers, but she likes to keep the family together – and of course I come in handy for minding my sister, 'cos the others are all at work. Anyway, you don't argue with my mom, basically.'

Anna grinned. Theo had cheered the place already. 'Have a good time,' she said.

Theo rolled his eyes comically in response.

'Won't be the same without him, will it?' she said to Jake when Theo had bounced out of the room. Ben slouched past with a steaming mug of something.

Jake's mind seemed elsewhere. 'Look, I don't think you should be staying tonight. You've had a bad month and it can get very moody round here.'

'I'll be fine,' Anna said firmly. 'I feel all right now – really. She just took me by surprise. Come on,' she joked. 'I don't think I need a minder.'

'Sorry.' Jake looked sheepish. 'Didn't mean to take over. But look, if there's any problem – ' He wrote on a piece of paper. 'This is my number. Call any time. I don't mind.'

'Thank you,' she said, touched. 'That's nice of you.'

Again he hesitated. 'Will you come round tomorrow? For that meal I was threatening to cook?'

Anna laughed, cheerful suddenly. 'Yeah – great. Thank you.'

*

Despite her assurances to Jake, when she found herself alone again she felt jumpy and apprehensive. What had happened in the kitchen seemed like a dream now, but when she went back in there much of the chaos Olivia had created was still in place. She thought it typical that Ben had apparently not even noticed. Jake had sorted out the kettle and replaced the packets which had not broken open, but the floor was still wet and there was a thick sludge of sugar and coffee on the table.

Convincing herself she felt calm, she found a Tesco's bag, shovelled the mess into it and wiped the table down. She was searching for a mop and bucket when she heard sounds from the long room next door. Heart thudding, she went in there.

'Oh Anna, hello!' Olivia produced a wonderful smile which, had it not been for the white binding on her hand, would have made what had happened earlier seem impossible. 'I'm so glad you're still here. We were afraid you would have given up on us and gone.'

'Er, no.' Anna felt disorientated. Krishna appeared too, charming her as if nothing had happened.

'Jake stayed for a while. He's only just gone.'

'Lovely boy, isn't he?' Olivia gushed. She went round the chairs, plumping cushions. 'And he's been such a good friend to Krish. It was such a shame he and his wife couldn't seem to get on – so many broken relationships about nowadays. There's a sadness about Jake, I always feel. Misses his little girl terribly.'

She tidied the music on the piano. 'Have the boys got back here yet?'

'Yes. Theo's off home tonight.'

Krish looked stricken. 'I'd forgotten! I'll just go up – ' He headed for the door.

'Yes, do go, and tell him not to leave without saying goodbye,' Olivia called.

When they were alone, Olivia said, 'I'm afraid you gave me a terrible shock earlier.' She looked across at Anna, an odd, closed expression in her eyes. 'What happened to her?'

'Cancer. She wasn't well for quite a while. I wasn't keeping it from you. I thought you would have known.'

'Darling – ' Olivia swept over to her and took her in her arms. 'You weren't to know what a hermit I've been. I'm so out of touch with things. And at least we've found each other now, which is a great, great joy to me.' She held Anna's shoulders. 'We'll have a lovely evening together, the three of us – you, me and Krishna. It'll be perfect.'

By some signal, presumably from Olivia, the three of them were left alone all evening, with no interruptions from the lodgers. Theo had said his goodbyes and gone earlier. Krish clearly didn't want him to leave.

They shared a simple meal of bread and cheese, salad and pickles. Olivia sat between the two of them at the table looking beautiful and was at her most charming, but Anna now found it impossible to relax in her company. She caught herself observing, questioning, tuning in to undercurrents beneath what Olivia was trying to present to her. She moved her chair away slightly from where Olivia had arranged it close by her side and watched the spectacle of what almost amounted to a courtship between mother and son.

'I'd so like you to think of me as family now,' Olivia said after they had eaten, talking mainly of practical things, Anna's teaching, Krish's course at college. 'I always so wanted a big family, growing up alone.' She leaned over to touch Krish's hand, as she had already done a number of times during the evening. He smiled back at her, his expression affectionate, adoring almost. At the start of the evening Anna had felt reluctant admiration for him, that he could cope with this woman and remain so loyal to her. But she was growing more exasperated with the pair of them, frustrated by what she saw as falseness.

'Wouldn't it be lovely to have a big sister like Anna?' Olivia went on.

'Oh, it would,' Krish said, with slightly too much enthusiasm. He gave Anna a dazzling smile, and she managed to bare her teeth at him fairly convincingly in return. 'The thing is, though, you've never told me about Anna before. Or Kate. I mean, we're not actually related are we?'

Olivia laughed. 'Not by blood, no. But Kate and I were closer than most sisters ever are. We adored each other. She was lovely, Katie was, when she was young. So kind and sweet. She'd have done anything for anyone . . .'

Anna listened, longing to be beguiled. She wanted to believe everything she was being given, to rest on the surface. And Krish was so interested and attentive, his eyes fastened on his mother's face, and she wanted to believe in that too, that this extraordinary affection was the whole story between them.

But questions kept nudging into her mind as Olivia talked and talked about her mother. 'Katie and I were inseparable at school.' Her face was glowing, her voice animated. 'And of course she loved my father. She used to come on holidays with us, because your grandfather, Anna, was a very upright man, but rather a joyless sort, I'm afraid. We had a marvellous time together, and then of course I went away to boarding school. But we wrote letters all the time, and all the holidays we just lived at each other's houses. We talked about anything and everything – quite openly for those days, I can tell you!'

On and on it went, Katie and I, Katie and I . . . Krish seemed to be drinking it all in.

'So why didn't I ever meet her?' he asked after a time.

'Oh, well,' Olivia said, face still bathed in a bright smile. 'The war came and changed everything. Nothing was ever the same. I joined the Wrens and Katie was here nursing and we didn't see so much of each other after that. And then after, I went off to London and I met your father . . .'

These last words were spoken with a worshipping tone that Anna found ridiculous. He was just a man, she felt like saying. Yet another one.

Olivia directed a wistful smile at Anna. 'If ever there was a love child – ' She leaned across and stroked Krish's head. 'Unfortunately Krishna, my Krishna, was already married. He was on a visiting lectureship, you see. He felt the only thing he could do was to return home. But he left me his child.'

Anna thought of Elizabeth Kemp, how she managed to put from her so many things she didn't like. She felt a rising anger and resentment. All this pretence at being honest and vulnerable, when all the time she was selecting what she would tell, giving her son these half-truths. And what the hell was he playing at anyway, listening with that fixed, devoted smile? She felt like a fly trapped in the syrupy atmosphere between them. She knew there were layers and layers to Olivia which made it impossible to know quite where the truth lay. Had she even been honest when she wrote her notes to Kate?

She felt tired of it all suddenly, with a frustrated urge

to smash through the brittle surface of things with which she had been presented all evening. She couldn't listen to any more.

She stretched and yawned. 'I'm sorry, I really am tired. You won't mind if I go up soon?'

'Of course not, darling,' Olivia said. 'You've had such a difficult time these last weeks and of course I hadn't even realized. Do go on. Krish and I will clear up.' She stood up with Anna, searching her face, but Anna found she couldn't meet Olivia's eyes. To have done so would have symbolized too much: an honesty otherwise quite lacking from the evening.

While Krish was carrying something to the kitchen she let the question force its way to her lips. Cheeks burning red she looked up defiantly at Olivia. 'Was Angus the father?'

Olivia's expression froze. There was a second of nakedness, fear flickering in her eyes. Then she said coldly, 'I've absolutely no idea what you're talking about.'

Chapter 35

Anna sat on the solid bed, her heart pounding. The tiredness had vanished and she felt wound up and unready for sleep. She unzipped the overnight bag and pulled out her long T-shirt and wash things, noticing as she did so that Olivia had left a small vase of flowers next to the bed, picked from the garden.

Deadly nightshade most probably, she thought. Knowing it was absurd, she found herself sniffing at the white daisies and the greenery around them to find out if there was anything amiss. Those looks she had seen in Olivia's eyes. At this time of night she could start to believe anything.

Restless, she pulled back the covers of the bed, then opened the window, lit a cigarette and blew smoke out on to the twilight air. Footsteps passed in the otherwise quiet street. After a time she heard sounds of movement in the long corridor outside the bedroom: the others coming up.

Leaving the window open a crack, she took her washbag and went out to the bathroom at the back of the house. The staircase ran up the middle of the building, joining the corridor upstairs which ran from front to back with a series of doors along it. Anna didn't know who slept where.

She washed, scrubbed her teeth, found herself thinking about Jake and the way he looked into her eyes.

Walking back to her room she admitted to herself how much she was looking forward to seeing him the next evening. A door squeaked somewhere along the corridor. Yawning, she went into her room, turned to shut the door and started with a violence that set her whole body trembling.

'What the *hell* are you doing?' she cried furiously. 'You nearly gave me a heart attack!'

'Sssh – don't let her hear.' Krish closed the door quietly and stood against it. His face was solemn and looked heavy from drinking.

'What d'you want?'

'To talk – without her.' He sat down on the edge of the bed and she thought how young he looked. 'Sorry,' he offered awkwardly. 'You obviously know a lot of things about my mother that I don't. She only tells me what she wants me to hear.'

'Yes,' Anna relented. 'I can see that.' She stood across the room from him, glad that she'd put off getting changed. 'What d'you want to know?'

'I don't know what there is to know. I mean I'd never heard all that stuff about your mom before. The only thing she talks about in the past, really, is my father.'

'And was that the great passion she'd like us to believe?'

Krish looked up at her warily. 'How would I know?'

'Of course, how could you?'

'She's got no letters though. He didn't keep in touch with her. She probably just wrapped herself round him like a creeper – the way she does with everyone.' Anna was disturbed by the harsh way he spoke.

'But downstairs you were – you seemed so close.'

Krish seemed uncomfortable at her mentioning this.

'We can be, sometimes. She's very good company, as you've seen. But there's something . . . She's just not normal, is she?' He spoke in a sudden rush. 'It probably sounds stupid to you but it's taken me until now to realize – these past couple of years. When I went to college I heard a lot about other people's mothers. At school she wouldn't let me go to visit other people. Wanted me to herself – ' He broke off. 'Look, can't you sit down?'

He sounded so wretched that she came and sat on the bed. 'It must have been very difficult for you.'

He sat looking down at his hands for a moment in silence, twining his fingers together. The next thing she knew, he was pushing her back on the bed, hands moving clumsily and hard on her thighs as he half lay across her, his tongue pushing into her mouth.

In reflex she drew up her knees and shoved as hard as she could. 'Who the *fuck* d'you think you are?' she yelled at him as he regained his balance. 'What is it with your family? You all think you can just take what you like. You rip into other people's lives . . .'

'Shut up for God's sake!' He rushed at her, clamping his moist hand over her mouth. 'She mustn't hear.'

Anna yanked his hand away. 'Don't do that to me.' She marched over and opened the door. 'Just get out of here, you stupid little git.'

Krish slunk out of the room. 'I'm sorry . . . I really did want to talk.'

'Don't ever try anything like that again,' she hissed at him. She watched him disappear into his room.

Turning, she jumped again, and with even more force. At the other end of the corridor, dressed in something long and pale, Olivia stood quite still, watching. Her face was set in an expression of such hatred that Anna felt her knees turn weak.

'So.' Olivia's voice snaked along the corridor. 'I can't even trust you.'

Anna felt something give in her, come flooding out. 'You're all bloody mad,' she shouted. 'All of you. I'm getting out of here.'

Starting to sob, she ran into the room and in half a minute threw all her things back into the bag. When she came out again Olivia was still standing in the same place, watching stony-faced as Anna ran downstairs. She pulled open the heavy front door and ran out towards her car, only just able to see through her tears.

The light was still on in the attic above Jake's shop. Standing outside in the deserted street, Anna realized she didn't know how to get in. There were two floors of the dark shop below, and it was as if he was out of contact with the street, high up there. She went to the door and looked for a bell. There wasn't one. Instead she tried the letterbox, which was fortunately well sprung and gave a resounding clap when she released the flap.

She waited. Outwardly, now, she was more composed, had had to control herself in order to drive. But she could feel a tight bubble of emotion inside her, only just held in. She could not have gone back to be alone in Kate's house tonight.

There were sounds from inside and she saw movement behind the glass door. He left the light off, cautious perhaps, and she could just see the washed-out blue of his jeans as he came to the door. It opened, brushing the mat. She felt she'd never been so relieved to see anyone.

'Anna?' She couldn't make out the tone of his voice. Surprised, certainly, but she thought she noticed in it a degree of pleasure, relief almost.

'I need to talk to you.'

'Yeah – of course.' He hesitated, not wanting to presume anything. 'It's too late for the pubs isn't it? Will you come in?'

'Here's fine.' She hadn't meant to sound so abrupt. As well as holding back her emotion over Olivia and Krish, she suddenly wanted Jake to hold her, and that wasn't appropriate, wasn't why she'd come.

Jake led her up through the dark shop with its comforting smell of wood polish, past the dark shapes of the furniture. Following, she thought how odd it was that she was here alone with him, somehow suddenly the closest person to her now apart from Roland. Their feet sounded loud on the bare staircase up to his attic.

When they reached the flat she forgot everything for a few moments, exclaiming, 'Jake, it's lovely up here!'

'I'm glad you like it.' He smiled. 'Only thing is, you have to go down to the next floor for the bathroom. I'm working on that. Might get a shower put in. But otherwise it does me fine.'

The room was lit only by the sidelight next to the bed, where Jake had evidently been lying. It was a long room stretching across the building, with a gabled window at each end. At the back Jake had his kitchen. The bed was at the front under the window. Music was playing softly in the background, the deep, rich sound of a stringed instrument.

In the middle of one side of the room was a wooden fireplace with space for a couple of easy chairs. Either side of it were long shelves striped with the coloured spines of books, records, tapes, and at one end a stereo. The walls were all painted a pale colour, except for the other long wall opposite the fireplace, which was a deep malachite green and covered from floor to ceiling with framed pictures.

Anna's attention was drawn to these straight away, postponing her need to talk. A section of them near the middle were photographs of a little girl: a baby, a toddler with a cap of fine blond hair and a cheeky smile.

'Is this your daughter?'

'That's Elly, yes. Of course she's changed again now.'

'She's lovely.'

'Yes – she's great.' He went to the fridge. 'D'you fancy a beer?'

'No thanks. I've drunk enough this evening already. Wouldn't mind a coffee.'

She sat on one of the chairs by the fireplace. 'I s'pose you'd rather I didn't smoke up here?'

'Sorry – I'd prefer it.'

'That's OK. It'll be good for me. I ought to give up.'

'I gave up when Elly was born.'

She twisted round to look at the pictures again. 'Are these all places you've been?'

'No. Places I'd like to go. Never had the chance, or made the chance, depending how you look at it.' He was nervous, unused to having anyone in the flat and having to be sociable.

She sat in silence for a moment, aware again of the music in the room, a melancholy cello.

'What is this?'

'Bach. Beautiful, isn't it?' He handed her her coffee and sat down.

'It sounds so sad.'

'I suppose it does. It's just what I seem to want to hear recently.' This was not spoken with self-pity, but Anna felt awkward.

'I'm sorry – I've barged in. Would you rather I went?'

'No, I wouldn't. I spend far too much time on my own.'

There was a pause, then he said, 'What happened?'

Anna put her mug on the floor and sat back. She let out a long breath.

'It sounds daft, but I'm not exactly sure what happened. Olivia came down after you left. She said she'd had a shock.' She told him about the meal, the fawning affection between Olivia and Krish. 'It was pretty sickening. I got more and more frustrated because I felt they were feeding me something, some image they wanted me to see, and I still hadn't managed to talk to her properly about anything.'

She told Jake what had happened with Krish, growing more emotional as she spoke.

'It wasn't him I really minded, though. The really horrible part was her. Krish is just young and silly . . . But when I saw her standing there, absolutely still, with that look on her face . . . I couldn't have stayed the night in that house. She'd have killed me, I'm sure. I could just see her coming round the bedroom door with a knife in her hand.' She looked across at Jake. 'I've never known anyone who's had this effect on me before. There's something – evil about her. You must think I'm being very hysterical.'

'No, I don't at all.' There was sudden quiet. The tape clicked off. 'But we'd better get hold of Krish tomorrow.'

'I'm not sure I ever want to see him again – or her, for that matter.'

'I think you'll have to.' Jake spoke gently but emphatically. 'Look, Anna, I don't know all the background to this as you obviously do, but I do know a lot about Krish. I didn't explain properly last time we talked. Your coming here has lifted the lid off something for them and it's him that's going to get the full rush of it. I know he shouldn't have behaved the way he did tonight, but you have to understand the kind of hold Olivia has on him. She's never let him out of her sight hardly, apart from school when she had to. But she wouldn't let him go out or have friends – let alone a relationship with a woman – God forbid. Anything that's started she's destroyed one way or another. She interferes in every part of his life. Possessive isn't a strong enough word to describe it.'

Anna frowned. 'But he's left home, hasn't he?'

Jake gave an ironic laugh. 'He's done three terms in London. During the summer before he went he overdosed because she made him feel so guilty about going. He was in hospital for three days.'

'But you said she wanted him to go – appealed to the university?'

'She did. But that's Olivia for you, isn't it? Nothing ever goes one way with her. Even in London she completely dominates his life. He has to phone every day, come home every other weekend. And there's barely a weekend in between when she's not down there. He's not allowed to see anyone else when she goes down. He has to devote his time to her. And if he doesn't ring there are tears, threats – the whole works, turning on the guilt. If she thought he was going out with anyone . . . well, it's almost unthinkable. I think he almost believes she can see into his mind. That if he was seeing anyone, she'd know, somehow.'

Anna listened, feeling forgiveness for Krish before Jake had even finished speaking. 'I can't imagine how he's coped this long,' she said. 'She's so terrible . . .' Her voice trailed off. 'But she does make you love her, doesn't she?'

'Better not to, I think.'

'She let Krish come and work for you. She must trust you.'

'I think I was partly to distract him from other things at the time. But we get on all right, me and Olivia. She knows I'm not going to be drawn into anything. She trusts me with Krish – like a sort of old uncle figure.' He shrugged, then looked at her seriously. 'And you know her because she was your mother's best friend who tried to do away with her baby?'

Anna shook her head. 'Sounds terrible, doesn't it? But it was my fairy story when I was little. "Tell me about you and Olivia when you were little girls." Bosom pals, complete devotion and all that. The stuff she left me to read telling me the truth about what happened was awful. She'd bring out all the good bits for me when I was a child. It was like – some mothers keep their jewellery box as a special thing to show their kids. All the shiny things inside. But with her it was Olivia.' She was crying suddenly, sobbing until she could barely catch her breath.

Jake got up, flustered, knelt down by her chair.

'I'm sorry,' she said, trying to gain control of herself. 'This keeps happening.'

'No, it's OK. Don't apologize.' He went to the kitchen end and came back with some squares of kitchen roll. 'Here – 'fraid I only have tissues in when I get a cold.'

Anna laughed, blowing her nose.

'I'll make more coffee – that's if you want? Or would you rather get some sleep?'

'No.' She handed him the mug. 'I'd like to tell you about it.'

He turned and touched her briefly on the shoulder. She felt the warmth of his hand through her shirt. 'No one should be alone with Olivia.'

She talked for an hour or more, telling him everything she could remember, trying, as Kate had done, to weave Olivia's account of herself into Kate's own. She told him about Angus, about her father, and Roland, trying to keep everything in the right order. When she reached the parts about Olivia's baby and Arden, she saw a look of shocked understanding on Jake's face.

'Does Krish know any of this?' she asked.

'I'm quite sure he doesn't.' Jake paused, trying to take it all in. 'I had no idea. Poor Olivia.'

'Yes, poor Olivia. But then you think what she did to my mother. I think Mom thought it was partly her own fault for bringing her to live in the house when I was on the way. At the time she didn't see what else she could do. But there was this huge splinter of sadness through her life. Looking back, I can recognize it more clearly. When you're young you don't always spot things, or know what you're seeing. I tried to ask Olivia about it tonight – about Angus. I was getting tired of all that sweet sugary crap between her and Krish. She just blanked me out. Gave me that evil eye look of hers and said she had no idea what I was talking about.

'In a way I don't know why it matters now anyway. Except that I think Mom wanted me to find out, to deal with it for her. I can't help thinking Olivia was lying, that he wouldn't have been disloyal to my mother, but they were strange times . . .'

'You may never get the truth now, anyway,' Jake said. 'Truth with Olivia is something that shifts around. What she wants is power over people. She knows she's got power over you because you want to know things, because you care about her. You see what she's done to Sean and Ben – let alone Krish. Don't let her get under your skin. It never leads to anything good.'

'Ben as well?'

'Ben's not in anything like the mess Sean is. He's very unsure of himself academically and he confides in her a lot. There's no doubt she's bright. She's supposed to be pretty well thought of for her knowledge of Bengali culture. She's very preoccupied with it because of Krish's father.'

'She even tries to sound Indian.'

Jake looked at the ceiling, exasperated. 'The whole thing, yes.'

Anna sat back in the chair, legs stretched out. Her head was beginning to ache.

'You all right?'

'Just tired. I don't think I can think about this any more tonight.'

'But you will see Krish?'

She hesitated. 'OK.'

'We could take him out somewhere. Get him away from there.'

'She won't want him going with me.'

'I'll think of something.'

Anna groaned. 'It's so late. I'm sorry. I must go.'

'Don't,' Jake said. 'There's no need and there's not that much of the night left – it's after three. Just sleep here. I've got a folding bed I use for Elly. I'll have that.'

She looked at him doubtfully, wondering for a few

seconds what this meant. The thought of driving back now was so dismal. 'Are you sure?'

Eyes full of warmth, he said, 'Of course. No problem at all.'

'My stuff's down in the car . . .'

'Give me the key. I'll get it.'

When he came back, Jake tactfully left to give her time to undress in this strange room, his pictures watching her from the wall. But she felt trusting, almost happy. By the time he came back she was already lying down.

He had changed into an old pair of shorts and a shirt. She looked at the firm lines of his legs, his arms. He pulled the folding bed open, settling it in line with her bed, tucking a sheet round its long mattress. She took in his slenderness compared with Richard's compact body.

He looked at her across the space between the two beds. 'Have a good sleep.' And reached over and clicked the light off.

'Jake,' she said drowsily. 'I wanted to ask you more about yourself. I'm sorry. I've been talking so much.'

'That's OK. There's not an awful lot to say about me.'

'I'm sure there is . . .' She felt her voice trailing off, sleep slipping over her in thick layers.

It must have been only moments later, but felt much longer. It began with a light pressure on her head, a stroking, soft as cobwebs in her hair, but then it was hard and she was in the dream and there was the terrible pressure, pushing, pushing so she couldn't move, and she felt her breath being forced out of her until she threw herself upright, whimpering like a tiny child, sweat breaking out under her arms and behind her knees.

'Sorry,' she heard Jake saying. 'God, I'm so sorry. Anna – it's OK. It's only me. I'm sorry.'

There was a click and the room sprang up round them again in the light. She squinted, bewildered, into Jake's face. He was sitting on the bed beside her, eyes wide with worry.

'I'm sorry,' he said again.

'Why?' She was dazed, couldn't think straight. 'I was dreaming. When I was little I sometimes used to dream I was being suffocated – pushed down and down. It's come back again since – since Mom died.' She remembered waking, as a child, out of the tight hold of the dream, gasping, with Kate's arms round her and her voice, 'It's all right, you're safe now. Quite safe with me.'

Jake was saying, 'It's just – I think it was my fault. I touched you. I was stroking your hair.'

'Were you?' She looked at him stupidly. 'Why?'

'Because . . . I don't know. I suppose I wanted to do something for you. I thought you were asleep. Sorry. I feel ridiculous.'

'No – don't.' She was moved by his care, felt a great need for it rise in her. 'You were being kind.' She looked up into his eyes. 'If I'd been awake I'd have liked it. I feel so lonely.'

He moved closer to her, put an arm round her and pulled her to him, so her head was resting against his chest. She heard his voice quietly, 'Me too.' He stroked her hair again, gentle as a parent, and she held his other hand and listened to the beating of his heart. After a time both of them slept, comforted.

Chapter 36

Birds, she thought, when she woke the next morning. Even before opening her eyes she knew she was somewhere new. The light was different, coming from high on her right, bright, no curtains.

The window had been opened above the bed, and moving air touched her face.

'Birds,' she said.

'Not the dawn chorus, though.' Jake came across, offering her a mug. 'Tea all right?'

She sat up, gratefully, trying to smooth her hair down. 'Oh, I need this. What's the time then?' He was already dressed.

''Bout half-nine. I've just been down to open up. Sleep OK?'

'Fine – thanks.' She felt herself blushing. She last remembered falling asleep leaning against him, and vaguely recalled him moving her, lying her down again. She thought of his touching her hair, of this area of need and intimacy which had opened up between them. She looked up and smiled shyly at him.

He sat down at the far end of the bed. 'Considering how little sleep we had last night, I don't feel too bad.'

'Nor me,' she said, though she did feel muzzy. Silently she sipped the tea, strong, with a tang of something, Earl Grey perhaps. A bee flew in through the window, bumped its way a short distance along the wall and back, then found the white air again and disappeared.

'Thanks for letting me stay.'

'No problem.' He smiled, face transforming. 'I was enjoying the novelty of having someone else around.'

She could tell neither of them was going to mention last night, now daylight had come, both embarrassed or afraid.

'How often does Elly stay?'

'Every other weekend usually. Unless that upsets some other arrangement her mother has made.'

Anna nodded. Jake obviously found the situation difficult to talk about and she didn't want to push it.

'What were you doing before this – before the business, I mean?'

'I told you – selling insurance.'

'What? Really?'

'Did you think I was joking?' He gave a reluctant laugh. 'I was training to be the man from the Pru. Nice safe job, suit, haircut, the lot. Life mapped out nicely.'

'And you couldn't stick it?'

His eyes moved sharply to her face, expression wary suddenly. 'You sound like Sal. Why? D'you think I should have done?'

'No!' she said, alarmed. 'Of course not. And anyway – it's none of my business, is it?'

'It's absolutely terrifying having your life stretching ahead of you like that, doing something you're indifferent to for the next thirty years. And I was doing OK at it. Personable, they called me. I was good at sales, always got on well with clients. But I got to thirty and I just couldn't do it any more. I was suffocating.'

'This seems much more you,' she said cautiously.

'I gave up work with the Pru when Sal was pregnant

with Elly.' Jake talked in a steady voice, eyes fixed on the floor in front of him. He talked about it as if it was something he just wanted over, needing to be told but best out of the way. Anna listened, the empty mug cradled against her chest.

'It seemed to rock the foundations of something for Sal. Some insecurity or expectation she had that neither of us had known about. My fault, I suppose. Not a good time when she was pregnant and wasn't sure how it was going to go with her own job. She works in admin over at the Poly. And I suppose she thought she was settling down with one sort of person and I turned out – in her eyes at least – to be someone very different. The business wasn't too good at first either, of course. So things were already wobbly. Then Elly was born and everything changed again.' He paused. 'I don't know. Too many changes all at once. We could never seem to reach each other after that. Even now it's not easy, having to keep seeing each other because of Elly. There's a lot of resentment. But we do it for her . . . I could never not see her.'

'It must be so difficult,' Anna said, feeling inane. Her mind flashed to Richard, to the miscarriage. What if she had had the baby? For the first time she was half glad. It would not have been right to have a child together.

Jake looked round and gave her a wry smile. 'Let's get off all that. Breakfast? It's toast or toast, I'm afraid.'

'In that case I'd like toast.'

She pulled her jeans on and quickly manoeuvred her way into the rest of her clothes as Jake sliced bread and clicked down the toaster.

'Shouldn't you be down in the shop?'

'There's a bell – rings up here too if anyone comes in. But yes, I should really. I'll just get this down me. I don't usually do a roaring trade at this time in the morning.'

They were eating thick, slightly singed slices of toast and honey when Anna suddenly exclaimed, 'Oh, no. What's the time?'

'Nearly half-ten. What's the matter?'

'Roland. I promised I'd see him this morning.' She was flustered, driven to action, flapping round the room, toast still in one hand. 'Anyway, I must go and let you get on.' She shoved her things into her bag with her spare hand. 'Listen, thanks ever so much.'

Jake stood up. 'No thanks needed. It's been a pleasure.'

'What about tonight – Krish?'

'Fancy a *balti*?'

'Love one.'

'I'll pick you up if you like. Seven-thirty?'

She gave him the address, then hesitated. Jake looked down into her eyes. There was a moment of awkwardness, of not knowing how to part.

Anna went to the stairs taking refuge in the need to hurry. 'Bye then. See you later.'

In the street she lit her first cigarette of the day, thinking that by now she would normally have had a couple already.

The growling of Jake's Transit van sounded incongruous in the suburban street. She climbed up into the cab, slim in jeans and a round-necked navy top which followed every curve of her.

Jake gave her a broad smile. 'You ready for this?'

'Doing my best to be.' As Jake reversed into Kate's strip of drive, she said, 'Does Krish know we're coming?'

'I phoned.' The van accelerated loudly. 'He sounded very low. Didn't say much.'

'But he's coming?'

Jake nodded.

'Did he say anything about last night?'

'No. He never says much on the phone. Always afraid she's listening.'

'What a life.'

Jake inclined his head in agreement. 'My guess is he won't have had the easiest of days.'

As they drove along the Alcester Road towards Moseley, the two of them talked rather abstractedly. Had she got to Roland's in time? Had he had many customers that day? Anna was feeling nervous about seeing Krish. Not because she didn't want to forgive him, to give him support, but because those feelings had somehow to be made clear.

They saw him waving to them from the corner of the road before they even reached Olivia's house. Jake braked sharply and Anna moved up into the middle seat of the cab. Seeing Krish again she was struck once more by the enormous appeal of his puppy-like looks.

'Been forced to camp out on the pavement now, have you?' Jake joked as they pulled away.

Krish seemed slightly breathless. 'I thought if she saw you two it'd make things worse. It's been bloody awful in there today.' He shifted uneasily beside Anna, avoiding her eyes. 'She's not speaking to me – not a single word. Ben's been out all day, so there's just Sean. Jesus, is he a moody bloke. Must be living with us that does it.'

He gave a nervous little laugh and turned to Anna. 'I'm really, really sorry about last night,' he said disarmingly. 'I got completely above myself and I regretted it straight away. Can you forgive me?'

Anna smiled. There was an adroitness in the apology which made her realize that he had become well practised at saying sorry, keeping things smooth. Living with her, no doubt.

'It's OK.' To her annoyance she felt herself blushing. 'I hope you didn't get into too much trouble over it?'

'I expect you've gathered my mother's rather possessive?'

'Don't worry,' Jake said. 'Anna's on your side.'

'I thought you'd fallen under her spell like everyone else seems to.' His voice was bitter.

'Not for long,' Anna said.

Jake parked in a side street off Stoney Lane, and they walked across to the little restaurant. The street was busy, most of the shops still open, with people milling in and out of the grocer's a few doors away, leaning over the rickety trestle tables outside to select from the boxes of green bananas, okra, garlic, oranges. A string holding paper bags shifted in the breeze. One of the passing cars blared Asian film music, a woman's voice reaching high. The evening air was warm and full of the smells of cooking.

Inside many of the tables were already taken and the atmosphere was busy, full of spice and smoke, a mixed-race clientele, the waiters holding dishes high, wriggling their hips to squeeze between the chairs. A huge white man sat alone at the back of the room pulling at *naan* bread with stumpy fingers. The waiter seated them with great courtesy, a metal jug of water and a small metal dish containing chopped onions in a runny white sauce rippled with tomato ketchup. Each table was covered by a sheet of glass with the menus tucked underneath and a sprinkling of paper napkins on the top.

'You familiar with this cooking?' Jake asked.

'Oh, yes. Richard was very keen on these places and got me hooked. I brought my mom here a few times.'

Jake smiled. 'And?'

'She loved it. Said it was the nearest she'd get to travelling now.'

They ordered Cokes and food.

'Kebabs,' Krish said. 'It has to be kebabs.'

Once they'd got past the activity of ordering, there was a sudden awkwardness. Anna asked Krish about his course, whether he was enjoying it.

'It's fine,' he said 'Really interesting.' She couldn't help feeling that this, too, was a stock reply.

'And the Bengali – you obviously already speak it?'

'Some. She brought me up almost bilingual – that was the idea. She speaks it very well herself.'

He changed the subject quickly then, asking Jake how the business was going, and the two of them talked through the starters. The main dishes arrived, the dark, well-used *balti* dishes like small woks, half filled with bright, sizzling food, and thick *naan* breads and rice alongside.

'Enjoy your meal,' the waiter said, retreating.

There was a long, embarrassed silence. They tore the bread, scooped up the spiced meat and vegetables.

'So things are bad again?' Jake said eventually, with a directness which suggested they settle down to the real business of the evening.

Krish nodded. Anna expected him to feel ill at ease with her there, but he seemed to trust her. She saw that as a measure of the trust he had in Jake.

'It's the longest I've spent in the house since last summer. A few days is OK. I can cope with it. Things don't build up too much.' He looked round at Anna. 'You might think I'm being very critical of her. Most people think she's marvellous – charming and sensitive, life and soul of the party. She is, of course, some of the time. In fact in some ways there's no one I'd rather have a conversation with. That's the good side of the lodgers being there. She's gifted with shy people – draws them out, makes them feel interesting and part of things. And she's very clever. I admire her a lot for all she's done. She had a hard time, bringing me up on her own and all that.'

'My mother brought me up on her own,' Anna remarked.

'Did she?' Krish looked intrigued for a second. 'But I expect she's a very different sort of person. My mother's had so much to deal with – me coming along, not only the bastard baby but the wrong colour as well, and her parents throwing her out ... She's heroic, really.'

'Why did they throw her out?' Anna asked, feeling compelled to interrupt this hymn of praise. She wondered what version of events Olivia had permitted Krish.

'Oh, they wanted her to have a nice little job, marry someone rich and influential. You know, all the respectable things. She wanted to play the piano – she's very gifted, you know – and study. Branch out. She was really a sort of Bohemian at heart.'

'I see,' Anna said, carefully. She felt Jake's eyes on her.

Krish pushed his chair back. 'I need a proper drink. Coke just isn't enough for the day I've had. Back in a minute.'

'There's an off-licence just along the way,' Jake explained as Krish disappeared. He looked at Anna. 'At least we'll be able to deliver him home safely.'

'What's going on?' Anna asked. 'We're back to the Blessed Martyr Olivia Kemp bit again.'

'He does that. When he's most angry with her he has to get all this stuff in first – how marvellous she is. It's a kind of pledge of loyalty, I think.'

'Before he says what he really feels?'

'Sometimes.' Jake offered her more rice. 'He doesn't find it easy to say anything bad about her.'

Anna refused the rice. She sat back in her chair. 'I feel I know so many things about her that he doesn't.'

'Then tell him.'

'D'you think it'd really be any help to him to know?'

Jake considered this. 'He only knows what she's chosen to tell him. Perhaps it would help to have another version of events.'

'I can hardly tell him here.'

'It's not ideal I know, but I don't think we'll get too many chances.'

Krish came back with chilled wine and a four-pack of beer. He pulled off one of the cans and drank thirstily.

'That's more like it.' He grinned at the two of them. 'Go on, help yourselves. Wine's open. I got them to do it.'

Anna took a beer and pulled the ring. Cautiously she said, 'Krish – how much do you know about your mother's life?'

'Hardly a thing,' he said, jovial suddenly. 'I mean, I have a sort of outline, without much detail. Great parents, nice house. Wrens in the war. London. My father – MY FATHER, in capital letters heavily underlined. The great Krishna Chaudhuri. Me. That's about it. Don't know what's missing – except a screw, in her case!' He laughed, loudly, but it was drowned by a sudden cheer from one of the other tables. Someone's birthday. Krish's dark hands played nervously with the red and green can. He drained it and took a second one. 'Go on,' he said to Anna. 'Let's have it, then.'

'We could talk about it later,' she said gently. 'Get out of here?'

'That bad, is it?' he said with a foolish giggle. 'What's she done then? Hasn't murdered anyone, has she? Sometimes, the look in her eyes, I think she could. I really do.'

Anna glanced uneasily at Jake as she started talking. She began with the early parts, the friendship, easing them in. Krish listened without interrupting. His cheeks had deepened in colour and his eyes were beginning to have a slightly glazed look. As she spoke, couching what she had to say in the gentlest terms possible, Krish drank steadily, ignoring the remains of his food. He sat back on the hard chair, eyes fixed on Anna's face. In the middle of her account he leaned over and picked up the bottle of wine. Jake tried to restrain his arm.

'Go easy.'

'Piss off, Jake,' Krish protested. 'What d'you think I bought it for?'

It was only when she got to the part about Arden he began to react. He leaned across the table, clutching the bottle to his chest with one hand like a teddy bear. 'So you're saying she's a loony. It's true!' He laughed almost triumphantly. 'I knew it. My mother's a loony.' He lifted the bottle and drank it back like fizzy pop. 'That's more like it.' He offered it round. 'Go on, have some.'

'Let's get out of here,' Jake whispered to Anna. He stood up. Between the two of them they put together enough money to pay the bill. It was a struggle getting Krish out between the tightly packed chairs. He refused to give up the bottle and kept letting out bursts of laughter so that people at the other tables turned and stared at them.

'My mother's a complete fruitcake,' he told one table amiably and Anna felt their eyes all momentarily swivel to her, trying to work out if she was his mother, then concluding she probably wasn't.

Outside, Jake held him round the waist and Anna took his arm. It was growing dark, the sky a very pale blue, edged with yellow, the street still full of life, cars passing.

'Come on, Krish,' Jake said. 'Let's get you to the van. It'll be OK.'

Krish stumbled along between them. As they reached the van he was still laughing, crumpling between them, tears running down his face. Alongside the road was a small park, open space behind a low railing. They stepped over, Krish catching his foot on the rail and making them sprawl on to the grass together, him between them. A rat scuttered away nearby. They sat Krish up between them. His head was in his hands, the bottle standing between his knees. More music blared from a house opposite.

'I'm going to end up like her!' His voice was high. 'I know I will. She's going to make me like her.'

'You won't,' Anna tried to soothe him. 'You're not a bit like her.'

'But you said it last night. "You're all mad." You said so.'

'I was just angry. I'm sorry.'

Krish was silent for a moment. 'I can't be what she wants all the time.'

'And what's that?' Anna asked him. Jake sat listening quietly, an arm round Krish's shoulders.

Krish shook his head helplessly. 'Sometimes I think she wants me to be my father.' He paused as a motorbike roared past on the road. 'Or she wants me to be a baby for her for ever or . . . I don't know. She justs wants me to be everything . . . that she needs.'

'But that's not reasonable, is it?' Anna said. 'No mother should ask that of a child.'

'She's not just any mother, though, is she?' Krish took more mouthfuls from the bottle. 'Thing is – I've realized gradually that she's not like other mothers. But I've always thought, well, maybe she's not that bad. No one else thinks there's anything odd about her. I've tried to kid myself she wasn't so different from anyone else – what happens with some of the lodgers . . . That she was just broad-minded, a free spirit or something. She's coped, after all. She's not got a psychiatric record – she must be OK really. So that meant I'd be all right too. But she's not all right, is she? She's even been in one of those places . . .'

'A long time ago,' Anna said. 'And for a good reason.'

Krish was barely listening to her. 'She'll drive me mad herself. She'll be the one. I can't do anything without her being part of it. I can't go out, can't have friends, can't see women. If I even get near a woman it all gets fouled up because I feel as if she's watching. I don't even want to do this bloody degree. I don't know what to do . . .' He was really crying now, taking deep gulps. 'I can't even talk about her normally because I feel such a shit if I do . . . And I'm scared. I'm so scared of being ill – in my head. Sometimes I think I'm not right. No one should think things like I do.'

Anna also put her arm round him. 'Krish, Krish . . .' The three of them sat close in the darkening evening. Anna felt Jake stroke her arm with the back of his fingers, behind Krish's back. She looked round at him and their eyes met, sadly, but with warmth in them.

'Let's get back,' Jake said. Krish was sagging between them now. 'He's past any more conversation.' He lifted the bottle of wine and held it up in the fading light. 'God, he's nearly drunk the lot.'

'We can't take him back there!' Anna said.

'He can come to mine. I'll drop you off first.'

'I'll come round tomorrow – first thing.'

They had to half drag Krish into the van. He sat slumped in the middle seat, silent now and unreachable.

'I didn't even tell him all of it,' Anna said to Jake, still outside.

'He's certainly heard enough for now, though.' Jake stopped by the door of the van. In the shadows his face looked longer, and thin, his expression anxious. He glanced in at Krish and shook his head. 'D'you think I was wrong?'

'No. I'd have had to tell him. He was going to keep asking me.'

They drove back in silence, Krish pressed against Anna's shoulder. He was asleep, but uneasily so, and kept stirring and giving long, groaning sighs. The silence between herself and Jake was not neutral either. She knew there was a pressure of emotion between them, of need and attraction. That each of them was waiting to see if the other would move forward first. Anna felt very alert, her emotions heightened, as if she could go on effortlessly all night with no sleep.

'He looks so vulnerable, doesn't he?' she said eventually, and the remark seemed to jar into the charged silence, a distraction from their thoughts.

Jake nodded. 'What you said about coming round tomorrow – that'd be really good.'

Anna smiled in the blue night light, hoping, knowing he did not just want her there because of Krish. 'I'll be round about nine-thirty,' she said.

When they stopped outside Kate's house, Jake jumped quickly out of the van and came round to open her side. He waited as she climbed down. Krish slumped further, half lying across the seat.

'Thanks for this evening,' Jake said, sounding uncertain now.

She jumped to the pavement and stood looking up at him. Each of them waited, taking courage to look into each other's face. Even in the dim light she could see the emotion in Jake's eyes, his searching her for a response. But she was afraid. It was too soon and the feelings too serious to hurry.

She looked away. 'Goodnight, then. I'll see you in the morning.'

'OK,' he said quietly. He leaned forward and gave her a brief, awkward hug. She was taken by surprise and had barely registered the feeling of him against her when he had let her go and was striding round to the other door of the van. The door slammed, the engine started up.

She stood waving as he drove away, seeing the white van recede down the street, feeling excited yet regretful.

'And who the hell was that?' a voice said behind her.

Things registered all at once. The car parked a little further along the street, the old blue Saab. The self-righteous voice. She turned to see his angry eyes behind her. Richard.

Chapter 37

He slammed Kate's front door behind them with such violence that the house shuddered. The force of it jarred Anna's nerves, set off her temper.

'Don't do that,' she snapped, switching on the hall light, then the kitchen. 'It isn't your house.'

'Oh dear.' Richard followed her into the kitchen, laughing sarcastically. '"It isn't your house,"' he mimicked. 'Just listen to you.'

Richard looked incongruous in Kate's suburban kitchen in his faded, loose-fitting trousers, grey shirt with the sleeves rolled to the elbow, the rumpled, wavy hair, hand reaching up to pass through it, a restless habit of his. She used to find his anger frightening. She wasn't used to male emotion, had once regarded it as something more valid and powerful than her own. She'd always been the one to try and stay in control and appease him; hold things together. Now she no longer cared.

'Don't imitate me.' She faced him, her tone very cold. 'I didn't ask you to come here.'

He stared at her. 'What's happened to your hair?'

'I got it caught in some heavy industrial machinery.'

Richard ignored this, already on to the next thing, pacing the floor. 'You go off one night with no explanation. You never answer the phone. I come over and you're always out . . . Anna, this is ridiculous. You've been here a month and you said it'd be a few days . . .'

'And you said you'd be home that night I came, and you weren't. I've had enough of that.'

'Look – ' Richard paced up and down the kitchen, palm outstretched as if explaining something really-very-simple to a perverse child. 'It was one of those things. We'd had a case conference – all sorts of added complications – one of the key social workers was delayed. It was a very unusual situation.' His rubber-soled shoes gave off a squeak as he spun round on the lino. 'It's just the way it is, Anna. I can't drop everything and come home just because you've got a meal ready, can I? There are wider concerns, and sometimes they have to come first, that's all.'

'Fine.' She could feel an ecstatic anger rising in her, her body tensing with the force of it.

'So what's going on? Why aren't you answering the phone? You must have finished packing up here by now. I thought it'd take a week, max. I'll give you a hand with the last things, if there's more to do. Take a carload to Oxfam or whoever first thing in the morning, and we can get back home.'

'And then what?' she asked, controlling her voice.

'Well – we can just get on with life again.'

After a silence, she said, 'I'm not coming home. I don't want to live with you any more. I don't love you. I want to be on my own.'

Richard stopped pacing, was actually listening. 'But you've got to be back at school any day now.'

'I've given up my job.'

He walked over to her and put his hands on her shoulders. She felt herself shrinking from him. Her life with him now felt like something from which she had woken – a trance in which she had lost consciousness.

His voice was soft and persuasive, eyes fixed on hers in a practised look of concern. 'Anna? You can't be serious? Look, I know it's been a bad month. Your mum and everything. But you can't let all this take over your life. You have to keep things in perspective. God knows, I see enough of the consequences of people letting things get to them too much. And you're too intelligent to let that happen.'

She let him have the full force of her fist on his nose, punching so hard she jarred her elbow. His eyes snapped shut instantly in pain, hands jerking up to his face. He held them out again, seeing them stained red. Blood fell in long strokes down the grey shirt.

'*Jesus*.' The hurt tone turned to fury. 'What is the matter with you?' He groped at the box of multi-coloured tissues on the worktop.

'We lost our baby,' she heard herself shrieking at him. 'And it was the worst thing that's ever happened to me in my life and you didn't say anything. Not one fucking thing. And my mother's dead and you couldn't even be bothered to come with me to the funeral. All the hours I've spent listening to you about your bloody job and you've never listened to me when I needed you to. I don't want to talk to you now – ' her voice grew quieter – 'I've got things to do. I've found Olivia and she lost her baby too and I want . . . I want . . .'

Incoherent, she found herself sobbing, bent over next to the sink, breathless with it, a pool of pain inside her draining out.

'Oh God,' she cried after a few moments. 'It's all so sad. Why is life so *sad*?'

Richard stood watching her warily, a pad of tissues pressed to his nose, blood on his chin.

'You didn't want us to have a child, did you?' She spoke with her back to him. 'It didn't mean anything to you.'

'I don't know. It was so sudden. It's not as if we planned it.'

'Planned it.' She turned, scornful. 'You can't just plan everything.'

'It was different for you. Maybe you were ready for it and I wasn't. And you could feel it. It wasn't real to me.'

'But you said you felt it – felt it flutter under your hand.'

'Sorry.' He gave a long sigh. 'Something I'm not very good at, I suppose. It's a long time ago now.'

'Eight months!' she flared at him again. 'What's eight bloody months? Some things stay with people for the rest of their lives, Richard, they don't just disappear all finished with. You can't just organize them away. How can you work with people like you do when you know nothing, you understand nothing?'

'My job's about practical decisions,' Richard said sternly. 'Not emotions.'

Anna turned away. 'I don't want to talk about your job. Not again.'

For a moment the only sound was Kate's clock, ticking across the kitchen.

'Look – ' He approached her again, though his voice sounded ridiculous because his hand was still clamping a pink tissue over his nose. 'You need some space, that's all. A rest. Come home and take it easy, even if you're not working. You can take your time, look for another job. We'll talk . . .'

'Richard.' She looked strongly into his eyes, her own red and still full of tears. 'I'm not coming back to

Coventry. I can't live with you any more. You and I are not good for each other.'

'Who was that I saw you with outside?' Richard's voice was even, but Anna could hear the suspicion in it. 'Is this to do with him?'

'The day I left home – not that you apparently noticed – was the day after the funeral. I'd never even met him then. I left home for myself.'

'But now it's to do with him, isn't it?'

She looked down at the floor, seeing spots of Richard's blood. 'I don't know. Maybe.'

'Who is he?'

'Someone I met through Olivia.'

Richard tutted, exasperated. 'And who the hell is Olivia?'

'Someone Mom knew.'

'Has he touched you?'

'Oh, don't be so bloody predictable.'

'Has he, though?'

She thought of that night in the flat. Jake's gentle hands. Touched, but not in the way Richard meant. 'No.' She felt humiliated having to answer these questions.

Richard stared at her, trying to decide whether to believe her. 'Five years we've been together,' he said finally. 'And now you want to go, just like that.'

'Not just like that. It's finished, Richard. I want my life to change.'

She found bedding for him and he slept in the front bedroom while Anna was in Kate's at the back. They parted for the night in morose silence. Anna lay in Kate's floral room aching with sadness, but too tired for more tears.

The next morning they were civil and distant, like acquaintances made the day before. They ate breakfast, discussed the Coventry house.

'We should sell it,' Anna said.

'You might want to come back.'

'I shan't come back. Anyway, I thought being a property owner made you feel uncomfortable.'

Richard frowned at a half-eaten slice of toast, trying to take in her decision, her strength. 'I could rent again, I suppose.'

'Or buy somewhere smaller.'

'You can't buy anywhere much smaller. Except a flat.' He looked across at her, appealing. 'Anna, this is horrible.'

'I know. I'm sorry.'

All the time she was holding on tight to her determination. Being alone there with him again it would have been so easy to slide back, not fight it, to go with him and settle into the old routine, the stifling habits. She felt she was holding her breath.

'You're not going to stay here, are you?'

The tone of ridicule in his voice riled her, brought back all her resolve. 'Probably not. I'll decide when I'm ready. I might move nearer the middle of town.'

'What about your job?'

'I've resigned.'

'Will you find another school?'

'Maybe. Maybe not.'

He put his head on one side. 'You loved that job.'

'I didn't. I put up with it. Felt I couldn't give up. I liked the kids – some of them. But I want a change.'

Richard looked concerned. 'Anna, who's behind all this? What's going on?'

Calmly she looked at him. 'I'm going on.'

He didn't stay long after breakfast. They spent some of the time in silence, some talking.

'I'll come over and collect more things,' she said vaguely. 'Don't know when. I'll ring you.'

She stood out by the old blue Saab in the bright morning as he prepared to go. She felt strong now, and certain, but Richard was suddenly emotional.

'Come with me – please? Give us another go, can't you?'

'No. I'm sorry, Richard.' And she was.

'I can't believe this.' He gestured helplessly. 'If you change your mind . . .?' He held out his arms. 'Is a hug too much for you?'

She accepted, kissed him sadly. 'Thank you,' she was saying, and then there came the sound of the loud engine, revving through the Saturday morning calm and braking outside the house.

She saw Jake's long legs emerge first below the door, then he appeared, his face white and tense, hair tied back in a short ponytail. He saw the two of them together and stopped, embarrassed.

'What?' Anna cried. 'What's happened?'

'There's trouble.' Jake made an apologetic gesture with his long hands. 'Look – sorry to interrupt. I think you'd better come.'

Jake's driving was jerky.

'What's going on?' Anna's heart was pounding, her head still thick from a night of broken sleep. She sat tensed on the slippery black seat.

'Ben phoned. It's Sean – he started a fire. I think they've sorted that, but he sounded awful. And Krish's only just functioning after last night, of course. I'd have left him to get some more sleep, but he made me drop him off home on the way.' Jake glanced at her anxiously.

'I wouldn't have come if – I mean, I haven't got your number. I feel a right clumsy idiot for barging in on you like that.'

'It's all right,' Anna said. 'Richard was just leaving. Actually I was relieved to see you. What's sparked all this off?'

'From what Ben said Sean and Olivia have been arguing half the night and no one's had any sleep. I don't know what goes on between them – some terrible version of teasing on her part, I suppose. But she's obviously pushed him too far this time. Olivia's asking for you, by the way.'

'For me?' She felt her heartbeat quicken further. 'Why?'

'I didn't ask. I thought in the circumstances I'd just do what she and Krish wanted.'

When they reached the house Ben was walking up and down, hands on his hips, elbows at an outraged angle.

'About bloody time!' he exploded as they leapt from the van. 'I shouldn't be left with all this,' he added petulantly. 'He's come down again now, too. I was all for calling the police, but Krish wouldn't let me. Sean's a fucking maniac.' Ben was quivering, babbling on as they stood by the van.

'I got up an hour or more ago. Found him at it with a lighter – stark naked, blood all down his chest as well. He was going for all those sari things – God knows what would've happened. He's completely out of his tree. And then she came down and they had another go at each other. It was disgusting, foul. I couldn't believe it . . .' Anna saw he was close to tears, the shock of it making him seem small and childlike.

'Then what?' she asked gently.

'I was the one left to put it out. Neither of them seemed to notice what was going on – they were too busy mouthing off at each other . . . I was dowsing it all down. Luckily nothing else caught.' He took a deep breath. 'Sean went upstairs saying he was going to pack all his stuff and he was going, and Olivia went to pieces. She tried to persuade him . . . crying, and she was all over him – horrible – but he said it was too late, he was going. All this time and I never saw it. I thought Sean was just moody, or – I don't know.' He shuddered. 'She's some kind of pervert. I can't handle this, Jake.'

'What about Krish?' Jake said. 'Where is he?'

Ben pointed. 'In there with them.'

With Ben following, Anna and Jake ran into Olivia's house. The front door was already open and the hall floor stippled with muddy water. In the long room they were met by a sight that Anna would never forget. The acrid smell of burning and of damp ash met them straight away. The front end of the room where the table stood was wrecked. Instead of the warm glow of light through the coloured silks at the windows, daylight poured through bare panes, harsh and white. At either side hung shreds of blackened cloth, and the wall was stained dark by the flames, as were the corners of that end of the room where there had also hung saris, which must have caught fire with the speed of tissue. The table, the floor, the sills were soaking wet and a black sludge of charred material lay at the edges of the room. Overturned on the floor were a yellow plastic bucket and a red washing-up bowl.

Olivia was sitting at the table, her elbows resting on the wet wood, apparently oblivious to the damp. Her face, stilled with shock and exhaustion, was that of an old woman, limp and grey. She still had on the long, pale pink nightdress in which Anna had seen her that night on the landing and her hair was loose round her shoulders.

Sean was standing in the middle of the room, a black Puma bag with red lettering on the floor beside him, stuffed so full of things that it wouldn't close. A pair of trainers were stuck in on the top. He had evidently just been saying something to Olivia and he was leaning slightly forwards, his body grotesquely angular and aggressive. At the other end of the room, Krish was sitting in one of the easy chairs with his legs drawn up close to him, chin on his knees, his eyes wide and staring.

Anna and Jake stood for a moment in the doorway. Jake stepped forward. 'What's the problem, Sean?'

'She's the problem,' Sean snarled. Anna was reminded of something wild: a wolf. Sean pointed a rigid finger at Olivia. 'She's sick – up here.' The finger jabbed against his head. 'Someone ought to do something about her.'

Olivia protested, her voice tremulous, 'But you loved me, Sean. You did.'

'You messed me up!' Sean shouted, his thin, pitted face contorted. 'You don't know what love is. You controlled me – sent me off my brain.' He turned to Jake suddenly. 'You ask her what she does. She leads you on and then turns against you – backwards, forwards, so you don't know where you are. She makes you so you can't get her out of your mind. You used me – ' He pointed at Olivia again. 'And last night she came at me with a razor blade, tried to slash me. Look.' Wrenching up the sleeve of his T-shirt, he showed them a ridge of Elastoplast along his shoulder. 'Wasn't deep. I got out of her way. You're a fucking crazy bitch!' he yelled at Olivia. 'People ought to know.'

Bending down, he snatched up the bag with such force that the things on top fell out and he had to stuff them in again. He backed out of the room, pushing past Ben, who was standing in the doorway.

'I should've burned the whole fucking house down. I should have burned her to death in her bed.'

The front door slammed. There was silence, then Olivia's sobbing. She covered her face with her hands.

Anna went to her, afraid to touch her. Then, tenderly, she stroked the dark hair, more streaked with white than she had realized, feeling the warmth of Olivia's head beneath it, the trembling of her body. She pulled out one of the chairs and sat down beside her, not heeding the water on it.

'Livy,' she said softly. 'It's all right, I'm here. Don't worry, my love.'

Olivia's body crumpled. She leaned over until she was half lying in Anna's lap, sobs breaking out, sometimes from a place so deep that she was rigid for a few seconds, not drawing breath. Then a great cry would come, high and terrible, and gulping sounds of distress.

And Anna held her, stroking her, trying to soothe her, tears running down her own face.

'Oh, Anna,' Olivia said when she could catch her breath. 'Anna. Anna.'

'It's all right,' Anna said again. 'I'm here. I'm here, Livy.' She was overwhelmed with tenderness, and with the peculiar sadness of that tenderness.

She didn't know how long they sat there together. She noticed nothing else. After a time Olivia sat up and put her face in her hands again. From behind them she said, 'I'm so alone.'

Anna saw Jake move across to her from where he had been sitting with Krish, beckoning her out of the room.

'I'll be back in a minute,' she told Olivia softly.

In the hall, Jake said, 'I've called a doctor.' Seeing Anna's face fill with panic, he added, 'It's just her GP. Krish told me he's occasionally given her something to make her sleep. I think he knows her quite well.'

They all helped Olivia up to bed as if she were a child. Her movements were slow and trancelike. Jake came back down to wait for the doctor and Anna was left with Olivia and Krish. Anna wanted to speak to him, worried by his silence, his troubled eyes, but somehow could not in front of Olivia. And she simply did as they asked her, lay down on the bed, her hair in waves round her pale face on the two thick pillows. There was a limpness about her, but her face was anxious.

'Krishna?' she said to him in a low voice. 'You do love me?'

'Yes, *mamaji*,' he replied.

Anna watched him lean over obediently to kiss her. His manner was exhausted and wooden. She felt very sad watching the two of them together.

'Sleep now,' Krish said wearily, as he went to the door. 'You'll feel better then.'

Distantly Anna heard the doorbell. 'That'll be your doctor.'

Olivia reached up suddenly and seized Anna's hand, gripping it very tightly. She raised her head off the pillow. 'The baby,' she said in a rush. 'My baby – I wanted to hurt Kate. I don't know why. She was always an angel to me. But I do that ... I've destroyed everything I've ever loved. The baby could have been anyone's. I never knew ...'

They heard feet on the stairs, and a man's voice.

Olivia fell back on to the pillow. Hoarsely, she said, 'Angus was completely hers. Not that I didn't try. But he would never have touched me.'

Anna smiled down at her, stroked her hand. 'Thank you,' she said.

'She'll sleep now,' the doctor told them, downstairs. 'Got herself into a bit of a state, did she?' He eyed the burnt curtains, evidently preferring not to ask.

'She didn't do that,' Anna said quickly.

'I know she's a bit excitable. Give me a ring if there are any more problems.'

'Where's Krish?' Anna asked when the doctor had gone.

Jake looked startled. 'Isn't he up with her?'

'He came down before I did.'

They searched the house. His room was strewn with books and papers, but he had gone.

'I expect he just wanted to get away from us all,' Anna said.

Jake frowned. 'Let's look at the top.'

They found Ben in his room with the door open, watching a portable black and white telly, its picture dancing up and down the screen. He jumped as they appeared.

'You all right?' Jake asked.

Ben stood up, clicked the set off. 'I'm leaving,' he said, standing with his hands pushed into the back pockets of his jeans. 'I can't stay here. I've never seen anything like it. It was disgusting.' He looked from one to the other of them, mole-like behind his glasses. 'I was really happy here. I don't understand what's happened. I could talk to her, and she was so lovely . . .' His voice started to break with emotion.

Anna was caught between pity and impatience. 'Olivia's had a very difficult life,' she told him. 'Things have just been stirred up for her a lot recently.' She looked at Jake. 'It's my fault, really.'

'No. It would've happened sooner or later.'

Ben watched them, uncomprehending. 'Where is she?'

'Asleep,' Anna said. 'Krish's gone off somewhere.'

'You're not going, are you? Leaving me alone with her?' Ben stepped forward in panic.

'I'm staying,' Anna said. 'Jake – have you got to get back to the shop?'

'It'll have to stay closed today. I can't leave you with all this.'

Anna looked at him in amazement. When Richard was forced to have time off it amounted to a tragedy. 'Isn't Saturday your best day?'

Jake gave an ironic grin. 'It's only money. Don't worry, Ben. We'll be here.'

'Good.' Ben picked up his sweatshirt from the chair with sudden energy. Petulantly, he said, 'Well, I'm off to find somewhere else to live.'

Anna and Jake stood looking round the long room, amid the mess and the sour smell. The house felt very quiet. There was an occasional drip of water in a corner by the window, a fly circling somewhere at the back.

'I wonder where the hell Krish's gone,' Jake said. He went to the front window, stepping on the squelching fringe of burnt cloth, and looked out.

'D'you think we should be worrying about him?'

'I don't know.' Restlessly he came back to her. 'God, Anna, what's going to happen to them both?'

She shook her head. 'They need someone else in on this, don't they? Help of some sort. Only it seems inconceivable after what she went through last time.'

'Things have come on a bit since then,' Jake said.

'I should hope so.'

They stood close together in silence in the desolate room. Eyes troubled, Anna saw the look in his, and she turned away, frightened by the frank tenderness she found. She stood half facing him, tousling her hair nervously with one hand.

'I suppose we ought to clear up.'

He didn't answer immediately, and she had moved to the table, started shifting the chairs away so they could work on the floor. 'Anna?'

She knew what he wanted – for her to turn and look at him, to go to him – but she felt perverse and raw. Too shocked by all that had happened. In the end, rather gruffly, she just said, 'What?'

Jake's mouth lifted gently into a smile. 'Nothing. You're right. We ought to clean up.'

They spent the next few hours sweeping and scrubbing and mopping. There was a huge relief in this activity, a physical outlet which helped ease the tension of wondering where Krish was and when Olivia would wake and what would happen when she did. And of the feelings each knew were gathering between them across the room, unspoken.

As they worked together, Anna was vividly aware of him even if she was not actually looking in his direction: of his shape, the long legs, the large, rough hands, bruised left middle fingernail, the lines of his thick brown hair. His movements impinged on her, pulled her mind off track.

Their conversation became foolish and self-conscious.

'It's a good job she didn't have carpet in here,' Anna said after a while. 'This should clean up all right.'

'Won't do the parquet much good though,' he replied. 'Might start curling up.'

'What a shame,' she agreed. 'Such a lovely room.'

They made sandwiches for lunch, talked about Krish, Anna smoking. By late afternoon, having cleaned the room from top to bottom with almost unnecessary thoroughness, they were running out of things to do. They stood surveying their work.

'I'll put the kettle on,' Anna said. Jake came to stand in the kitchen doorway, one hand resting on the frame.

'Olivia's been out for hours now,' Anna said, turning. 'I suppose I ought to go and have a look in on her.' She looked at him, shyly. 'I'm sorry. This is so stupid.'

'Look, Anna . . . I can't believe this.' He searched her face for a response. 'Can't you say something?'

'I don't think I know what to say.' She put her head on one side. 'Could I have a hug?'

Laughing with relief, he came to her and they held each other tightly. His body felt very warm and lean, its closeness a comfort. She rested her head against him, felt his arms round her back.

'I feel so clumsy, so nervous.'

'What of?'

'Making a mess of things again. And – ' He hesitated. 'I suppose of you not wanting me.'

She leaned her head back to look at him. 'But I do. So much.' And grinned suddenly. 'Pretty unusual all this, isn't it?'

She felt his big hand gentle on her head, drawing her closer until their lips met. Anna closed her eyes.

There was a slam of the front door, and Ben's anxious voice calling 'Hello?'

They released each other quickly, exchanging a half-comical grimace. 'We're here!'

Ben strode in, morosely. 'Well, nothing much doing. Looks as if I'm stuck here a bit longer. You're not leaving now, are you?'

Chapter 38

At six Anna went to Olivia's room and found her stirring, eyes closed, her head moving from side to side. Her face was haggard. Anna waited, sitting on the chair near the bed. She watched as Olivia eventually opened her eyes, for a moment unfocusing and bewildered after this long, unnatural sleep.

Her gaze fixed on Anna, stopped, and stared hard. Anna felt a chill run through her at the dark, flinty expression.

'Anna?' She gave a faint smile. 'You've been waiting for me? That's nice.'

'We've been here all day,' Anna told her.

Olivia frowned. Then, wearily, she said, 'Sean.' She closed her eyes again. There was a pause before she spoke again. 'Where's Krishna?'

'He went out. I expect he'll be back soon.'

In a small voice Olivia said, 'Will you help me up?'

Anna pulled her gently to a sitting position. As she helped her out of bed she saw the hem of the pale nightdress was stained a grubby grey from the mess on the floor downstairs. Olivia stared at it.

'Jake and I have been cleaning up,' Anna told her. 'You won't have much of a problem, really. Just need new curtains.'

Olivia didn't seem to be listening. She leaned forward slowly and nipped the leg of Anna's jeans between finger and thumb. Anna resisted the impulse to pull her leg away. Olivia stared at the washed-out denim.

'When I was your age we never dreamt of wearing such things,' she said wonderingly. 'You're all so much freer.'

'Mummy told me you always had lovely clothes.'

'I had beautiful things. The best, if possible. My father always saw to that. Proper, tailor-made things . . .'

Olivia still had about her the aura of a past age, Anna thought, as she started helping her to dress. Kate had adapted to the years, had worn large squarish glasses, kept her hair conveniently short, shopped at Marks and Spencer, wore comfy slacks, as she called them, when she was not at work.

But she couldn't imagine Olivia in slacks. There was still a formality about her approach to clothes, the way dressing was still an activity carried out at certain points in the day rather than something incidental. And there was the dark mahogany dressing table with matching silver-backed mirror, hairbrush, clothes brush, items all formally laid out, and a passive acceptance of Anna's help which spoke of maids. Her limbs seemed to be heavy and she was slow and lethargic. Together they put on the cotton skirt in which Anna had seen her play the piano, and a white blouse. Anna fastened the buttons, her actions accepted without protest. She brushed Olivia's hair, feeling its thick softness. She saw herself in the mirror behind Olivia, her eyes serious, a sad, almost reverent expression on her face.

'Will you plait it for me?' Olivia asked. 'Then I can just coil it up at the back.' And as Anna did so, she added, 'Your hair is such a lovely colour. You should grow it long.'

Once they had walked slowly downstairs together,

Anna went to help Jake prepare food – pasta and salad – from what was available in the house. Olivia ate a little with them. She remained subdued, apparently detached from what had happened, and content to sit and watch television. They sat with plates on their knees, relieved at having the telly, at not having to talk. Every so often, though, Olivia roused herself and looked round restlessly, saying, 'I wish Krishna would come back.'

By the time it got to nine o'clock, Anna and Jake were giving each other uneasy glances. They knew Krish had few friends, had not been allowed them. 'Perhaps he's gone to see Theo?' she suggested. 'They get on pretty well, don't they?'

Olivia looked doubtful. 'We could telephone,' she suggested.

'Let's give him a bit more time,' Jake said. 'After all, it's not exactly late yet.'

They sat through the news, each of them taking little of it in.

The phone rang at ten-thirty. Jake leapt up and went to the hall. Anna heard his voice, solemn, saying mostly, 'Yes ... yes ...' He asked something, said yes again, then rang off.

He appeared at the door, his expression unreadable. 'Anna, can I have a word?' Olivia watched impassively as Anna left the room.

Jake pulled her urgently along the dark hall. 'That was Selly Oak Hospital,' he whispered. 'They've got Krish.'

'I must go to him.'

Anna expected Olivia to be hysterical, to disintegrate. Instead, she and Jake watched her transform herself. She gathered herself, seemed to gain stature, dignified and unbending as a bird of prey.

'They say he's going to be sleeping it off for hours yet,' Jake told her. 'They wouldn't let you in at this time, anyway.'

'I need to be with him. He'll want me beside him.'

'Olivia,' Anna insisted gently, 'he's unconscious.'

Olivia stood in the middle of the long room, her face set in lines like stone. She was very composed, as though all her energy was concentrated in one burning point in her mind, consuming any other thought or feeling.

'What did he take?'

'They didn't say,' Jake said. 'They only gave the barest details.'

She fired out the questions relentlessly, as if forcing herself to face the worst. 'Where was he?'

Jake drew in an uneven breath. Anna could see he was feeling terrible. 'Kings Heath Park.'

'Where in Kings Heath Park?' Impatient, as if Jake was an idiot.

'They didn't tell me. Sorry,' he added helplessly.

'He was lying there all alone in the park,' Olivia said. 'Anyone could have found him.' She turned her head fiercely. 'Who found him? Who touched him?'

Jake took a step back. 'I don't . . . They only said he was in the park. We'll be able to ask tomorrow.'

'Sit down both of you,' Anna said firmly. 'I'll make us a drink, and then sooner or later we're going to have to get some sleep.'

'Sleep!' Olivia dismissed her scornfully.

'We need to sleep.'

'I've been asleep all day. I shall sit up for him.'

Anna's eyes met Jake's. With his he motioned her

into the kitchen. As she prepared coffee she heard their voices in the other room, Jake's soft, reassuring, and Olivia's monosyllabic replies.

'I've told her we'll stay,' Jake said, when Anna appeared again.

'Of course. That's no problem.'

'We could take it in turns to sleep,' Jake suggested. There was no protest from Olivia. 'D'you want to go and get some first, Anna?'

'I'll take this up with me.' She picked up her mug. 'Wake me at three or so?'

'OK. I'll see how we're doing.'

She went to kiss Olivia's cheek, but she moved away, sitting very straight on the edge of her chair. 'No, don't touch me.'

Anna shot Jake a look which said 'good luck' and left them.

She settled down in her clothes, having nothing else, and knowing she would be up again soon. Climbing on to the high, unyielding bed, she dreaded being unable to sleep and left most of the coffee undrunk on the table. She thought of Krish unconscious on a hospital bed, nurses coming to check him through the night.

The next thing she was aware of was Jake sitting on the side of the bed. She shot up, heartbeat speeding in panic.

'What time is it? What's happened?'

'It's all right. Don't worry. It's nearly four.' His eyes were red. 'I was falling asleep downstairs, so I thought I'd better come and get a bit of proper kip before tomorrow.'

'You should have woken me earlier.' Anna looked fearfully at him. 'How's it been? What's she doing?'

'Not a lot. It's been fine, really. She's just been sitting

there – we had the TV on. No dramatics. She's quiet. She seems stunned.'

'I suppose she's not tired?'

'All right for some, eh?'

There was silence, then Anna said, 'Poor Krish.'

Jake sighed. 'Yeah.'

Anna pushed back the sheet. 'Here – it's nice and warm for you!'

'Sounds wonderful. It's a great shame my getting in means you have to get out.'

He stood up and reached out his arms and they held each other. 'I didn't want to wake you,' he said. 'You looked so lovely.'

She smiled up at him. 'That's a nice thing to say.'

He leaned down to her slowly and they kissed. His hands moved across her back, drawing her to him. Then he lifted his head again and looked anxiously into her eyes, watching for her response. 'I keep thinking, we have to be careful with each other, not take things too quickly. I don't want to steamroller you. It's taken me by surprise feeling so ... strongly, already. I didn't expect it, and I don't know if you ...'

She put her hands on each side of his face and pulled him towards her without speaking. He seemed startled by the force of her kiss, its reply to him.

'Seems almost wrong,' he said after a moment, 'feeling so happy with all this going on.'

'I don't know.' She held him close. 'Maybe. I just know I'm glad. Everything's been so sad for so long.'

After they'd stood together in silence for a moment she stepped back. 'Come on – you need some sleep.'

'I know. It's OK. I just wanted to touch you.' He stroked his fingers down her back, then released her.

'I'll tuck you in.'

When he was lying down she kissed him again, before his smile took her to the door.

The rest of the night passed, strange and dreamlike. Olivia sat upright in her chair, not leaning against the back of it, as if performing a penance. Anna made hot drinks to keep herself awake, and Olivia accepted those offered to her with a nod, but usually left them untouched. Most of the time she sat in silence, staring across the room towards the window at the back where the light began faintly to appear.

Anna kept feeling herself on the point of dozing off, and then Olivia would suddenly speak and she would be jerked into full consciousness again.

'Did Katie show you my letters?' she asked, soon after Anna came down.

'Yes. Some of them.' She wondered if now, finally, they were to have a proper conversation. 'Not all, I don't think. She didn't *tell* me anything, you see, she wrote it and left it for me to find.'

'So you know all about me.' Her eyes still didn't meet Anna's, but her voice was wretched.

'I know what you chose to tell her and what she chose to tell me herself.'

She thought Olivia was about to speak again, but there came only a clearing of her throat, then silence. She was still beautiful, Anna thought, the dark eyes in that lined face.

'D'you mind if I smoke?' Anna asked timidly. She knew it would help keep her alert.

'Do what you like,' Olivia said absently.

A moment later, she said, 'May I have one?' Anna stood up and gave her a cigarette, clicking the lighter for her, the cigarette tucked between her dry lips.

'I've never seen you smoke before.'

Olivia dragged hungrily on the cigarette. 'I have – on and off. For years.' There was a pause, then she said, 'Katie must have told you about my father?' She narrowed her eyes, breathing out smoke. 'I ruined his career. I know Kate thought he'd do anything to advance himself, but it wasn't true. He was as soft as an egg inside. When he lost me he just lost his spirit. Gave it all up – the politics, public life. Packed me off to London. He was sweet to me after the baby. Sweet and tender. He cried. My mother didn't cry – not in front of me, anyway. But he couldn't bear to have me near him, not the way I was.' She shook her head slowly. 'He got such comfort from me, you see, all those years. My mother worshipped him – really, genuinely worshipped him. Couldn't stand herself you see, so she poured it all out on him. But she closed down emotionally. I was the only one who loved him properly. I've never felt quite as much for anyone as I did him.' She looked round sharply at Anna. 'I don't want to give you the wrong idea. He never laid a finger on me in any way he shouldn't have – nothing like that. He was very honourable in his way, and besides, he was far too busy touching up all the maids or anyone else who came his way. It was more that I was an idea, a fantasy. Something he saw as pure, that he could love without all the humiliation he went through with my mother. Sometimes, the way he held me – the two of us warm and safe together – it shielded us from anything else. I should have just gone on loving him like that. But I couldn't. I spoilt it, you see. I'd seen too much, heard too much of things I shouldn't have heard or seen. I lashed out. I was dirty.'

Anna wondered if she would become emotional but

she gave no sign, just stubbed out the cigarette in her saucer. Not knowing what else to do, Anna said, 'I'm sorry – for all you had to go through.'

What seemed much later, as the light was lifting the colours round the room and the birds were coming to life outside, Olivia said, 'You were such a darling, darling baby, Anna. So sweet and pure. I wanted to keep you from it all, you see, keep you as you were. You and Krishna.'

'We don't normally let visitors in in the morning,' the nurse told them. She was petite and pretty, a black fringe curling out from the front of her white cap, but her manner was chilly and suspicious. 'Are you friends of his?'

'I'm his mother,' Olivia snapped.

The nurse looked startled. She'd probably expected a timid Asian woman with limited English. 'His . . .? I see. I'm sorry. I suppose as you're here . . . Would you follow me?'

Her feet clip-clipped on the polished floor. She led them to a little room aside from the main ward.

'We put him in here out of the way.' Her tone was ambiguous. Anna and Jake exchanged glances. Overdose: a nuisance taking up a bed. 'I'll tell him you're here.'

Olivia stood between Anna and Jake, watching the nurse give the door a shove. She looked very small in the yawning hospital corridor. Anna had wanted to take her arm, but sensed that she did not want to be touched.

The nurse went over to the bed by the far wall. Peering through the small, reinforced window, Anna could just see Krish's dark hair and the shape of his body under the bedclothes. He was turned away from them, facing the wall. Anna saw the nurse bend over and speak to him. Krish's body moved, curling almost convulsively so that his head disappeared underneath the bedclothes. The nurse tried again, then gave a light shrug and came back to the door.

'I'm sorry. He doesn't want to see anyone at the moment, I'm afraid.'

'But I have to see him.' Olivia's voice was high, the desperation barely controlled.

'He's rather distressed.' The nurse's voice was gentler now, taking on a tone of one addressing a patient instead of a visitor. 'You have to understand, he's not long come round and he won't be feeling very well for a while. Give him a bit more time.'

Olivia broke away from them and ran towards the door of the side room. 'Krishna, Krishna!' She had it half open, and they all had to restrain her, pull her away. Jake took her by the shoulders, led her off as her sobs filled the echoing space.

Anna stood with the nurse. 'Is he going to be all right?' she asked.

'He should be,' the nurse said. She looked at Anna curiously. 'Are you a relative?'

'No.'

The nurse nodded her head in the direction in which Olivia and Jake had disappeared. 'He was pretty adamant about not seeing her.'

Anna didn't feel confident in speaking to this young woman. 'Their relationship is complicated,' she said.

'I don't know, though.' The nurse's tone of disapproval returned. 'He may look all of a heap now, but soon after he surfaced this morning he opened his eyes, looked at me and said, "Titty." Can you believe it?'

'Don't worry,' Anna said, despising her petty outrage. 'He wasn't after you. Actually Titty is a person.'

When they went back that afternoon, Olivia had dressed in her bright blue sari and plaited her hair.

'Let's hope to God he'll see her,' Anna whispered to Jake as they left the van and walked across the car park.

By the side door of the hospital they met Theo. He looked shocked, preoccupied, was walking staring down at the ground and jumped when Jake called his name.

'Hi.' He nodded at the three of them. 'Hello, Olivia.' He looked away, then back at her. 'This is bad. Really bad.'

'You've seen him?' Olivia said eagerly. 'Is he talking?' Hope shone in her face.

Theo shifted awkwardly from foot to foot. He was dressed in a blue tracksuit and trainers and looked huge and muscular, but Anna could tell he felt terribly put on the spot, that there were things he couldn't say in front of Olivia.

'He's not saying much,' he told them, avoiding Olivia's piercing gaze. 'I think he's still a bit – you know – sleepy.'

'Well, he's bound to be!' Olivia's voice held a note of desperate cheerfulness. 'But he's going to be all right, isn't he? He's awake and he's seeing people. Let's go on in.'

Theo looked at Jake. 'He asked for you.'

As they parted, Theo gestured to Anna to stay behind. 'Thanks for phoning me, Anna. This is . . .' He shook his head again. 'I'll come again tomorrow, right?'

'Thanks Theo. It's an awkward journey for you.'

'No problem. The bus is OK. I can get to the outer

circle.' He stared at her. 'He won't see her, you know. What the hell's going on?'

'I'll tell you' – Anna put her hand on his dark wrist – 'when there's time.'

She watched Theo lope off across the car park.

Jake and Olivia had waited for her just inside. She took Olivia's arm as they climbed the stairs to the ward. Anna felt sick with nerves, and with sorrow at the sight of this little woman dressed up in her borrowed sense of identity, looking sad and eccentric in her sari, her gait wrong for the clothes, clinging to her hope that this costume might bring her closer to her son. She wanted to say something, warn Olivia that Krish still might not be ready, but it was too late before she could find the right words.

When they reached the middle corridor, Olivia took in a deep breath, preparing herself.

'Perhaps Jake should go first,' Anna suggested, as they pushed open the swing doors to the ward. 'Tell him you're here and you want to see him?'

Olivia hesitated, then nodded. 'All right,' she said, her voice husky.

But on looking through the window of the side room they saw that the chair next to Krish's bed was already occupied by a tall, thin man, his white coat open to reveal a moss-green shirt. Krish was still lying down and they couldn't see his face.

After a short time the doctor glanced round at the door. They saw a chiselled face with dark, serious eyes. Seeing them watching, he came out, closing the door softly behind him.

'Good afternoon. I'm Dr O'Connor.' His voice was soft, Irish. He looked from one to the other of them, trying to work out who to talk to.

Olivia could not contain herself. 'I want to see my son,' she erupted, harshly.

'You're Mrs Kemp?'

'Yes, of course I am.' She seemed suddenly enraged, as if she resented his presence there.

'We're friends of Krishna's,' Anna explained. 'I'm Anna Craven and this is Jake . . .' In confusion she couldn't think of his name. For a second she saw the bizarre nature of the whole situation, that she was here with these people who a week ago she hadn't even met.

'Morrell,' Jake finished for her.

'Ah, Jake,' Dr O'Connor said. 'Krishna asked just now whether you were here. He'd like to see you.'

'What about me?' Olivia wailed, her fragile collectedness disintegrating. She went to the door again. 'Krishna, my darling – *mamaji* is here!'

Anna felt Dr O'Connor observing them all. She went to Olivia and gently held her arm. 'Livy, why not let Jake go in first, if that's what Krish wants, and he can tell him you're here and perhaps afterwards . . .'

Jake looked at Dr O'Connor who nodded at him. He slipped into the room and sat by Krish's bed.

'I should explain,' the doctor said. 'I've been called in to see your son. I'm the duty psychiatrist.'

'No!' Olivia recoiled from him. 'No. We don't need you. Don't you go near him. Just let me talk to him. What he needs is to be home with me. We're all right when we're together. We're safe. We don't need anyone like you . . .' Her voice was reaching higher, barely controlled.

The doors of the main ward swung open and a woman in a green overall pushed a huge, rattling trolley past them without giving them a second glance.

'Mrs Kemp, let's go into the side room here,' Dr

O'Connor suggested. 'We can talk about this more privately.'

'I'm not going anywhere with you,' Olivia almost spat at him. 'I'm not moving. I'm waiting here to see my son. *My* son.'

'Mrs Kemp – ' Dr O'Connor seemed to experience actual physical discomfort in bringing out his next words. 'Krishna has told me very clearly that he is not ready to see you just at the moment. I know this is terribly difficult and I'm sure he's not trying to hurt you deliberately. At a time like this people sometimes react most strongly against the people they're closest to. I shouldn't like to have to forbid you to see him. For Krishna's sake it would be helpful if you could respect his wishes. He's in a very low state and we're assessing him to see whether he needs some more specialized care. We may need to transfer him to a bed over in Rubery . . .'

Rubery Hill. The psychiatric hospital on the southern fringe of Birmingham. Olivia's face froze. In no more than a whisper she protested, 'No . . . No . . .'

Watched by Anna and Dr O'Connor, she moved to the door of Krish's room, crumpling against it, her hands splayed on the wood each side of the window. 'Krishna . . . *my Krishna* . . .' His name spilled from her mouth over and over, as if she couldn't stop, her forehead pressed white against the glass.

Chapter 39

Krishna and Olivia both went to Rubery Hill Hospital: Krishna as a voluntary patient. Olivia was not given a choice in the matter.

Anna and Jake were Olivia's only visitors over the next month. Theo went to see Krish with sombre faithfulness.

Krish's first questions now were, 'How is she? What's she saying? Is she blaming me?'

It was only recently though that he had started to talk at all. At first he had remained in a paralysed state, almost completely dumb except for whispered replies to the most basic questions regarding his needs. Anna and Jake visited every other day and Krish sat in inscrutable silence. He had been assigned a psychotherapist, and stonewalled him for hours at a time. No one could detect any maliciousness in this, but simply a need to withdraw, to be out of things. He had refused absolutely, and was still refusing, to see his mother. The hospital staff deemed it right to keep them apart.

After three weeks he had gradually begun talking to Steven, the psychotherapist. Then to Theo. Then Anna and Jake. One day when they approached him, Anna carrying a box of Rose's chocolates, Krish looked up and, very softly, said, 'Hello.' He looked exhausted, his face drawn, black shadows under his eyes. He told them he wasn't sleeping. He talked in sudden jerks about his life with Olivia, sitting childlike in pastel green pyjamas, his voice so quiet they had to concentrate hard to hear.

'I've hated her so much.' He was weeping into his hands. He shook his head from side to side as if to dislodge the thought of her. 'I do love her – but she makes my life impossible.' He looked up at them through his fingers. 'God, what the hell are we going to do?'

He held his hands out in front of him, palms down in a despairing gesture, watching their slight tremor. 'Look at me. I can't do anything any more. I can't even make a cup of coffee by myself.'

Afterwards, gloomily, they drove away from the hospital in the van. Finally Anna said, 'Well – at least he's speaking.'

The last time they saw Olivia was in mid-October. Anna took flowers to her that day: a bunch of vivid blooms, blue, yellow, pink, deliberately chosen to shout at the pallid walls of the hospital. This outcry of colour was in part an expression of her own guilt, her protest against helplessness, despite the reassurance of Dr O'Connor and the other staff that they had done the right thing. The only thing.

Olivia looked old. Older than Anna had ever seen her, the skin of her face flaccid as if something in her very being had collapsed. She was brushing her hair. Brushing and brushing. It was newly washed, long and wild looking.

'It's so grey,' she said, giving Anna and Jake no other greeting as they sat down. 'So terribly faded. I'd be grateful if you'd buy a rinse for me, Anna. Something subtle of course. I don't want to look cheap.'

In her mind there seemed to be only a small circle of illumination left, kept alight to pick out practical details. Everything else was off stage, out of sight.

'Did Ben pay his rent before he left?' she asked. She raised the brush over her head and strands of her hair lifted with it, crackling with static electricity. Her thoughts jabbed at Ben's rent book. Then at the tap in the upstairs toilet. Could Jake be a darling and fix it? Because she was sure it was leaking, and it was the hot one: such a drain on the tank . . .

'And Anna, I don't seem to have my Access card here and I'm sure to need it. Could you check in my handbag when you get back to the house? It's in the little cupboard at the side of my bed.'

These enquiries were low key, the drugs keeping her just a fraction away from calm. She didn't mention Krish.

Two days after that, Olivia walked out of the hospital. Whether by luck or canniness on her part she chose a time during the morning when the ward was unlocked, the staff busy and there was a general air of bustle in the corridors. She may have followed an instinct which told her her only mistake would be to hesitate.

She must have made her way, unchallenged, right down the drive of the hospital, wearing her blue dressing gown and sheepskin slippers. From there she was walking along the bypass, a busy, fast-moving artery feeding the M5. Who would challenge a woman in a blue dressing gown and slippers on the A38 bypass?

Just over a mile and what must have been half an hour later, she walked on to the nearside platform of the railway station at Longbridge. Within five minutes an Intercity train, moving at shrieking speed past the back of the Rover car works, dashed into a body clad in a cornflower-blue dressing gown, which was lying with a neat sense of purpose across the track.

Chapter 40

December, 1981

'Off somewhere nice?'

Anna put her bag down and watched Roland's rotund figure advancing towards her along the street, obviously anxious not to miss her.

'A day out – with Jake and Elly. Sort of winter picnic. I'm sure you'll tell us we're mad.'

'Not at all. It's a marvellous day. You'll be all right well wrapped up.'

They stood outside Kate's house. It was a dazzling morning, water droplets on the grass catching the light as last night's hard frost was beginning to melt. At one corner of the drive a freshly painted white post had been driven into the ground, topped by a 'For Sale' sign.

'Any offers yet?'

'It only went up yesterday,' Anna protested. 'Give them time.'

'And have you started looking for a new place?' Roland's attempt to sound detached and cheerful failed miserably.

'I'm not looking far away – just a little further into town, but still Kings Heath. I'd like something a bit older.'

Roland chuckled, his face reddening. Since Kate's

death his emotions seemed to come upon him even more overwhelmingly.

'Look, you're the only family I've got,' she told him. 'I don't want to lose you – if you can put up with me, that is!'

Roland laughed delightedly. 'I'm very relieved you're not planning to take off and leave me again.' He frowned. 'What are you going to do, actually? Look for a new teaching job?'

Anna stared at the house opposite, giving an absent-minded wave to a woman stepping out with a shopping bag. 'I'm not sure what I'm going to do at the moment – and I'm rather enjoying not being sure.' She took in a satisfied breath of the icy air. 'I feel as if I can start again. Use some of my earnings I never had time to spend. I think Jake's infected me with his travel bug.' She turned to Roland. 'What about you?'

'Oh – I shall potter along no doubt.' Without self-pity, he added, 'Nothing will be the same now she's gone.'

'Oh, Roland,' Anna said. 'I'm so sorry.' She went to him, and was taken up into one of his bear hugs.

She felt his breath on her hair as he spoke. 'But my dear, nothing could make me happier now than knowing you're going to be just up the road.'

Jake's van grumbled along the curving roads out into the Warwickshire countryside. Bare branches spiked black against the untouched blue sky, the fields ploughed or left to pasture. Bright, low-angled sunlight gave the furrows and tree-trunks a hard edge of shadow so that the landscape looked vivid and assured.

Between Anna and Jake, strapped to the seat with her plump legs stretched out straight, sat Elly. She was wearing a little denim skirt with woolly red tights and a blue coat with a red lining, squeezed over layers of jumpers. Her round face was edged by a mesh of fine blond hair.

'Daddy, where are we going? We've been driving for such a long time.'

'Soon be there,' Jake told her. 'Just another mile or two, and then we can have our picnic.'

Elly turned to Anna and gave her a mischievous, trying-it-on smile which showed a deep dimple to the left of her mouth. 'I want some of that chocolate.'

Anna grinned back at her. She'd taken to Elly immediately and already they'd had a couple of outings together. 'Don't worry. I expect we'll leave you a little bit.'

'Not just a bit!' Elly was outraged. 'I want lots. I want *this* much.' She held out her arms wide, red mittens dangling on strings from her coatsleeves.

'Sandwiches first though,' Jake told her firmly. 'Let's hope we're not going to freeze.' He looked away from the road at Anna for a second, giving a smile which she returned. Happiness surged through her, made her feel like singing. She had woken that morning in his bed, held by him, their eyes meeting each other's, and seeing she was loved.

They rounded the bend beneath the rise, from where she knew she had glimpsed Arden out of the taxi. She saw trees snagging at the blue, but between them a sudden shock: where the crouching shape of the hospital had stood before, there was nothing now but the naked sky.

'It's gone!' she cried. 'They've already done it!'

'What's gone?' Elly peered through the windscreen.

'There was a building there – on the hill.' Anna pointed. Still hardly believing it, she went on, 'And now it's not there.'

'Why?' Elly frowned. 'Did somebody steal it? A stranger?'

'Yes,' Anna said. 'Several strangers, I should think. And some machines.' She felt desolate. It had felt important to come back here. 'Oh, well. Can't show you now then, can I?'

'Never mind,' Jake said. 'I'll have to try and imagine.'

The stone arch at the entrance to Arden was, however, still standing, a large green and white sign next to it announcing the name of the demolition company. The arch was too narrow for the bulldozers and they had cleared a way in through the boundary fence, leaving a gash of crushed bushes and white, snapped twigs. Their tracks had mashed deep ruts along the drive, the surface churned aside and now frozen hard, still white with ice behind the broken shadows of the trees.

They left the van just inside the entrance and jumped down. Anna was disorientated. 'I was here four months ago,' she calculated as they reached into the back of the van for the picnic bags. 'I suppose it was obvious they were going to do it soon, but I still can't believe it's just gone completely. I thought it would take them longer.'

'Not once they get going,' Jake said.

They picked their way along the rough path, Anna and Jake each carrying a bag and Jake with a rug draped over one shoulder. 'Mind how you go,' he called to Elly, who was skipping ahead in blue wellies. 'Hold my hand or you could twist your ankle. It's rough here.'

'I want to hold Anna's hand,' she said. Anna felt the woolly fingers grasp hers and was flattered to be chosen. Elly looked up at her, eyes huge and grey like Jake's. 'You're Daddy's girlfriend, aren't you?'

'Yes,' Anna said solemnly. 'Is that all right with you?'

'Oh yes,' Elly said. 'I think that's all right – so far.'

'Thank you,' Anna said. She and Jake laughed together, their breath misting the air.

'You look like dragons,' Elly said, puffing a breath out herself and laughing too. Jake came and put his free arm round Anna's shoulders.

As they walked round the final bend of the drive Anna found herself feeling nervous, as she had the first time she was there. She had expected something to remain: bricks, plastic tape, skips: something of the paraphernalia of demolition. But there was nothing. The site had been cleared with great thoroughness, the rubble carted away, the ground bulldozed and flattened, so that the only thing now visible was the long area of earth frozen iron hard.

Anna walked on to it. There was almost no sound. She could feel the rays of the sun on her face. Elly loosed her hand and danced off over the inviting space.

'It was very big.' Anna pointed, swinging her arms to try and explain it. 'All across here. That wing over there had been burnt, but there was a lot of the front left – here. And it was beautiful – the façade of it, anyway – like a Victorian stately home. And there was a water tower about here. Square thing, all black . . .' She picked out as best she could the places where she thought there had been airing courts, wards, filling in the shape. They walked round in silence for a few minutes, turning, staring, trying to imagine.

As she did so Anna saw something incongruous trapped in the earth at her feet. Pale blue, icy, pressed down and half hidden. She fished a knife from her picnic bag and prised it out of the ground: a round, plastic bead, its hole for stringing blocked with a brown thread of soil. She turned it round in her fingers, cleaning the outside until it felt warm and smooth.

Olivia's voice came to her: 'I wish I had something to hold on to: a bead, a stone, a strand of hair, anything to call mine.' She slipped the bead into the pocket of her jeans.

She walked slowly over to Jake and saw him watching her, taking in the sight of her as she came to him.

'After I'd seen this place I knew I couldn't condemn her,' she said.

Jake nodded, put his hand on her shoulder, and she turned, reaching up to kiss him.

But then Elly was pulling her arm, impatient. 'Come on. Let's do something.'

'You're right,' Anna said. 'Let's get the picnic going.'

They found a spot on the grass not far away and put the rug down, laying on it French bread and cheeses, crisps and *samosas*, fruit and a Thermos of coffee. Wrapped in their coats and scarves, they sat looking across the countryside, at the gentle swell of the land and brown, scoured fields, oblong farmhouses like Lego pieces, dots of bushes. Elly was quiet, eating crisps with sudden concentration.

Anna sat back, feet stretched out, the wind ruffling her hair. She had bitten into a *samosa*, delicious spiced potato, plump peas.

Even up here there was very little for them to say about Kate and Olivia that they had not said many times already. There had had to be an inquest after Olivia's death. At the funeral Anna had been startled by the intensity of her own grief for Olivia. And for Krish struggling with his guilt, his new sense of release. She thought of him now almost as a brother to whom she owed protection.

There came to her a feeling of peace, of standing outside time, as if she could walk along the ridge of

Krish's life from up here and see that he would live through this, would surface again.

'He's going to be OK,' she said to Jake. 'I think.'

'Yes.' He unscrewed the lid of the Thermos, steam billowing out. 'Eventually.'

After their meal they shared the chocolate. Elly took her squares, relishing them slowly. She delighted in the huge flat area laid out there for her to run around on, and was soon skipping up and down in delight, her mouth ringed like a clown's with chocolate.

'Don't choke!' Jake warned her. 'Here – the Frisbee!'

He spun the thin yellow disc towards her and it lifted and arced on the breeze, Elly following as it hit the ground and wheeled away down the incline.

'Daddy, Mummy,' she cried, 'I'm flying!'

Anna laughed and turned to Jake, flinging her arms round him, feeling his tight round her. She settled, leaning against the padded shoulder of his jacket. 'She's lovely, Jake. A great kid.'

'She's coming on,' he agreed. There was pleasure in his voice. 'She's really taken to you.'

'I'm so glad.' She twisted her head to look up at him. 'In a strange way I'm glad about everything.'

He looked down into her eyes, his long face serious. 'Are you?'

'Very, very, very. Come here.' She pecked his nose, teasing, then found his lips with hers, trying to show him with a kiss. After a moment he drew back and looked at her again.

'What's the matter?'

'I don't want to lose this, Anna. It's just – we haven't said anything, actually said what we feel.'

'Didn't I show you last night?'

'Yes.' He looked down. 'You did. I know.'

She took his face in her hands, pulling him close to her so that her breath was warm on his ear. 'I love you. Thank you for making me so happy.'

He laughed and they sat for a long time side by side, watching Elly flying after the Frisbee as it curved and bucked in the air. Her cheeks were winter-pink and she chatted to herself in a constant stream, calling out to them, happy so long as they were watching.

Anna's eyes followed her, smiling. Her thoughts drifted from image to image, splinters of melancholy and joy all gathered in this place. She conjured up Arden as it had been: the handcarts, the long, sealed corridors, all the people whose lives had faded into shadows glimpsed on its walls. She watched the skipping rhythm of Elly's feet, her child's absorption and happiness. And brought before her two other children skipping there, one blond with heavy, black-rimmed glasses, the other fragile, waif-like, long hair curling, both laughing as they reached for each other's sun-warm hands.

'Daddy, Daddy!' Elly's voice floated across to them. 'It's lovely here. Can we stay? I want to stay here for ever!'

She ran and gave a leap of pure joy, her body rising, arms flung high, and the bright, gauzy hair lifting to catch the light.